HARSH REALITIES

THIEVES' GUILD BOOK THREE

The Thieves' Guild Books
by C.G. Hatton

Residual Belligerence #1
Blatant Disregard #2
Harsh Realities #3
Wilful Defiance #4
Darkest Fears #5
Arunday's Convergence #6

Kheris Burning LC#1
Beyond Redemption LC#2
Defying Winter LC#3

www.cghatton.com

HARSH REALITIES

THIEVES' GUILD BOOK THREE

C.G. HATTON

First published in paperback in 2014
by Sixth Element Publishing
Arthur Robinson House
13-14 The Green
Billingham TS23 1EU
United Kingdom
www.6epublishing.net

ISBN 979-8-806157-55-4

British Library Cataloguing in Publication Data. A catalogue record for this book is available from the British Library.

For Hatt

1

"Do you know where he is now?"

He sat there in silence, breathing in the tendrils of aromatic, narcotic fumes that were winding a lazy dance into the darkness of the room, staring into the flames of the fire blazing in the hearth beside them.

"You must know," the other urged. "He is your protégé."

The wine was hot and potent, far, far stronger than anything he'd ever served up in his own chambers.

The Man took a sip from the goblet, savouring the consistency of the thick, silky liquid. He looked at the face regarding him.

"He is," he deigned to agree. "Indeed he is. But understand this, the situation in this galaxy has always been precarious. The nature of these fragile beings is tempestuous at the best of times. We set these events in motion, it is my protégé as you say that has had to deal with the consequences, harsh consequences. He is still young and he is still learning."

A massive fist punched into the side of his face. He felt blood vessels burst, sparks flaring behind his eyes.

He'd felt the intention behind the blow before he felt the force of it but he was restrained, upright, arms bound behind his back, ankles manacled to the legs of the chair he was sitting on. A cloth blindfold was tied around his eyes and a needle stuck in his arm was dripping what he recognised as Banitol into his bloodstream.

He was about as far from the safety of the guild as it was possible to get.

Another blow to the jaw sent his senses reeling. When sounds started to filter back into his awareness, they were of weapons being readied, a distant beeping and harsh voices. Footsteps echoed.

Cold water hit his face. He lifted his head slowly and spat blood off to the side.

"Let's try again," a voice said, up close, quiet. Earth accent and a mind that was cold and dark. "Where are they?"

"I don't know what you're talking about," he said softly with a faint smile, keeping his heart rate under control and feeling the Banitol spread its tendrils into his subconscious.

A hand slapped him across the back of the head.

He felt the guy in front lean in close and whisper, "Come on now, NG, you're in no position to act dumb."

He blinked, feeling the rough cloth against his eyelashes. They'd hit him hard when they'd taken him down and the dull pounding at the base of his skull was getting steadily worse.

"You're making a mistake," he said calmly, just loud enough for the other three in the room to hear. He was aware of four more, patrolling outside. For hired muscle, they were above average, he'd give them that. He'd goaded them until they'd knocked him unconscious again and they still hadn't slipped up. On the whole, the situation wasn't going well.

He sensed a presence move close in by his side and felt a slight tug on the needle taped to the crook of his elbow. A sharp jab hit the side of his neck, another drug on top of the crap they were already pumping into his veins to get him to talk.

It would take more than that.

He let his head drop and heart rate slow, hearing the echoing beep of their monitors respond with a shrill alarm.

He drew back from attempting to read anything from them. It was tough enough trying to neutralise the drugs filtering into his system and dampen down the pain. He had no idea where he was, where they'd taken him, but it didn't have the feel of a medical facility. It felt more like an aircraft hangar. Cold and empty with a lingering smell of engine oil.

And it was doubtful that anyone at the guild even knew he was missing.

The mercenaries surrounding him were cold and focused on their mission. Yet even though he was bound to a chair and beaten half senseless, they were still wary of him. Very wary. It appeared that his reputation had preceded him and it would have been almost flattering if they hadn't been so intent on torturing the crap out of him.

There was no hint in their surface thoughts of who had hired them and until he could make physical contact with one of them, he couldn't find out anything more, couldn't get as deep as he needed to pull the information from their minds.

He twisted one of his hands slightly. The restraints were tight and a gloved hand clamped around his wrists, another delivering a blow to the back of his head. He flinched, feeling the hairline fracture shift and propagate with the impact, having to concentrate to ease the throbbing pain that was rebounding around his skull in waves.

A hand touched his arm. It was a woman at his side, he could sense that without trying. She was thinking that she didn't really give a damn about their instructions. She wanted to kill him. Slowly. He turned his head slightly towards her, chin still down, shoulders slumped, willing her to take off her gloves and feel his pulse for herself.

She was close. He could hear her breathing.

She reached a hand to the back of his neck and stroked gently with a gloved thumb, pressing suddenly to engage a device that stabbed into his neck with a piercing sting.

He bit down on a gasp. A hand pushed down on his shoulder from behind. The woman touched his leg, a soft glancing caress, and another needle of hot pain lanced sideways into the knee joint. It took all he had not to scream.

The man leaned in again, touched his cheek with a gloved hand and whispered, "Where are they, NG?"

He shivered as a piercing pain hit another pressure point. It was difficult to admit, impossible to even dare let the dark little voice in his head whisper it, but he was starting to think he might have underestimated the danger he was in.

"You don't know what you're messing with," he managed to say between sharp breaths.

She touched his elbow softly, wrist, temple, ribs, each time leaving behind an agonising shard of pain.

"Much more," she whispered, "and you'll be begging us to let you talk."

He'd never begged anyone for anything and this bitch wasn't going to be an exception.

"You haven't said the magic w…" he said before another stab of white hot pain took his breath.

It took him a second to gather enough wits to shut it out.

She pressed a finger against his lips, resting it there for what felt like an eternity with a soft, "Sshh." Finally, she pulled his shirt open and pressed an inert device against his chest, over his heart, and murmured in his ear, "You really don't want me to activate this one."

She was enjoying it.

He'd been enjoying a Mai Tai in a bar on San Pedro before they'd hit him over the back of the head, and he still had no idea how he hadn't seen it coming.

"The council," the man said. "We know you meet with them. Where are they?"

They had no idea that he was neutralising the Banitol in his system almost as fast as they were feeding it to him but for the moment he needed them to think it was working.

He shook his head slightly and focused all his attention on delving into the woman's mind. The room vanished. Pain gone, at least for the moment. He went as deep as he could without making physical contact, reading the immediate details of the mission from her thoughts. The impatient, arrogant greed was chilling, her motivation only hard cash. She didn't care who he was. They had orders to deliver him alive and deliver intel on the council if they could. She wanted to kill him, that was dominant in her thoughts as she inflicted each new escalation of pain. It wrapped around her mind, stifling her sanity.

As far as he could tell, she didn't know who'd hired them.

They demanded his attention by punching a fist into his face again and it was impossible not to slam back into the nightmare.

"This situation is not going to get any better for you, NG, unless you start to tell me what I want to know," the man said, voice drifting as he backed away.

The heat of the pain spiking into each of the pressure points rose as the woman murmured close up, "You want this to stop? Just start talking…" She pressed a hand against his chest and the device there sparked into life.

As dark as her mind was, he'd been in worse places. Far worse.

He breathed, slow and steady, riding it out, surviving. They had nothing in their arsenal that would ever make him betray anything about the guild. He just needed to bide his time until theirs ran out.

It didn't take long. The woman was tracing a finger along his jaw when the shockwave of a high velocity round cut through the air in front of his face. She fell back.

Flash bangs exploded all around, reverberating detonations filling the massive hangar, multiple breaches occurring simultaneously. He sat completely still in the centre of it, head bowed, aware of the slick coordinated efforts of the extraction teams, sensing the cold brutality of the supporting assault troops spreading out around him, and not needing to see the red flashes on the armour to know that some of them were the Man's elite guard.

The Senson embedded in his neck was shielded with a dampening patch but he didn't need to communicate with these people. They knew what needed to be done.

More shots – short, controlled bursts, minimum effort, maximum effect – broke through the chaos and noise, followed by the sound of bodies falling and rapid footsteps pounding towards him.

He felt someone he recognised as Banks run up behind him, fumbling to untie the restraints at his wrists and saying, "We got the four outside."

"I know," he muttered. He'd felt them die. Each life extinguished like a light being switched off. "Glad you decided to join the party."

The device was pulled from the back of his neck. Banks and Martinez were supposed to be on special assignment. He felt Martinez kneel in front of him, gently disengaging the rest of the devices, reaching up to pull down the blindfold.

She smiled. "Hey boss."

NG stood. His limbs felt like jelly and for a second, he thought his knees might buckle but Martinez placed a hand on one arm, Banks steadied him on the other side and they walked with him as he made his way over to the three guys and the woman kneeling on the floor. Four of the Man's elite guards were standing over them, rifles held casually but unmistakably pointed at the captives who were still shaking.

NG nodded to the guild personnel and looked down, seeing the leader of his captors for the first time. A dark switch in his mind flipped.

"Who's paying you?" he asked quietly.

The leader looked up defiantly. "I'll tell you nothing."

He heard himself say softly, "You don't need to."

He grabbed the man by the throat.

His fingers connected with warm flesh and there was a panicked snap of horrified tension as the guy tried to flinch away. Futile resistance as it took the merest instant to pierce the mind and negate any instinct to fight.

The mercenary's head slumped to the side.

NG wasted no time then. It was as easy as accessing a data file. He extracted, viciously and ruthlessly, every last vestige of information from the deepest recesses of the mind he was invading, taking the guy's most deep-rooted memories from the moment of birth to this very instant in a rush of subconscious transfer that was almost overwhelming. He trampled through the man's head with no regard for the damage he was causing, receptors and neurons sparking and dying in his wake.

He felt Martinez behind him, watching. He didn't waver. These people had taken a contract to capture him but it was more than that. Whoever had hired them was targeting the guild.

The four guards were cold, pitiless pillars of support on either side, watching unmoved.

In the space of seconds, all that was left of the man was sufficient brain activity to keep the basic biological functions operating. All the higher functions, any trace of the man that had been, were gone.

NG stepped back. "I'm done. We're leaving."

"What do you want us to do with them, boss?" Banks said.

He started for the door, fatigue beginning to burn in every joint and muscle. "Put him out of his misery. The others are of no interest."

The sense of relief from the captives was almost palpable. "You're letting us go?" asked the woman. "After what we did to you?"

He stopped and turned. "Letting you go?" he said, incredulous. "What made you think I was letting you go?"

The shots rang out as he walked away. Three more lights going out in the dark.

No one messes with the Thieves' Guild.

It was cold outside, cold and dark. They stood in the shelter of the doorway for a moment, Banks on one side, Martinez on the other, waiting for the officer in charge of the Man's elite unit to give them the go-ahead to make a move for the ship.

NG shivered. Someone had given him a thick combat jacket and he was still cold. Now that the drama was over, he felt a bone-deep tiredness begin to take hold as the darkness receded from his mind. It was getting hard to keep his eyes open. Martinez had fussed at the head wound but he'd shrugged her away.

He hadn't got the answers he wanted from that mind as it crumbled beneath his touch but he'd got enough to suspect who was behind this.

Banks was talking to someone on the guild ship, fast and

furious, updates on status, the sharp edge of intense focus starting to ease now they had him, safe and almost sound. There was another ship in orbit that they were tracking. He could hear the flow of intel as they communicated through the implants quite clearly even though he wasn't in the loop.

"Get its ID," NG muttered, trying to ignore the pain that was still pulling at the base of his skull, the nausea that was swirling knots in his stomach. Soft tissue was easy for him to manipulate and heal. Broken bones and fractures were hard work. A skull fracture with concussion was sending him sideways now the adrenaline had worn off.

Banks glanced at him. "We're on it, boss." He was thinking that it had been too close. Way too close.

NG could feel a sharp edge of anxiety in his two bodyguards. Martinez was staring at him. He could read from her mind that they'd been sent here expecting to be too late and that they'd find him dead. She was desperately relieved to have found him alive, wanting to get him back to the safety of the Alsatia.

He felt like he'd been caught running away from home.

He pulled the jacket tight, trying to think back and round to what had happened, how he'd screwed up badly enough to be caught that easily, and he had no idea.

He listened in as the mercenaries' contact broke orbit and fled.

Martinez touched a protective hand to his shoulder. "Okay, we're good to go. Let's get you out of here."

There was a summons to the Man's chambers waiting for him when they docked. NG leaned his head against the wall of the private lift and closed his eyes as it took him up through the levels. He'd slept half the way back and used the rest of the time to heal, leaving the visible bruising around his eye to run its course, and concentrating whatever energy he had left down to cellular level to fix the internal damage. He hadn't quite managed it but he'd made headway and didn't feel quite so crap. A chewing out from the Man was the last thing he needed though. He'd made a serious mistake somewhere and it was obviously too much to hope that he might have had time to resolve this mess before the Man heard about it.

He had his hand on the elevator button for level twelve, trying to decide if he had time to go shower and change when an urgent request for attention nudged through the implant. It was official but tagged with one of the codes his staff used when they wanted to talk privately, in person. Decision made. He hit the button and rubbed a hand over his eyes, leaning back into the corner as the lift took him up.

Evelyn was waiting with a cup of hot tea for him, massively relieved to see him intact, but an uncharacteristic agitation buzzing around her that made his head ache again.

"We have a problem," she sent straight away, tight wire through the Senson, as private as they could get.

"I know."

She frowned.

"I'm fine," NG said cautiously, knowing he didn't look it and not sure why she was so fraught.

Evie bit her lip and touched his arm gently.

He read it from her mind an instant before she spoke. "Mendhel's dead."

2

"He is talented," the other commented, "very talented, I would not dispute that. I question whether he is too headstrong and yet not strong enough to be what we need."

"He is impetuous and mischievous," the Man replied. "He is a child, even now. Much of what he has achieved so far has been play. His only weakness is that he cares deeply. But he protects his own and can be ruthless with others. As we need. I admit, he does not yet truly comprehend how powerful he is." He took another sip of the wine. "We underestimated the voracity with which the disparate factions in this galaxy would protect their own and take such dire offence at any threat, however ill-perceived."

"With hindsight," said the other, as she reached for the jug that was resting on the small table between them, "would we have considered other stratagem? Would any other strategy have had a different outcome?"

"No," the Man said. "We have always had limited resources at our command. I stand by the guild and I stand by our decisions, however unpredictable the outcomes have proved to be."

"That's not all," Evie said, ushering him into the office. The grief he could feel tugging deep inside her mixed with the confused disbelief that he couldn't shake. He was tired, still hurting and still pissed that he'd been caught like that.

"What happened?" he said, digging deep to find some energy from somewhere to deal with this. He didn't want to deal with anything. What he wanted was to crawl into a dark corner and lick his wounds alone.

She pushed him through towards the door to his quarters.

"Someone killed him," she said. "LC's missing. We just had to rescue Hilyer from someone who shot him down and took him captive. And the Assassins have accepted a contract on you. Drink your tea."

A hit out on him? He took a sip from the cup. It wasn't just tea. She'd put something in it that sent a warm feeling into his joints. She steered him to the bathroom and started the shower running.

He started to shrug out of his shirt and turned back. "What tabs were they on?"

"We don't know," she said. "There's nothing logged. They were both supposed to be here on down time. We don't know who killed Mendhel. We don't even know who managed to capture Hil but apparently he's a mess. They're bringing him in now."

She watched as he stripped off, frowning at the bruises. "You shouldn't have gone out alone."

He ignored her. He'd gone out with a cast iron ID. No one should have been able to associate him with the guild.

She folded her arms. Not impressed. "Do you need to go to Medical?"

"No, I'm fine. Is this contained?" He needed to limit the dissemination of information on this.

"Yes, of course it is. Do you know who it was?" She was thinking that it couldn't have been the Assassins' Guild who'd got their hands on him or he'd be dead.

He kept quiet, stepping into the stream of hot water and scrubbing off the blood and dirt. He had an idea who it could have been but it wasn't something he could let her into. No one else in the guild, with the exception of the Man himself, even knew about the threat. The Thieves' Guild wasn't the only organisation playing across the lines and they'd crossed swords before, with plenty of people, plenty of times. But this was an escalation. A chill settled deep inside despite the heat of the water. Mendhel Halligan was their best handler. LC Anderton and Zach Hilyer were their two best field operatives. NG rubbed a hand over his eyes. He'd been out on a routine meet and greet. Nothing he hadn't done a thousand times before. It had checked out but his cover had been broken and someone had openly attacked him in an attempt to get to the guild's council of elders? At the same time that someone killed Mendhel?

He turned off the shower. "I need to talk to the Man," he said quietly.

"Yes, you do." Evelyn said, throwing him a towel.

He caught it and wrapped it round his waist. "Is Hilyer hurt?"

"He crashed. Skye's a mess too. Apparently Hil has amnesia. That's why we don't know what happened. He can't remember."

"Who's bringing him in?"

"Hetherington and Wibowski."

"Hurt badly?"

She nodded, hesitant, thinking he couldn't ignore a summons from the Man and knowing that he was going to if she said what she was about to. She said it. "The Chief is waiting for him in the conference room with Legal. I haven't told them yet that you're back."

Christ, it was tempting to leave them to deal with it but he couldn't. Knowing the Chief as he did and knowing that Hil was hurt. "Give me a minute," he said. "Get Media and Science in there too, total blackout, and tell them to wait for me."

He intercepted Hilyer in the hallway. The extraction agents had reported the amnesia but they hadn't mentioned the full extent of the injuries Hil was carrying and the fact that the kid's Senson had been torn from his neck. Hil hadn't been given the luxury of showering and the kid looked bruised and exhausted, eyes glassy and a haunted look on his face that matched the confusion in his mind that was making NG feel dizzy, on top of the throbbing headache.

"It's good to have you back, Hil," NG said softly, grasping the kid's hand in a firm shake and using the contact to read quickly what he could and give enough healing energy to keep Hil on his feet. It wasn't much but it was something. "We're in the shit and I really need to know what you can remember."

Hilyer was one of the best field operatives they'd ever handled, second only to LC right now. He was fearless. Obnoxiously arrogant was the way some people in the guild put it. But Hil could handle himself whatever was thrown at him. Except now he looked like he could pass out at any minute, standing there shivering and on the verge of going into shock. They should have taken him to Medical first.

NG shut out the pain he was picking up. It was bad enough that he had his own half-healed wounds to deal with. Being a telepathic empath was great until you were suddenly in the vicinity of a hospital case. He didn't have much more energy to spare but he put a hand up to the back of Hil's neck, carefully manipulating at base level to bring down the anxiety and nudging him gently into motion down the corridor.

He felt Hil calm within a few steps.

"I… they…" Hil was struggling to speak. "NG, I'm sorry, I don't remember anything straight." He stopped to take a breath and NG was hit by a twinge of sharp second-hand pain shooting through the ribs before he could block it again.

Hil looked up through hooded eyes. "What happened to Mendhel? Has someone told Anya?"

NG kept his face impassive. He hadn't even thought of Mendhel's daughter. He was struggling himself to keep track of the implications of all this. Evelyn would know where she was.

For the moment he shook his head. "We'll go through a full debrief later. Right now I need to know whatever you can remember. You okay for this?"

They stopped at the door to the conference room. He could hear Hil screaming, 'No', to himself inside his head. It didn't take much manipulation and the kid said, "Yeah," a touch of that natural belligerence sparking back into action.

NG nodded and pushed open the door.

The section chiefs of Acquisitions, Legal, Media and Science were already in there. The total blackout he'd ordered meant no display screens and no monitoring of the meeting. This was going to be private. There were too many rumours doing the rounds already.

He steered Hilyer to a seat and took his own place, careful not to let any intrusions into his thoughts yet. The four others at the table were strong personalities – they had to be to control the four main divisions of the guild – and as much as he wanted to know what they were all thinking, he wasn't ready for an outright assault from all four of them. He'd talk to them all separately later. None of them knew what had happened to him and he wanted to keep it that way for now.

He looked across at the huge man sitting opposite Hilyer. "Chief," NG said, "do you want to take this up?"

The Chief was a big man, one of the best they had, and as head of Acquisitions he was responsible for the handlers and the field-ops. He had a right to start this.

The Chief shook his head, placed his hands out flat on the table in front of him and leaned forward towards Hilyer. "Where the hell have you been and what the hell have you been doing?" he said coldly.

Straight to the point. As calm as he was outwardly, NG had never seen the big man this distraught. They'd never lost an active handler before. And more than that, Mendhel had been a good friend to them both. It was hard to shut out raw emotions that were so close to his own.

"We get word Mendhel is dead," the Chief was saying to Hil, "your emergency beacon yells for help and suddenly we can't contact LC. We were hoping he was with you but obviously not. Tell me the three of you weren't out on a tab that we didn't know about."

Hilyer looked confused, blood draining from his face, thinking that no one would ever take an unauthorised tab, why even say it?

It was a genuine emotion.

NG looked around the table. Legal was staring at him, a faint smile creasing the corners of her lips that deepened as he caught her eye. He could guess what she was thinking without having to delve into her mind. He definitely wasn't ready to go there yet. She maintained the contact for a moment longer then cast her gaze over to Hilyer suddenly, a subtle change in expression. She didn't have much respect for the way the field-ops worked – not enough discipline in her eyes.

"We've found evidence of a tab at Mendhel's safe house on Earth," she said coldly to Hil. "He was handling an assignment that had not originated from the guild. What do you know about that?"

There was silence.

NG looked back to Hilyer, looking deep inside and seeing nothing but confusion. He'd encountered people with amnesia before and it was disconcerting to share that twirling chaos of jarred synapses. Hil had it badly. NG broke away before the dizziness could take a hold and watched as they gave the kid a hard time, Hil looking desperately from face to face as they threw questions at him. It was difficult not to break in and rescue the kid from further interrogation but the possibility that Mendhel could have been running an illicit job with his two top field operatives was too serious to handle in any other arena.

Hil was struggling.

The Chief was done, hitting the limit of his patience with this kid who was usually one of his cocky young superstars. "Let me set this straight," he said finally. "You left here with LC. That's logged. It is not in dispute and don't deny it. What the hell were you two doing?"

The complete and utter perplexity that crossed Hilyer's mind was impossible to miss. NG couldn't help but snap his head round to stare. They'd been assuming the amnesia had been caused by the head injuries from the crash but they hadn't realised the extent of it. It was abundantly clear that Hil had absolutely no intact memory of the last time he'd left the Alsatia.

"You don't remember leaving with LC," he said quietly.

Hil looked hard pushed to find any comfort in the fact that someone believed him. It was getting harder to filter out the pain and NG was tempted then to call it, get the kid out of there and down to Medical. It took him a moment to realise that Legal was nudging for a connection through the Senson. He ignored her. It wasn't etiquette to hold private conversations during a conference and he wasn't sure he could handle her inside his head right now. Not aching the way it was.

She flashed him a glare and pushed a data board over, the thin display screen flickering with a not too discrete demand to allow her access.

He sent her a quick, "Devon, we can talk later."

"We need to talk now," she sent back, no disguising the irritation in her tone. She was staring at Hil. "You should send Hilyer to the lock-up."

He had a bad feeling she was right, but he sent, "He should be in Medical."

"They were running an unauthorised tab, NG. We can't let that go. I know, I know, they're the best field-ops we've had in generations. Since the legendary Andreyev. I know the stories. But, NG, face it – these two are rogue. God knows what damage Anderton is doing out there right now."

She broke the connection and turned back to Hil, Media joining in the questioning. Science didn't say much. Science tended to keep to themselves, taking the technology the field-ops brought in and playing with it as it suited them. They didn't mix well and the head of Science was possibly the worst of them all.

It didn't take long before they were down to squabbling amongst themselves. NG braced himself to break it up. Hilyer didn't need this, fading out, sitting there with his eyes closed.

"Get him out of here," NG sent privately to the Chief. "I'll send a guard detail down to Medical. Don't let Devon get anywhere near him."

The Chief nodded. "I don't know what the hell is going on," he sent, "but they wouldn't betray us. I know them."

"I want them both off the standings board."

It was a drastic measure and the order got a raised eyebrow but no argument. Damn right there would be no argument. LC and Hil had a reputation for breaking the rules and that was what kept them at the top of those standings. But whatever was going on, no one messed with the Thieves' Guild, field operatives included.

NG glanced at Hil and looked back at the Chief. "Let me know if you hear from LC. And for Christ's sake, don't authorise any tabs right now without running the list past me first."

Devon waited for everyone to leave before she stood up. She was wearing black, as always, immaculate bearing and turn out. She always made him feel scruffy.

He stood up and walked past her, sending a silent, "Walk with me, Devon," to her through the Senson.

She sidled into step alongside him, eyeing the array of bruises that hadn't quite faded. "Been fighting in the playground, NG?" she sent softly back with the ever-present edge of sarcasm.

He could smell her perfume, a clean subtle scent that was as sharp as the concealed knives she carried. Old habits die hard.

"What have you got?" he said without breaking stride.

Devon smiled. "On Mendhel or you?"

They reached the lift and NG turned to face her as they waited for the doors to open.

This was the game they played in private. Devon wanted his job and she knew he knew it. She'd never been granted audience with the Man but she'd used the channels she could access to make it very clear that she was NG's successor and ready to take over.

NG met her gaze, reading the satisfaction there. She thought she had one up on him, that he'd finally screwed up.

"Five hundred," she said. "Million. I wouldn't go out alone again any time soon, if I were you, NG."

3

"Was it a risk to let one such as Devon get so close?"

The Man smiled. "How could I stop it? Powerful individuals, strong characters, such types will always find each other whether they search for it or not. The guild needs personnel and it will always need the very best."

"But a risk nonetheless?" she said with raised eyebrows.

He tilted his head and considered his goblet, offering it for a top up. "Every time we open the door and let someone in," he said, "be it a high achiever or a waif and stray, we take a risk. Anderton. Hilyer. Mendhel himself. All have been high risk. These creatures are complex. They are short-lived and the ones that are special tend to have experienced life fast and hard. They are not straight forward and Devon was never an exception to that. An exquisite individual, extremely efficient, very clever and intuitive, with an edge about her that has served us well. But a risk to let her get close? It was inevitable. Had I tried to intervene, I suspect I would only have driven them closer."

She left him standing there when the doors opened. He stared after her before following.

"Half a billion?" NG said, a note of scepticism creeping in. "Are you sure?" He looked sideways at her through narrowed eyes as the elevator doors closed, trapping them together in that enclosed space. "Are you tempted?"

She laughed. "I'm retired. You know that. And yes, I'm sure."

She hit the button for eleven and held out a data board. "Everything I have on Mendhel is in here. We've recovered Hilyer's ship. There was a phony package on board – empty – and it looks like she's missing memory modules. It's going to be a long night. And really, NG, you look like shit."

He ignored the snide comment. He felt like shit and his head was still pounding. He didn't manage to keep the tiredness from his voice as he asked, "What about LC?"

She shook her head, a trace of contempt flitting through her mind. She didn't like LC and she didn't hide it. "No sign."

The lift stopped at her level. She held her delicately manicured hand on the button to stop the doors opening.

"I know how much everyone here adores you, NG, but this is serious. Someone wants you dead. You need to be careful out there," she said, a glint in her eyes. She was thinking how fortunate it would be for her if he got himself assassinated.

A dark whisper deep inside reminded him that it was only a small step in logic before she started planning how she could arrange for that to happen herself.

NG couldn't help the small smile that crept out. Devon hadn't retired from the Assassins – he'd made her a better offer.

"I have a good team around me," he said softly.

She knew exactly how good. She didn't know that he knew that Evelyn was one of hers. Her eyes bore into him. "You know, NG, smiling at me like that doesn't always get you what you want."

He knew what he was doing and let the moment hang. "… Yeah, it does."

She smiled, razor sharp, eyes sparkling. "Come find me when you're done." She slid through the gap in the doors and vanished as soon as they opened.

"What happened on Earth?" the Man said, voice undulating gently from within the dark shadows of the chamber. It was hot, humid and a notch warmer than usual.

NG was still standing. No invitation to sit so hopefully it would be swift; he wasn't sure he could handle a drawn out inquisition.

"We don't know yet," he said.

"The Assassins have accepted a contract on you," the Man said, no hesitation in going for the jugular. "Unprecedented."

NG kept his gaze straight, heart rate steady. It was unprecedented and he'd been trying to figure out what he'd done to upset someone, what the guild had been doing to upset the balance, that was so bad someone was prepared to pay that much to take him out. There was nothing obvious.

"And yet those mercenaries didn't kill you outright which means someone else wants you alive," the Man said quietly, changing topic with lightning speed and beckoning him to sit. "I wonder, NG, if you fully appreciate the risk you take every time you go out alone."

NG sank into the chair, the aches making themselves known and it took some effort to keep the discomfort from his mind.

"They weren't going to kill me," he said, the absolute confidence in that statement belied somewhat by the defensive tone he failed to temper. "They didn't want me, they wanted the council."

The Man stood and moved away from the desk. "We have stirred emotions in some treacherous territory. I fear this is the work of the Order."

There was a clink of bottles from the rack on the far wall. NG didn't turn, staring at the grain in the flat wooden surface of the desk.

"Our old adversaries are far more dangerous than you realise," the Man said, finally settling on a vintage that suited his mood and wandering back to the desk. "They resent our reach. You risk too much."

NG bit his tongue. He'd never hidden within the confines of the guild and he'd be damned if he was going to start now.

He felt a hand touch briefly against the back of his head as the Man passed, low down on his skull, the pain dissipating completely, instantly. He hadn't appreciated how bad it was getting until it vanished.

The Man sat. "You are far more important than you will allow yourself to accept." He opened the wine and poured the dark red liquid into a jug before looking up. "The Order has had tendrils snaking amongst man's corridors of power throughout human history. The guild is young in comparison yet they have never before managed to breach our defences. Why now?"

NG stared, unblinking. If Banks and Martinez hadn't pulled him out, he could have been one step closer to finding out.

The Man pushed forward one of the goblets. "You would have been dead," he said dryly. "They would not have hesitated to kill you once they had what they wanted. They have attacked us. Openly declared war. Find out which faction of the Order, which individual, is behind this. Find them and end it. Then find out which fool has had the temerity to place a price on your head."

He was alone when he woke, nowhere near rested enough and a demand for attention pulsing insistently at the Senson.

"Boss, I know you didn't want to be disturbed…" There was something strange about Evie's tone. "Legal has turned up something against Hilyer. She wants to throw him in the lock-up. The Chief is standing his ground but it's getting nasty. Media needs to know how you want the situation on Earth handling. Science want you in the Maze to sign off on some prototype. And Sean O'Brien is waiting in your office."

He sat up, disentangling himself from sheets that still held a faint scent of Devon's perfume.

He had a hangover. He could neutralise most substances but not the fine black powder the Man mixed with his wine to create the warmth and fumes that always set the atmosphere in those chambers. To open the mind, the Man said. It did that alright but it was tiring.

The section chiefs could manage without him for another hour. Sean though? Sean O'Brien was one of the best outside agents they worked with and she was great company but he was exhausted. He could still feel the edge of the narcotics from the wine so he couldn't have been asleep long.

He scrubbed a hand over his hair and sent back gently, "Can't it wait?"

"Someone's put a bounty out on LC."

It was so absurd, it didn't register. "What?"

"Twenty million. It's gone galaxy-wide in hours. O'Brien thought you'd want to know."

It didn't take long to shower and shake off the cobwebs. Evie had set the lights in the office low and put a tray on the table. She knew how to look after him after he'd been in there for a session with the Man.

Sean was already sipping at a cup of tea. She was looking well. She stood and stuck out her hand as he approached. He shook it with a smile. It had been a while since they'd had her on the books but she was one of his favourites and it was good to see her again, despite the circumstances.

"How's the old man?" he asked, waving her to sit.

Sean smiled. "Fishing in a boat off an island on some deserted planet he found in the Between. He built a cabin there. It's very peaceful."

"Sounds tempting."

"It's good for him. You'd hate it."

NG smiled as he poured himself a cup of tea. He couldn't imagine Frank O'Brien spending his days fishing.

"He's threatening to come out of retirement for this one," Sean said. "I told him to stay where he was."

"Twenty million?"

She nodded.

"How do you know it's on LC?" The field-ops never used their real identities when they went out.

"It's in his name," she said simply, pushing a data board across the desk. "LC Anderton. There's a physical description and the contract cites the Thieves' Guild. There's no doubt. And it's the highest bounty ever posted on a single individual. It's going crazy out there."

NG sipped at his tea and flicked through the screens. There was information there that couldn't have come from anywhere but inside the guild.

He put the board down and looked up. "Just LC?"

"As far as I know," Sean said carefully.

"Dead or alive?"

"Alive, as far as I can tell. But I have heard rumours that it may change."

Sean was good, possibly the best bounty hunter currently working, on both sides of the line. That she was sitting here, that she'd brought this to him, spoke volumes. It was unheard of that the Federation of Bounty Hunters would accept a contract on a member of the Thieves' Guild and it wasn't hard to make a snap decision.

"Standard rate plus expenses," he said.

Sean smiled. "You'll need to give me more information on him."

"I can do better than that," NG said. "I can give you the field operative he was with when he went missing."

Hilyer wasn't impressed at being sent out with a bounty hunter and Devon wasn't impressed at losing him and losing the chance for Legal to get one over on Acquisitions. But hiring Sean made sense. According to Media, news of the bounty was spreading faster than they could contain it. "We've never seen anything like it," she'd said. "This could be really awkward."

When Media said something could be awkward, she meant catastrophic. Nothing was a problem as far as her department were concerned, every challenge merely a fantastic new opportunity to exploit. He'd told her to wrap up on Earth and go after the Federation. They'd always had a more than civil arrangement of mutual respect with the Federation of Bounty Hunters, which now looked like it had gone to hell.

Worse than that, they had a breach. As huge as the guild was, it had never before been compromised. Somehow, personal intel on LC had been leaked. And someone had blown his own cover and the location of that meet and greet to a bunch of mercenaries.

NG stared at his desk. He'd initiated an internal investigation and sparked a massive guild-wide review of procedures. He still had a pile of routine work to clear and a stack of special assignments to set in motion. Half the specials were pie in the sky long shots to try to smoke out something on the Order, not that he could reveal that to the personnel involved. There were a couple of active theatres that needed attention, conflicts they had security forces involved in, but the rest could wait – he had too many people on Mendhel and LC.

There was also an encrypted grey-tagged file sitting there, something he couldn't explicitly confide in anyone, something no one else could even access. The Man's special project, compartmentalised and well beneath any radar.

The Man had gone. Taken off in his ship, taking all the elite guards, off to do whatever it was he did. Meeting with the rest of the council, as far as anyone else was concerned.

NG stood up and stretched, nipped across the office and switched the pot of tea for a bottle of whisky. He needed to find out who'd trashed his cover. He looked at the stack of work and poured out a shot. First things first. He dealt with the grey, always the priority, meticulously entering the intel into the matrix, then worked his way steadily through the rest. It was all complicated and it was frying his brain.

He picked up the last board that was tagged urgent and stared at it, not sure he could face it. He decided not, sat back and put his feet up on the desk, tempted to close his eyes for a moment.

Evelyn appeared outside his door, hovering, trying to decide if she could disturb him.

"What is it?" he sent.

She popped her head round the door, a tinge of bemusement in her mind, wondering how he did that, if he had sensors somewhere she didn't know about. "Science really want you in the Maze. Why don't you do that then sack it for the day. I'll fend off anyone else."

NG sat up. "What's so urgent with Science?"

Evie shrugged. "The message I got was that they want to implement some new drone in the Maze and want your go ahead."

"Tell them to go ahead."

"They want you to see it. Go on, it'll take a minute." She smiled. "You know what they're like."

He knew fine well what they were like. Out of all the guild personnel, they were the hardest to handle. Science played at the bleeding edge of technology, so much so he'd swear they'd sacrifice goats if they thought it would give them an advantage. The guild gave the field operatives a lot of leeway because of their particular talents; the guys in Science got even more because of theirs. It was like babysitting an entire ship of child prodigies. Science had been working on this automated patrol drone for months. If they needed him to see it for no other reason than to impress him, then he needed to see it.

It was cold in there so NG pulled an extra shirt and gloves from his locker before logging in. The Maze was the training ground for the field-ops and, himself aside, no else ever went in there except the techies for routine maintenance and Science when they wanted to dabble. It was a playground, as dangerous as you decided to set it, safety protocols almost foolproof. There were still areas where you could fall thirty feet and Medical were always complaining about the number of broken bones from reckless disrespect of the zero gravity in the Sphere.

It was his favourite place on the Alsatia and he hadn't realised how much he needed to stretch his legs.

The two guys from Science were already logged in. If nothing else, he needed to get them out of there so the field-ops could get back in. Fights and altercations in Acquisitions always increased if the Maze was out of bounds.

He caught up with them at the entrance to the Catacombs, halfway through the Maze and a nightmare if you had no sense of direction.

"Don't tell me you're thinking of deploying them in here," he said as he walked up.

Both the Science guys jumped, IQs at the top of the scale and nerves as edgy as mice in a snake pit.

They spun around, leaving the two drones hovering at head height behind them. They weren't expecting him. They weren't expecting anyone and they didn't know what to say, horrified to see him.

Whoever had sent the message up to his office hadn't told these guys and was probably pissing themselves laughing.

"What have you got there?" he said softly to put them at ease.

One of the Science guys blinked, tongue still tied, hands fidgeting with some kind of gadget.

The other one stared wide-eyed for a moment then turned slightly to wave a hand towards the drones. "It's the new auto-sentry," he said, careful with his words. "We've just powered them up. We're about to run a field test."

"I know," NG said slowly. "You want to show me what you've got?"

They both grinned then and turned back to their toy. "It's a completely self-reliant decision-making weapons platform," the wide-eyed guy said. "Fully autonomous, AI about equivalent to a shark. We've modified the model from the original specs to make it more intelligent, faster, and loaded weapons with FTH, low stun so we don't piss off the field-ops too much. They're going to be hard pushed to beat these fellas." He turned back to NG with a shy smile. "You want a demo?"

He nodded. Why not?

The hum emanating from both machines deepened with a click as weapons engaged. They were intimidating as hell. With a whirr, the two drones spun, targeted and fired at the two scientists, shots to centre mass, both lethal, the two pops of dark void as they died hitting NG like a hammer blow.

4

"Could you have protected him more?" she asked.

That was a difficult question and one he had pondered long and hard. The Man stroked a hand over the soft leather on the arm of his seat, absorbing its warmth, enjoying the company he was with. He enjoyed these comings together. Appreciated the rituals of sharing with an equal in such splendid and intimate surroundings. He looked up. "It took me a long time to find him and it has taken me a long time to nurture him into what he is now. But such a valuable asset is of no use to us whatsoever if we mollycoddle and smother him to keep him safe. His very nature demands he face adversity head on."

"Should we not have dealt with the other guilds more effectively?"

"We dabble. We guide a lot of organisations, subtly from within. A guild as small as the Assassins? I made the decision to leave them alone. To have infiltrated them would have been to take them over and I have never had a desire to perpetrate such outright cold-blooded murder. It doesn't sit well. I considered them in hand. I was wrong."

Automatic reactions kicked in. NG dropped and rolled, shots hitting the wall behind him. The drones moved fast, sharp precise realignments to target him as he dived desperately out of the way. He fell more than ran into the Catacombs and scrambled through into the tunnels. He didn't have a clue what these drones were fitted with. It was dark but presumably they had infrared and motion sensors, and they were packing live rounds, no doubt about that. He was screwed.

He ran, bullets ricocheting all around, expecting a shot in the back of the head at any moment. He scraped his arm against the walls until he found the gap he was looking for. He squeezed through, something hitting his trailing arm with a sting, and they had no chance to follow, slamming up against the walls, motors squealing, firing volley after volley in there after him until they gave up and flew off.

He took a moment to catch his breath and reached around to his arm, pulling out a tiny injector dart. The bastards had hypos as well as guns and they were artificially intelligent, no life signs, no emotions, nothing he could sense or track.

He tried to remember the layout of the tunnels and reckoned he had about two minutes before they'd work out a route round and catch up with him. Keep moving was the only plan he could come up with and he started to run, initiating a link to Evelyn.

She answered immediately, concerned. "What's wrong?"

"Why the hell is Science…" he sent, skidding around a corner, "…using live ammunition in the Maze?" He could hear a distant hum vibrating through the chill air.

"They're not," Evie sent. "Why would they? Oh god. Are you okay?"

He started to say he was but his breath caught in his chest and he thought he heard the noise up ahead switch in pitch. He slowed to a walk.

"Boss?"

She sounded miles away. He slowed again and leaned a hand against the wall, feeling a weakness in his knees. He was still clutching the tiny dart and as he brought it up to look at it, his vision swam and it was impossible to focus. He slumped against the wall, feeling his heart racing. Poison. Why would Science kit out an auto-sentry with poisoned darts?

He didn't mean to but he must have sent that last thought because Evie sent back, "They wouldn't. NG, where are you?"

It was a potent toxin and he couldn't help sinking to the floor. He slowed his heart rate and threw everything he had into countering it. If he passed out, he was dead.

"He's in the Maze," he overheard Evie send to someone else. "Get someone down there, for god's sake."

By the time he could see straight again, he had no idea how long it had been.

He got to his feet, swayed and reached to the wall to steady himself. He'd slowed the poison but it would take longer to neutralise it completely. He needed to get out of here.

There were two ways out of the Catacombs – the Shaft or the Chamber, so it was climbing or swimming. Backtracking to the entrance was a simpler option but he had no idea where the drones were.

"NG!"

"I'm fine," he managed to send, starting to work his way slowly back.

'*You're dying*,' the little voice in his head whispered. '*That was far too easy for them*.'

"NG, listen to me," Evie sent. "Science deny that there are any live weapons on those drones."

"Hate to disagree," he muttered weakly.

She didn't say it but he could almost sense what she was thinking through the connection. The drones had been programmed to kill.

He leaned his head back against the wall for a moment. In all the talk of Assassins and contracts, no one had once considered he might be at risk here, on board the Alsatia.

"We'll have Security in there in two minutes," Evie sent.

"No you won't," he sent, pausing as he heard a faint hum ahead. "Get to the control room. Keep a lid on this and keep everyone out. These things are going to kill anyone who comes in here."

He backed away and ran as a stream of bullets raked across the wall.

The Catacombs were full of narrow gaps he could squeeze through, leaving the drones trapped behind him each time they started to close in. Twice he ended up on his knees and the third time, he sprawled, out cold, and it was only Evie screaming in his head that got him up and staggering out of the way of another barrage.

There was no way he could face a vertical climb so he stumbled past the entrance to the Shaft and headed for the centre. The tunnels leading to the Chamber were all wide and there was nothing he could do but run for it, vision mostly gone, muscles trembling and coordination shot. The drones closed in fast and he ran into the open and dived into the pool amidst a hail of projectiles.

He hit the surface and plunged into the still water, feeling a pulse of pressure each time a bullet or dart pierced the water close by.

He sank into a cold world of absolute silence. He knew he should swim but he couldn't get his limbs to move. He was leaving feathery trails of red blood in the water and could feel poison spreading into his bloodstream from his leg and neck, burning pain in his shoulder. He'd moved fast, reflexes faster than any normal human otherwise they would have killed him in that first instant. The poison would probably have killed anyone else in seconds.

He couldn't do anything but sink, slowing his heart rate, slowing his breathing and relaxing every muscle from instinct more than any conscious plan.

It was a peaceful eternity until a splash from above sent a pressure wave billowing down towards him as the mass of the drone dived into the pool.

It closed in and followed him down, emanating an eerie hum that resonated under the water, weapons platforms spinning out streams of tiny bubbles.

He stared at it with the weird feeling that it was staring back at him, waiting with its smart as a shark intelligence for him to die. He slowly reached and pulled out two of the tiny darts, letting them tumble from numb fingers that could barely grip.

He drifted in the cool water and shut down.

Awareness came back with a jolt. There was no sign of the drone. He spun around in the water then kicked for the dark mouth of the flooded tunnel that led away from the Chamber. He swam, chilled through, muscles weak and shoulder burning, but still alive. Slowing the heart rate and dampening life signs was a trick they taught the field-ops, but nothing to that extreme. He'd dropped into a state of almost total suspended animation and it seemed to have fooled the drones.

He swam steadily, slowly, favouring his right arm. They always kept the water cold. It was designed to be testing and the tunnel was longer than anyone could naturally hold their breath. It seemed to take forever.

He finally made it through and surfaced into a smaller pool at the end of a narrow corridor. He was half expecting a drone to be there waiting but it was quiet.

He struggled to ease himself up out of the water and sat on the edge for a moment, dripping, breathing coming back slowly and painfully. He pushed a hand against his shoulder. It was still bleeding. So much for FTH.

He knew he needed to move but lying down for a minute seemed like a good idea.

"Evie," he sent tentatively, lying there on his back, legs dangling in the pool.

"NG, we thought you were dead," Evelyn sent, a slight shake in her tone. They were probably watching the life signs monitors from the control room. "There's a drone heading for you. Don't move. We're sending Security in."

"Don't," he sent, careful to keep the pain from his own voice as he pushed himself up onto his feet.

He started walking, becoming vaguely conscious of life signs moving within the Maze. "Evie, get them out of here."

"Boss," she started to send, breaking off as a distant echo of void popped through his awareness.

Three more pops followed in silent succession.

NG could still feel the poison coursing through his system but the edge of it had gone and he broke into a run. "Evelyn, listen to me. I need you to disable the safety protocols and initiate the patrol bots in the Block."

"Boss…"

"Don't argue with me, Evie, and for Christ's sake, don't send anyone else in here."

After that she just gave him a steady commentary on the positions of the drones. They went for the bots, fooled by the artificially transmitted life signs the small machines were designed to emit to train the field-ops in the use of sensory equipment. He managed to reach the stairs leading up to the Void before one of them switched targets and came after him.

"You need to move faster," Evelyn sent, calmly, and started counting down the distance as the drone closed in on him.

He was trying. There was no easy way out of the Maze. That was the whole point. Whoever had planned this had been smart. Very smart.

The Void was enclosed by locked blast doors. If he could get in there, it would give him time to come up with a plan.

He ran up the stairs, stumbling a couple of times and hearing the resonating hum of the drone behind. The best field-ops could break this lock open fast. LC's record was two minutes fifty. NG could do it in three and right now that was three minutes too long. Fortunate then that he had a personal assistant in the control room. He heard the lock disengage ahead of him as he ran towards it, as Evie counted down to ten metres and closing. He slipped through the gap and flinched as shots from the fast approaching drone peppered all around.

As the door slammed shut behind him, he stopped, heart pounding, the residue of the poison pumping through his bloodstream, and turned to face the beam that extended out into the darkness of the Void. It was three hundred feet long, only four inches wide and a fall of a hundred and fifty feet straight down if you slipped. Snakes and ladders. If you got across, it cut the time through the Maze in half. If you fell, you tumbled almost back to the start.

There was a crashing thud behind him then silence.

"It's gone," Evelyn sent. "What do you want us to do?"

"Find out from Science who the hell had access to these drones."

"I mean now, to get you out of there."

NG sat down on the beam, almost tumbling over the edge as he lost his balance for a second. He worked on getting his heart rate under control again before sending quietly, "Find out if anyone's controlling these things. And get a patrol bot to meet me at the far end of the Void."

He quickly went through with her the only plan he could think of, then stood, took a breath and ran the full length of the beam.

The Void led to the Block which led to the Sphere, all on the line of the Straight, the fastest route through the Maze.

There was a bot rolling along the floor towards NG as he ran out from the Void. He didn't stop, reaching down and scooping it up in the palm of his hand as he ran past.

He ran up the stairs to the Block, struggling again by the time he reached the top, hearing the echoing blasts of gunfire up ahead. The drones were going ballistic. Finance would go spare. The patrol bots cost a small fortune and from the sound of it, there weren't going to be any left.

"I hope you know what you're doing," Evie sent.

"Just be ready on that button," he sent back, climbing up onto a walkway that ran around the outside edge of the Block. The Block was a maze within the Maze – corridors and walkways on multiple levels with access via vents, shafts, ladders and narrow staircases. Both drones were in there. The trick was going to be to get one alone then switch off the life signs from the rest of the bots and hope he could get out of the way fast enough.

He chose one and ran towards it, shrugging off the fatigue that was draining his energy faster than he could fix it. He slid down a ladder, ran along a narrow walkway and jumped over a handrail, ten feet drop to the walkway, perfectly timed to land behind a drone that was darting after targets in front of it. It sensed him there and whirled, guns firing as he threw himself to the side, a round clipping his arm, before it spun its attention back to the bots. He almost dropped the bot he was holding, shutting out the pain and going into auto to struggle to his feet and jam the bot into the drone's exoskeleton.

It spun again, catching him on the side of the head and knocking him flying. He rolled with it and tumbled off the walkway, shots ricocheting off the deck.

"Now!" he sent to Evie and the firing stopped abruptly, the whirr and hum of the drone the only noise in the echoing space. This was the danger point. There'd be only two life signs in the Block. If they both came after him, he was screwed.

He could hear the drone above spinning, actuators screaming as it tried to home in on a life sign that moved as it moved.

"The other one's going for it," Evie sent. "Get out of there!"

NG started running, hearing gunfire from above as the second drone targeted the life signs from the trapped bot. There was a flash and a boom, and the shock of an explosion threw him off his feet. He rolled and staggered forward, running for the exit.

A long narrow corridor joined the Block to the Sphere. NG ran, footsteps echoing loud in his ears, feeling like his limbs didn't belong to him. He was losing blood again but there was nowhere to hide out and he was about done with being in here. The door to the Sphere loomed in the distance as he heard the remaining drone turn into the corridor behind him. It was a helluva risk.

The door slid open up ahead and he increased his pace, the drone speeding up in response, weapons whirring.

"Don't screw this up," Evie whispered.

'*You couldn't screw up more if you tried*,' the dark voice echoed.

He shut it out.

The Sphere was another trap – get it right and you were on your way and running, get it wrong and you were on your way to Medical. NG picked up the pace again and ran full tilt at the doorway. The drone started firing, shots winging past his ears. Something hit the back of his neck with a sting and he almost stumbled, managing somehow to keep his momentum and race headlong through the door into the zero gravity of the Sphere.

He curled into a ball and shot across the vast space, inertia keeping his trajectory true to the other side. He scraped through the opposite doorway and hit the deck with a skidding roll, weight returning with a thump. He had no control and crashed into the bulkhead, tumbling into a heap.

He heard the door slam shut behind him and felt more than heard a shudder that vibrated through the deck. There was a loud crash from inside the Sphere, then silence.

5

"How did they manage to infiltrate the Alsatia?"

"We were betrayed," he replied dryly.

"How?"

The Man leaned across and stoked the fire, flames dancing and sparks flying. "Ask not how, ask why."

She was thinking it was obvious, there was five hundred million on offer and in the scale of human greed, that was more than a lot, it was obscene. Of course they would chase it, whatever it took, but she humoured him. "Why? Why did the Assassins dare attack our stronghold?"

He regarded her for a moment. Thought not just of this assault on board the cruiser but of all that had followed. Every tumbling action, reaction and over-reaction that these events had precipitated.

"Hubris," he said finally, simply. "These creatures thrive on it. To infiltrate and undermine the great and mysterious guild of thieves? To steal away our very heart from under our noses? That would have been truly gratifying."

"Yet this attempt failed? I thought the Assassins never failed."

"They failed because they underestimated. In every capacity. They calculated in terms of normal human boundaries and we are far, far beyond those."

Everything hurt. NG lay still for a moment then stirred, sitting and reaching to his neck to pull out the dart.

He leaned back against the bulkhead, clamping a hand around the wound in his right arm and slowing his heart rate to slow the poison.

It didn't take long for Evelyn to come running up, three paces ahead of a team that looked like it contained personnel from every division of the guild.

"Didn't I say to keep a lid on this?" he sent to her privately, tired and not exactly wanting company.

She slowed to a walk and strode up, arms folded, looking down at him and along the corridor towards the Sphere.

"Less than ten people know about this, NG. I'm not sure what we're going to tell the cleaning crew."

He followed her gaze. Blood was smeared in streaks all along the deck.

The medic in the group kneeled by his side and started fussing with trauma patches and injectors.

NG leaned his head back and closed his eyes. "I need to talk to everyone who had access to the drones," he sent to Evie.

"NG," she replied hesitantly, "Science is adamant that no one could have tampered with them."

She sent that, the medic hit a sore spot and something snapped inside. NG felt every muscle tense, anger flaring as a dark mist flashed across his mind. He swatted the medic away and glared at Evelyn, eyes hooded.

"Get Science into my office now," he sent without thinking, cold and scathing. "I'll start with him."

She stood her ground, startled but foolhardy enough to defy him. "You need to go to Medical."

"I need to see Devon. Get her up there as well."

He felt someone pull open his shirt, shoving a trauma patch up against the wound in his shoulder and NG almost lost it, grabbing the guy's wrist as the patch activated with an agonising stab of burning pain. He bit down on a gasp and tried to brace himself to fend them off, coming up against a soft touch from Evie on the back of his neck and a calming whisper in his ear. He sagged back and closed his eyes again, the heat of the moment gone. Control returning.

Evelyn took hold of his hand and he squeezed, holding onto her like a lifeline, drawing strength from the connection.

"Come on," she said softly, "let's get you up to Medical."

He still protested but she insisted. He won the argument that he could walk by persuading her in his own way, not hard with her hand still holding his arm. It wasn't often that he did that to Evelyn but there was no way he was going to wait for a med team to bring a stretcher. While he was in her mind, he checked her out. She was the one who'd sent him down here but she was clear. Worried. About him and about the breach in security. He knew she always carried a concealed weapon but she'd added a sidearm, he noticed as they walked.

They had four members of the Watch with them, in full body armour, and somewhere along the way, Banks and Martinez joined the entourage.

They were all patient with him, waiting without a word every time he had to stop to catch his breath. He shouldn't have been so stubborn, but someone had cleared the way because they didn't encounter anyone else until they reached Medical.

"We've doubled the Watch," Evelyn sent through a private link, staying close as he was led into a private room and steered towards a bunk. "The Alsatia is on lockdown, no one in or out and maximum security across the cruiser."

So much for containing the fact there was a contract out on him.

"The Chief thinks this has to be related to Mendhel," she sent. "What's the chance this could be a coordinated attack?"

NG perched on the edge of the bunk and let a medic help him shrug out of his sodden shirt, wincing as the guy started to prod and clean the wounds in his shoulder and arm.

"I don't know," he admitted, keeping the connection private and having trouble concentrating enough to switch off the pain. "Let's be careful. Give me a couple of hours and we'll come up with a plan."

Evie frowned at the suggestion that he'd be fine in a couple of hours.

"Trust me," he sent. "And get me some dry clothes, would you?"

Evelyn disappeared. She was more worried than she was letting on. NG lay back. She should be. The Alsatia had never been attacked before. Ever.

The medics left him alone finally and he closed his eyes, going as deep as he could to heal while still keeping an awareness of his surroundings. They'd left a guard on the door, but he still didn't want to rely entirely on anyone else. Not until they identified how the drones' weapons had been tampered with. Scanning for life forms, he had a range of about a mile. Reading someone's immediate surface thoughts he could easily manage at ten feet, twenty at a push. Going for intentions and emotions that were buried deep, he needed to be close if not touching. It was going to be one hell of an operation to scan every single member of the guild until they found the leak.

Devon came by after a while. He opened one eye and looked at her as she wandered over, throwing a bag onto a chair, a smile creeping across her face when she saw he was awake.

"Hey," she said.

He smiled back, well aware that it could have been her.

She shook her head, eyes flashing, the smile turning into a grin. "Do you know how rare it is for someone to survive an attack by the Assassins?"

"They'll have to try harder than that. What do you think they'll go for next?"

"If it was me, I'd use a high powered rifle over distance. Large calibre rounds to the head rarely fail."

She was smiling but she was deadly serious. Devon had been one of the most successful Assassins in a generation. The only thing that had lured her over was the promise of more power. The Assassins' Guild was tiny in comparison to the Thieves' Guild. She had no chance of progression there. Here on the Alsatia, she had her own empire.

"Science is denying that they've been breached," she said dryly. "They're still analysing the poison." She gestured at him to sit up. "Let me take a look. You got one in the neck?"

He obliged and sat patiently while she stroked a finger over the tiny entry point. More gentle than she usually was but even so it was still sore. He took the chance with that brief contact to read her thoroughly, as deep as he ever wanted to go with Devon. She was clean. Annoyed that someone had stepped over the line into her territory. But nothing to do with arranging it.

She stepped back, shaking her head again, but frowning this time, puzzled. She wanted to say something but didn't, biting it back and saying instead, "The Assassins have full biometrics on you."

That shouldn't have been possible. He couldn't even start to figure out how his biometrics could have been acquired by anyone; as far as he knew that data wasn't even stored anywhere. He had his own reasons for needing a level of anonymity even amongst their own.

"I'm trying to find out how they have so much information," she added. "What did those mercenaries do to you?"

"I have no idea."

She was thinking that the intel was too good; she'd never been able to find out so much as his real name in all the digging she'd done herself, here. And he knew she'd done a lot. There simply wasn't a file to be leaked.

"What did they do, NG?"

He took a deep breath. "Devon, I was unconscious half the time. They could have done anything. But they didn't want me; they wanted a way to the council."

"Well, someone wants you and they want you dead." She turned to go and waved towards the bag. "Evelyn sent a change of clothes. She reckoned you wouldn't be wanting to stay here much longer." She left with a wink. "Watch your back, NG."

It was a relief to know that Evelyn and Devon were in the clear. That was two down, the two most obvious, a couple of thousand to go.

NG took his time dressing, sore and feeling a weakness that went bone deep inside but Evelyn was right. He didn't want to stay in Medical.

Media came in as he was trying to figure out if he could make it up to twelve without flaking out. She perched on the edge of the bed next to him and frowned, looking more serious than he'd ever seen her.

She skipped the pleasantries. "The Federation is closing ranks against us, NG," she said. "Someone has a paid a lot of money to buy their cooperation, on top of the bounty they posted on LC. It's as if they pre-empted our response and went to pains to make sure there was no way we could interfere. Someone wants to get hold of our boy really badly."

"Offer more to get him back alive," NG said.

"No go. They have a clause in the agreement. Someone is determined that we're not going to have a say in this."

"What about Mendhel?"

"It looks like it was a professional hit. I'm sorry. Probably not the Assassins because there was no registered contract. And we still haven't been able to contact Anya. It doesn't look good." She squeezed his hand. "I hate to bring this up," she sent privately, tight wire, "but there are mutterings about Devon over this."

This being someone tampering with the drones.

The last thing he needed was an outright war between the section chiefs.

"She's clean," he sent back, holding on to her small hand for a moment and using the contact to check her out and reinforce the message. "Trust me."

NG leaned on the bench. He was tired. Science didn't have any chairs in his lab and as much as it was tempting to take this conversation back up to twelve, he had no desire to drag it out for longer than necessary.

He'd spent three days screening every member of personnel in Science. He had a splitting headache that wouldn't shift but he'd found nothing. Not a trace of anyone who could have tampered with the drones and not a scrap of evidence as to how someone had gained access to Science or the Alsatia.

They still had no leads on the Assassins, no leads on Mendhel, and there was still no sign of LC. And no sign of the Man returning.

"I don't know," Science said finally, reluctantly, resenting that his section was under suspicion. Few other personnel ever went into Science so yes, it was his people they were looking at. And he knew it.

It wasn't easy to be patient. NG looked up through hooded eyes, spinning through his fingers some kind of gizmo he'd picked up out of the pile of crap on the workbench. Before he'd been appointed as head of operations, the Man had insisted that he experience every aspect of the guild first hand. Science hadn't been his favourite posting and his stint here hadn't ended well, no tolerance for the tedious intricacies of scientific method back then and even less now, especially with this latest chief who was even more aloof than the previous two.

They'd trawled through the records, isolating all personnel who could have got to the drones since the last time they were checked. A list of thirty four names were still outstanding – twenty nine on leave, five with no reason to be missing. It was more than disturbing to find a section with that many personnel awol and no one even aware they weren't here. It wasn't the way the Alsatia worked. They'd got complacent.

He glanced over his shoulder. The two guys from the Watch were standing a discrete distance behind him. This wasn't the way he worked. The incident with the drones had set everyone on edge.

"Find them," he said simply, pushing forward the board containing that list of elusive names.

Science scowled and reached forward, snatching the gizmo defensively and ignoring the board. "We will."

At its most inherent level, every aspect of guild operations was embedded firmly in the collection of intelligence; intrigue and subterfuge were threaded through every action, every section and department. Yet that scrutiny had never been directed inwardly before. There had always been security, a hidden code of integrity wrapped in a healthy paranoia and fierce internal competition that never failed and now somehow it had. Science was the core of guild operations, and as much as he didn't like it, he knew it was their beating heart. It might be Acquisitions who went out there to bring in the intelligence and technology but it was Science that worked their magic and made the advances that kept them one step ahead.

"Could someone have breached your security?" NG said bluntly.

Science was affronted and didn't bother to hide it. "One time," he snapped. "And not once since that..." ...little bastard Anderton, he was thinking, pausing abruptly and biting off his tirade as he realised the implications. NG could hear the thought processes ticking through that extraordinary brain; if someone else had broken in, that meant it might not have been one of his people, but it meant they had been breached. Science was calculating fast, analysing the odds and asking himself which was worse, and as he caught NG's eye, he averted his eyes quickly – whichever it was, one of his prototypes had almost killed their head of operations and that was unacceptable.

'*Damn right it's unacceptable*,' the dark voice inside chided. NG rubbed a hand over his eyes, feeling the pull in the shoulder. The two bullet wounds were healed, superficially, but sore still. And he was still tired. It was taking a long time to get over the effects of the poison, longer than it should have. It was frustrating. He wasn't used to feeling so weak, right on the back of the skull fracture. And the Man wasn't here, not that he would have run in there for help anyway. So he felt like shit again.

Even so, he didn't need Science to be feeling guilty and paranoid – that would just lead to more mistakes.

"What are you working on?" he asked, switching on a calm that was hard work to maintain but immediately effective in setting Science back onto an even keel.

The tall section chief took a visibly deep breath.

He stared for a moment, regarding NG with slight suspicion and trying to gauge if he really wanted to hear what they were working on.

"Stealth," he said suddenly, an almost child-like eagerness to please winning out.

Sitting through an hour-long explanation of the latest in stealth technology was the last thing he needed, and guaranteed there'd be no hospitality offered, but NG nodded.

Science grabbed another board and placed it on top of the pile of crap between them. "We're integrating spatial ambiguity theory with undetermined Agram's engineering principles."

It took a moment to realise that the guy had stopped speaking, waiting for approval.

"Agram's?" NG said, for want of a better response.

"We acquired tech on a tab last month that brought some new equations to bear. Controversial. Impressive but not as impressive as when we combined it with irreconciled SAT."

NG blinked. Irreconciled spatial anything made his head pound. "Field applications?"

Science nodded. "We're working on scale invariant deviants."

It took too long to think of a response and Science added, "Individual-personal and ship-scale," with a slight arrogance to his tone and the clear suspicion in his mind that NG had no idea what he was talking about.

"Work with the Chief and Quinn. We need this in the field," NG said, not knowing what the hell they were talking about. The Senson in his neck engaged with a gentle query as Evelyn nudged for his attention. "What's up?" he sent.

"Legal has a client asking to see you."

"Now?" It was an escape from Science but even so, facing a client was the last thing he needed.

"She thinks we might have a problem."

6

"You should have known."

It was a blunt accusation. He took a slow sip of the wine, feeling the chemicals in the narcotic touch on the receptors in his brain with a teasing embrace.

She pushed it further, leaning forward to emphasise her point. "If there was a breach in security, a traitor in our midst, why did you not know? Could you not have simply looked into the minds of your personnel for yourself? Are you not aware of such potential actions before they occur?"

"I'm not omnipotent," he said simply.

NG leaned his back against the wall of the lift. It was two levels up to Legal and he was taking the lift.

It was pathetic.

It was also his own fault – a stubborn need from his side to prove there was nothing wrong. No one messes with the Thieves' Guild and he was damned if they were going to run scared because someone had taken a pot shot at him. He was regretting it now but he'd ordered business as usual as far as clients were concerned. Heightened security measures and increased surveillance on any visitors but access nonetheless.

That Devon was insisting he attend a meeting with a client wasn't just mischief from her end. She was showing him first hand the trouble that was causing them.

He made contact as the lift rose.

"It's Silas," she sent back. "You need to be on your toes for this, NG. Are you sure you can handle it?"

He could tell that she wasn't happy.

She wasn't concerned for him; she was worried that he was going to screw up one of her most valuable contacts.

"Do I have a choice?"

"No. He wants you. Don't think I haven't tried to mitigate this already. Watch yourself with him. I don't like this."

He didn't like it either. He didn't like dealing with Silas at the best of times.

He rubbed a hand over the back of his neck, flexing the tension out of his shoulders.

Martinez was watching his reflection in the door, worried that he looked tired. Banks was checking in with Security on eleven. They didn't usually stick this close to him on board the Alsatia but between them and the Watch, he hadn't been alone for a minute.

He caught her eye, caught that look of concern, and straightened up, shaking off the fatigue as the lift doors opened onto Legal's marble hallways. He stepped into the cool ambiance of Devon's domain and walked, pulling energy from somewhere to complete the transformation. He still felt like shit, and he'd pay for it later, but for the minute he'd be as bright and sharp as everyone always expected him to be.

He took the offered board from the girl waiting for him and followed her through to a light and airy atrium. Real plants interwove their greenery around glass columns, tables and chairs set out café style in the centre. It gave the impression of a public area, relaxed and open but in reality only one client was ever entertained here at a time, confidentiality at a premium, clandestine seclusion guaranteed. It was an illusion that Devon nurtured.

It was also an illusion that they were alone – at least five guns were aimed into that central area. More than usual.

Banks and Martinez stayed at the door, another two guns watching his back.

Silas was sitting casually at the centre table.

NG walked forward.

Let the game commence.

“Nicely done.” Devon slipped into the chair opposite once their guest had gone, placing a data board on the smooth marble table top between them. “I’m impressed.”

NG raised his eyes. He was tired and not exactly needing her approval. He’d spent long enough working in Legal to know how to handle a client, not that she knew that. She was impressed that he’d pulled off a gambit that she was thinking could have cost them severely if it had backfired.

She stared at him, a smile dancing across her eyes as if she was pleased at her own judgement in him.

“Don’t,” he muttered.

“Don’t what? Don’t be impressed that you just nailed Silas to the wall?”

“I don’t like being threatened.” He didn’t like being summoned by a client who was bragging that they could get an acquisition completed and delivered at a fraction of the price demanded by the Thieves’ Guild and was sitting there insisting he match it.

He hadn’t. He’d threatened instantly to sever all ties and refuse to ever work for them again if they took this contract elsewhere.

High risk strategy.

Devon smiled and beckoned to her staff, sending a silent message through the Senson with an order to bring over drinks. “You dealt with it just fine,” she said out loud. “Silas was a fool to bring that in here. He should have known better. No one else in the galaxy has the kind of operatives we have here.”

She said ‘we’ – not so long ago that would have been ‘you’.

NG leaned forward. “Why the hell are the Merchants offering to run acquisitions, Devon?”

“Because Ballack is an arrogant, overconfident and smug son of a bitch who doesn’t care about anything but hard cash.”

Ballack had been president of the Merchants’ Guild for over three decades. He ran an old boys’ network of sycophantic supporters across both sides of the line and the guy had fended off pretenders to his throne with ease time and again. The Thieves’ Guild had always maintained an uneasy understanding with him. Business at arm’s length and a mutual distrust and reluctant respect for each other's particular skill sets. But never outright conflict.

NG shook his head. "He's offering acquisitions, direct to the client, at a price that will, to quote Silas, 'blow the Thieves' Guild out of the water'? It doesn't make sense. Where's Media? Why the hell did we not see this coming? We shouldn't be finding out about this kind of crap from a client, for Christ's sake."

There was something in her expression that made him stop.

"What?" he said.

She slid the board across the table. "This just came in."

NG looked down. It was a typical tab, filtered through a system of intermediaries to reach them. Objective, location, drop off, details for a preliminary pick up of intel regarding access – it was all there, along with Zach Hilyer clearly identified as the operative required to carry it out.

It was unheard of. Clients didn't request specific operatives. No one outside the guild should even know the names of any of the field-ops. It was another breach.

He rubbed his shoulder. Someone tried to kill him right here on the Alsatia, the Federation was touting around a bounty on LC, the Merchants were acting directly and openly against them and now a client asked for Hilyer by name? It felt like all their protections had been torn down and shredded by someone they couldn't even see. The Thieves' Guild was centuries old and it had never been exposed like this before.

Devon was quiet for once.

A tall thin guy brought over a tray of drinks, silently setting each glass down on the table with a napkin and backing away respectfully.

She waited until he was gone then reached to tap sharply on the board. "This enquiry is from the same source as the tab we found at Mendhel's house on Earth."

NG looked up. "How do we know?"

"We backtracked to the same courier and followed the money. It's a corporation."

"Which one?"

"NG, if I knew, I'd be telling you." She was exasperated. They were all frustrated and they were all tired. "We're good, but we're not psychic. The trail ends. Abruptly. Whoever they are, they're very good. And they know how good we are." She threw up her hand to stop him speaking. "Don't say it. We'll keep at it and we'll find them. Are you going to pull Hilyer back? You should use him as bait. That would speed up the process." She sat back and folded her arms.

When she pushed like this, it drove her crazy when he didn't respond. "Is it the same source as the bounty on LC?" he said simply.

He could hear her cursing him inside her head. "We don't know," she said, a muscle twitching along her jawline. "It could be. It probably is but we're nowhere closer on that." She leaned forward. "Speaking bluntly, NG, Acquisitions have made mistakes in the way those two were handled. No disrespect to Mendhel, but Anderton and Hilyer have been a disaster waiting to happen."

"It's how we work, Devon. You know that."

She wasn't about to relent. "You have an issue with discipline, NG. They went after something out there, freelancing. Hilyer turns up with his faked amnesia and Anderton disappears. You want to know what I think? They were bought. The package in Hilyer's ship was a decoy and Anderton has the real package. God knows what it could be but it looks like someone wants it back badly enough to place a price on Anderton's head in the millions for stealing it."

NG picked up the glass and took a sip. It was malt whisky, expensive from the taste of it. He shook his head. "I know them. They wouldn't betray us."

"Hilyer's record is appalling and I don't know how Anderton has managed to scam you all into letting him get away with murder…"

She said it without thinking and cut off her next comment, the glare softening. He'd heard the rumours.

"You know I don't believe that," he said quietly. LC was a handful and needed a particular type of care, which wasn't surprising considering his background, but he wasn't a murderer and there was no way he would have turned against Mendhel.

"I didn't mean it literally," she said, frustrated again. "No one seriously thinks that's what happened, whatever the rumour mill is saying. But listen to me, NG. You have operatives that can get away with behaviour like that here and you send them out there alone with no idea who could get to them. They were bought and they weren't smart enough to pull off the scam."

She was thinking that LC and Hil were the breach themselves. And he had to admit it was a possibility. Someone knew far more about the guild than had ever been public knowledge and those two field operatives were right in the middle of the whole mess.

"These people," she said, tapping the board again, "dare contact us to demand Hilyer. Give him to them."

NG nodded and drained the glass. He'd already decided what to do. He had an ulterior motive. There was no such thing as coincidence. If a corporation was behind this, responsible for assassinating Mendhel, he wanted to know if it was connected to the price on his head, and ultimately to the Order.

"Send out a Black on Hilyer," he said. "O'Brien is checking in regularly – she'll see it. Using him as bait isn't a bad idea."

There was an acrid smell of burnt out components still hanging in the air despite the tang of cleaning fluid. NG stood at the doorway to the Sphere, slouching, hands in pockets, watching the maintenance crew tear damaged panels from the surface of its curved interior bulkhead.

He hadn't seen the estimate for the repairs yet but they were going to have to bring in specialists. The wrecked drone had been taken out in pieces. He traced a finger round a bullet hole by the door.

"You were damned lucky," the Chief said, walking up to stand next to him.

NG shook his head. "I thought we were secure."

"I heard the price is half a billion – that much cash on offer and people will find a way to you, whatever we do."

NG glanced back down the corridor. Two of the Watch were there, heavily armed, still shadowing him at all times.

"That was one helluva trick," the Chief said.

"The gravity?" Evelyn had slammed the AG on to maximum as soon as he was clear of the Sphere. The collision hadn't just destroyed the drone, it had annihilated the integrity of the zero gravity field.

"No, the stunt you pulled in the pool. Christ, NG, we all thought you were dead. Do you know how long you were out?"

NG shrugged. He knew exactly how long he'd been out but they didn't need to know that. He'd told Evelyn that he must have blacked out. He turned away from the Sphere and said, "I need to talk to you about Quinn."

The Chief walked with him. "He's good with it."

He'd better be, they had no choice. Asking Quinn to take on Mendhel's field-ops had the potential to be disastrous. The two men were – had been – their two best handlers. Mendhel's operatives topped the standings by virtue of the fact he'd always taken the most difficult tabs for them, higher value, more risky, more rewards if they pulled them off. He'd also always had a way of getting the best from the most difficult characters who tended to be the most talented. LC was unpredictable, reckless and impetuous. Hil had a temper that was as much frustration at himself and everyone around him as any real anger. Sorensen was arrogant – quiet but condescending to anyone he felt was beneath him. Mendhel had always had the knack of being able to put them all at ease in their own way so they wanted to do well for him.

Quinn, on the other hand, was cautious with little tolerance for anyone he thought of as precious. His operatives were the solid ones, mid-ranking, steady and reliable.

The other difference between the two was that Quinn had never been a field-op himself. That was going to be the real sticking point. Operatives like LC and Hil tended to find it hard to respect anyone who hadn't been out there themselves. What they didn't know, what Quinn had asked him to keep private, was that

Quinn was ex-special forces – twenty years in the Earth military.

"Good," NG said. "We have no choice. A tab has come in for Hil. Same source that got Mendhel killed. Asking for Hilyer by name. We're going to use him as bait. Quinn's going to be handling one of the most sensitive tabs we've ever accepted."

7

She sat back, resting her goblet on her knee, slender fingers wrapped around its stem of twisted metal. "This corporation knows a lot about us – is the situation irreparable?"

"Considering what has happened since, no, it is not."

"Your little protégé is not subtle at times."

"He does what is needed. And he is prepared to take risks. That is a rare quality in these times. It is too easy to live and let others take on the daemons that surround us."

"But his actions cause ripples, noise. He alerts others to our distress. And the danger is that once the cracks are seen to appear," she said, "it is very easy for the malicious and small-minded to be manipulated."

The Man shook his head with a pah. "They are like vultures circling. They are watching and waiting. They don't need to see an alert to know what is awry. He does what is necessary. He has more patience than I when dealing with these creatures."

It was another two days before O'Brien brought Hilyer back in. NG gave clearance for them to dock and sat in Ops with Quinn, waiting. They'd gone over the plan with the Chief and whichever way they looked at it, there was a risk but they could see no other way. They had no other leads.

The Man had docked that morning, with no summons, no orders, no word or comment on what had happened, simply replacing the Watch who were shadowing NG with two elite guards.

Those guards were now standing outside, alongside the guys from the Watch that NG had briefed with his own orders. He hoped to hell this didn't go down the way he was anticipating.

Quinn was sitting motionless, almost to attention, at the table.

"Go hard on him," NG said. He was perched on the bench along the wall. He wanted to set Hilyer on edge. The kid had had enough time to get over whatever had caused his amnesia. Sean had taken him to see Badger and if he was fit enough to run the gauntlet of hostilities on Redgate, he was fit enough to face up to whatever the hell it was he'd been doing with LC. "Let's see if we can shock it out of him."

A slight twitch of a smile tugged at one edge of Quinn's mouth. The big man was still firmly fixed in anger over Mendhel. They'd served together. And he was yet to be convinced that it wasn't LC and Hil who had caused his death. Going hard on Hilyer wasn't going to need any acting.

NG tapped the board he was holding against his thigh. He could sense Hilyer approaching, a complicated mix of emotions, flanked by a cold presence on either side. The guards outside the door tensed, stepping aside as Hil's escort joined them, directing the field-op to enter the briefing room.

NG waited while Hil pulled out a chair and sat down, temper brewing. The kid refused to look at Quinn, furious at everything that was happening to him. Hilyer liked to be in control and it was gnawing at him that he didn't know what was going on. It wasn't easy to absorb that kind of raw sentiment and rather than try to ease him, NG had to let it go. He needed Hil to be unsettled to be able to read the truth in his mind beyond the haze of pain and confusion that he was still carrying.

He threw the board down onto the table before anyone could say a word. "Mr Quinn here is your new handler," he said. "You have a tab."

Hil almost started hyperventilating. Oh god, he was thinking, panicking, Skye isn't ready.

She wasn't. She was still in the repair bay. Hilyer had never worked with any other ship and they were close; she was probably more like a mother to him than any human family the kid had ever known.

NG carried on before Hil could say anything. "Skye isn't ready, we know. You'll be going out with Genoa. Kase and Martha will be running escort for you. This isn't a usual tab. These aren't usual circumstances."

Hil picked up the board with his left hand. His right was encased in a brace, nestled in his lap, pain throbbing from the fractured bone in his wrist.

NG had a moment of hesitation. There was nothing but confusion and panic in the kid's mind. Normally they'd never dream of sending an operative out into the field in that state. He could sense Quinn steeling himself.

It wasn't easy for any of them.

Hilyer's hand started shaking and he quickly put the board down, hoping they hadn't noticed, embarrassed at the physical state he was in.

"Am I back on the list?" he said, confrontational. "The Chief said I was grounded."

NG jumped down and pulled up a seat at the table.

"This isn't a normal tab," he said again. "This has come from the same source as the one Mendhel was handling from Earth." He threw that in quickly and watched Hilyer for his reaction.

"How do you know what, where…?"

"We know. Don't ask how, it's complicated. But we know. Trust us. We know that it was a professional hit on Mendhel. And we haven't been able to contact his daughter." Another fast barb thrown in.

Hil looked horrified.

NG carried on relentlessly. "You left here with LC presumably to meet Mendhel about this tab. He turns up dead, Anya is missing, LC is missing and we're still trying to piece together what that job actually was. We want to sort this out. No one messes with the guild. We're not going to let them get away with this. This new tab is definitely from the same source. And they're asking for you… by name."

That made the kid turn white. "How do they know who I am?"

"Hil, like I said, this isn't an ordinary tab. Whatever happened with Mendhel, these people now want you. We want you to take this tab and then we'll see what happens."

"So I'm bait?"

Smart, despite whatever it was that had screwed with his mind. "Yeah," NG said bluntly without rising to Hilyer's blatant insubordination.

Hil faltered slightly and his voice was shaking as he said, "Does the Chief know about this?"

"It's not his decision. We want LC back and we want that package." It was almost a bluff. They didn't even know if there was a package. But if there was, if Hilyer knew there was, there was no harm stressing the point. NG pushed it further. "You know what we have to do, Hil. You know we won't let anything happen to you but the integrity of the guild is everything. You know that, don't you?"

Hil nodded, an automatic response.

"Legal are trying to trace whoever is behind this but they're embarrassed at how long it's taking them to get anywhere," NG said, standing up. "And as far as this tab goes, Quinn will handle things from this end."

He looked at them both and walked to the door. "I'll leave you to sort out the details. But be aware that we are still investigating Mendhel's death and we're running an internal investigation. And however this goes down, we won't be losing anyone else."

He left the room, leaving behind an atmosphere that was dangerously edgy. Whatever happened next could lead to Hilyer's immediate execution. If he slipped up. If the kid let a single thought enter his mind that incriminated himself.

NG felt cold. The two guys outside the door had been briefed to wait for his word. They both had their hands on their guns. He told them to stand ready and casually reaffirmed their orders, mostly concentrating on following Hilyer's train of thought, easy enough to listen in to at this distance.

Quinn was good and he quickly provoked the young field operative into a reaction. To be fair, that wasn't hard with Hilyer. NG felt the pure frustration-fuelled anger that sparked in Hil as

Quinn played the game. Combined with the pain he was picking up from the kid, it all made his head ache with a pulsing burn. And nothing was clear, not until Hilyer's memory started to flash on scenes of Earth – Mendhel and LC, and LC scared and hurt. LC was never scared, Hil was thinking, oh god, what had happened?

It was genuine.

"Stand down," NG said quietly. He turned to the two elite guards. "Stay with him, don't let anyone near and keep him away from Legal. I want him intact."

They both nodded, synchronised small, curt motions.

NG turned back to the door. Quinn and Hilyer were inches apart, Hil with fists clenched, struggling to hold back an intense agitation that was about to explode.

NG pushed open the door, releasing the tension in the room before it came to blows.

Quinn glanced over, eyes switching from Hilyer to NG, not making a move until NG shook his head slightly and sent privately, "He's clean."

The relief in the big handler was immense but he showed nothing in his face. He stepped aside. Hilyer almost sagged behind him, shoulders dropping. His hands were shaking again and he stuck them in his pockets to hide it, slouching and glaring at Quinn's back.

The kid's headache had intensified into a dense black migraine that was spilling over and eating at NG's concentration.

"Sit down," he said to Quinn. "Hil, go up to my office and call into Medical on the way for some painkillers, for Christ's sake."

Hilyer left, slinking out and picking up his bodyguards with resignation rather than resentment.

NG sat, exhausted. Quinn was a cool presence opposite, easy company in the circumstances.

"Give him whatever he needs," NG said, rubbing a hand over his eyes. "Get him out there and do whatever you have to do to nail the ID of this corporation."

He looked at Quinn, reading a calm readiness in the big man's mind, mission prep and a cool, clinical need to go after the people who had killed his friend. "I've cleared it with the Chief. We want you to handle Hilyer. Only Hilyer."

Quinn's only response was to raise his eyebrows.

"We'll juggle the rest of your field-ops for the time being. Some of them are due to take leave anyway and we can handle the others. I want your attention on Hil. Is that clear?"

It was a question in wording only and Quinn knew it. He had no choice and NG didn't want his opinion on it. It was decided and yes was the only answer.

"Yes," Quinn said with a small smile. He didn't like Hil but he respected the kid's abilities. It was in the method that they'd clash. And he was thinking that Hilyer was going to have a problem taking his orders.

"I'll get everything sent to Ops," NG said. "Give me an hour with Hil. He'll be fine. If he ever wants to get back on the list again, he'll have to be."

He poured himself a whisky and stretched out on the sofa. His head was pounding. Whatever Hil had going on, he wasn't trying to hide anything. Not consciously. If anything, it was the opposite. The kid was frustrated that he couldn't remember what had happened. It just wasn't inside his head. Or rather it was, he just couldn't get to it. Yet.

NG closed his eyes. It was hard work venturing into that kind of maelstrom.

When Evelyn interrupted, she didn't connect through the Senson, she just knocked at the door with a single clear rap and walked in. She wasn't happy.

"You have a message from the JU," she said and dropped a board on his desk.

NG sat up. "Jameson?"

"He wants to see you. He's demanding that you go to Earth. Now. No delays or he will, and I quote, 'cause you so much fucking trouble, you'll wish you'd never even heard of the JU'. You want me to tell him you're busy?"

Damn, he should have thought of Jameson.

NG jumped up and downed the last of the whisky in the glass. "Tell him I'll see him but at RV2. We can get there in what? Two days?"

Evelyn considered arguing with him but thought better of it. She really was good in a crisis. No tea, but she walked briskly over to the cabinet and picked out the exact whisky he was drinking. Who was it in this office that was supposed to be the telepath?

"I'll set up the hospitality room," she said, topping up his glass.

By that, she meant the high security suite they used whenever there was a risk in bringing outsiders on board. Isolated, physically and electronically, sterile and fitted with a security system that was impregnable.

"He won't like it," she continued without waiting for him to speak, "but if Jameson's January Unit is anything like it used to be, they'll know what's going on. That's what worries me."

NG shrugged.

She glared at him. "Half a billion will tempt even someone like Jameson."

"He knows he'd never be able to put me down and walk away alive to enjoy it."

"Let's not put that to the test," Evie said, not realising that she sounded more like the covert bodyguard she was than the PA she pretended to be.

NG smiled. Matt Jameson was one of their closest allies. Jameson's January Unit paid the Thieves' Guild well to both keep their hands off Earth military business and to run tabs on the other side of the line for them. It was the only Imperial military unit they ever dealt with. Anything Earth wanted from the Thieves' Guild went through the JU. Jameson knew fine well that NG took payment from the Wintrans to do exactly the same but that was the game. It was a valuable service and one they did well. Not so much industrial or military espionage, rather a delicate balancing act to maintain a steady level of technological advancements within the two powers and everyone in between.

Evelyn's worries were probably unfounded. Whenever Jameson wanted to see him, it was urgent. The guy didn't have any other setting. It would be some routine tab. But Evie was right. Chances were he could know something of what was going on. Any intel from that direction was always welcome. And Jameson usually brought more than information. Good whisky and real coffee went a long way out here.

It wasn't routine. Jameson threw one punch and had NG around the throat, pinned to the bulkhead, before anyone could react. Sometimes knowing what was about to happen before it did just sucked.

8

"Ah. The might of the Imperial military. Its peculiar relationship with our guild has always fascinated me."

The Man reached for the jug. "It is a disgustingly arcane and stifled organism that believes it is untouchable."

"Winter is no better."

"No, it is not. But at least the Wintran corporations are transparent in their greed."

"You sent Zach Hilyer into the hands of the corporation that mocks us. Was that fair?"

"No. What in any of this has been fair?"

She looked up. "I must say, I am pleased to hear that Zachary did not betray us. He is one of my favourites. What did the good Colonel Jameson want?"

"What he always wants. The Earth Empire is insidious in its need to control and its desperate desire to regain its former glory. Jameson has always seen our guild as a means to wield power across the line. It is a delusion we have nurtured. But one that has come back to bite us."

"Stand down," NG sent calmly on a shared link to the security detail, Banks, Martinez and Evie included. He hadn't stopped Jameson or ducked out of the way because he wanted to know what the hell had freaked out a guy he thought of almost as a friend. "He's just pissed. He's not going to kill me."

They didn't like it but they all lowered their weapons.

Jameson glared at him, nose to nose, fingers squeezing and shutting off his air. NG breathed slowly and kept eye contact, calm, no resistance.

"You've gone too fucking far this time, NG," Jameson hissed. "You bastard thieving son of a bitch. What the hell do I pay you for?"

NG let him vent, riding with it and using the physical contact of the hand around his neck to look deep as Jameson slammed him up against the wall with another punch. Evelyn and Martinez snapped their guns back up, two perfect stances aiming at Jameson's head. Jameson's own holster was empty. He'd been thoroughly searched and hadn't bitched when he'd been told to leave his guards on his ship. Not that he needed a weapon. He was thinking how little effort it would take to snap NG's neck, fingers twitching and weight shifting slightly in readiness. The thoughts that flashed deeper were more disturbing.

"It wasn't us, Jameson," NG said softly, throwing a subtle spanner into the midst of the man's anger. "It wasn't us."

Jameson's grip eased slightly, confusion replacing the surface fury.

NG strengthened the suggestion, calming, taking the heat out of the colonel's emotions.

Jameson sagged and shoved NG to the side, turning and looking around as if he was noticing for the first time the full force of guild personnel surrounding them. He threw his hands up, glared at Evie, then spun on NG again, pointing. "I swear," he said, voice raised, "no one else could have got near. It was your operatives, you son of a bitch."

Evie sent, "Hilyer and LC?"

NG gestured her to stand down. "Jameson, it wasn't authorised," he said. "We have two rogue field operatives out there that we're trying to find ourselves."

Jameson narrowed his eyes. He didn't believe it. He didn't want to believe it. He'd come in here expecting to have caught them off guard, fingers in the cookie jar.

"Sit down," NG said calmly. "We're as much in the shit here as you are." He gestured towards the conference table and sent privately to Evie, "Get Devon in here. It looks like our boys hit the JU."

Jameson sat and unbuttoned his jacket. He was wearing a civilian suit. Unofficial. His relations with the guild didn't exactly go through regular channels.

Evelyn brought tea and a decanter of whisky, setting three shot glasses on the table. She backed off and joined the circle of security surrounding them.

NG poured two shots of whisky and waited for Jameson. The colonel stared at him without making a move for the cup. "We had an agreement, NG." He was still furious, distrusting, but the edge was gone. "What the hell happened?"

NG picked up one of the cups and nudged the other. Jameson still ignored it. It was obvious that the colonel was now very aware of the security around them. And he knew why, amused to see NG having to take such precautions.

"We don't know yet," NG said. "Mendhel was killed."

Jameson nodded. "We heard. Is that connected? Jesus." He hadn't put the two together and now it was laid out, his mind started ticking over. He picked up the shot glass and downed it in one.

NG followed suit and topped them both up, filling the third as he sensed Devon approaching.

Jameson recognised the significance of Legal joining them and stood. Old Earth manners.

She smiled as she sat and raised her glass. They didn't toast; it was more a silent acknowledgment to each of their positions. Three of the most powerful individuals in the galaxy and one of the worst breaches in trust and security NG could recall.

"Half a billion is one hell of a price, NG," Jameson said, going on the offensive. "Who else have you been pissing off?"

NG smiled, refusing to rise to it.

Jameson looked around theatrically. "Worried?"

"No one can get to me," NG said nonchalantly, cocky, feeling Evelyn and Devon both tense inside. They'd never let on to someone like Jameson that the Alsatia had already been compromised. He kept his gaze steady. "What did they steal and from where?"

Jameson stared from NG to Devon. He still thought they were playing dumb.

Devon leaned forward. "Whoever got to our field operatives killed their handler, Colonel Jameson. One of our best handlers. We're not involved and the sooner you stop assuming that we are, the sooner we can all find out who is behind this." Her tone was cold but not as withering as it could get. She could be a softie when she needed to be with outsiders.

Jameson was smart. You didn't get to that kind of position in such a specialist unit within any military without being very good. He considered them both then reached for the shot glass, holding it up for a refill.

NG played the game, topping up all three cups.

Jameson took a sip and placed the cup very deliberately on the table. "I cannot divulge that information at this time," he said, the formal words tripping off his tongue with infinite ease.

Devon laughed. "Come on, colonel. You've admitted it was your facility. You want your stuff back? Tell us what it was."

He was still suspicious but NG started to pick up an underlying uncertainty. It was obvious that his superiors hadn't told him what it was. Jameson didn't know what had been stolen and he'd been expecting to find out by coming here.

"We don't have it, Jameson," NG said cautiously. "And we want our people back. Someone is working against us both. Tell us what you know. We'll tell you what we know."

There was a long moment of silence then Jameson said, "It was a research facility," conceding but giving away nothing of value because he didn't know any more himself. "High end, top secret. Hell, we don't even know what the researchers were doing in there."

He looked up, from NG to Devon again. "Honestly. Your boys got away with something that we've never even seen. There are no records. And guess what? The lab was destroyed by an explosion after they got out." He sounded pissed again. "Who was it?" he said aggressively. "No, let me guess – Anderton?"

NG nodded. There was no need to deny it. Jameson was smart.

He hadn't plucked LC's name out of thin air, he'd heard about the bounty. It didn't take much to put it all together and the guy was suddenly thinking, hell, this was someone else. He'd come to the Thieves' Guild expecting all the answers, pissed at the idea that NG had betrayed them and now it seemed like it was an unknown. An enemy out there, not a betrayal by an ally after all.

Jameson shook his head, disbelief crossing his mind. "And you have no idea why he did it?"

NG sat quietly, non-committal. Devon was as still as a statue, willing him to give Hilyer to Jameson. They'd sent the kid out to confront the corporation with half an army of extraction agents at his back. Setting the Earth military after them as well wouldn't do Hil any favours but it might tip the chances of them catching the bastards.

"One of our other field operatives was there as well," he said. "We don't know why but we think the two of them were freelancing for a corporation. He made it back here." He considered what else to say. "The corporation sent in an anonymous request asking for him – to finish the job, we think. We're assuming they think he has the package. Him or LC. And they've put out a price on LC to try to find him."

Jameson nodded.

"We've sent him out on the tab," NG said coldly, feeling satisfaction from Devon and dismay from Evie. "We can tell you where but we want him back alive."

Jameson smirked and reached for the shot glass. "Deal."

He left Jameson with Devon to work out the details and walked to the elevator flanked by Evie, Banks and Martinez, two of the elite guards a step behind.

Evelyn was quiet until they got into the lift, too quiet because he could feel she was itching to say something.

"You don't like it?" he sent finally, privately on a tight wire.

"No."

"Don't make this personal."

She was still scowling as the door opened onto twelve.

He stood aside to let her out first but she stopped and looked at him.

"I trust Hil," she said quietly. "Everyone does. I don't believe he's betrayed us."

"LC?"

"The same."

That was personal with her. He knew she'd hooked up with LC a few times and the worry she was feeling wasn't just that for a work colleague.

"Someone got to them," he said.

"There'll have been a reason," she sent privately and walked out. She was thinking that he'd thrown Hilyer to the wolves. She could be right. It was never easy to sacrifice a piece for the bigger picture. But sometimes that was the only way to win the game.

He followed her and went towards his office, headed off by Martinez who respectfully nudged him aside and went in herself first, to check that it was clear. He knew there was no one in there but that was hardly something he could say. He humoured them but he was starting to feel claustrophobic. He stood at the door and watched Evelyn go to her desk, watched the look on her face as she picked up a board that was waiting for her. She glanced up at him and put it down quickly.

"What is it?" he said.

She shook her head and shuffled the board into the others sitting there. Not every board went across her desk before it hit his, but when they were this busy, a fair few did.

She was bothered. Thinking that there was no way she could give it to him until she'd spoken to Devon.

He beckoned with a finger. She tried to look calm and neutral but he listened in as she sent an urgent warning to Devon that she was needed here fast.

Martinez appeared at the door, content that there was no threat, and waving him in. He beckoned Evelyn again and waited until she picked up the board and walked over, walking in ahead of him without a word.

She watched him as he sat at his desk and then gave it to him, folding her arms and unimpressed at his reaction even though he hadn't reacted yet.

It was from one of his deep cover agents. Domino was one of their best, owner of a repair shop and scrapyard that was one of the busiest in Winter, high profit, perfect cover for gathering intel. The message was encrypted. He had a vessel matching the ID of the mercenaries' ship. In for repairs and he wanted NG to go see for himself.

"It has to be a trap," Evelyn said, knowing that she was stating the obvious.

NG read it again. Of course it was a trap. On the surface it was a simple communication. But there was a trigger word in there that negated everything else in the message and another hidden deeper that warned in no uncertain terms that Domino was in trouble, NG had to stay the hell away and if the guild sent anyone, they'd better be armed to the teeth.

It was a safety measure, a contingency they'd never had to use before.

NG looked up. "I know."

9

"He went after the Order?" The surprise in her tone was belied by her neutral expression as she watched him sprinkle the black powder into the wine.

"They were taunting us. What else was he to do?"

"I am surprised that you sanction such action."

He hadn't just sanctioned it, he'd given free reign, in fact made it a priority. "At the time we didn't know what it was that had so stirred them." He added another pinch and watched the steam billow upwards. "We have been at loggerheads for some time but it has been simple to avoid or deflect the weak blows from such a sprawling and obtuse organisation. I misjudged how effective they could be with some focus behind their actions."

"And he set the Earth military against the corporation that called for Hilyer? Foolhardy, was it not? Some are saying that was the moment the war started."

Poppycock but he didn't say that. He looked up, through the swirling vapours. "He did not know at the time the allegiance of the corporation, but I am sure that even if he had known, he would not have hesitated. He is bold. He needs to be."

They picked up a tail as soon as they left the shuttle terminal. NG threw his bag into the back of the rental car and went as deep as he could to read the guy who had followed them out into the half light of Ten Yarin's dusk.

Traffic from the orbital was heavy even this late. The colony was the type of place he hated, civilised to the point of obnoxious and big on bureaucracy of the most hypocritical kind. It was a haven for every underworld operation that liked to play the pretence of legitimacy and run their games close to the wire of respectable trade. It was the perfect place to entrap a quarry. All visitors entered the atmosphere via one of five orbitals, and no freewheeling down to the surface because an unforgiving net of security, second only to Earth and Winter themselves, surrounded the planet that would see you impounded if you so much as wobbled from a given flight path. So it wasn't surprising that they'd chosen this place and had someone watching arrivals at the capital city.

He was working on the theory that these people wanted him alive and in a way that made their job much harder and his a breeze. He had Banks and Martinez with him and the plan was simply to trip up the people sent to trap him. Devon had argued then told him he was a cocky bastard and welcome to get himself killed if he insisted on going in without backup. But Ten Yarin wasn't the type of place you could hit heavy-handed. He'd compromised and agreed to an assault team from Security posted on standby in orbit but he wasn't intending on needing them. This time, he was expecting trouble.

He'd already tried to reach Domino through the Senson, with no response so they had no way of knowing if he was even still alive.

NG reached into his bag for a gun, throwing a glance to Martinez that sent her reaching for her own. They'd had to smuggle the guns in. Ten Yarin had a simple single-minded blind philosophy on weapons – none in, none out. What happened on the surface was something else, but you'd better not get caught with any. He quickly and calmly unpacked the concealed components and reassembled them deftly, as he concentrated on the man a few vehicles over who was being infinitely careful not to watch them openly.

The mind he read was cold, a step up from the last lot of mercenaries he'd encountered. NG caught the intention there and overheard a fast, tight wire communication, "Got him. Kill the family."

Shit.

He sent, hard and fast, to Banks and Martinez, "They have Domino's family. Take this jerk out and get over there," as he calmly closed the door and walked round to the driver's side.

They didn't argue and he didn't wait to see what happened.

Domino's yard was out in the plains about twenty five miles from the city limits.

NG drove, fast, the lights of the city flashing by, and headed out into the rapidly falling darkness of the hinterlands between the coastal city and the foothills.

He still couldn't contact Domino and as he got closer, he started to scan ahead. There was a force of ten men at the yard. He could sense their intentions even at this distance and it wasn't good. There were no customers and none of Domino's usual workforce. He could feel pain pulsing at the weak life form he recognised as his deep cover agent.

He put his foot down on the accelerator and drove towards the yard, dark shadows from the massive hulking forms of dead and abandoned ships looming up all around. He didn't slow down, navigating the chaos without lights, spinning the car across the desert floor and weaving through the scattered debris of the junked superstructures.

He cut the engine and used the slope of the ground to freewheel in, coming to a skidding stop next to a pile of scrap some distance out from the high wall that surrounded the inner enclosure of the yard.

They didn't have watchers out, relying with an arrogant confidence on the guy who was supposed to be tailing him and a sophisticated life signs scanner that should have warned them as soon as he got within a mile of the place. High end kit but no match for the guild equipment he was wearing.

He got out, leaving the car door ajar. It was dark, all the floodlights out, and eerily quiet. A damp chill hung in the air. He reached for the bag and assembled another gun, thumbing rounds into magazines as he checked around. There was one guy on each exit, three roaming the yard and five with Domino. He pulled out the rest of his kit, strapping holsters to each thigh, slipping a knife into his boot and attaching ammo pouches to his belt.

The Senson engaged as he sensed the full force of a blow to the stomach, second-hand pain and a desperation emanating from Domino that was heart wrenching.

Martinez's tone was unemotional but heavy. "Boss, the family are all dead. Wait for us."

That wasn't going to happen. He started walking towards the wall, feeling that dark spot inside stir with a chill.

There was another blow, a spark of defiant resistance and a vicious shard of agony that cut through it.

NG broke into a run, drawing weapons.

It was pitch black inside apart from a small circle of light around Domino, strung up by his wrists, hanging from a chain in the centre of one of the massive cages down in the workshop.

NG crouched on the walkway that ran around the outside edge of the underground chamber, a gun in each hand, heart rate slow and steady and a tension in every muscle that was pure anticipation.

The intruders were all wearing armoured combat gear, black night vision glasses hugged close to their heads like fly eyes, high end kit with electronics as advanced as anything available on the blackest of markets either side of the line.

Even so, it had been relatively easy to avoid the five patrolling outside and he'd slipped straight past a giant of a man guarding the entrance to the workshop, guild stealth gear negating their detectors close up and every tiny movement as slick and silent as it was possible to be.

There were three men in the cage with the guild operative, one watching and two playing with knives inflicting wounds with practised precision.

Domino hadn't given away a thing. NG could read it clearly from his mind, through pain that was excruciating.

He shut it out and switched to the man watching. That mind was cold, waiting patiently, letting his men amuse themselves to pass the time. They'd baited their trap and were simply waiting for NG to walk straight into it.

Domino screamed.

The thin black thread of control snapped.

NG moved fast. He ran silently along an overhead beam, ducking amongst cables and pipes and began punching release controls. Chains clattered loose, spilling crates and baskets that scattered salvaged components and massive ship parts with a crash onto the floor of the workshop. He didn't stop, yanking pressure gauges as he ran leaving a trail of open valves behind him that started to vent steam and gases in billowing clouds. The intruders started at the sudden noise and commotion. They'd been waiting for their trap to spring and battle readiness sparked as they realised they were under attack, the anticipation of completing the mission clear and confident.

They were going to be disappointed – they'd never attacked the Thieves' Guild before.

NG ran towards the cage and dropped down, twisting in midair and firing both guns before his feet hit the floor.

The two tormentors fell, knives clattering, blood spraying. The leader of the mercenary unit spun and fired, rounds raking through the air as NG ran, skidding into cover. One hit with the sting of an FTH. So they did want him alive. He shrugged off its effects easily, taking its energy and absorbing it for himself. He could sense the buzz of conversation between the eight men, picking up their thoughts as they used implants to communicate, rapid bursts with military efficiency.

Eight left.

They should have brought more.

NG stood, turning and firing, taking down the giant with one shot to the head then spinning to wing the guy in charge with one shot to his gun hand. He didn't wait to see if the giant fell, running in to the cage to down the boss with a tackle that sent him crashing to the floor. A quick forehand blow to the head with the butt of the pistol smashed the night vision goggles and sent the guy senseless. NG hauled him backwards towards Domino, pausing only to raise a gun and fire once through the door and down the aisle, a clean long range snapshot that took the fifth guy between the eyes as he was stupid enough to risk a glance out from cover.

The five guys outside were closing in, more cautiously now they couldn't contact their buddies.

Domino was struggling. Dying. NG released him from the chains and eased him gently to the floor, sitting between the two men, his operative and the man who'd been sent by the Order to snatch him. He tucked his hand up against the back of Domino's neck, hushing him as he tried to talk. He was too far gone to heal. The black fog deepened.

NG placed his other hand on the throat of the guy who'd been leading the mercenaries and squeezed until he came round with a choked breath. It was easy to softly ease Domino's pain away and throw it into the other body sprawled by his side.

The man began to whimper. NG tore every memory and scrap of knowledge and awareness from the guy's mind, every bit of intel about this mission, fast with no care for the damage he was causing. He took everything.

The man screamed and died in agony. Domino's agony.

That bloodcurdling howl spurred the remnants of the attack force into an all out assault.

NG eased Domino to the floor and stood, holding the guns loosely by his side and waited, head down, sensing the adrenaline pulsing through the five approaching bodies.

When they moved in, their tactics were coordinated, slick and doomed to fail. They didn't dare switch to live ammunition. NG had the luxury of using armour piercing.

He took the hits from FTH rounds without flinching, spinning and returning rapid fire each time they exposed so much as an inch of flesh from cover. He took two down with head shots, the third with a double tap to the heart and the fourth with a bullet that ripped out the jugular. The last man didn't stand for long, screaming abuse and running straight in. It was too tempting to let him get close, feel the fear and absorb the hatred. He ran into a bullet, arms outstretched and inches from NG's neck, and fell back with a thud.

NG stood there, breathing in the swirl of void from so much death. The silence was laden with pure black emotion, the noise from the steam vents a chaotic backdrop to the carnage.

No one messes with the Thieves' Guild.

'No one messes with me.'

He sank to his knees, dropping both guns to the floor. His heart was racing, breathing ragged, vision clearing as if a fog was lifting. He sat there, head bowed, drained, the scent of blood heavy in the air.

Footsteps echoed.

He didn't move.

Someone stopped in front of him, another figure behind, and the cold barrel of a gun pushed against the back of his neck.

10

"Most impressive. Ruthless."

"As I said, he is fierce in protecting his own."

"Can he control it?"

The Man paused as he reached for the jug.

She was watching him intently. "Can you control him?" she asked, the two questions hanging in the warm, thick air between them.

He poured the wine slowly, topping up each goblet, watching the blood red wine splash and swirl within the curved metal. He placed the jug carefully on the table and nudged her goblet slightly. He took his own and sat back, settling himself before looking up.

She smiled, understanding clear in her mind that she was not going to get an answer to either.

"He is what he needs to be," he said again. "There is more to him, much more, than any of us could ever truly comprehend. Even I."

As he began to take stock, he could sense Banks and Martinez close by. More vehicles, armed men, the two guild operatives escorted into the compound at gun point and held at the gate.

He vaguely became aware of an urgent query pounding at the Senson.

"I'm fine," he sent back to them. "Wait there."

The figure standing before him was a dark presence that stared down at him with a swirling mix of contempt and anger. "NG."

'*My god*,' the dark voice inside his head murmured, '*you have a name, Nikolai, why don't you use it*?' Condescending. Dripping with disdain.

A corrosive whisper that ate at his soul.

NG looked up, raising his head slowly, a trickle of blood dripping into his eye from an injury he couldn't remember.

"Pen," he said quietly, blinking. Back in control but not completely back up to speed.

Pen Halligan was legendary amongst Mendhel's field-ops. They adored the guy. NG had never seen it. Pen made no secret of the fact that he hated the guild and its hold on his brother, had no time for its games and did not rate NG.

The big man stood there, a massive shadow in the darkness. "Who killed my brother?"

'He blames you for what happened.'

He probably had every right to.

"We don't know," NG said.

A switch was thrown and the cage flooded with light that stung the back of his eyeballs. A hand grabbed him by the scruff of the neck and hauled him to his feet.

Pen wasn't convinced. He had a gun in his hand, held low down by his thigh, and he was tapping his finger against the trigger guard.

NG didn't need to delve into Pen's mind to know that this larger than life underworld boss wouldn't hesitate to put a bullet in his head if he played this wrong. It was hard to know how to play it at all. He couldn't influence Pen. Never had been able to. Spec-ops trained minds were one thing, Pen Halligan was something else again.

"LC's missing," NG said quietly.

It was a gamble to mention it.

Another dark cloud crossed Pen's mind. He thought of LC and Hil as family. Strays who needed someone to take care of them. He would do anything to protect his own and it had always been clear that he didn't count NG in that number. It was easy enough to read that he knew the shit the Thieves' Guild was in, about the bounty on LC and he knew about the price on NG's head. The big man raised his left hand, finger pointing, anger barely constrained, dark eyes flashing. He didn't say what he wanted to, that NG might as well have pulled the trigger and killed Mendhel himself, that NG had been a damned fool and pushed the line too far this time.

"You had this coming," he said finally, voice low and controlled, thinking that he'd told his brother, told Mendhel time and again that the damned Thieves' Guild would get him killed. "What happened?"

It was a knife's edge as to which way this was going to pan out.

"We don't know," NG said again and felt the gun barrel push against his skin.

Pen stared back, wanting to throw his own gun aside and lay into NG with his fists. He was also thinking, tempted but no real intention behind it, that he could kill NG right here, right now. Order Yan to pull the trigger. Claim the half a billion. Why the hell not? He had no allegiance to this cocky son of a bitch standing here in front of him, this son of a bitch who'd got his brother killed. "You're upsetting some dangerous people, NG."

This big man himself was dangerous people and the way he said it had an edge that NG had heard before.

Pen gestured around them. "Who are these bastards?"

NG didn't move or say a word.

Pen took a step forward. "You come into my territory and you start killing people, I want to know. Who are these bastards?" He kicked at one of the guns lying at his feet. "They were trying very hard not to kill you."

Pen and his guys had been watching. He'd had people watching the terminal and had followed him here. They'd stood back, watched him take out these mercenaries with ease and waited until he was done before coming in. NG read it clearly from Yan's mind where there was a new level of respect there that he'd never get from Pen. Even so, they wouldn't have cared if he had been killed.

"Is this connected?" Pen said coldly.

To what had happened to Mendhel and LC, he was asking. If it was, Pen wanted to know. If not, the only decision was whether to let him go.

"I don't know."

Pen wasn't impressed but he sent a curt tight wire order to Yan to stand down. He wouldn't trust anything NG said anyway and they had enough to go on to find out themselves. The pressure on his neck eased suddenly as Yan lifted the gun and moved away.

Pen laughed harshly and shook his head. "I don't trust you, NG. I don't like your guild, that's no secret, and believe me, the Thieves' Guild is not in a good place right now. Anywhere." He stepped forward and put his hand against NG's chest. "I do not for one second believe that you have no idea who killed Mendhel. But, NG… if I find out that you had anything to do with it, I will hunt you down and kill you myself. And I'll do it for free."

His eyes glistened. He pushed gently, the brute strength behind that hand trembling with restraint. "Your cute manipulations don't work here. Stay out of my way and stay out of my territory."

Pen turned and walked away, Yan following, neither of them looking back.

NG stared after them, feeling cold. Losing Mendhel had hit hard. Losing Domino like this was almost unbearable. He fixed a resolve deep inside and opened a link to Banks and Martinez. "Let Pen go," he sent. "Domino's dead. Wait here, secure the yard and call in a clean up crew. I need to go to Winter."

It took one short jump to get there. NG knew exactly where the meeting was to take place and who it was he needed to contact. He hadn't just taken the guy's memories, he'd taken his ID codes, armour, weapons and their ship. No AI so there was no issue over ownership and he had the codes to gain access. Martinez and Banks hadn't been happy to let him go without them but orders were orders and he'd pulled rank on them.

He needed to do this alone.

Someone had outsmarted them. There was no way anyone should have been able to tie Domino in with the guild.

There was no way anyone should have been able to get to their handlers and field operatives, no way anyone should have been able to gain access to the Alsatia to try to kill him. But someone had.

He made orbit and waited until nightfall in the capital city, requesting permission to land using the stolen codes and watching the sprinkling of lights below spread as the craft flew down towards the surface.

It was the warm season, the ship stats informed him. Only five degrees below zero in the capital.

NG scrubbed a hand over his eyes. He hated Winter. Hated everything it stood for and despised everyone who played their games of politics to wrangle positions of power within the phoney structure that passed for government. It wasn't surprising that the trail had brought him here. Ennio Ostraban had managed to play chairman and hold together his tentative coalition for long enough now that it was bound to have attracted the attention of the Order. It would have been surprising if they hadn't extended their writhing mass of tentacles out this far.

And Winter had an elaborate and convoluted system of law enforcement that was part militia-run and mostly esoteric corporate nonsense that was corrupt as hell and more than likely to change on a whim if someone could profit and someone else was prepared to pay enough. Perfect when you had dirty work to be carried out.

He hated it.

And he hated being cold.

'*You're too soft*,' that dark voice murmured maliciously, deep inside.

"I'm not in the mood," he said out loud, reaching a hand to flick the ship into manual and increasing the rate of descent.

Time alone with no one to distract him from his thoughts had been hard. He wasn't going to start listening to the doubts now. It wasn't often that he lost control completely but it was happening more and more frequently.

And when that darkness descended, it was getting harder and harder to temper it.

'*Listen to yourself. Hate is such a powerful emotion. Use it.*'

NG threw in another command and disabled the safety parameters.

He accelerated hard, every ounce of concentration needed to keep the craft level and steady.

'Coward.'

He cut the engines and plummeted towards the planet.

He let the craft freefall for about a thousand feet further than it was sane to do, playing chicken with that part of his mind that still had a modicum of self-preservation, and fired up the engines only when ground control began to initiate emergency procedures. The response to the access codes he was using said a lot about the sway these people had over the Wintran establishment.

He was directed down to a private runway, asked politely if he required assistance and ushered through to a groundside berth that bypassed customs and entry protocols with the slick efficiency of a VIP arrival.

There was a car waiting at the berth, blacked out windows, empty, no surprise that the codes he had started the ignition. He turned up the interior heating, glanced back at the bundle he'd thrown on the back seat and set off to the rendezvous.

The warehouse was quiet. Abandoned. Dark. And cold. NG stood in the shadows behind the door of the empty office, the cold weather gear he'd raided from lockers in the ship not quite enough to keep the chill from seeping through to his bones.

He waited, motionless, breath frosting in the cold, clean air of corporate Winter. The office was mothballed in perfect sterile preservation, waiting for the next proprietor to take ownership of the warehouse. He'd set a spotlight and a single chair in the centre of the room and initiated a tight radius shield.

Then he just had to wait.

It was exactly thirty minutes after he'd sent the designated signal that the car pulled up outside. It was an efficient operation, far superior to the last set of hired help he'd encountered. That was what you got as you moved up the food chain.

Five men got out of the car. The man he was expecting plus four armed guards.

NG tensed, picking up their thoughts and emotions, readying himself for another fight, but only the main man walked up to the warehouse, dismissing the others into guard duty with an arrogance he'd regret.

The outside door banged and footsteps resounded with a sharp echo as the man approached, emanating calm confidence with an air of impatience.

Another mistake.

He made his way through to the office, humming to himself. NG could hear the off key tune, hear the underlying self-satisfaction of the man as he anticipated the reward of accomplishing this mission.

NG didn't move.

The door banged open and the man who walked in was exactly as he remembered, older, more grey in the hair, more expensive wool coat hanging on the thin shoulders, but the same cold aura of self-interest. The man walked in, eyes having trouble adjusting to the dark, and stopped when he saw the prone hooded form on the floor lit by a single angled spotlight. There was doubt then and an intense irritation that flared in the man's chest.

"What is this?" he said, disgusted, voice hollow in the empty space. He turned and squinted into the shadows trying to make out NG as he stood there. "I stipulated alive. If he's dead, you don't get paid."

The old man took a step forward and kicked at the body, nudging it over, distaste mixing with a burning curiosity. NG watched from outside the circle of light as he knelt and pulled the hood from the head.

The man reeled backwards, standing and scowling.

NG slowly pushed the door behind him closed with one outstretched hand and stepped forward into the light.

"Hello A'Darbi," he said in little more than a whisper and felt the recognition hit with a pang of ice in the old man's stomach. "How's Ostraban these days?"

11

She took the goblet and inhaled the vapours deeply. "Into the heart of the Wintran coalition itself? Alone? Was that wise?"

He regarded her with slight disdain.

"Did you know what he was doing?" she said.

This was not an interrogation, or even a debriefing, nowhere near the intensity of the questioning he inflicted on Nikolai. He was not obligated to answer. But these sessions, as with those in his chambers, served to clear the mind, put situations into perspective.

He laced his fingers and looked deeper into the question. He didn't reply, saying instead, carefully, "Ostraban is gathering a dangerous momentum."

"He is," she conceded. "Do the corporations truly support him or are they paying lip service to the ideal because they need to be seen to do so?"

"They support him exactly as far as it serves their own ends. It was no surprise to find out that the Order is fuelling his success."

It took a moment but A'Darbi wrestled back his self-restraint. "NG," he said, swallowing awkwardly, taking a step backwards, eyes darting to look down at the body of the mercenary leader he'd hired. He tried desperately to contact his men and couldn't, no response, starting to realise that he was in real danger for the first time in his privileged life.

"You look like you're doing well for yourself, A'Darbi," NG said quietly. Taynara A'Darbi was one of Ennio Ostraban's oldest and closest advisors. They'd met before and last time the guy had been a minor official, nowhere near important enough to have been recruited by the Order. How things change.

"NG," A'Darbi said again, mind racing in embarrassed desperation to find something to say that would mitigate his having been caught in such a compromising situation by someone as dangerous as NG.

It was almost worth a smile.

He was close. This man that was squirming there in front of him had been instructed to arrange his abduction. NG felt like he had a wriggling catch at the end of his line. A catch that would lead directly to the Order.

"Sit down," NG said quietly. He could see the cold calculations that were sparking within this elder statesman of Winter as he sat and adjusted his expensive coat as if he was about to begin business negotiations.

A'Darbi opened his mouth to speak but NG hushed him with a casual wave of the gun in his left hand and a shake of the head.

He didn't need to let the old man speak. He could acquire everything he needed to know brutally and quickly.

A'Darbi put up a hand. "Now look here, NG," he said, dropping into his stern voice as if that could save his life. "You're out of your depth, son. It's the council we want to speak to."

NG took a step forward. "You killed one of my men."

A'Darbi shook his head, affecting a concerned expression. He was used to taking the podium to deliver reasonable deniability. "Casualties are unfortunate – avoidable if your council would only answer our requests for open discussion." He spread his hands. "That's all we ask."

There was a nervous tick fluttering in the man's mind, more than anxiety at his current predicament. He was hoping like hell that NG didn't know something, praying that the Thieves' Guild didn't know.

NG took another step closer. "Why now, A'Darbi? Why are you moving against us now?"

To give him credit, he was a fast thinker. You didn't get that high in any organisation without being able to bullshit.

"Winter doesn't move against you, NG," he said in a perfectly contrived tone of condescending reassurance. "Why would you think that, son? Everyone on this side of the line values the role your guild plays."

'He doesn't even lie well. Why are you listening to this, Nikolai?'

"I'm not talking about Winter," NG said slowly, ignoring the darkness, listening in as it dawned on A'Darbi that if he wasn't talking about Winter, he could only be talking about the Order.

A'Darbi set his face, jaw clenching. "Put the gun down, son. You don't know what you're talking about. You don't know what you're dealing with here."

It was only a matter of time before his men realised something was wrong.

NG made a show of checking the gun. "Tell me about the Order, A'Darbi."

It was like flicking a switch.

The composure drained out of the old man like water swirling down a drain. "No," he said, barely more than a gasp.

"I know you're working for the Order, A'Darbi, and I know that the Order has declared war against my guild. Why now?"

The thoughts that flashed through the old man's mind were jumbled, tumbling. "What do you want? I can pay," A'Darbi whispered, a trickle of sweat running down his face.

NG shook his head slightly.

'This is pathetic,' the dark voice whispered at the back of his mind, *'you should just kill him.'*

He could sense the old man's heart pounding, feel the panic that this was out of control, this wasn't supposed to happen like this.

Suddenly A'Darbi said quietly, maliciously, "Tell your council their days are numbered," and NG caught the edge of his intent a fraction of a second too late.

He moved fast and caught the old man with a firm grasp around the jawline as A'Darbi bit down on a suicide capsule. The poison flooded his system and NG was hard pushed to halt it, freezing the moment, and freezing A'Darbi in an instant of lethal agony. The old man's face contorted in a last tortured realisation that death wasn't going to come quickly.

NG took his time getting everything he needed.

'Nice. Let him suffer.'

He had to keep his emotions in check as the old man's brain released its knowledge of events and consequences, a trail of revelations that NG took carefully and stored away, gathering every ounce of intelligence on the Order, its relations with the Assassins and the Federation, its links with the Merchants, Earth and Winter. A'Darbi was high up, not as high as NG needed but far more senior than anyone he'd encountered so far. And the intertwining threads of activity that had impinged on the guild were knotted in a convoluted and devastating mess.

And in amongst it all, a vicious satisfaction that the Thieves' Guild was meeting its match with the sheer volume of money and resources pitched against it. Zang Tsu Po was nothing but a renegade who had no idea what he had precipitated in his foolish blackmailing of the Thieves' Guild but at least he was putting his own money up for grabs with the bounty on the two rogue thieves.

NG was another matter. A'Darbi would have been more than happy to back any suggestion to put half a billion of the Order's reserves on the table to be rid of him, but as far as he knew it wasn't the Order who had contracted the Assassins. No, they wanted NG alive, wanted that connection with the council, wanted him on his knees so they could bleed every last secret of the Thieves' Guild from him with excruciating exactness. An Assassins' knife in the back was far too fast for their liking.

A'Darbi writhed in agony as his memories were torn apart and NG's heart started pounding as he realised the implications of it all.

He pushed the old man away when he was done and watched the body crumple to the floor.

He had to get back to the Alsatia.

Evelyn was waiting for him when he docked, unimpressed, concerned and relieved all at once, a flurry of emotion that made his head ache.

"Hilyer's missing," she said, offering a data board and dropping into step beside him, two of the Man's elite guards a step behind her.

NG hoisted his bag over his shoulder and took the board. "What happened?"

"The tab on Abacus was a disaster. We lost him and we've had word that there's a bounty out on him now as well. Wibowski and Hetherington have gone awol." She was also thinking about Domino. "What's going on, NG?"

It wasn't a rhetorical question. NG kept walking towards the lift. Martha Hetherington and Kase Wibowski were two of the extraction agents he'd assigned to watch Hil's back so if Hil had skipped out and they were awol, with luck the three of them would still be together. Field operatives often had to go deep and he couldn't think of a better two to have with the kid.

He pressed the button to call the elevator and made another decision, very aware that he was running on instinct but they had no time to waste on prolonged analysis of potential scenarios and strategies here. "Send out a Black Rogue Seven on Hil and LC."

"We've already sent out a Black," she said, thinking, oh shit, a Black Rogue Seven is going to cause chaos.

"I don't care," NG said. "We need them back. Someone is screwing with us. We have to stop it. Right now."

Devon sat in her usual seat at the conference table and kept her face immaculately neutral, hiding her anger. "Zang? Are you serious?" she sent privately. "Do you know the figures Zang posted last year?"

He'd keep the briefing short, not in the mood for a long drawn out inquisition, and he wanted to get back out there to follow the lead he'd squeezed from A'Darbi. The four chiefs had got the basics, no details of the Order, only the fact that it was Zang Tsu Po who had ordered an attack on Mendhel and forced Anderton and Hilyer to run an unauthorised tab.

NG looked around at the chiefs who kept his guild running.

Media was flicking through the board in front of her as if she could find something he'd missed if she went through it all faster and faster. "At least we know now that Hil and LC didn't betray us willingly," she said. "What did Zang send them to steal?"

"I've told you everything I know," NG said. "Christ knows what they went after. We wouldn't have taken the job. Not against the JU. Zang must have known that. And he knew no one else could pull it off."

Devon didn't look at him as she sent, privately, "And did they pull it off?"

NG reached for the jug to top up his tea.

"Did they?" she sent again.

"We have to assume so, Devon," he sent back, "because if they didn't, Jameson would have hauled the two of them back here in chains. I don't know why LC ran. But if the bounty is still out there on them both, presumably Zang hasn't found them either."

She glared at him and sent, "We lost some good people on Abacus," insinuating that he'd made a mistake by tipping off Jameson.

He looked up at her. Evelyn hadn't been exaggerating when she'd said the tab they'd sent Hilyer out on had been a disaster. They'd been caught up in an outright battle between the corporation they now knew was Zang and Jameson's heavy-handed response. Earth versus Winter. With Hil and LC right in the middle of it. Hil had disappeared and five extraction agents had been killed, caught in the crossfire.

The Chief was sitting there smouldering. "What about Domino? Was that Zang?"

NG poured out half a cup he didn't really want. "I don't know. How close are we to finding LC?"

They all looked to Media. As much as it was the Chief who was coordinating the search teams, rumour-mongering was her department. She shook her head. "We're not," she said. "O'Brien has stopped sending in updates. The bounty is escalating and we have nothing but unsubstantiated rumours. He's vanished."

"Have we sent someone to Kheris?" he said, knowing it was a long shot before he said it.

"Yes," Media said, unimpressed that he'd had to ask. "And no, there's no sign of him. Come on, NG, you know he'd never go back there. We've checked every known contact. There are a lot of rumours and we're doing our best to quash them to take the heat out of this but there is a ridiculous amount of money on offer."

LC doesn't have a chance was what she was thinking but she'd never say that. And she was right, he knew Kheris was a long shot. LC would never go home if he had any say in the matter.

NG curled a hand around his cup. "Have we got people on Sten's?"

Media pursed her lips and looked to the Chief who stared NG in the eye and said, "We've got people everywhere," defying anyone to make an open accusation of negligence.

Acquisitions was taking the brunt of this whole drama. NG looked at Devon, picking up an air of contention between two of his chiefs. She didn't react, blinking lazily and daring either of them to make an issue of it here. He ventured beyond her surface thoughts, not something he did lightly, not in these surroundings. Christ, she'd thrown in a proposition to dissolve Acquisitions and take control of their affairs into Legal.

The Man would never go for it but give her credit for having a go.

NG picked up his cup and sent privately to the Chief, "Keep Quinn on Hil alone. I'll sort out the list. We need to get our operatives back. Rein in everyone else and put all resources into finding Hil and LC. And whatever happens, trust me, okay?"

The Chief didn't reply but he met NG's eye and nodded almost imperceptibly.

NG took a sip of the tea and placed the cup on the table. "We're going after Zang," he said out loud. "On all fronts. Hit them where it hurts." He could go after Zang and the Order, and use all the resources of the guild. Money and power. They were the lifeblood of the guild and no one could match the Thieves' Guild when it came to acquiring them.

12

"A Black Rogue Seven?"

The incredulity was justified. Never before had a head of operations instigated such a drastic course of action without his explicit approval.

"Desperate times…"

She raised her eyebrows. "Did Nikolai actually appreciate at the time just how desperate?"

"He has an acute talent for reading a situation and an ability to anticipate, pre-empt, almost foresee an outcome."

"More even than you…?"

He reached for the wine with a wry smile. "He understands these creatures far better than I. He is the worst of them and the best of them. The Black Rogue Seven was drastic and, I admit, caused ripples we have still not yet repaired. But if he hadn't dared make such a timely and audacious move, I fear the consequences could have been far worse."

They talked for another five hours, planning, bringing every section of the guild into play against Zang – Legal to fight and escalate every corporate litigation action Zang were fending off, Science to undermine every patent application and attempt at innovation or advancement, Media to launch a blistering propaganda campaign and Acquisitions to do what it did best, hit them in their pockets.

Evelyn brought in coffee and on the third round, she placed the fresh jug on the tray and slipped a board in front of him without a word.

NG scanned the brief and scrubbed a hand over his eyes. It

wasn't often that the Man sent him direct orders. He looked back at the message. He didn't have much time.

"Evie," he sent privately as she walked out, "find out where Ballack is for me, would you?"

According to A'Darbi, Ballack's first secretary was Order. The higher the chain went, the more insidious the whispers into the ears of the galaxy's powermongers. No wonder the Merchants' Guild was working against them.

Evelyn sent straight back, "You haven't been watching the news streams, have you? He's on Redgate. The Merchants are threatening to pull out."

NG looked up. Christ. The supposedly neutral presence of the Merchants' Guild was the only stabilising factor in that region. If they left, it would be almost impossible to run any kind of operation from there any more.

"Have we heard anything from Badger?" he asked out loud, interrupting the ongoing discussion, knowing the answer but needing to work his way through the logic.

"No," Devon said.

"And what have we got on the Merchants?"

"Why?" Devon's tone was still confrontational.

"What have we got?" he said again.

"It's a problem we've been trying to mitigate, NG," Media said. "Like Silas said, they're offering acquisition work. Packaged up differently but you don't have to look too far beneath the surface to see that they're touting for tabs that we would normally get without question. We've had contracts pulled that were done deals except for the signature then suddenly the client doesn't need us and we find out they're talking to the Merchants. Having Hilyer and Anderton at the top of the Federation's most wanted list isn't doing our reputation any favours." She paused, hesitating to add that his own name on the Assassin's list was an added instability that didn't help market confidence. She leaned forward. "In the long term, they can't match us. No one has a pool of operatives that even come close to ours. And that will show. But immediately…? They're making promises and laughing at the fact that clients are even listening to them. And they are. Silas isn't the only one."

"Why do you ask?" Devon said again, suspiciously.

"What about Redgate?" he asked, directing the question at Media and ignoring Devon.

"It's a war zone. Worse than ever. The Merchants are losing control because some Wintran corporation has gone in there and is throwing cash around. You don't think that's Zang, do you?"

NG stood up. It didn't matter if it was Zang or not. What mattered was that if Ballack was on Redgate, then his right hand man would be there.

Devon sent privately, angrily, "NG, what's going on?"

He picked up the board. "Keep at it," he said out loud, glancing round at all four of his section chiefs. "I want our boys back and I want Zang. Whatever it takes." And he walked out.

Devon followed, striding after him silently and stalking him back to his office.

He threw the board onto the desk, not caring that she was right behind him, and walked through to his quarters.

His bag was still on the bed where he'd thrown it when he got in.

Devon was fuming. She stood in the doorway, the board in her hand, glaring at him.

"NG, what's going on," she said again.

He tipped the contents of the bag into the chute and started to pack a clean change of clothes.

Devon frowned as she realised what he was doing. "Where are you going?" she said incredulously, disbelief that he was going to skip out again mixing with a tantalising thought that she was going to be left in charge again.

"Redgate," he said, throwing a couple of handguns into the bag.

"What about this?" She held up the board.

He ignored her, turning and rummaging in a locker. "Cover for me."

She slammed the door shut and walked up close to him. Her perfume stung the air. She slapped the board against his arm. "Direct orders, NG. I know that discipline isn't one of your strong points here but for god's sake, when the Man says to stay here, stay. What the hell are you thinking?"

He closed the locker and turned abruptly so that her face was inches from his. "I'm going to Redgate," he said softly, taking the board from her and tossing it aside.

She was horrified but she hid that from her expression, eyes narrowing. "What's going on, NG?"

He shook his head slightly. "Don't ask."

"Is it personal?"

"No."

"If it's guild business, why doesn't the Man know about it?"

"He does."

She clenched her jaw, frustrated. "NG, you're not the only one who got a message from the Man. We have direct orders to keep you here."

'The Man knows you too well.'

NG pushed the darkness aside. So the Man was expecting him to chase the Order. It wasn't a rebellious streak that made him throw the board aside – he knew what needed to be done. For all the Man's seemingly omnipotent presence, he didn't always appreciate the frailties of the human race. How petty minded and self-destructive humans could be when power and money were at stake. Whatever delicate balance of mutual tolerance had existed between the Order and the Thieves' Guild had been blown apart. By something. It was a race to get the upper hand and right now the Order was winning. They'd follow the trail of bodies he'd left fast enough. He couldn't sit and wait for their next attack. That was what the Man didn't understand. The Man planned in terms of centuries. Humans lived in the moment.

Devon was trying to decide whether to throw him onto the floor or throw him onto the bed.

"I don't have any choice," NG said quietly. "I'll deal with the Man when I get back."

"You won't get out of Redgate alive," she said, eyes flashing.

"I'm not going to hide."

"I know the Assassins, NG. They're out there looking for you. The last I heard was assholes like Ki and Brandon, even Sceznei, bragging about who was going to get to you first. And you know what's more disturbing?" She didn't give him time to respond. "My contacts have stopped talking to me."

She glared at him. He could feel how hard it was for her to have that connection severed for good. Over him.

"We've already been breached," she said. "Right here. Walking onto Redgate will be suicide." She folded her arms to stop herself reaching out to hit him.

'She cares about you. How touching. And if you leave, the bitch will be in charge. But let's face it, she can't screw it up any more than you already have.'

He bit his tongue to stop himself saying anything out loud.

"NG…"

"You don't understand," he said softly, knowing that was the wrong thing to say.

Her eyes flared wide. "So tell me! For Christ's sake, NG."

He shook his head and turned. Devon instinctively grabbed his arm and twisted, pushing him against the locker door. She was strong. They always played rough. He let her pin him there, feeling her heart pounding against his chest.

"If you get yourself killed, I'm left with the mess," she whispered harshly. "Don't leave me in the dark to handle the fallout from your screw up, NG. Tell me what's going on."

'Or what?'

"I'll be fine," he said stubbornly.

"You'll be dead."

"You can't stop me."

It crossed her mind to incapacitate him, right there, a single lightning fast move that would leave him out cold on the floor, and when she moved he almost reacted, sensing her intention just in time as she grabbed the back of his neck and pulled him into a kiss.

"There's an organisation called the Order," he said, brushing her hair from her face.

'You're making a big mistake.'

Devon stretched, arching her back, the edge of the sheet slipping to expose a smooth shoulder. "Now I get an explanation?" she said, her voice soft despite the edge of nonchalant sarcasm.

"You're right. I might need help so you need to know."

'You're pathetic, you don't need help from anyone.'

She twisted around and looked up at him through long lashes. "Go on. I'm intrigued."

"They've been around for millennia in one form or another, going by various names over the centuries. We have fingers in a lot of pies, you know that. Trade agreements, alliances, relationships that go back generations. The Order has that and more. We don't know who they are. They don't know who we are. We've no doubt crossed swords in the past, but never openly." He paused, watching her reaction.

She looked sceptical. "A secret underground organisation? Like the Illuminati? Come on, NG, you expect me to believe that? The Illuminati are a fairy tale, they don't exist."

"In some areas, people say the Thieves' Guild doesn't exist."

"Fair point." She paused for a second. NG could see the turmoil in her mind. She couldn't tell whether he was screwing with her or being serious. "Suppose for a second you haven't lost your mind, why has this secret organisation suddenly decided to declare war on us?"

NG was leaning on one elbow. It felt like he'd pulled a muscle in his back. Devon was never gentle.

"NG? Talk to me."

He shifted his weight to ease the ache and tried to figure out what he could say.

'You shouldn't say anything.'

"My real name is Nikolai," he said suddenly. As far as he was aware, only two individuals alive knew his real name. He'd always used different names when he moved postings. Or let people tag him with a nickname.

Devon raised her eyebrows, lips twitching into a smile. "Nikolai?" She leaned back, staring at him in bemusement, fully appreciative of the honour he'd just bestowed on her. "Okay then, Nikolai, talk to me."

"In everything we do," he said cautiously, "we aim for balance. You understand that?"

It was one of the first things he'd explained when she'd come across to them. There was more to it than that, much more that no one but the Man appreciated, but balance was the underlying philosophy that everything else rested on.

She nodded, eyes narrowing.

"The Order pushes for war. Constantly. They profit from conflict. Keeping the scattered populations scared and weak is what keeps them in their positions of power."

"So they see us as a threat?"

NG shrugged. "The Thieves' Guild directly opposes what they are trying to achieve. We nurture advancement through cooperation, dissemination of information to encourage progress and evolution." By stealing it and sharing it out. He didn't say why, couldn't quite bring himself to tell her why that was so important. "We undermine what the Order strives so hard for. I don't know why but something has made them act against us. They've screwed up. They've revealed themselves for the first time and now I have something to go after."

"They want to get to the council? Why won't the council just talk to them?"

He leaned in and kissed her, long and hard.

There wasn't a council but that wasn't something he could admit to her. The council of elders was a smokescreen, obfuscation, stuff and nonsense to hide the fact that the guild was just the Man. And it had worked. Everyone after him so far had been trying to get to the council.

Problem was, Devon needed to think she was part of a bigger organisation, that was what he had tempted her with. She didn't need power and control, she needed something to strive for, always something higher, further from her reach to aim for. She didn't need to know that the guild was just him and the Man. No one did.

She laughed and pushed him away. "Are they Earth or Winter?"

"Both."

"Zang?"

He nodded. "Zang is, or at least was. Seems he's gone renegade. I'm not sure if that works for us or against us, but it's the first crack I've seen in their armour, and trust me I've been looking for a long time."

"Why Redgate?"

"I want to talk to Badger."

She looked sceptical.

"And Alek Ingarssen," he admitted. "Ballack's sidekick. He's Order. He's as high as I've managed to track down. I need to know who's pulling the strings."

"Ballack will recognise you."

"I'll stay out of his way. It's Ingarssen I need to get to and he doesn't know me."

Devon traced a finger across his chest. "Why now?" She was genuinely intrigued. She'd caught the hint of a new enemy and now she knew, she wanted to join the hunt. Her touch was soft on his skin as she circled the scar from the bullet wound but her soul was cold as she contemplated the implications of taking on an organisation more powerful than the guild she'd adopted as her own.

"They made a mistake," he said.

Killing Mendhel and Domino, he heard her think. She stared at him and said, "NG… Nikolai… you can't go to Redgate alone."

"I'll take Banks and Martinez."

"Take Evelyn as well."

He did smile then. "I don't think I'll need a PA with me where I'm going."

Devon frowned, wanting to explain but not wanting to lose the advantage of what she thought was her secret. "I don't understand why it has to be you to go. Let me send someone."

No one would ever be able to understand why it had to be him.

Only the Man knew anything about his abilities. He had no choice but to go himself. No one else could strip away the truth directly from Ingarssen's mind as he thought it.

NG shook his head and cheated, using the physical contact to give Devon no choice but to concede the argument.

"Give me everything you've got on the Order," she said.

"I just did."

There wasn't much else he could say. And it wasn't like there was a file he could hand over.

She moved closer, stroking her hand along his bare skin to the bicep muscle and the second scar. "You heal fast," she murmured.

"I'm invincible."

'You're soft, Nikolai,' the dark voice whispered maliciously, *'and you shouldn't have told her a thing.'*

13

The disbelief deepened. "He knows the council to be a fabrication? Why, in all of this, why would you want him to know he is alone?"

"He is alone. It does him no good to live a lie."

She stared at him, eyes wide. "The concept of a council of elders has served us well. Why can it not serve Nikolai? You are hard enough on him. You say he protects his own, does he not deserve his own form of protection?"

"He is not like any other, any of us, any of his own. He is alone and it will do none of us any good if he is cosseted to believe otherwise."

She was his conscience, this woman sitting opposite him, staring and so unimpressed.

"You put the pressure of the entire guild on him," she said, "the full weight of the special projects, the responsibility for the future of a whole race..."

"And he thrives on it."

"Does he? Does he not get closer to cracking every time the handle gets cranked another notch?"

"He gets stronger. He has no choice."

They walked off the ship into a snowstorm and an armed guard. NG pulled his collar close. He was wearing black, not exactly business clothes but not exactly combat gear, body armour and warm weather layers and he was still cold. Banks and Martinez stayed close, flanking him on either side.

They'd used guild-seeded corporate IDs to gain entry permission, old and hard-earned IDs that had extensive authentic provenance.

It was a difficult decision to expose such an established corporation that had been so useful for such a long time but it was one the Merchants were familiar with, one that had no discernible link with the guild, and he couldn't risk using a less stable cover. It was risky enough just to be here.

They'd scanned the security system from orbit before they'd committed to landing and he'd calculated the risk to be worth it. The terminal's auto-visual ID system was down, as it had been for years – few visitors to Redgate wanted to be readily identified – they had a mobile disruptor to knock out any real-time camera feeds, and there was no reason any of the staff here should recognise him. The only danger was Ballack himself and his immediate personnel, Ingarssen excepted. NG had never met the guy. He just needed to avoid Ballack, get in, get what he needed and get out.

He blinked snow off his eyelashes, nodded to the officer in charge of the escort and received a curt welcome. They were taken across the runway and into a terminal, fast tracked through arrivals and led into a lounge. It looked like power was on emergency back up, lights flickering and heating struggling to keep up with the drop in temperature. The whole place was more run down than he remembered from his last visit, years ago. No wonder Ballack wanted to pull the plug.

The armed guard left them there with a handful of other travellers who were waiting to be processed, all corporate types, a few bored regulars and a couple of nervous newbies. Life carries on whatever the rebels were planning and Redgate needed to maintain its supply chains.

Martinez pulled coffees from a vending machine, extra sugar masking the tang of the artificial flavour.

In most Merchants' Guild facilities throughout the galaxy, the coffee was real, straight from Earth, no expense spared. The Merchant's airfield on Redgate had every look of a place that had been low priority for a long time and was fast reaching the end of its effective life span.

A far off rumble echoed through the building.

One of the nervous women clutched at her companion. "It sounds like thunder," she said.

"Sounds like fucking artillery to me," Martinez muttered.

NG hid his grin behind the coffee cup.

A Merchants' Guild official scurried in after a while, waving the others to wait and smiling at NG's group, so their IDs must have checked out.

"Orientation talk is basically this: don't leave the perimeter of the airfield if you want to survive this business trip," he said and laughed. "No, seriously, you've requested passage to the south. That's fine. You'll be able to leave in the morning, probably. I'll have someone let you know. This isn't a good time to be visiting Redgate but hey, I'm sure your competitors daren't chase up trade here right now so why not take advantage, huh?" He handed over a bundle of documents. "Keep these with you. Snowstorm is due to let up some time soon. Hostilities to the north are getting worse. Check in at the desk if you want to book an armed guard. You all have rooms booked at the Wellbeing and they can sort you out with transport if you need it. Have a good trip."

NG went through the motions of checking the documents. He had no intention of leaving the airfield.

The official watched until NG nodded his approval then led them back out into the cold and pointed them in the direction of the Wellbeing, an array of lights that cut through the white out of the snow.

Banks clapped his hands together as they walked. "Jesus, why the hell do people fight over this place?"

"Money and power, bud," Martinez said. "Imagine how hard the bastards would fight if they had year-round sunshine."

Badger was already waiting in the suite of rooms they'd booked for the night. He'd ordered enough room service for them all and brought in a load of kit that he'd spread around the lounge.

He didn't look up as they walked in, dark glasses perched on top of wild hair and a handful of tortilla chips on the way to his mouth as he ran data through five boards at once with the other hand.

NG dropped his bag and perched on the arm of the sofa, reaching for a beer. "I want you on something new."

"Uhuh." Badger spun a board around and pushed it across the low table. "You need to see this."

The image wasn't clear but it was clear enough. "Is that Hil?"

"On Aston. With at least five sets of bounty hunters after his ass. They didn't catch him as far as I can tell. But he's pushing it."

"What about LC?"

"Nothing since Palmio."

Banks and Martinez were at the dining table, spreading out cloths to clean weapons. NG popped open the beer. It was good to see Badger again. It had been too long just hearing the reports from him second-hand as the field-ops brought the intel back.

"What have you got on the Merchants?" he said.

"Nothing new. Ballack threatening to pull out is trash talk. He's in full negotiations with this corporation that is ploughing so much into making more of this place than it's worth."

"Is it Zang?"

Badger looked up, curious. "Why?"

NG took a swig of the beer. It was cold and reminded him of old times on tough assignments where the only alcohol was cheap beer that you always hoped like hell was cold enough not to taste like ditch water.

"It was Zang that had Mendhel killed," he said carefully. "They probably posted the bounties on LC and Hil."

Badger looked down, fingers flying across his boards. "What about the Assassins?" he said.

"That's what I want you on," NG said. "We don't know. I want you to find Ki and Brandon, and some guy called Sceznei."

Badger laughed and cursed at once. He finished what he was doing then pushed the boards away, grabbed a beer and another handful of chips and sat back. "What's going on, NG?"

"Honestly? I have no idea. We have a breach in security and I have no idea where." He nodded towards the table stacked with boards. "I want you to wrap up here, get that intel back to the Alsatia then go find the assassins. Do anything you have to do."

The fact there was a Black Rogue Seven out there causing mayhem flashed across Badger's mind. He looked at NG with a bemused, questioning expression.

NG downed another mouthful of beer. "Whatever it takes."

Alek Ingarssen was tall and thin, sitting with legs stretched out, confidently sprawled in the shabby armchair. He held his hand up and rubbed his thumb and fingers together, smiling. "That's what it's all about," he said. "You can do well here."

NG held up his tumbler of whisky and nodded. The Wellbeing was struggling to live up to brand standards but no one could complain considering the circumstances.

A sealed package left at the desk for Ingarssen didn't take long to illicit a response and as they sat negotiating an under the table deal packed with backhanders, NG read the guy's mind as easily as if the jerk was recounting every thought out loud. He was arrogant, blatantly self-interested and had no problem in assuming that his visitors were as corrupt as their bribe had suggested. He'd arranged a meeting according to their request, private, discrete, no need to mention their presence to Ballack.

It had been a calculated gamble but Ingarssen turned out to be exactly the type of right hand man they had anticipated – one who watched his own back and feigned loyalty only so long as it met his own ends.

And he was proud to be Order. It resonated through every fibre. He was even considering inviting NG to a meeting of the Low Guard, some introductory low grade recruitment organisation used to feel out potential future members.

NG had said everything Ingarssen wanted to hear and kept back just enough to sound like he was cautiously secretive – exactly the kind of upcoming merchant operator the Order saw as a future asset.

The booming noise of the distant artillery ebbed and flowed, the low lighting in the room flickering as the back up power struggled. They were sitting in a private chamber, an inner sanctum that was warm, much warmer than the rest of the Wellbeing. Rank has its privilege and Ingarssen was milking it to its extreme.

Banks and Martinez were waiting outside and they were all hoping that Ballack would keep his distance. Ingarssen certainly had no vested interest in his boss being privy to this meeting, they'd made sure of that with the offer they'd presented.

"You'll do very well," Ingarssen said again, more than contented with the deal, leaning forward and offering his hand.

NG took the bony hand in a firm grasp and took everything he needed, freezing the moment, gently teasing out the information and leaving Ingarssen undamaged but reeling as if the alcohol had suddenly taken its toll.

'*You should melt his brain*,' the dark voice whispered.

It wasn't worth the risk. They needed to walk away from this one quietly with no trail blazing behind them.

Ingarssen blinked and laughed, sitting back and shaking his head slightly. The man of the Order had no idea what had happened and NG had a lead that went right to the heart of the Earth Empire. Easy.

He opened his eyes to darkness, adrenaline rushing and heart pounding.

'*Enemies at the gate…*'

NG sat up reaching for his gun. He was still fully dressed. Badger had left. Gone to secure his den and bug out. They'd decided to stay the night to maintain their cover, taking turns at watch.

It looked like that had been a mistake.

It took a second to scan around and focus in. Martinez was at the door, gun out, about to open it, hostiles in the corridor outside, Banks asleep in the other bedroom. NG sent a fast sharp warning to them both. He ran out into the main room, hauling Martinez aside as the door exploded inwards.

Debris rained down on them. They both twisted round,

firing at the armoured squad that was bursting in. NG picked their orders from a mind that was clear and focused – it was an advance team, four guys, night vision kit, expecting their shock tactics to catch the target unawares. All four hit the floor with a bullet through the throat. Martinez was up and pulling NG to his feet before the smoke cleared.

Banks was already at the window. "Shit," he said and turned.

NG scanned around quickly. There were vehicles pulling up outside, more troops piling out to surround the Wellbeing, heightened emotions and slick communications. There were more moving rapidly through the building. Whoever had called this in knew what they were doing. According to the information he'd dragged from A'Darbi, the Order wanted him alive. But surely there was no way they could have known that he'd be here. Even if they'd found A'Darbi's body and made the connection.

He ran back into his room and grabbed his armoured vest, shrugging into it and running back out.

"The corridor," Banks said. "Up."

The roof was going to be the only way out. They moved fast, evading an increasing force assaulting the hotel with no regard for collateral damage. NG had no idea who'd given them away. Definitely not Ingarssen. And he'd been scanning every individual they'd encountered from setting foot on the planet. Nothing. He was absolutely sure that no one had recognised him.

'Someone did. You screwed up.'

He ignored the doubt niggling deep inside and ran.

They reached the roof and crouched in the shelter of the doorway, watching troops land, dark shadows spilling out of gunships and into the snow, spreading out into search patterns. From the look of them and their equipment, they were probably a mercenary unit rather than local militia.

'You've really blown this one.'

"We need to move," Martinez murmured. She had a hand on his shoulder. He hadn't had time to grab his coat and the driving sleet had soaked quickly into his shirt. Martinez was worrying that everyone and their dog was going to hear the commotion and come join the party. She wanted him out of there. He wanted out of there. So much for quietly in, quietly out.

Artillery strikes were still hitting the north shore off in the distance. They gauged their move and ran, jumping across to the adjacent building and rolling to their feet, Banks a shade behind and Martinez veering left to cover. After that, they made their way steadily around the complex, leaping gaps between buildings and running across rooftops to the main terminal, avoiding the massive spotlights that began to flash in sweeping arcs.

More gunships were starting to close in, thrusters roaring, shouts from the ground echoing through the night. A shell hit close by, the blast sending out a shockwave that shook the building beneath their feet.

"Oh shit," Martinez sent, glancing round as they ran, "they're attacking the airfield. Does the whole fucking planet know we're here?"

'*Well done, Nikolai.*' Deep inside, that dark niggling voice was laughing. '*You've just thrown a spark into the powder keg.*'

A gunship raced overhead, swooping down and skidding to a halt on the rooftop up ahead. Troops piled out.

"Who are these guys?" Banks muttered and sent tight wire, private, "Shit, Martinez, we need to go to ground, girl. This is getting out of hand."

He was right and NG caught the unease in Martinez's reply, listening in to their exchange as easily as if he'd been included in the loop. He didn't resist as Banks grabbed his shoulder and herded him towards the edge of the roof. As good as NG was – he'd looked after himself far longer than he'd known any one person in the guild – keeping him alive was their job and they'd proved themselves to be very good at it, many times. He had no reason to doubt them now.

They ducked low and worked their way round to a point where lower buildings edged onto the main terminal, dropping down and jumping from roof to roof until they were low enough to climb down to ground level. They moved fast, using the cover of the buildings and stacked transport containers. An icy cold wind whistled viciously through the narrow alleyways sending the snow and sleet into wild flurries, sucking out any residual heat he had left in his body.

They could hear sounds of fighting close by. An outright attack had been initiated on the neutral airfield simply by the presence of so many armed soldiers attacking the Wellbeing. That was all it had taken. Ballack would be furious.

Martinez stopped suddenly, gesturing them to get down. Banks closed in defensively, instinctively sensing danger as NG detected the presence of a figure emerging from the darkness behind them.

He turned.

Martinez spun, gun up.

NG read the intention and time seemed to slow as the figure moved in a fluid dance, the knife flowing from graceful fingers to cut through the storm in a perfect trajectory. An incendiary shell hit the building to their left, the bright flash of flames illuminating the figure. NG started to twist away. He was fast but he knew he wasn't going to be fast enough, the knife flying straight and true towards his throat.

Except that Banks shoved him aside. The knife hit home and Banks fell.

NG stumbled to his knees, feeling the shock of the stabbing pain second-hand. Martinez was firing but the figure had vanished.

Another artillery shell hit near by.

More figures were appearing at the edge of his senses, far too many to determine individual intentions. Gunfire started to ricochet along the narrow gap. A shot punched into his chest sending him tumbling backwards, crunching into a wall, breath forced from his lungs.

Martinez was scrabbling to get to Banks and for a second NG couldn't move, sharing the effects of the toxin from the knife as it slowly spread through Banks, paralysing.

He shut it out and staggered to his feet, staring across at them, glancing left and right, watching as Martinez dragged her partner to the opposite wall, leaving a dark smear in the snow. She crouched there shielding him and holding one hand against the ragged wound in his neck, returning fire with the other.

NG covered them, firing towards the shadows at the far end of the alley, heart sinking, chest on fire.

Banks coughed, trying to reach his gun, unable to move his legs. "C'mon Angel, help me here," he muttered.

NG glanced across at them as Martinez quickly pushed her gun into Banks's hand, closing his fingers around the grip. She pulled out her second weapon, looked up and sent calmly, "NG, get away. We'll hold them."

He caught a flash of intention from multiple hostiles moving in and another shot grazed his arm. He flinched and managed to mumble, "No," feeling the pain mix with that emanating from Banks, then the dark mist descended and it became a blur, snow and darkness, flashes of searching lights, shots and explosions, Martinez yelling and a vague awareness of each punch of void that hit as he turned and fired with perfect precision, one shot, one kill.

It was like he was watching from a distance, sound muted, no control over his limbs. This had happened before but he'd never felt so lost, so far away. He fought to get back control.

"No chance," he heard himself say, voice cold, calmly ejecting the spent magazine and reloading amidst gunfire and the flash of grenades, smoke mingling with the drifting snow.

Banks took a hit, pain flaring, managing to fire steadily at the advancing troops. "Go. Angel, get him away from here."

NG felt himself turn. '*No*,' he thought, a chill settling deep inside that had nothing to do with the storm.

His heart was pounding.

A grenade exploded close by, throwing out shrapnel and kicking up the snow pile. He didn't flinch.

'*Don't do it*,' he thought desperately.

He glanced back at Banks and Martinez, knowing what he was about to do and unable to do a thing to stop himself.

He could feel that Martinez was torn. He watched as she hugged her partner, tight and fast, whispered something in Banks's ear, then pushed herself to her feet and ran to him. "Go!" she yelled, grabbing his arm and pulling him away.

He let her, breaking into a flat out run and screaming inside.

When they stopped finally, he sank into a dark corner, awareness coming back slowly. With pain. He could hardly breathe, feeling a fluttering in his chest that was pulsing in agony.

He'd left Banks to die.

'I left him to die. You weren't strong enough and we're still not out of this.'

They were inside a warehouse, dry but freezing cold. Martinez knelt by his side. She lifted his chin and stared into his eyes. She was willing him to come back, as if she knew. It was difficult to focus and she didn't let go until he'd managed it.

He reached gently and wiped a smudge from her cheek.

That slight movement sent a spark through his chest and he couldn't help coughing, tasting blood in his mouth, grey closing in at the edge of his vision.

Martinez froze. "Oh shit," she said softly, "you were hit." She unfastened his vest gently, inhaled sharply when she saw the damage and pulled a trauma patch from a pouch, tucking it inside his shirt where the armour piercing round had done its job.

He flinched as her cold fingers touched his skin and almost passed out as the sting from the patch hit home.

'Heal yourself, you fool.'

NG half-heartedly pulled energy from somewhere to stem the internal bleeding, aware that the crushed metal of the bullet fragment within his flesh had shattered a rib.

He looked up. "Who knew we were coming here?" he said, voice ragged.

Martinez secured the vest again. "No one," she said abruptly, not in the mood for conversation and chiding herself viciously every time she caught herself wanting to look around for Banks.

NG shifted his weight, trying to figure out if he could move. Devon and Evelyn knew. His stomach turned at the thought of it. He'd been sure they were clear.

He coughed again and a stab of pain shot through his chest. "Pull it tighter," he mumbled.

Martinez tugged on the straps. She was cursing, violently, silently, to herself, furious and scared that she was going to lose him too. She fumbled around in her pockets and pulled out an injector, punching it against his neck, three times in fast succession, antibiotics and two shots of Epizin.

He caught hold of her wrist and said, "I'm fine."

She took a deep breath, looked at the blood drenching his sleeve and reached for another patch for his arm. She looked him in the eye. "We need to get off this shit-hole of a planet."

NG nodded. "There's something I need to do first."

14

She shook her head, the disapproval in her mind outweighed by a sadness in her eyes. "I hear in some quarters that Redgate is setting itself up as a new centre of power to oppose Earth and Winter. Could that ever be so?"

"Of course not." He was quite scathing and didn't temper it. It was bad enough that Nikolai had disobeyed his direct orders, worse that the boy had almost got himself killed. And to lose one as valuable as Banks was always annoying.

He drank, the wine most pleasurably hot and the drug firing his hostility towards such nonsense as Redgate. "The Order will never let that happen," he said. "They may be content to watch as despicable characters such as Ballack play their games and will most likely profit from such ventures. But as a new power base? The Order has need of only two adversaries and they are content with the ones they have. Redgate is a tolerated amusement, a source of lucrative contracts, and one that will be quashed in an instant if it is deemed to be gaining any real power."

She helped him to his feet and they turned. A single figure stepped out of the shadows by the door, unmistakable stance, knife in hand.

It was an assassin. NG hadn't sensed him there, the pain too much of a distraction. Damn, he needed to get his shit together.

Martinez raised her arm and fired without hesitation, the shot resounding through the empty space.

The assassin vanished.

They stood, breath frosting in the chill air.

"Who the fuck is that?" Martinez muttered. "Assassins here?

As well as half a fucking platoon of mercenaries? Someone told all these bastards that we were coming here."

NG was pretty much spent but he wanted to get to Ballack.

"Someone inside?" she asked abruptly, emotions burning. "One of ours?"

It must have been but it was hard to admit. He could feel the assassin now, essence cool and confident, moving round on them. The fighting outside had shifted over to the main terminal, sirens wailing and tanks rolling around the perimeter. There was at least one assassin, a rebel army and a private mercenary outfit between them and the ship.

"Let's go," he said, breath catching in his chest as they walked slowly, directly towards the advancing assassin, NG directing Martinez through the Senson.

Assassins hated their invisibility to be breached and when Martinez raised her aim and tracked him through the shadows, the guy broke and ran, sly recalculations flashing through his mind.

"Is this a good idea?" she sent. "We should get the fuck out of here."

NG wasn't going to slink away so easily.

He'd already found Ballack. The guy had a Senson Five, top end for the commercial market. He responded immediately to NG's request for a link.

NG didn't reply to Martinez but he included her in the connection.

"NG," Ballack sent back, "you know, we take care of our guests much better when they don't lie and deceive their way into our midst."

"You have a snake in your camp, Ballack," he replied, splitting his concentration between tracking the assassin and putting one foot in front of the other. He trusted Martinez to watch out for other hostiles. They both had weapons out, a gun in each hand, walking cautiously out of the warehouse. "Tell me who betrayed me and I'll tell you who it is."

"I'll do better than that, NG. I'll give you an armed escort back to your ship and you can tell me who put this ridiculous price on your head."

Martinez muttered out loud, "I don't like this. Don't trust him."

He didn't trust him but Ballack couldn't afford to make an enemy of the Thieves' Guild. Not openly. Behind the scenes subterfuge was one thing but outright public enmity was bad for business.

True to his word, Ballack cleared their way to the ship and followed them on board, leaving his escort on the runway as instructed.

The bulky leader of the Merchants' Guild put his hands up in mock surrender when he saw Martinez standing there tracking him with a gun.

"All a misunderstanding, right?" NG said quietly, just about managing to stand without shaking, arms folded around his chest, keeping the pain from his face.

Ballack shrugged. "It's been chaos," he said. "We're pulling out, I'm sure you've heard. Redgate just isn't worth the trouble any more."

"Redgate's always worth the trouble," NG said softly, "you just never understood why."

Ballack smiled. He'd lost and he was trying not to lose face.

"Who was it?" NG asked, needing to know how he'd screwed up and lost one of his best men.

Ballack's expression was unfathomable. He was a master of manipulation and kept his position in the Merchant's Guild through a complex mix of deceit, paranoia, charisma and a sharp intelligence to see opportunity and seize the moment. He shrugged again. "Half a billion is bound to bring out the worst in people, NG. People hear about that kind of cash, they're going to be watching out for you. I'm surprised you risk yourself like this."

"Business is business," NG said.

Ballack smiled again, this time a wolf's smirk of satisfaction. "So who is the snake in my back yard? Let me guess, Newton? Ingarssen? No? Ronson? They're all snakes, NG. Believe me, I don't need you to tell me that."

It was still hard work to concentrate and read anything from the man beyond surface thoughts, hard to do anything much other than standing his ground.

Ballack rubbed his hands together as if that was it, deal done and down to the real business. "Now this little escapade of yours, NG, has cost us," he said. "There are those who think they can take advantage of any incident on this damned planet. You being here has cost me. I want compensation."

NG nodded. He was expecting as much. "One of my men died here, Ballack. I want him returning to us."

"I'll see to it myself. You don't look so good yourself, NG. Why don't you come inside? Hospitality isn't up to much, I'm afraid." He paused for effect as a barrage of artillery hits boomed in a thunderous succession outside. "No? I won't take offence." He smiled at Martinez before looking back to NG. "Now, I take it this unfortunate incident hasn't affected relations between our two guilds."

"Back off, Ballack," NG said softly. "Stick to what you know best. Leave the acquisitions to us."

Ballack shrugged, shoulders twitching, smug and self confident as if there'd never been a problem. "We all do what we do best, NG. Survive. You take care of yourself now."

It seemed to take forever to get to Earth. Martinez tried to protest that he needed medical attention and should go back to the Alsatia but he'd pulled rank and insisted they didn't have time. He needed to get to Earth.

They landed at RDJ, anonymous documents getting them past customs. No one knew they were coming here and there were no problems getting in despite a heightened security around the old planet. They secured a car and drove out into the city.

It was hot and humid. NG let Martinez drive and wound down the window, feeling the warm breeze on his skin.

She'd watched him like a hawk since Redgate, fussing at the injuries, bitching as she'd cleaned up the bullet wound in his chest and refusing to talk about Banks. "Shit happens," she'd said, shutting him out. She'd deal with it in her own time and her own way. That was the way his staff worked. It was the way the whole guild worked.

They were stopped at two roadblocks, different IDs and a wad of hard cash getting them through with no questions. They drove up into the hills and at the third roadblock they had to leave the car. Martinez was nervous, more nervous that Devon and Evelyn would roast her alive if she got NG killed, but she spoke to the guards like a native and smiled, and they offered her coffee, laughing and saying she could stay for more if she ditched the white boy.

They had to walk from there, taking it steady up the steep steps. He had to stop half way to catch his breath, chest still burning like it was on fire, and she waited patiently, sitting on the step next to him staring out over the bay, emotions wrapped up cold and hard inside. She didn't question what they were doing.

"Martinez…" he started.

"Don't say it, boss. I'm here to keep you alive. I knew the risks when I signed on for this. So did Banks. Move on, keep your head in the game," she paused and met his eye. "Just don't let what happened to Banks be for nothing, okay?"

He nodded and she turned away.

A canopy of leafy vegetation wound overhead, thick knotted trunks weaving amongst the green, birds singing, and it was good to be planetside amongst so much life. He'd been too cold for too long and the warm air was easy on the lungs.

'All I can smell is the putrid decay of the human race. You're wasting your time.'

He refused to acknowledge the inner voice, pushed himself to his feet and struggled up the rest of the brightly coloured steps.

Arturo was waiting for them at the top, leaning on his walking cane and smiling. The old man was as sprightly as ever and led them along a winding pathway that was half strangled with twisting tree trunks and through to a terrace. There was a table and chairs set out, a jug and glasses waiting.

Arturo waved them to sit, looking intently at NG. "I would

swear you get younger every time I see you," the old man said with a mischievous smile then frowned. "Tell me, how close have they managed to get?"

Arturo was old school Thieves' Guild, maintaining deep cover on Earth. He didn't miss much and was thinking that NG was hiding an injury.

"Not close enough to cash in just yet," NG said softly.

The old man stared for a moment then laughed and reached to pour from the jug. He pushed the glasses across the table, ice clinking. "I heard about Domino," he said. "Bad business."

"We know who killed Mendhel now," NG said, taking a long drink of the liquor. It was strong, rum and lime with sugar.

"Zang. I heard that too." Arturo leaned forward. "I also heard that Luka is out in the mining colonies. Don't worry about that boy – he can look after himself. Bastards come back in every day claiming they've seen him and no one yet has managed to catch him." He chuckled to himself again. "What's the bounty up to now? Eighty five million? And half a billion on you? We live in exciting times, my dears."

Martinez was keeping quiet. She was just sipping at the Caipirinha. Arturo reached out and patted her hand. The last time they were here, Banks had been with them and he didn't need to ask to know what was wrong.

The old man looked back to NG. "So what can I do for you?"

"The High Court. I need a way in."

Arturo raised his eyebrows. "We can manage that. You care to tell me why you want to put your neck into the hands of our dear Emperor?"

Martinez turned in for the night early. It was the first time since they'd left the Alsatia that they were in friendly territory and she was content that he was in safe hands. Arturo kept his place well but subtly guarded, fiercely loyal people who adored the old man and were completely dedicated to the guild. NG had scanned them anyway.

They were safe.

He sat on the terrace and watched the moon rise. It had been a long time since he'd been on Earth.

He hadn't given Arturo the full story, just that he needed access to the Advisor for Trade, and the old man hadn't pushed. He'd patted NG on the back, like a fond grandfather, and headed inside to make arrangements.

It was a warm night, insects humming. The scent of rainforest filled the air. Tiny lanterns cast arcs of soft light amongst the undergrowth. It felt safe and he could almost imagine he was alone with no worries, the weight of the guild and its dramas far away.

'Don't be a fool.'

Breathing was hard for a second, the pain of the broken rib breaking through his barriers. Christ, I don't need a reminder, he thought.

'You obviously do,' that dark voice warned and the pain intensified.

He concentrated to shut it out, nullify the pain and dampen down the self-doubt.

'Oh my, have you not worked it out yet?'

His vision started to narrow, darkness closing in.

'I'm not you, 'NG',' the voice whispered maliciously. It laughed harshly. *'Pay attention now, Nikolai. You don't really exist, you know, you never did. And I want control back.'*

He was hallucinating. Exhaustion and one injury after another, one assassination attempt after the other, had taken its toll and the rum had tipped him over the edge.

He lay back, staring at the stars and breathing slowly, feeling the darkness nudge from within. Every time he'd lost control, he'd been in extreme violent danger, some kind of automatic reaction. He was now lying on a grassed terrace in one of the safest spots in the galaxy on a peaceful and warm night with friends close by and no enemies in sight.

'You really think? Do you really think I can't just take over whenever I want?'

NG tried to open his eyes, tried to sit up but he couldn't move.

It felt like he was paralysed, asleep but dreaming that he was awake.

He tried to shout out but he had no control. He felt himself stand and pull his gun from the holster on his thigh.

He heard Martinez call his name from behind and felt himself turn.

'*Don't*,' he gasped.

She walked up slowly, cautiously, saying his name again. He felt his finger twitch on the trigger and he fought to take back control, managing to use the pain to snatch himself back from the brink.

Martinez reached out a hand and took the gun, stroking his other arm gently until he snapped out of it, then she led him back to the table and nudged him into a chair.

She was the only person who'd seen him like that and she didn't judge, didn't condemn. She was thinking that she'd seen worse in some of the marines she'd served with, guys who clicked into berserker mode in combat and wept and screamed like terrified children in the night when the nightmares began.

NG rubbed a hand over his eyes. Martinez was also thinking that she missed Banks and it was hard to be close to that raw emotion.

He looked up. "Shit happens, right?" he said and she laughed.

They sat quietly after that until Arturo came to join them, cane tapping along the stone pathway.

He sat and smiled at them both. "Beautiful evening, is it not? It was the Imperial Advisor for Trade you wanted to see? Yes?" He placed a board on the table. "It would seem that he wants to see us too."

The information listed on it was a typical request for contact from a potential client to the guild, relayed through multiple sources, originating from Earth, encoded and seemingly from the Emperor's Advisor for Trade himself.

Martinez took the board. "Is this for real?" she said.

"Looks like it." NG looked to Arturo. It felt bad to have to read the old man for any deception but there was no such thing as coincidence. There was nothing there to doubt. "Can you set up a secure livelink?"

"Of course."

"Do it. Let's hear what His Excellency has to say."

The temple grounds were peaceful, a gentle cool breeze chiming the bells, carrying the scent of incense from the fires. NG stood, breathing in the faint narcotic and wondering how easy it would be to walk away. Just leave. Vanish into the shadows like the assassin on Redgate, drop all responsibility and disappear.

It had been hard to leave the warm sanctuary of Arturo's place and fly half way around the planet to take up the trail but they were so close now. Advisor Trent had spoken to Arturo briefly, requesting a meeting with the head of Thieves' Guild operations. Arturo had laughed and said he didn't know what the esteemed minister could possibly mean. The guy had flushed. It was impossible to read thoughts through the long distance link but the body language was unmistakable. "I know NG is coming to Earth," he'd said curtly, uncomfortable, nervous and looking over his shoulder anxiously. "And I know that I'm next. They're going to kill me. I want to come over. I'll tell you everything but you have to protect me."

They'd stayed up the rest of the night planning. The Advisor had specified a time and a location, the Temple of Heaven. No weapons, no surveillance, the only time he was allowed privacy. Arturo's people in Beijing had identified some old, disused subway tunnels that ran nearby. It wasn't great but with only a few hours to gather reconnaissance and come up with a plan, escape through subterranean tunnels was the best of their limited options. Martinez had argued against it, thinking it had to be a trap, and offered to take a team to grab the guy, but that wasn't the point. NG wanted thirty seconds of Trent's time – that was all – there was no way he was going to risk an extraction if someone was trying to kill the guy. "Fast in, fast out," he'd said and Martinez had muttered, "Didn't you say that last time?" Arturo hadn't joined the argument. He'd arranged a team of six agents and the logistics necessary to get into Beijing and out again. With Advisor Trent if possible, with the information they needed if it wasn't.

If it went to plan, they'd be back in RDJ inside six hours and away from Earth in eight.

NG watched the flow of people through the courtyard. It was quiet despite the numbers, gentle laughter mixing with the sound of bells and soft words floating on the breeze.

There was only a slight stir in the throng as the Advisor for Trade walked into the grounds of the temple surrounded by an entourage of armed bodyguards. It was routine, a ritual he honoured every week, and they honoured his right to enter the temple alone. Martinez and four of the six agents were positioned around the grounds, the other two in the tunnels. Only NG was unarmed and he was waiting casually by the entrance to the temple.

Trent spoke briefly with his guard then walked alone across the courtyard to the steps. He didn't make eye contact until he reached the top then he looked desperately at NG, turmoil churning in his stomach and naked fear tearing at his mind. NG read what he could through the distress. Trent was convinced the Order had already posted his termination. A'Darbi led indirectly to him and that kind of breach in the chain wouldn't be tolerated. He knew it was only a matter of time and he knew his superiors couldn't fail to see the connection. He was pre-empting his fate and almost scared to death that he couldn't avoid it.

If it was an act, he was a damned good actor.

NG glanced at Martinez. He was the briefest touch away from reaching deeper into the organisational structure of the Order.

He took a step towards the Advisor.

A single sharp crack tore through the peace and tranquillity. The high velocity round hit Trent in the head, he jerked, gone in that instant, body slumping to the stone paving.

NG moved automatically, lurching forward and catching him as he fell. There was nothing but cold void. He knelt there for the briefest of instants, feeling a wave of shock flow over the people watching.

Someone screamed.

He started to stand but something hit him in the back of the head, low down at the base of his skull, a punch of dissipating energy that snatched at his nervous system. FTH. He shook it off but another impact drove him back to his knees.

He could hear footsteps pounding up, feel a dark panic rising.

Martinez sent, "NG."

"Go," he managed to send back. "Get back to the guild. They need to know what's happened."

Another FTH round hit him in the back. The intense pain that flared fed the darkness and NG was pushed roughly into the background. He felt himself turn and stagger to his feet, watching the scene through a mist. He saw himself grab the first guard to reach him with a hand around the throat, squeezing and destroying the mind in a single stroke. He dropped the husk to the floor and spun to the next. More bodies were pressing in and he inflicted excruciating pain and agony on every ounce of flesh he managed to touch.

NG watched, struggling to gain back control. A rifle butt smashed into the side of his face, sending his senses spinning. His knees buckled and a weight hit his back, driving him down to the floor. They were screaming at him not to move, twisting his arms behind his back, malicious sons of bitches who had just seen their charge eliminated right in front of them, team mates drop dead all around them. A vicious kick landed against his ribs and he was thrown back to the fore, the mist gone, but he couldn't do anything then but concentrate on breathing.

Another blow hammered against his head.

He closed his eyes and sank into an oblivion that was far more welcoming than the darkness he'd been drowning in.

15

"I don't understand," she said. "Surely we could whisper in the ears of the powermongers as easily as they, if not more so. Why do we play such games with thieves and rogues? We made the decision to make our stand here, why do we let others walk openly in those corridors through which we sneak in shadow?"

The Man placed another log on the fire, drinking in the warmth of the glowing embers. "To do so would set us directly at odds with the Order."

She leaned forward in her seat, earnestly, firelight flaring in her eyes. "We are at war with the Order."

He met her gaze and raised the stakes. "We are at war with a race of beings that will destroy every planet in this galaxy should we allow it to happen again."

The cell was cold. NG sat quietly, controlling the pain, dealing with the internal injuries the best he could. His wrists were clamped in manacles, safetycuffs that were attached to a device at the centre of the table. They'd given him water to drink but no food, Earth hospitality at its finest, and after four or five rounds of interrogation it was getting harder to bounce back.

They'd brought him to a secure facility, off world. Two armed guards were in the cell watching him now, another two outside the door and more watching through the monitoring system. They weren't taking any risks. And as far as he could tell, they were Imperial Security, no hint of the Order yet. But if it was the Order that had assassinated the Advisor, they wouldn't be far behind in realising who the ISA had in custody.

The door opened and a medic walked in. NG didn't move but

cast his eyes up to look at the surveillance camera tucked high in the corner of the cell wall. The woman who had been supervising his incarceration was watching remotely from an adjoining room. She was uneasy. She wasn't Order but that didn't mean they weren't pulling the strings somewhere in the background.

The medic set his case on the table. He pressed an autoinjector against NG's neck then took hold of his arm. They'd already been through this. He felt the cocktail of drugs hit, more potent than anything they'd hit him with so far, and didn't move as the medic took another blood sample, filling ampoule after ampoule from a vein in the crook of his elbow.

NG kept his gaze fixed firmly on the camera. They were watching his stats remotely. He could sense the woman staring at him, thinking that this was her career on the line, why did this have to happen on her watch?

The medic finished up, packed away his kit with care and walked out. The drugs had a variation of Banitol in there, inhibition relaxant, strong and potentially lethal from the size of the dose they were giving him. He let it flow for a moment then neutralised it fast.

"We've taken him to level five," she sent through a secure connection to someone. NG listened in easily enough. "Nothing. He hasn't even flinched. He hasn't said a word except to ask for Jameson. You want me to go to six, I want clearance from the Executive."

"He knows about the JU?" the someone sent back.

"Apparently."

"Who the hell is he?"

"We have no idea. Every ID check we've run has come back negative. He isn't on any list. He's carrying recent gun shot wounds, one serious, and he has a Senson Six."

"Wintran?"

She hesitated. "We don't know."

NG closed his eyes and let his heart rate start to drop. It triggered an alarm. If they let him speak to Jameson, he was clear. If that spooked them, he was done.

"Get Jameson in here. Shit, the colonel is pissed enough as it is, let's give him another headache."

They sent in a medic to make sure he wasn't going to drop dead and then left him alone to wait. It didn't take long. He felt Jameson's anger approaching as soon as the colonel entered the facility. He had troops with him. The JU didn't do anything by halves.

Jameson stopped outside the door. "This had better be good," NG heard him say.

The woman's mind was both fraught with hope that Jameson would take her problem away and anxious that she'd screwed up by bringing in the JU before they knew anything more about this charge they had in custody.

The door opened.

NG looked up.

Jameson took one step inside the cell and grinned. "Oh my, you've just made my day." He snapped at the woman, "Get him loose for Christ's sake and send all your records to the JU. You've never seen this guy, we haven't been here and you know nothing, understand?"

She nodded, relieved, and the cuffs popped open.

Jameson was wearing a tuxedo, medals gleaming in neat rows, immaculately starched white dress shirt, black bow tie undone and hanging round his neck in that casual formalities over for the night way. He'd been drinking but it had been a while ago. His men were in full combat readiness, chameleonic body armour shifting patterns as it adjusted to match the surroundings. They formed a cordon around Jameson and NG as they marched, NG trying to keep up and not struggle too badly. It was possible he'd just jumped into a worse situation but anything had to be better than being locked up and waiting for the next session of interrogation.

Jameson's mood was difficult to read and what he was picking up made NG's head ache even more than it had been. The colonel was pleased with himself, and not just because he had NG in his pocket now, that the Thieves' Guild owed him big style. There was something else there.

They walked out of the secure facility without ceremony and straight onto a drop ship, engines running, crew meeting them as they boarded. They left the troops in the main terminal and Jameson steered NG into a forward compartment, gesturing him to take a seat.

It was good to sink down but the rumbling of the ship as it prepared for takeoff rippled through every aching and torn muscle. He shifted awkwardly to get comfortable, aware that Jameson was watching, the colonel settling into a chair opposite and smiling as he hooked the restraints into place.

"Incredible," Jameson said, smug, the smile turning into a grin. He leaned forward. "So does this mean the Thieves' Guild is taking on assassination contracts now?"

"I didn't kill him."

"Not what the report says."

"Jameson, I didn't even have a weapon on me."

"The official report says you did. They've matched ballistics." Jameson's tone changed, serious now. "Can I ask why? What did Advisor Trent have to do with anything?"

NG leaned his head back and closed his eyes. He was too tired to argue.

The engines fired up for launch, the rumbling deepening as it took off and accelerated hard.

"You said you'd talk to me, NG, so talk. This is a real shitstorm and you're right in the middle of it."

NG opened one eye.

"As it happens, I've just been speaking to one of your boys," Jameson said. "We know who sent them to raid our base."

NG didn't need to read it from his mind. "Zang."

Jameson nodded. "Hilyer turned up on our doorstep and turned himself in. He's leading us to them. I'll be damned if we don't get Zang and the damned package back. What does Trent have to do with anything?"

The drop ship pulled a manoeuvre that sent NG's stomach lurching. He faded out for a second.

'Don't tell him a thing.'

He had no intention to. He was reading loud and clear from Jameson's mind that the warship they were on their way to dock with was going to Winter after Hilyer and Zang.

Jameson laughed again. "Shit, I always knew you were a tough bastard, NG, but level five? Jesus, most people don't make it past three."

They docked amidst a chaotic clamour of battle-preparation. NG shut it all out. Jameson had told him to wait on the drop ship so he waited, listening in as the colonel briefed a team to escort their guest to medical.

"Give him the VIP treatment," Jameson sent through a tight wire and the marines laughed, thinking that they understood fine well what their commanding officer intended. Jameson paused as he realised their intention and added, "No, you fucking morons, I mean look after him."

NG held in a smile, sensing the discomfort of the JU marines as their sergeant snapped a "Yes sir" in reply.

The staff in the warship's medical facility were more gentle, settling him into a secure bay before they undocked.

NG lay back. He had no choice but to comply, go for the ride and get what he could while he was here. He didn't need to break into any systems – he just needed to listen in to the thoughts of every technical operator, specialist, researcher and officer on board and he could get the JU's most intimate secrets. Nothing he hadn't done to Jameson, many times. But there was no harm in getting up to date.

He closed his eyes, let his energy levels recover and set to work.

Jameson called for him to be brought up to the bridge as they approached the Wintran facility.

NG dressed slowly, still sore, most of the damage healed. He'd been careful not to heal the superficial injuries, leaving the bruising and abrasions. He was in enough shit as it was; a miraculously fast recovery wouldn't do him any favours in this company.

The tension in the warship was rising, the anticipation of battle heightening emotions to an edge that was difficult to share. On the Alsatia, each section had its own characteristics and distinctive aura – Legal curt and factual, Media imaginative and inspiring, Acquisitions daring and irrepressible, Science reckless and curious. Never on board the guild's cruiser was there such a mass brewing of raw aggression.

NG followed his escort through the warship and shut out the onslaught, fighting a darkness deep inside that wanted to revel in it.

"I thought you'd want to see this," Jameson sent privately, gesturing him to come stand at his side.

Hil had offered Zang, LC and the package to Jameson, all wrapped up neatly in one place. Knowing Hilyer, it would never be that simple. There was no way he'd hang LC out to dry. Jameson didn't care. He wanted Zang to pay. If he didn't get the package, he'd carry on hunting down LC and Hil until he got it. But in the meantime, the colonel had been given a target and he was planning total annihilation.

"I want Hilyer out alive," NG sent.

Jameson smiled. "You're in no position to make demands, NG. This is my show. You get to sit back and watch, my friend."

They all knew fine well the implications of this attack – an Earth force assaulting a Wintran colony – and they were committed to it. Zang had attacked an Earth facility first so it was justified. That's what they were telling themselves. NG wasn't convinced and whatever the hell Hilyer was planning, the kid wouldn't have done it lightly.

Bombers were already bombarding the colony, drop ships on their way down to the surface with troops.

NG watched coldly. It went against everything the Man had been working for, striving to keep peace and steady advancement within the two power bases.

Jameson was a calm commander, controlled and confident.

NG stood next to him, close enough to touch. He could reach out and give the colonel enough doubt to call a halt to the assault.

'*Too late*,' the dark voice whispered deep inside. '*The attack has started already. Even if Jameson pulled back now, the damage is done. Earth just declared war on Winter and there's not a damn thing you can do.*'

It was chilling to watch. The Earth warships dominated the space around the orbital, demanding total cooperation, all traffic frozen, media black out, hundreds of smaller Earth fighters and gunships buzzing in a swarm around the colony.

Hil was down there somewhere. They had a transmitter on him. NG listened in to the secure communications as they tracked him deeper and deeper into Zang's facility. No reported sightings of LC yet. But Zang Tsu Po himself was in there somewhere. That was another catch they wanted.

The attack was brutal.

NG listened, detached. There would be a way to turn this around to their advantage, somehow, but he couldn't do a thing here.

He watched as they tracked rogue vessels, shooting down anyone that didn't respond fast enough, bringing in reinforcements to chase stealthed wraiths.

The warships rained down a furious and unrelenting fire.

It was a show of absolute Earth military supremacy the like of which hadn't been seen in generations.

Until they lost Hilyer.

Jameson didn't react, didn't move as the reports came in. Hil had vanished. Simply gone, the transponder no longer transmitting.

Jameson turned slowly to look at NG, no emotion on his face, anger seething inside. "No," he sent privately, "no, no, no, you're not going to get away with this, NG. You son of a bitch. What is this? You think you can fool us? Where's my damned package?"

NG stood his ground, staring at the bank of monitors and screens.

"Get him out of here," Jameson growled.

The soldiers standing guard at NG's side jumped into action, quickly taking hold of an arm each and manoeuvring him away from their colonel.

He went without a fight but couldn't resist the smile that slipped out.

16

"Earth versus Winter," she said. "Exactly what we don't need."

"These creatures are unpredictable."

"You feel responsible for them."

"I am responsible for them. They are fickle and temperamental, wild and uncouth."

"Yet you want to save them."

He poured more wine. After everything that had happened, he was wondering why.

She pushed forward her goblet for a top up even though she had drunk barely half. "Because you see their potential," she said. "And it irks you that they do not see it in themselves."

"Nikolai is proof of their potential and see how they treated him."

"And," she pushed as she watched the wine tumble from the jug, "because we must stop it happening again, whatever race it is that is unfortunate enough to become the latest prey."

They took him down into the depths of the warship and locked him in a cell. He stretched out on a cold bench and listened in to the rest of the conflict at a distance. They didn't find Hil, LC or Zang and took out their frustration on the colonists and any ships that refused to respond to their lockdown.

Jameson came in after the assault had entered its final cleanup stage. He stood with his arms folded, fuming, mind racing with the only way he could figure out to deal with NG and the damned Thieves' Guild.

"You think you're smart?" he sent through a tight wire. This conversation wasn't anything he wanted on record.

NG sat up, keeping eye contact.

"Where's my package?" Jameson was thinking that he could keep NG locked up down here as a hostage to force the guild to cooperate.

NG kept his breathing slow and steady, reading every thought that crossed the military man's mind as clearly as if the guy was shouting it.

Jameson growled. "Don't give me the fucking silent treatment, NG. You want to see what level six feels like? See how tough you are then?" It was a real pisser. He'd been so sure he had the Thieves' Guild securely in his pocket for saving NG's ass from Imperial Security. If he had to threaten NG to get the package, he'd lose any leverage that had given him.

NG stood up slowly. "Matt, I don't even know what your package is," he said with a laugh.

The colonel snapped, "You expect me to believe that?" He narrowed his eyes. "How much are you worth, NG? How much does your precious Thieves' Guild value you? Enough to hand over that package to get you back?"

There was no way he was going to be held hostage. He took a step forward. "You have no idea what you're dealing with," he said quietly. "You think you just gave Winter a bloody nose?" Another step closer. "You just screwed up, Matt. You have no idea."

The colonel snapped and went for NG's throat, same move he'd pulled in the Alsatia's hospitality suite.

This time, NG didn't hold back.

He'd manipulated Jameson before, subtly, nothing too overt, gentle suggestions, the way he worked with most people. It wasn't that he put thoughts into someone's head, it was more that he worked with what was there already. Manipulating emotions. It's easier to make a decision when you suddenly feel good about it, when that choice feels intuitively so much better than any alternative possibility.

NG didn't give Jameson any room to feel anything other than scared shitless about the thought of risking the wrath of the Thieves' Guild by holding him for ransom. Suddenly the idea of maintaining a civil and respectful relationship with the guild wasn't just appealing, it was the only sane option.

Jameson froze, confusion flashing across his eyes. He couldn't remember why he'd been so angry. He seemed to realise with a start that he had his hand around NG's throat and let go, letting his hand rest on NG's shoulder instead.

"You owe me, right?" he said. "Zang's not going to get away with this?"

"No," NG said softly. "No, he isn't."

Jameson exhaled the breath he was holding. He leaned close and whispered, "Get off my warship, NG. Before I think of a reason to throw you back to the ISA."

Evelyn and Martinez, flanked by two of the Man's elite guards, were waiting this time when he got back to the Alsatia.

Despite the whirlwind of drama he was stepping into, it felt good to be back.

Evie stepped forward first to meet him. "Hilyer's here," she said, dropping in alongside him and matching his stride. "He's in Medical. Skye brought him in a few hours ago."

"Skye?" She was supposed to be grounded.

"Quinn sent her out after Hil. We got word from Pen, NG. They took out the guy that killed Mendhel then Hil took off for Earth." She was trying not to stare at him. "Are you okay?" Martinez had told them about the gunshot wound on Redgate and the incident on Earth.

Evelyn was worried about him but it was hard to look at her without thinking she could have betrayed him.

"I'm fine."

"The Man wants to see you. Do you need a full debrief or the short version?"

"I need to see Hil."

"From what I heard, he's not in a fit state to see anyone. There's a full report on your desk."

"Any sign of LC?"

They stopped at the elevator.

"Rumours, nothing more." She paused, biting her lip and frowning.

"What?" he said, reading it from her mind and trying to keep the dismay from his face.

"We have a real problem, NG," she sent, switching to private again. The relief she'd felt at seeing him alive was overwhelmed by the dread of having to tell him what had happened, the intel Hil had brought back with him. "We know who betrayed us."

"Who?" he said softly, needing her to say it.

"Hetherington, Wibowski…" She paused again, looking deep into his eyes and feeling lost. "And Genoa."

That was the real kicker. An AI. Bad enough that two extraction agents had gone rogue but to be betrayed by an AI…

He glanced back at Martinez.

She knew and she was furious – she knew Kase Wibowski and Martha Hetherington well.

Evie touched him on the arm. "That's not the worst of it."

"Just tell me, Evie."

"NG, it was Anya. Mendhel's daughter is the one who betrayed us to Zang."

'Killed by his own kin. How ironic.'

He couldn't breathe for a minute. They'd kept Anya away from the guild after her mother had been killed. For her own safety. He was the one who'd persuaded Mendhel that was for the best.

That dark spot of self doubt inside was churning, mocking and deriding. *'All this tracks back to one bad judgement call?'*

Evelyn squeezed his arm. "You look tired."

He felt sick. He used the contact to check her out again, feeling bad that he had to and guilty that he'd doubted her when it still looked like she was clear. That just left Devon and the thought of that made him feel worse.

"You want me to field it while you get some rest?" Evelyn said.

He shook his head. "I need to deal with this now."

"Who do you want first?"

"Hil," he said again. He needed to know what had happened down on that planet.

NG stopped at the door to the Man's chambers, hand against the warm wood panel, hesitating to knock. His head was pounding. Hilyer had been hard work, in pain from injuries sustained during Jameson's bombardment, and belligerent, still thinking everyone was against him. But he'd given up the whole story, as much as he could. The kid still claimed not to know what the package was and not to know where LC was, and in a way NG had no choice but to believe him – the information simply wasn't in Hilyer's mind because he'd taken a crap load of very specific drugs to wipe his memory and make sure he couldn't remember.

NG stood there, half tempted to walk away.

"Come in," the Man called from the depths of the chamber beyond the heavy door.

He stood for a moment longer then pushed open the door and stepped into the fray. The Man was at his desk, the room dark except for the light from dancing candles, the scent of spices and oils from all corners of the galaxy mingling into a warm intoxicating concoction.

"You disobeyed my direct orders, NG," the Man said softly. "You are lucky to be alive by all accounts."

The Man had contacts that went far deeper than any of the people NG and his team dealt with. It wasn't worth considering from whom those accounts may have come and in a way it was chilling to hear, as if the danger had been far more grave than he'd appreciated.

"These are dangerous times and our enemies grow in strength. Contrary to your own opinion on the matter, NG, you are not invincible. Do not exacerbate the risk to yourself by this irrepressible need to confront those who seek to undermine us."

The Man looked down at his desk, returning his attention to his work.

NG stood there, just inside the door, perfectly motionless, overheating in the stifling air. There was no way the Man was going to let him off that lightly.

"I understand we have Hilyer back," the Man said without raising his head. "What about Luka?"

It wasn't often that the Man ever referred to LC by his real name. It added a weight to the atmosphere.

The Man looked up. "Where is he now?"

It was second nature to nudge for a look into any mind asking a question, to gauge the intention there, to see what was expected before replying.

"Don't try to read me, NG."

His heart was pounding. He hadn't meant to. "We don't know," he said finally.

The Man nodded towards the heavy set wooden chair in front of his desk. "Sit down."

Devon stood in the doorway of his office, watching. The lights were soft, temperature set to low. NG gave up trying to focus on the document he was dealing with and looked up.

"You need to sleep," Devon said softly.

He hadn't stopped since he'd got back and the marathon debrief sessions with Hilyer then the Man were taking their toll. He rubbed his eyes. "We need to screen everyone."

She looked dubious, wandering in and taking a seat. She rested her elbows on the desk and leaned forward, peering at him, thinking that the scar on his cheekbone was new.

"Everyone?"

NG nodded. He couldn't do it by remote. He wanted every single person on board the Alsatia to traipse in so he could read their intentions and see their loyalty for himself.

"Not going to happen," Devon said casually. "But we've isolated active guild operations from shipside business. You could start trawling your way through Acquisitions if you're set on it. That seems to be where the problems lie. We've grounded the AIs, as you ordered. They're objecting."

That was an understatement. From what he'd picked up, they were close to rebelling. AI sensitivities were always difficult. They were a minority, tetchy at the best of times and always expecting special considerations. But grounding them was no different to locking down Acquisitions and refusing to let the field-ops and extraction agents leave the cruiser. They all complained. The guild demanded high levels of performance and its people operated on the edge of brilliance. None of them liked to be reined in.

The problem with the AIs was that he had absolutely no way to be sure.

"You control their contracts," he said, "remind them of that."

Devon was surprised at his tone. She sat up. "Media is working on the hypothesis that it was Ballack who hired the Assassins to kill you."

Her eyes had a sparkle to them. She was trying to provoke him into talking because she was thinking that he was being irrational. Media could work on whatever she wanted; someone had put a ridiculous price on his head, he wasn't going to run and hide. Media was also working hard to reclaim their kudos with clients and mitigate the damage from Ballack's crass attempt to undermine their standing. But Devon was also thinking that it actually wasn't an unreasonable theory to consider that Ballack and the Merchants had the most to gain from the downfall of the Thieves' Guild.

"I'm not the guild," he said. "Taking me out doesn't destroy it."

She bit off the comment she was tempted to make, wisely, and sat back instead, looking at him with a wry smile.

In the time he'd been working with her, she'd come closer than he'd allowed anyone else in his entire life.

"I want Hilyer," she said suddenly.

"No."

"He's overstepped the mark, NG. We can't let this go with a slap on the wrist."

"I'm pulling him out of Acquisitions."

Devon stared. "What?"

"The Man wants a special projects team."

"To deal with the Order?"

NG didn't move and didn't reply.

Devon narrowed her eyes. "NG, what else haven't you told me about?"

The Man wanted a special team to accelerate his preparations for fending off an alien invasion.

NG kept his expression neutral. That was hardly anything he was ready to share.

"Stay away from Hil," he said. "He's been through enough. We all have."

Devon stared at him, about to snap back and argue her case, catching herself and backing down. She decided he was tired. She wasn't usually big on empathy but she was staring at the scar on his cheek and wondering what else he was carrying. His chest was still aching. The Man hadn't offered any healing this time.

She stood and walked around behind him, gently starting to knead a hand across the muscles in his shoulders. She'd missed him, physically not emotionally. He had no delusion about that. She didn't care that he was goosed and half intoxicated still. She hit a knot and a sore spot, leaning in to whisper in his ear, "What happened on Earth?"

"We were set up."

"I mean to you, Nik."

NG didn't reply. It wasn't often that Devon showed concern and it wasn't somewhere he wanted to go.

He stretched forward, folding his arms on the desktop and resting his head down.

She considered pushing the issue but decided not to, dropping it and shifting her massage up to his neck. Her hands were warm, her touch soft against his skin. Her mind was not somewhere he wanted to go but he went in there anyway. She hadn't betrayed him. While he'd been away, she'd lodged a motion to have him suspended, to take Acquisitions into Legal, and dissolve the autonomy of the handlers, but none of it had been malicious and she was genuinely glad that NG was back, safe if not completely sound.

He closed his eyes.

Wherever the breach was, it wasn't here and for now at least he was in good hands.

It took days to screen all the personnel from Acquisitions. NG sat through the last interview, a headache hammering behind his eyes.

The Chief was asking the questions, reluctantly and in poor humour. They'd had a stand up argument when NG had demanded that all the Chief's personnel be screened. Neither of them had handled it well. He'd been impatient and unimpressed, the Chief defensive and unrelenting, both of them hurt that people they'd considered their own could have betrayed them. NG had felt the harsh reality of it – he'd lost Banks and was still sore from Earth's hospitality – and for the Chief to stand there in the safety of the Alsatia and accuse him of over-reacting had flipped him over the edge.

It had been a long week.

Micah Sorensen answered the questions easily. His thoughts were simple to read. The field operative was relieved that Hil was back, it took some of the pressure off him to vie for that top spot in the standings, felt like life might get back to normal.

The Chief glanced at NG.

Sorensen was clear. They'd all been clear.

It had been draining but he knew for certain that Acquisitions was clean.

He nodded.

The Chief gave Sorensen permission to leave, watched the tall field-op walk out then sat back, glaring at NG. "Satisfied?"

NG stood up and walked to the door. "I will be when we've gone through Legal and Media."

The Chief stood, regretting his attitude, relief diluting his temper. "NG…"

He didn't stop. He didn't need to babysit the section chiefs and he had no inclination to soothe egos. LC was still missing, Mendhel's daughter had vanished and Zang was still at large and no doubt plotting against them. And god only knew where Martha Hetherington had crawled back to. Never mind the Order, who weren't going to forgive and forget the recent blows he'd dealt them, and the fact that he still didn't know for definite who had set the Assassins after him. The Chief could relax but the guild was a way off being settled yet, if it ever would be again.

Quinn was waiting outside, leaning casually against the bulkhead. "All clear?" the big man said, more lightly than he was feeling. There'd never really been any doubt about Sorensen so it was a justified assumption.

NG nodded and turned to go. It would be good to give Acquisitions a miss for a while. Emotions tended to be high in here at the best of times – lately it was becoming unbearable.

Quinn stood up to his full height and took a step forward, his bulk blocking the way.

"Not now, Quinn," NG said softly.

"Does this mean we're clear to get back out there?"

"Not yet." He had to go through everyone who had any connection to the tabs they ran, Legal mostly but some divisions of Media too, before he could initiate the list again. There was too much risk otherwise.

Quinn didn't like it. "We're boiling over down here, NG."

The headache banging behind his eyes peaked. He stared at the handler with eyes that he could hardly keep open. "I'm not prepared to risk losing anyone else."

But you can risk yourself, Quinn was thinking, biting his tongue not to say it. "I want to go after Anya," he said instead, willing NG to give him the go ahead to take Hilyer and get out there. They'd already spoken about the special projects team. Quinn was usually the most stable of the handlers, steady and meticulous in his planning. The man standing there in front of him was itching to join the hunt for Mendhel's daughter, just to get out there and shut down the breach.

"We will," NG said, "but we need to do it right. Can you get in touch with Pen?"

Quinn nodded. "He's been avoiding us but if you let me go, I'll get through to him."

NG rubbed a hand over his eyes. "Give me a chance to talk to Hil and I'll clear a trip to Aston. We need Pen in on this."

Talking to Hilyer hadn't gone well. NG stood under a torrent of hot water, leaning his head against the bulkhead and letting the water flow over him. He needed to sleep but he needed to shower away the tension first.

He hadn't been able to face the idea of fighting an insubordinate and obnoxious field operative who'd been cooped up in Medical for a week so he'd ordered the kid into the Maze to work off his pent-up energy before sending for him. The interview still hadn't been easy, Hil slouching, mistrusting everything that was said and seriously thinking that the Alsatia was the last place he wanted to be. It had been hard to soothe, even with a damned good whisky. The promise of a special projects assignment hadn't done so much as pique Hil's curiosity and only the prospect of going back to Pen had done anything to get him on side.

It was frustrating.

'You pander to their whims and wonder why they screw you around,' that dark voice of doubt whispered. *'You should kick Hilyer out on his ass. See how the child fares then.'*

NG tipped his head up, eyes closed, feeling the water splash over his eyelashes and onto his cheeks. Like tropical rain. The kind that fell suddenly, drenching, cleansing. He didn't want to move. The Alsatia in this state wasn't the safe and calm sanctuary he could usually run back to. There was an undercurrent of instability that he couldn't calm.

'You're losing it. Have you not grasped that yet?'

A sharp stabbing pain lanced into his ribs suddenly. Pain from the flesh and bone that had been shattered by the armour piercing round, the wound he'd worked hard to heal. NG slumped against the shower wall. He had no control over it. All the aches and pains he'd been shutting out, all the old injuries he'd healed, started to filter back into his awareness.

'You abuse this body, Nikolai. My body.'

It felt like his reality was unravelling. He bowed his head, water running down the back of his neck. Breathing was hard work. He tried to close it down, focus in to cell level but he couldn't concentrate.

'You're too weak to fight me.'

The water was steaming hot but there was a cold chill deep inside that was spreading. He could feel the dark mist swirling and for the briefest of instants he was tempted to give in to it. Give up. Stop trying to do well by everyone. Why should he care? Who the hell had ever cared about him?

It was a dark place to be and he was sinking into it. A distant part of him felt Devon and Evelyn nudge urgently at the Senson, both coded, demanding his attention.

The mist receded, pain gone in a flash that left him gasping.

He stood there for a long moment, water flowing over his skin, the warmth returning slowly. He scrubbed a hand over his face and sent to them both, not bothering to keep the weariness from his tone, "If it's not urgent, I'll deal with it later."

Evelyn replied first. "Sean's found LC," she sent. "She wants to see you."

17

"And it all comes together..."

He raised his eyes. "The fortunes of the guild I created should never – ever – have rested so precariously on the actions of so few individuals."

The corners of her mouth turned up. "But they are such an extraordinary few."

She was teasing him.

He swirled the jug and rested it on the table.

"Is that not what history relies upon?" she asked. "That the few sacrifice for the greater good of the many?"

Poppycock again. The few rarely sacrificed anything. The few were mostly the few who fed off and profited from the many for their own ends.

She pushed again. "Is that not what you attracted in the very essence of the guild you created? Gathering the special, the outcasts, the exceptional to challenge the norms of society in this galaxy of such self-centred creatures? You are frustrated by their actions but surely, you could not have expected anything less, anything different from them? Each roll of the dice was weighted, and it was you that fixed the odds. Don't deny that."

Frank O'Brien had good taste in hideaways. NG sat on the cabin's porch with Sean and watched his two field operatives wander back along the dirt path from the beach. The sun was setting, long shadows stretching out from the wooden cabin, the shade bringing an edge of chill to the day's warmth.

Hil and LC were quiet, walking slowly as if neither of them really wanted to return to face the crap they'd been running from.

They were both hurting, Hil physically, LC reeling from the news that it was Anya that had betrayed them. Hilyer hadn't been subtle in telling him.

NG stretched out one leg and leaned back on his elbows on the step. It hadn't been easy to listen in but he wasn't about to give them any privacy, not when he was this close to bringing them both back in. He'd brought Hil along for two reasons – one, to get him away from the tension that was brewing on the Alsatia and two, to cushion the meeting with LC. Luka looked exhausted, tense, dreading going back to the guild. He was walking along next to Hil because he was caught in the momentum, otherwise he would have turned and run.

"He had a bad reaction to some stuff he was drugged with," Sean said softly, still concerned.

NG caught a hint of more than concern there. She'd given him a brief run down of what had happened, how she'd caught up with LC on some freighter out in the mining colonies and stayed with him until the kid had finally admitted who he was. Sean was embarrassed that she hadn't brought LC straight in. It was complicated, was the way she'd tried to explain it, completely failing to justify even to herself why she'd let LC persuade her to let him hand himself in to a bounty hunter. She felt bad because she hadn't been able to convince LC that the guild was safe.

They'd had a tough time by the sound of it and NG had taken more from her mind than Sean had admitted to openly. LC had a tendency to charm without meaning to. Evelyn wouldn't be impressed to see that she had competition.

Sean touched NG's knee. "I'll leave you to it. Be gentle with him." She stood, waved to Hil and LC and headed into the cabin.

LC was fraught, heart pounding, eyes tracking Sean as she disappeared inside. Hilyer gave NG a brief acknowledgement, held LC by the shoulder for a second then jogged up the steps and followed Sean.

LC stood awkwardly, not sure what the reception was going to be. He'd lost weight, his hair was cropped short and his eyes had a haunted look to them, a drastic shade paler than they used to be. He was dreading being hauled into Medical, so god knew what he'd done to change his eyes like that. A tiny metal tag was pierced through the top of his left ear. Sean had touched on their encounter with bounty hunters, the tag physical evidence that LC had been caught somewhere along the line. She'd admitted that she'd reprogrammed it so technically LC belonged to her. That wasn't exactly what he'd had in mind when he'd hired her to find the kid.

"Sit down," NG said gently, an invitation rather than an order.

LC sat on the step. He was trying desperately not to think.

NG placed a hand briefly on the back of the kid's neck and gave him as much healing warmth as he could spare, calming and reassuring. He felt LC take a deep breath and relax, still scared deep down but that trembling anxiety easing.

They both sat there, breathing in the fresh sea air and staring straight out towards the sea.

"It's good to see you're alive, LC," NG said finally, softly, non-threatening, no trace of anger or retribution.

He felt LC's breath catch in his chest, a panic as the kid thought of his handler with a depth of grief that was almost overwhelming. Mendhel wasn't alive and it was his fault, he was thinking desperately.

NG said quickly, "We know what happened, Luka. You had no choice. We know it's been a hard time, and believe me, the guild hasn't had an easy time of it either, but we want you back."

It was too easy to read his mind, emotions laid open. LC wanted to blurt out everything. There wasn't even any need to maintain a physical contact. The kid wanted to explain but he was tying himself in knots because he couldn't. NG could read the thoughts there easily, the dilemma about the package. It all came back to the package Zang had sent them to steal. He was the package, LC was thinking, how could he admit that?

What the hell did that mean? It was frustrating, tempting to just grab the kid's arm and take what he needed to know.

Just tell me where the damned package is, NG was thinking, biting his tongue not to say it out loud, not to spook the kid.

He felt the touch of LC's mind with the shocking realisation that he was being read.

LC was scuffing the toes of his boots against each other, staring at the ground. "I don't know where it is," he said.

NG turned his head slowly. Apart from the Man, he'd never met anyone ever who could do that. It hit him like a physical blow.

He felt LC reflect that shock back, the adrenaline rush fast, heart racing.

LC turned to look him in the eye, trying frantically to throw up a shield and shut down his thoughts.

"You didn't say that out loud, did you?" LC whispered, starting to shiver.

NG stared at him, thinking clearly, 'What happened out there, Luka?' Simply thought it, not using the Senson, just mind to mind in the way the Man hated.

LC's face flushed, horrified, as he tried to not think. He was good but NG was better. Whatever defences the kid tried to build were easy to break through. LC was terrified that he'd been discovered but there was also a tinge of incredible relief that he wasn't alone.

NG stood up. It was hard not to grab hold of that feeling and cling to it. He'd always been alone. "Come on," he said, "let's walk."

The sun was sinking gradually down to the horizon, darkness creeping in across the calm expanse of sea. They walked slowly, random thoughts tumbling from LC as he flashed on memories from the past, how he'd come to the guild, how Mendhel had rescued him from being shot on Kheris when he'd been stupid enough to get caught, and how NG had welcomed him in to the Alsatia. Anything but what had happened at that lab with Hilyer.

'He's rogue,' the dark voice mocked, *'and he's more powerful than you realise. I should kill him.'*

NG shut it out fiercely. There was no way he was going to lose control here. "Talk to me, LC," he said.

"What do you want me to say?"

LC had a reputation for being reckless and he suddenly opened his mind, flashing back to the lab, getting hit with some kind of virus, the agonising after-effects, getting shot on some back of beyond station and almost dying, sharing the void of each death at Zang's facility – a whirlwind of painful memories thrown relentlessly at NG.

He took it all, the whole story, no need for a drawn out debrief. LC had an eidetic memory and sharing that intensity of information left a mass of data seared into NG's mind.

The virus, or whatever it was that Zang had sent them to steal, was rampant in every part of the kid's body – a living, swarming organism. Fast cell regeneration, immunity to poisons, increased mental capacity. No wonder Zang was desperate to get his hands on it.

But the side effects...

LC was left doubled over, gasping for breath, system about to go into shutdown. Sean had said he'd had a rough time; she had no idea how rough. And the kid was still hurting, no matter how much he tried to shut it away.

NG stood next to him, watching the sun set, holding a hand against the back of LC's neck and using that contact to help ease the pain, settle the bone-deep ache that was tearing at the kid's soul.

"The Earth lab was destroyed after you got away," NG said quietly. "And chances are Zang didn't know exactly what it was he was sending you in there for. Does anyone else know?"

LC hesitated, a series of faces and snatches of conversation flashing into his mind, giving NG his answer without a word. Christ, this was going to be complicated.

"We need to bring them in," he said. "Do you understand?"

LC nodded reluctantly and said hesitantly, "Anya's with Pen."

NG nodded. "We'll deal with Anya." He paused. It was going to be dark soon. "Are you ready to come back?"

It was a rhetorical question.

LC had no choice and he knew it.

"Good," NG said. "There's someone I need you to talk to."

They walked back to the cabin in silence. LC was firmly in automatic mode, putting one foot in front of the other, keeping his head empty of thoughts, feeling safe for the first time in a long time simply because NG was there. It was a hell of a responsibility. The bounty on the two field operatives was escalating, the Assassins' contract was still active, and Zang and the Order were upping their game against the guild. There was no room for complacency but for the moment, he could allow LC to relax.

It was dusk by the time the cabin came into sight. They both saw the smoke rising from the chimney and sensed the presence of another person at the same time, LC hesitating, panic flaring.

It was Sean's father. No need for alarm. Conversely, he felt LC's stress level rise as the kid picked up on the thoughts that he shared freely.

'Don't worry,' he thought. 'Frank won't betray us. Even if he is the most successful bounty hunter of all time.'

"Oh shit," LC muttered, heart pounding again, thinking of Sean and not even caring about the price on his head. He backed away a step.

NG couldn't help the grin that slipped out. "Frank's a teddy bear," he said gently. "Unless you do anything to hurt Sean, then he'll come after you for free."

He nudged LC down the path.

The night sky was pitch black, no artificial lights, no scurrying mass of thinking minds spilling emotional garbage on all sides and absolutely no risk of an assassin's dagger in the back.

NG leaned against the railing of the porch, resting a half empty bottle of beer against the wooden bar. Both the field-ops had been visibly relieved when he'd accepted Frank's offer to stay the night. They'd been expecting to get hauled straight back to the Alsatia but one night away from the dramas of the universe wouldn't do them any harm.

It was hard not be envious of this peaceful lifestyle that Sean's old man had earned for himself.

'Don't fool yourself. You can never settle, you know that. We need the thrill of adversity, you and I.'

He lifted the bottle and drank, unable to argue with that dark muttering deep inside.

The door banged open behind him, soft voices filtering out and footsteps approaching.

Frank O'Brien was a rare man with cast iron principles and a strength of spirit that was good to be near. He joined NG, leaning on the railing next to him with a bottle of beer in his hand and a smile on his face.

They clinked bottles.

"So those two youngsters are the best of your infamous field operatives?" Frank said, teasing gently.

NG nodded. He'd known Frank a long time, a trusted associate of the guild who never asked any questions and always delivered. Sean was doing a good job of carrying on that legacy. Except she might now have crossed that line. It was a difficult decision to make but it might be time to ask her to come in. She was far closer and knew far more than any outsider would ever be privileged to.

"My daughter seems smitten with the pair of them. One more than the other," Frank said, insight and intuition as sharp as ever. The man might be retired, but the instincts hadn't faded.

NG smiled. He knew that LC was listening in, worried about how Sean was going to react to her father meeting him, like he might not come up to their standards. Christ, LC Anderton fretting about what someone might think of him. That was a first.

"They're good kids," he said.

Frank didn't look impressed. "First thing I ever taught her," he said, "don't get involved with the target. And she goes and falls for one of yours."

"I have another job for her if she wants it," NG said softly.

Frank looked at him, eye to eye for a long minute, then nodded. "She will. I get the feeling no one is going to manage to cash in on these contracts. Jesus, NG, eighty five mill each on those two and five hundred on you? Who the hell have you all been pissing off?"

NG paused with the beer bottle half way to his lips, aware that LC had picked up on that five hundred. "It's a long story."

Frank didn't push it. "I was sorry to hear about Mendhel," he said after a while, genuine emotion. The guild didn't mix with many people in the outside but when they did, loyalties and friendships tended to run deep.

NG drained the last of the beer. "We've lost some good people," he said quietly.

It was weird but as much as they were all relieved at this temporary respite from the chaos and drama, all he could pick up from Sean's dad was a burning curiosity, a yearning to leave this sanctuary and get back out there himself.

"We might have a job for you if you're interested," NG suggested, nonchalantly. "If we can tempt you away from the fishing."

Frank laughed and clapped him on the back. "Come on, we shouldn't leave those two reprobates alone with my little girl for much longer."

The three of them looked up as NG and Frank walked back in. More logs had been stacked onto the fire and they were sitting around the table messing about with a pack of cards.

Frank pulled another couple of beers from the fridge, giving one to NG and sitting at the table. He settled himself, took a swig from his bottle and looked directly at LC. "So have you slept with her?"

Sean had a mouthful of beer herself and almost choked.

LC flushed, bright red, fumbling the shuffle and spilling cards onto the table.

Hilyer grinned and stood up, excusing himself and limping out to the kitchen, sending silently to LC, "Don't blow it, bud."

NG followed, smiling.

Frank's kitchen was well stocked, homely in a way the mess on a ship could never quite manage.

Hil leaned against the counter, pulling a pack of painkillers from his pocket. "So what happens now?"

"Frank'll give LC a hard time then if he likes him, he'll welcome him into the family."

Hil smiled and popped a couple of the pills. "You know what I mean."

They hadn't talked a lot on the way out here, not knowing what they'd find, what state LC would be in. Now the kid was wondering where they went from here.

"We need to hold Skye in quarantine, Hil. We have no choice. After what happened with Genoa, we can't make any exceptions."

Hil stared at the floor. He was tired out, feeling that he had no fight left.

"We have some loose ends to tie up," NG said.

"Anya?"

"Anya. Zang. That bastard's not going to let up until he gets hold of you both." He looked at Hil. So far nothing had been said about the incident at the lab except that LC had been infected by something. Hil was assuming it was a failed experimental bioweapon that LC had somehow recovered from. "There are also some people LC encountered while he was out there. We need to bring them in."

Hil looked up, puzzled, wondering why. NG didn't say anything but the kid was smart enough to put two and two together, thinking shit, he knew LC had been screwed up but to have revealed his connection with the guild to anyone was bad news.

"We still off the list?"

NG nodded. "Special projects."

Hil took a beer out of the fridge, holding his side as he leaned over. "We should go rescue LC."

"I think he'll be fine. He's still wearing her tag – on some planets that's virtually a wedding band."

18

She took a sip. "I do like Hilyer and Anderton," she said without looking up. "They have such an indomitable spirit. Did you suspect that Zang's mysterious package could be carrying such a significant secret?"

"If I had," he said dryly, "I would not have acted any differently. We have enemies. We confront them. This, this... package... that had the entire galaxy chasing after our missing operatives, no one knew what it was. Even Earth didn't know what they had. However," he raised a finger, "if we had known then what its origins were, I..."

"Hindsight," she interrupted sternly. "As you say, you – we – are not omnipotent. How did Zang learn of it and we did not?"

"The Order, I presume. And therein lies a greater question. How did the Order know of it, and we did not?"

It was a brief respite, reality waiting as soon as they set foot on the Alsatia. Evelyn was standing almost to attention, arms behind her back, flanked by two of the Man's elite guard.

There was something wrong.

She didn't move, expression neutral, eyes flicking from NG to LC as they walked off the ship.

NG was a step ahead and he turned slightly to the others, gesturing them to wait and saying softly, "Stay here," not liking what he was reading in Evie's mind.

He felt a flutter of panic in LC, felt him reach out cautiously with an automatic self-defensive need to assess the danger around him. Christ, the last thing the kid needed was to get sucked into the disturbed psyche of the Man's elite guards.

NG threw up a shield to block him instinctively, switching to direct thought. 'Luka, don't. Don't even try to read these guys. You don't want to go anywhere near their minds, you understand?'

LC frowned and the banging headache that was emanating from behind the kid's eyes peaked with an intensity that almost made NG's eyes water.

NG squinted at him. 'LC, do you understand?'

'No,' the thought came back. LC was vague, dazed almost. 'Shit, NG, how do you deal with this?'

'Shut it out,' he sent back brusquely. He didn't have time for it. 'And for Christ's sake, don't try to read the minds of the Man's guards. That's somewhere you don't want to go. I'll explain later. Okay?'

LC nodded, swaying. Sean steadied him with a hand to his back and it was impossible to miss the flare in Evelyn's thoughts as she saw the gesture.

NG turned away. He definitely didn't have time for this. "Stay here," he muttered again and walked up to Evelyn.

She was still staring at Sean and LC as he approached, snapping her gaze directly to NG's eyes as he came to a halt in front of her.

"Winter has attacked an Imperial mining facility," she said. "Ostraban claims it wasn't sanctioned and Earth is making diplomatic noises at the moment but they're shifting their fleet into the Between. Media wants to see you – she thinks this could be an opportunity."

NG nodded, irritation building, waiting for the rest.

"Ballack has lodged a complaint against you. The staff in Legal want to know how you want to respond. And the Chief needs to see you."

She paused.

There was a lot more to all of it, all swirling in ordered circles around her thinking as she filtered the information she decided he needed to know right now. The alert he'd sent out had caused massive ripples, compromising too many of their operations to mention. She decided the Chief could cover all that with him and set her expression back into neutral, report over.

NG narrowed his eyes. She wasn't getting away with it that easily. "Where's Devon?" he said bluntly.

Evelyn sucked in a breath. "She left a message for you in your office before she went. She didn't tell me where she was going."

NG felt the anger rising and bit down on the comments that flew into his mind. It wasn't Evelyn's job to keep Devon in check. But he'd left Devon in charge and it wasn't just irritating that she'd skipped out. It had been a relief to get LC and Hil back within his grasp, was it too much to hope that he could keep a grip on his people again? And finding out that Devon wasn't tucked up safe and sound on the Alsatia as he'd thought was more unsettling than he'd expected to ever feel.

NG held out his hand and Evie passed over the board she'd been holding behind her back. The orders were explicit in their simplicity. He read through them quickly.

'No rest for the wicked…'

He turned to LC and Hil. They were both hanging back, hesitant. Sean was standing close to LC, still protective towards him, still disturbed by the emotional attachment she hadn't managed to avoid.

The Man wanted to see him. And the Man wanted LC and Hil confined in his own medical facility, on board his ship. Quarantined. Like he'd guessed they'd have the package and it was never going to be as simple as delivering up a sealed container with the goods inside.

As far as NG knew, no one except himself and the Man's private staff and security had ever been allowed to set foot on that ship before. And the Man never left it. The ship docked with the Alsatia and left, as far as anyone else knew, to liaise with the rest of the council that supposedly controlled the Thieves' Guild from afar like omniscient puppet masters. And now the Man was inviting, ordering, their two recalcitrant field operatives into his sacred domain.

The two elite guards stepped forward.

"Go with these guys," he said, feeling another pang of panic in LC. This was going to be a minefield. Hiding him away on the

Man's ship was a way they could keep the kid isolated and protect his sanity. For a while at least.

"Trust me," he said. "It's the safest place for you right now. Don't argue. Don't say anything to anyone. Understand? Play dumb. They'll run a standard medical, just like post-tab. Nothing more. Then they have orders to keep you secure. Don't do anything stupid." He had to wait for them to nod, sensing the caution and distrust and sharing it. "Sean, go with Evelyn. You can wait in my office. This might take a while."

The Man had a twisted sense of humour at times. Playing chess with a being that could read your mind was challenging; playing chess while presenting a debrief from one of the worst situations the guild had ever had to manage had been almost impossible. And it hadn't just been a game. The Man was ruthless in teaching his lessons and the end game had been hard, emotionally as well as strategically.

NG cradled the goblet of hot spiced wine in his hand, resting its weight against his knee, still not sure how much longer this was going to last. He'd met with the section chiefs before coming in here, more to grab some intel on LC's story and issue some fast orders he wanted actioning immediately than to hear what they had going on, and he was very aware that events were unfolding out there while he was sitting in here playing chess.

He took a sip of the wine. The alcohol was laced with a narcotic far more potent than anything the Man had ever given him before. It had already been a long session, the Man pushing him for information, insights, even going as far as trying to spark that supposed latent telekinetic ability that he'd never managed to find. It had been tough going.

He was having trouble focusing, eyes heavy, the fallen chess pieces that were lying discarded on the desk blurring, the queen he'd sacrificed so ruthlessly to win staring up at him from her blind, intricately carved eyes.

It seemed to be his fate to sacrifice those most valuable to him and it never got any easier.

The Man leaned forward. "Zang Tsu Po is a worry. The bounty has doubled. He acts directly against us. Where is he?"

"Vanished." NG drained the last of his wine. "Jameson is looking for him, Ostraban is looking for him, we have people on it and we have people watching them. With tensions this high and emotions this charged on both sides of the line, there aren't many places to hide."

"We have enemies, NG," the Man said softly. "We must take care. Zang's wild actions are making him more dangerous than we anticipated. Find him." He paused, rubbing his thumb across his fingers and glancing at the single candle illuminating the dark chamber as if he was about to snuff it out. That would be the end of the session.

NG stared at that tiny burning ember, the glow turning into a blur of orange, willing his boss to extinguish the stuttering flame.

"Yet…" the Man said.

NG blinked, concentrating his focus back onto the figure sitting there in front of him, a being who wielded such sway over the future of the human race.

The Man's eyes were dark. "I fear there may be more to all this. Tell me again of the freighter and its captain."

He'd been through it all once.

"Tell me again."

NG rubbed a hand across his eyes. "William Gallagher. Claims to have been shot down by aliens. He lost his ship and was lucky to survive. Everyone out there thinks he's mad."

He felt the touch of the Man's mind as a gentle nudge, hypnotic. It was hard not to fall into that embrace and let go completely, let the Man read whatever he wanted.

It was LC's memory of a vague contact with Gallagher's mind that the Man was manipulating, gently teasing the information from NG's mind third hand, seeing what Gallagher had seen, what LC had subconsciously seen hidden deep in the old man's memories, what the kid had then thrown across to NG without even knowing it.

It wasn't painful when the Man did that, but it was wearing.

Time had no meaning. Hours could have passed. NG opened his eyes, not realising that he'd closed them.

The Man was staring at him, a gleam in his eye that was a mix of anticipation, dread and satisfaction. "I want that freighter and its crew," he said, something in his voice NG had never heard before.

The Man stared without a word for a while longer then suddenly picked up his fallen king. "Work with Luka," he said. "Zang Tsu Po has delivered right to us, through his greed and morbid fear of mortality, the very answer to our ultimate dilemma. Use it."

It being the virus, the catalyst, whatever it was that Earth had managed to discover and lose without even knowing what it could do. No one knew what it could do and the idea of letting it loose was chilling.

"It is loose," the Man said scathingly.

NG dropped his gaze, staring down into the dark depths of the empty goblet. LC hadn't just let slip knowledge of the guild while he was on that ship in the mining colonies, he'd spread the virus to at least one other that he knew of. What had happened since the kid had left was anyone's guess.

The struggling flame of the candle flickered.

"Zang," the Man said eventually, breaking an ominous silence, "was chasing rumours of an elixir of life. Eternal life. This quirk of human biochemistry that gives us the weapon we need against our enemies is, I suspect, not simply a serendipitous side effect of an artificially created virus. But wherever it originated, it is one that has landed in our lap and one upon which we must capitalise. You say Luka has the potential to be stronger than you? We have to know. Isolate the active element of this elixir and use it. We need to know what it can do, what our people can do when it is given to them."

NG raised his eyes, working hard to keep his breathing even, trying not to react, concentrating to avoid the temptation of looking into the Man's mind to read his full intentions.

"Hilyer, Sorensen and Essien," the Man said.

Their best.

NG hesitated to argue outright that it was madness to infect three of their top operatives based only on LC's account of his experience and anecdotal evidence of the effects on another, without initiating some kind of test protocols.

The Man frowned and shook his head slowly. "Tests take time – time, based on the experience of Luka's freighter captain and the very arrival of this DNA in our galaxy, that we do not have." He said again, "Hilyer, Sorensen and Essien."

NG nodded, the slightest of movements in acknowledgement of the orders. He could be sentencing three of his best people to death for all he knew.

"Nikolai," the Man said quietly, "from here on, there will, I fear, be much more we will have to risk and sacrifice in order to accomplish our ultimate goal."

The words weighed heavily and he couldn't help glancing at the forlorn queen.

The Man kept his ship dark. Warm. NG sat in the anteroom to the Man's chambers waiting, elbows on his knees, head resting in his upturned hands. After the session with the Man, he'd made his way back to his office, brain fried, senses scrambled, wanting nothing more than to crawl into bed. Instead he'd had to talk to Sean, fend off the Chief and work out a series of orders with Evelyn. Devon's message had been ridiculously cryptic but to give her credit, she'd left a command structure in place that was managing to be as slick and efficient as he'd expect from Legal.

Sean had taken the job of chasing down Anya after some persuading, concerned about LC and reluctant to leave him but too stubborn to leave unresolved a mistake like letting Anya go and still furious with herself that she hadn't brought LC straight in. The Chief had kept his report brief – they were in the shit and it wasn't getting any easier out there. And Evelyn had patiently plied him with tea while they worked out priorities.

Sleep hadn't featured in any of it.

He'd sent for Micah Sorensen and Lulu Essien and headed back to the Man's ship, sending word for LC and Hil to be brought to him. The Man wanted to speak to them all. He was hardly asking for volunteers but he was honourable enough to feel the need to explain before condemning them to become lab rats.

NG rubbed his eyes. This was what they'd been working towards, striving towards. A weapon that would give them a chance. And now it was within reach. As rumours of alien sightings and alleged incidents increased, an Earth scientist managed to engineer an elixir, as the Man called it, with the exact properties they needed to take on the alien race they knew was fast approaching its new feeding ground? Coincidence? Christ, there was no way it was a coincidence.

He looked up as he sensed the four figures approaching, shaking off the fatigue and standing before they rounded the corner.

Luka looked exhausted, hands stuck in his pockets, head down as if he didn't dare look up in case he accidentally encountered someone who would melt his brain. God knows what the Man's medical team had been doing to him.

The others were quietly curious, well aware of the honour they were being granted in being brought here, in awe of their surroundings. Hilyer veered towards the shelves lining the room, gawping at the artefacts. He peered at one piece, a carved instrument of some kind, and muttered under his breath, "Holy crap, that's one of mine." It was a revelation, like he'd never considered before where their acquisitions ended up.

The kid looked round and couldn't resist reaching to touch a medallion that was mounted on a stand, delicately and almost reverently holding the tarnished metal, stroking his thumb over the intricate, knotted design. "Hey LC, isn't this the amulet you stole from that place on Winter."

LC glanced over, memories of pain and flight flashing into his mind. That tab had almost killed him. He managed a half-smile.

They were like children.

NG suddenly felt really old. It was hard to be sharing this. He waited for them to gather round and took a deep breath. "The man you're about to meet," he said quietly, "is the head of the

Thieves' Guild. Don't say a word." He looked at Hilyer. "Don't touch anything. Don't move an inch unless he tells you to." He looked at LC and dropped into direct thought, 'And for Christ's sake, don't even think about trying to read his mind. Are you okay?'

LC raised his eyes and nodded slightly. He wasn't okay by a long way but he wasn't going to admit it so there was still some of that incorrigible spirit there.

"Understand?"

They all nodded then.

NG turned to the door. The Man watched the activities of the guild personnel closely but from a distance. This was the first time he would meet any of them in person. NG rested his knuckles against the warm wood of the door. It felt like he was on test. Like everything he'd ever done would be judged on what happened in the next few minutes with these four individuals standing behind him.

He rapped gently on the door.

19

"You are hard on him. You are hard on them all."

"We do not have the luxury of time to be soft."

"They are young," she said softly, "and the young do not comprehend the intricacies of the universe in the same way as you or I. You gambled with this virus, this elixir. Did it pay off?"

He couldn't answer that question. It could be years, centuries, before the effects were seen fully.

He steepled his fingers in front of his face, felt his warm breath on his hands as he exhaled. "I had no choice," he said eventually. "Knowing what was to come, I had no choice. And Nikolai had no choice but to obey."

"And deal with the consequences."

LC sat, leaning his elbows on the table and slumping forward. "So what do we do now?"

The lights in the office were low, temperature set to cool. They'd left Hil, Sorensen and Lulu in Science. For once Hil hadn't argued and NG wasn't sure if that was the influence of the Man or the fact that the kid realised the significance of the moment. The Man had kept the interview brief but he'd told them about the Order, Zang and the virus then sent the others to Science and ordered NG to take LC in hand. "Work with him," he'd said ponderously. "Push him."

'I'll push him alright.'

LC glanced up.

NG was standing, rifling through messages on his desk. He quickly dampened down that niggling voice inside. It was disconcerting to have to guard his thoughts. It was second nature to listen in to other people but the only place he'd ever had to be careful to shield his own mind was in the Man's chambers.

"We wait," he said.

"You should both get some sleep," Evelyn said from the doorway, walking in and setting a tray onto the conference table.

NG sent privately through the Senson, "Any word from Devon?"

"No," she sent back, pouring tea for them both and squeezing LC's shoulder as she turned away. She dropped a couple of boards onto the desk. "Ostraban is asking to see you."

"Not now," NG said. "Fend him off."

She nodded. "Also, Science are sitting on a package that one of our couriers brought in for you. They want to know what you want them to do with it."

"Addressed to me?"

"Yes. It's shielded. No origin. They're worried it could be a bomb or some kind of biological weapon."

For Christ's sake. "Tell them to open it."

Evie nodded again. She backed away, glancing over at LC as if she couldn't quite believe he was back. He'd dropped his head down to rest on his folded arms, eyes closed but far from asleep.

"Let me know if you need anything," she said softly and left.

NG picked up the two boards. Ostraban was investigating the death of Taynara A'Darbi. That message wasn't subtle. He threw it down on the desk. The other was a stack of personnel assessments from Legal's staff, one for every AI and a list of complaints at being grounded from the AIs themselves. It was a headache he had no inclination to address, not yet. He dropped the board onto the pile and searched through the drawer for a pack of cards.

LC looked up as he sat at the table.

'Why don't you trust Skye?' LC thought at him.

NG reached for his tea. He closed his mind down. Abruptly.

LC got the message.

They were in a difficult position. He'd never worked this closely with anyone in the guild except Devon maybe, Evelyn at times.

Certainly no one who could read his thoughts the way the Man could. But he was still the head of operations, head of the guild as far as anyone was concerned. And LC was just a field operative.

'Oh no, no, no, don't fool yourself. This child sitting in front of you will never be just a field operative again.'

LC leaned forward. "Why don't you trust Skye?" he said quietly, out loud, little more than a whisper.

NG looked up. "Has Hil told you about Genoa?"

LC nodded.

"We screened everyone in Acquisitions, did you hear about that?"

Another nod.

"We have no way of screening the AIs."

LC frowned. "But Skye…?"

"LC, I have no way of screening the AIs," NG said bluntly, emphasis on the 'I'.

The kid got it then. "Ah." He was trying to think if he'd encountered an AI since he'd contracted the virus and another piece of information clicked into place. Elliott. He flushed, trying to remember if he'd mentioned Elliott in his debrief.

He had but NG had taken the whole story anyway in those few brief moments at the coast when LC had thrown open his mind. Elliott was one of the reasons the Man wanted the crew of that ship bringing in.

He shuffled the cards and said casually, "Tell me about the freighter you ended up on."

"I put in all in the report," LC said quietly. "You know everything."

"Tell me again. I need you to think about these people as you go through it – I need to know everything, even things you've forgotten."

LC bit his lip, trying not to argue. He took a deep breath but still didn't speak.

"Start with Elliott," NG prompted.

The kid looked tired, worn out and caught out. "He was some kind of tech guy," he said wearily. "The Duck belongs to

Gallagher and he swears blind it doesn't have an AI but this guy Elliott controls the systems like it does." He stopped and bit his lip again. "It was weird. I couldn't read anything from him. Nothing. Even after I started getting the hang of it. It's like there's a dark void when he's there in front of you." He raised his eyes, knowing that NG knew all this and resenting the fact that he was being forced to go over it again.

Apart from AIs, there was no living sentient being that NG wasn't able to read in some form or other. It would be interesting to meet Elliott.

"He's a jerk," LC said in response to that thought. "And he knows about the virus. He fixed me up after I got shot on Poule. I should have died."

"Which is why we need to bring him in," NG said softly. "What about the others?"

"Hal Duncan was Earth marine corps," LC said. "He saved my life on Poule. He got caught up in some kind of petty mob family squabble when we got back to Sten's World. He was dying. It was Elliott who said I had the only way to save him. We infected him with the virus. I had no choice."

"Do you know his background?" Hal Duncan had been a breeze for Legal to research. The guy had an impressive military record to his name.

"Some of it."

He knew more than some of it but he didn't want to go there. Duncan had served in the front line of colonial enforcement actions, heroically by all accounts, but LC had seen some of those battles from the other side and they weren't memories he wanted sparked.

"What were the effects of the virus on Duncan?"

LC exhaled a breath he was holding, exasperation barely constrained as he said quietly, "NG, I've told you all of this."

In the light of the Man's recent orders, he wanted to hear it again. He wanted to know what was likely to be going on in Science with three of his own people.

"Tell me again."

LC's eyes flashed with frustration. "He was wasted for four days then woke up reading minds. What was I supposed to do? He knew about the guild before I realised what he was doing." He drained the last of his tea and spun the cup on its base.

One thing the kid didn't mention out loud was that Duncan had recovered from the effects of the virus faster than he had. Way faster. It wasn't resentment that kept him from saying it, it was a really bad feeling deep down inside that he'd released something, something he was managing when it was just himself and as soon as he spread it to Duncan, he lost control. Out of the two field-operatives, Hilyer was the control freak. And it was freaking LC out that he was freaked out about it.

"Tell me about DiMarco."

LC groaned softly and started tapping at the tea cup. His opinion of Gallagher's pilot was mixed. "He's even more of a jerk than Elliott," he said but felt bad saying it. "He used Gallagher's ship to run guns." To outlaws in the Between, and there was the dilemma – LC had been on the run himself when he ran into them. It had made for a strange camaraderie that the kid was still feeling guilty about.

"Does he know about the virus?"

"No, I said he doesn't or least he didn't when I left them. I don't know what Hal might have said."

"Can we trust DiMarco?"

LC choked back a laugh then met NG's eyes with a serious consideration. "Yes. Maybe. Shit, what can I say? He's a pirate but he didn't sell me out when the bounty hunters found us on Tortuga."

"If he knows about the bounty, he knows about the guild," NG said bluntly.

It had been cited in the original contract that was touted around publicly. That was one of the most difficult factors in the mitigation of this whole situation. Media had had a nightmare trying to damage control their reputation.

LC went cold. He hadn't known. He didn't think DiMarco had known while he was there but Tierney, the leader of the colony, would have found out. The place had been teeming with bounty hunters when they left. His hand started shaking.

They'd find out soon enough whether they could trust DiMarco when the guy was brought in.

"What about the others?" NG said.

"They don't know anything."

No wonder Mendhel was the only handler they'd ever had who could manage LC. It was trying. "Tell me about them anyway."

LC pushed the cup away. "Bill Gallagher owns the Duck. He's a freighter captain." Decent guy was the assessment sitting there in the kid's mind. Too decent to pull him into anything to do with the guild. He didn't want to say any more because he didn't want to make Gallagher a person of interest to NG. But, considering the Man's reaction, something from that initial burst of information that LC had thrown out when they were talking outside Frank O'Brien's place had already tagged William Gallagher as being of interest to the guild. Immense interest. More than Elliott or Duncan in the scheme of things.

"What was his story?" he asked softly.

LC looked up, dismayed that NG knew. "He claimed he was shot down by aliens out in the Erica system. It was some kind of accident. He had his papers pulled. Everyone said he was mad. I thought he was okay."

"Any details?"

"He never talked about it much. Why is that so important?"

NG ignored the question. "What about the other engineer? Garrett?"

LC rolled his eyes. "Oh Christ, Thom is just a young kid who covered for me, NG. Why do we need to pull him in?"

Thom Garrett was more than just a young engineer. LC knew that and he answered his own question. "Gallagher."

Garrett was old Earth military. Legal hadn't been able to find definitive evidence but it looked like the kid was from one of the oldest and most reputable military families on Earth, a Rear Admiral's grandson who'd disappeared from all records two years ago. They had no idea why he was out in the mining colonies.

"I thought he might have been a drop out," LC said quietly, "but I knew he was wired with a Six which is pretty high end hardware for a drop out. Nothing added up, but nothing was adding up about anything." And I was just trying to stay alive, he didn't add. He had a headache pounding behind his eyes.

NG blocked out the niggling second-hand pain he was picking up and reached for the jug of tea, aware that LC was watching him, frowning, wondering how he'd just managed that.

"Try it," NG said.

"What?"

"You need to learn to control it." NG picked up the cards, shuffling and laying the deck carefully on the table between them.

LC was staring at him, wanting to go get a beer, wanting anything but to face up to this.

NG gestured to the stack of cards. "Take one."

LC rubbed a hand across the back of his neck, wanting to argue, but he took the top card, glanced at it and placed it face down on the table.

NG read it easily, feeling the barriers the kid tried to throw into place but breaking through without any effort. "Three of hearts," he said, reaching forward and turning the card over.

Three of hearts.

"Again," he said.

It took three more cards before LC started to put up any real defence.

'Pathetic.'

LC looked up, confusion flashing in his eyes.

NG ignored it. He slid a card off the pile, took a brief look and placed it face down on the table.

He felt a tentative reach from the kid but then LC dropped his gaze to the card and shook his head.

"I don't know."

'You're a fool to even let him come close.'

"Try harder."

LC was pale, thinking that he didn't know how to try harder, he didn't even know how this worked, try harder at what?

"So don't try," NG said softly, still keeping his guard up. "Just take it."

LC raised his eyes slowly, heart pounding, half-heartedly trying to read the information from NG's mind.

NG fended him off easily.

"I can't beat you," LC said quietly.

"I'm not asking you to beat me – just tell me what the card is."

LC stared, resentful and tired, but then he blinked, slowly.

That time the intrusion was sudden and brutally clean.

The shock hit them both simultaneously.

Something snapped inside.

NG reeled, shoved violently aside by the strength of the darkness deep down at that split second instant as the unexpectedly powerful attack broke through his defences.

He felt himself take hold of LC's mind and hold fast, matching power with power.

The kid jerked backwards, breathing fast, trying to break free, knowing he'd overstepped a boundary and frantically wondering what the hell had just happened.

NG felt like he was slipping away. The scene faded, blurring as if he couldn't quite focus.

He fought to keep control but it felt like he was pinned under water. He couldn't breath, couldn't move.

He heard himself say, "Oh, now the fun begins," hardly recognising his own voice.

"NG…?" LC muttered.

'*Don't*,' he tried to think but the words wouldn't form inside his head. He was trapped and mute. It felt like he was drowning.

He felt the power of the force aimed at LC build slowly, the kid starting to squirm as the pain increased.

'*Fight it, for Christ's sake, LC, fight it.*'

LC gasped, grinding his palm against his forehead.

NG could do nothing but watch. He was numb. He could see that LC was struggling, curling up, clasping both hands to his head, and he could feel himself maliciously increase the assault.

LC looked up, a trickle of blood dripping from his nose, eyes bloodshot. "NG," he gasped, desperately trying to block it and failing.

"I'm not your 'New Guy'," NG heard himself say, sneering. "Didn't you figure that out yet?"

NG felt cold and helpless, locked away. He couldn't access the Senson, couldn't so much as twitch a finger. He felt himself stand up slowly.

LC flinched away, scrambling to his feet, stumbling. "NG, don't."

"I have a name… " Cold and malevolent.

"Sebastian," LC whispered. He backed into the corner. "Where's NG?"

'I'm right here!' NG screamed.

He felt himself smile and take a step forward. If he touched LC, the kid was dead and there was nothing he could do to stop himself.

20

"Ah, I understand now why you wished to see me."

The way she was looking at him was not quite pity, not quite sympathy.

"Sebastian," she said. "In all you have told me so far, I almost saw this coming. Why did you not?"

"I should have."

"Did Luka survive?"

There was a coldness there too. As she had said already, he knew she had a great fondness for these creatures, especially the ones so talented, the young ones that had experienced such hardship before finding their way to the fold.

"From what we know of the virus now," he said, avoiding her question, "it seems to adapt to maximise the strengths of the host. Luka has always been sensitive – bold and reckless, yes – but always highly perceptive. And driven. Nikolai warned me that the child had the potential to be strong. Sebastian found out how strong."

NG felt the power of the attack increase, unrelenting, until LC cried out, doubling over and clutching his chest. He felt the power surge, sending the kid flying back against the bulkhead with a sickening crunch.

"Come on, fight me," he heard himself say in that mocking tone. "You think you're so powerful, prove it."

LC crumpled to the deck with a gasp.

He felt himself laugh, taunting, slowly squeezing closed the veins in LC's beating heart, shutting down the airways of his lungs one cell at a time.

The rush of power was overwhelming.

'NG, what the fuck are you doing?' the kid sent fiercely, bracing himself, flicking into survival mode and sending a shockwave of force back at him.

It hit like a physical punch.

NG felt the assault waver with the strength of LC's resistance. He took the chance to fight, trying to wrestle back control from the overwhelming darkness.

It turned its full attention to him then, derision eating at the core of his very being. *'You don't even exist, 'NG'. How can you possibly hope to confine me again?'*

'You're not real.'

'You're the one that isn't real, Nikolai.'

LC threw in an all out counterattack. NG felt his senses go spinning off in a dizzying whirl. He got control back suddenly, dropping to his knees as all his strength dissipated like fleeting mist, heart pounding as the full pain of LC's attack hit home full strength.

He took it for a second then threw up a barrier, feeling the mocking laughter recede deep down inside.

Whatever he'd sparked in the kid was unrelenting, the shared pain escalating and threatening to break through.

NG looked up, trying to disengage gently from the conflict, resisting an instinctive urge to fight back. "LC, Luka, it's me," he said.

LC didn't let up, eyes glaring, nerves still strung tight, pain still flaring. Eventually he decided it was safe and threw his mind into neutral, slumping back into the corner. "Who the fuck is Sebastian?" he muttered, voice ragged, wiping the blood from his face, a hand still hugged against his chest.

NG felt numb. He shut down all emotion and reached out a hand.

LC looked at him suspiciously before taking it, gearing himself to try to stand and failing.

"Don't move," NG said. It felt as if hours had passed. They were both exhausted. He could feel the agony pulsing through the kid's mind and body, the torn muscles, burst blood vessels, heart labouring, lungs threatening to shut down. He used the contact to send a flood of healing energy into the field operative he'd just almost killed, managing to repair some of the worst of the damage he'd caused.

LC looked up finally, eyes still hooded and shot through with red, biting back a comment, trying and struggling to control his breathing.

"Can you stand?"

LC nodded and accepted the help to get up. He swayed slightly as he got to his feet, a trickle of blood running from his ear. The virus in his body was running riot trying to fix the physical damage but he knew how close it had been and he was thinking, my boss is fucking insane.

He flushed as he realised that NG had heard it.

That dark entity deep inside laughed. '*It won't be so easy to stop me next time.*'

NG took a step back defensively. "Get out," he said to LC more harshly than he intended, for the kid's safety more than anything.

LC glared at him, bewildered, and started to back away, absently wiping away the blood trickling down his neck.

"Luka, get out," NG said again, voice trembling. "Go to your quarters and stay there."

He felt his senses start to spin again.

"Go!"

He heard the door slam.

'*You've blown it, Nikolai, face it. You're history.*'

No. He wasn't giving in to insanity that easily. He gripped the edge of the table, head down, keeping his breathing slow and steady.

'*The next time I get near Anderton, I will kill him before you even know I have control.*'

The door opened.

"Get out," NG snapped without looking.

'*I could kill Evelyn now…*'

Her hand reached to his shoulder and he spun, brushing her

away. She recoiled as he glared, hand up in warning. "Leave me alone," he yelled, anger overriding the fear of seeing her there.

"NG...?"

He backed away, crashing into the chair and turning to run straight into the Chief who had his hands up, expression dark. NG pushed him aside violently, stumbling into a run for the door.

He made it to the lift without killing anyone and sagged against the wall as the doors closed.

He'd almost killed LC. After everything that had happened, he'd almost killed the kid in the safety of his own office.

He punched his fist against the lift door until it opened onto the dark corridor that led onto the Man's ship, pushing through the gap and breaking into a run.

Two of the elite guards were up ahead, standing shoulder to shoulder to stop him.

Before he even reached them, he shoved them out of his way with an explosive burst of power, armour clattering as they slammed against the bulkhead, and ran on unhindered to burst into the Man's office, uninvited, unannounced and unwelcome.

He came to an abrupt stop, two steps into the dark chambers, chest heaving.

It was almost pitch black in there, four massive figures in full armour standing motionless in his way. The heat was stifling, way hotter than he was used to, and a trickle of sweat ran down his back as he struggled to stay his anger.

The Man's voice resonated through the darkness. "Let him through."

As they stepped aside, a tiny orange ember flared and danced into flame.

The Man was sitting at his desk.

NG blinked, head bowed, heart pounding, no idea what to say.

"Leave us," the Man said and the guards backed away, the door slamming shut after them.

NG swayed. He was breathing heavily, exhausted, as if he'd run the Straight three times in a row.

"Sit," the Man said.

NG walked forward slowly, not even sure now he was here what he was going to do.

"I must admit," the Man said, leaning forward to light another candle on his desk, "that I have been expecting this day for some time. I apologise, Nikolai. I should have anticipated that exposure to another telepath could precipitate this situation."

NG raised his eyes slowly and considered the man in front of him. It felt like he knew nothing, as if reality was unravelling around him.

The Man met his gaze with dark, glinting eyes. "You have questions?"

Damn right he did. "Who the hell is Sebastian?"

There was a long silence. Time meant nothing here in these chambers but right then it extended into an eternity.

The Man was an unmoving statue, fingers entwined and lips pursed. Eventually he nodded. "I found Sebastian when he was five years old and locked in a cage, treated no better than an animal. Humans frighten easily and become savages when threatened. He was a child and his talents were beyond the comprehension of those around him. Even caged, he could still reach out and he had no idea of the harm he could inflict."

NG stood, clenching his fists by his side, a dreadful queasiness pulling at his stomach. "I don't understand," he said. "Who the fucking hell is Sebastian?"

The heat was almost unbearable.

The Man ignored his confrontational tone. "Sebastian was a complex child and he learned quickly how to torment his tormentors. I only regret that I was too late to save him."

NG took a step forward, frustration spilling over, voice low and dark as he said, "That doesn't answer my question. I just almost killed LC."

"Sebastian almost killed him."

The frustration exploded into an anger he'd never directed at the Man. "What the hell does that mean?" he yelled. "It was me in that fucking office. I almost stopped his heart for Christ's sake."

"It was Sebastian," the Man said calmly, serenely.

NG hit the back of the chair in front of him. "I'm not Sebastian."

"No, you are not," the Man said, ignoring the violent outburst. "You are kind and empathic. You use your talents to help people. You are stronger than Sebastian in many ways and it is your strength of character, that determined selfless nature I created to harness your talent, that is the very basis of the future of all my plans."

Breathing was difficult suddenly. The words, 'I created', resounded around his mind, nonsensical, like a bizarre dream sequence. "What?"

"I created you," the Man said, an element of sadness in his tone that NG had never heard before. "I had to. I had no choice but to imprison Sebastian in his own body and give control to a new and distinct personality, you, Nikolai, so that you could utilise your potential to grow and develop."

"What are you saying? I'm not real?" It was a realisation that dawned with a sickening clarity. He stepped back, feeling Sebastian stir maliciously, vying for control amidst a despair to give up that was almost overwhelming.

"Nonsense," the Man said abruptly. "You are no more or less real than any other being. Sebastian could not survive in this turmoil of human society and he knows it. He toys with you now because he enjoys your discomfort and you do not realise the power you have. Really, Nikolai, do not disappoint me."

It was dizzying. And he realised suddenly that they'd been here before.

The Man nodded, weary, regretting that it had come to this.

NG felt the probe as a gentle pressure. "No," he shouted, backing away, instinctively throwing up a defensive shield, forcing the Man out of his mind with a violent deflection. "No! Stay out of my fucking head. And I swear, don't ever do that again."

"NG, sit down."

"No!" He was trembling. "Don't. Don't call me that." Thinking about it, the Man rarely used his name, preferring to use the stupid nickname the guild personnel had given him when he'd turned up as the new head of operations, when no one here knew him any more and he'd turned up out of nowhere – it fitted – all part of the game, the charade.

NG took another step away. "When?" he said aggressively, fighting the despair with anger. "When the fuck did you 'create' me? What am I? Five minutes old because you decided you didn't like the previous owner of this body? You just made me up? Is my whole life a lie? Is everything a lie? Jesus Christ."

The implications were too wrong, too twisted to be comprehended. He could feel the blood pounding through the veins in his head. "What about the fucking alien invasion? Is that all a lie as well?"

"Sit down," the Man said, gently, no coercion, inviting him to be sane and calm.

He shook his head, standing and holding onto the rage because that was all he had. It's a hell of a thing to be told you don't exist.

The Man lit another candle. "You do exist and you are more powerful than you know. Your life as you remember it is your own, Nikolai. Everything you have experienced is real. Very real. You want to know when I created you?" He took a deep breath. "When Sebastian was five. He was already beyond saving, yet his potential was too valuable to me to destroy him. Your potential is too valuable to me." He leaned forward and placed the queen from the chessboard in the centre of the desk.

NG stared at the Man, shadows dancing from the candlelight, anger tugging at every cell in his being. Nothing he'd ever known was real.

He wasn't real so what the hell was the point in anything?

He glared at the carved figure. All the noble sacrifices he'd had to make, every decision, every hard fought battle, they were all meaningless.

A chill settled deep in his chest.

"I quit," he said coldly and sent the queen flying off the desk, papers and artefacts scattering, every flame in the chamber extinguished, plunging the room into utter darkness.

For a heart beat the universe froze, then the Man's voice was a deep murmur in that black void. "If you leave here now, I will not be able to protect you from Sebastian."

He didn't care and he walked out without looking back.

21

"Nikolai was well within his rights to be angry. You have demanded a lot from him. Used him." She stopped short of reminding him that she had warned him before, many times on many occasions, of pushing the boy too hard.

The Man picked up his goblet.

"This is not the first time he has confronted you," she said. "Why so different now?"

He swirled it by the stem, watching the dark waves tumble and crash within. "Dealing with one instability is a mere distraction, two or three at the same time an inconvenience perhaps a frustration. Having so many at once, against an exponential increase in occurrences warranting our attention…? I have stopped him before because he was not ready. Because we had time. This time… I had no choice. After the encounter with Sebastian and Luka, he was stronger. Far stronger than I have ever seen him. The truth is that I could not stop him."

NG stood in his quarters, heart still pounding, daring Sebastian to try something.

There wasn't so much as a sneer.

'*What? Nothing? Was that the best you can do?*' he taunted. He threw a bag onto the bed. '*You want your body back? Take it.*'

Nothing.

He pulled a change of clothes out of his locker and stuffed them into the bag. He looked around. He didn't own much and he wanted to take nothing else from here.

None of it mattered.

He wandered into the office and knocked back a fast whisky.

He'd take Ghost, he decided. It was the fastest ship they had, no AI and no one would dare stop him. No one would miss him. The battle with the Order would go on to the end of time. That was the nature of mankind. Greed and paranoia, power and fear. That's all it boiled down to. The Man had created the Thieves' Guild to maintain balance within the disparate factions of humanity, to nurture and nudge the human race to get it ready to face a supposed alien attack? Well, they could do it without him.

He downed another whisky, rooting around in the desk drawers for a couple of sets of ID and some credit sticks, no idea where he was going to go, throwing out handfuls of accumulated crap he'd forgotten he'd been hoarding.

He stared at the desk, strewn as it was with junk that meant nothing anymore. He didn't want any of it, all the anger and frustration welling into an intense ball of fury that boiled over before he could contain it.

Everything flew off the desk in a flurry, boards and books, papers and reports, and a damned good bottle of whisky. He cursed and stood quickly, reaching out somehow and managing to stop the bottle in mid-air, concentrating to hold it there, everything else falling to the deck with a crash. He heard the knock on the door, heard it open, aware that Evelyn wasn't waiting before coming straight in, and he lost it.

The bottle fell and smashed into pieces.

Shit.

He looked up into Evie's eyes and froze.

She was trying to figure out what to say, finally saying softly, "NG, you need to come to Science."

Looking down from the observation balcony into the controlled environment of the lab, the package was simply a small silver box, wisps of dry ice spiralling lazily into the sealed atmosphere.

"Did you run the DNA," he asked coldly.

"NG,' Evelyn bit back the words that sprang to the tip of her tongue, thinking that she'd worked with the Assassins for eight years and they had never been thwarted in the completion of any contract she'd ever heard of. She was also thinking that she'd kill anyone who hurt him, or LC, or Hil. Or Devon. "We're running it now. The results should be back soon."

The finger that lay in the box had a tiny red ribbon tied in an immaculate bow around its knuckle joint, the manicured nail still perfect.

It was Devon's. He didn't need a closer look or any DNA results to confirm it.

"Where's the note?"

He followed Evelyn to a small office, ignoring the stares of Science personnel as they passed. He felt numb.

The sheet of parchment paper was suspended within a clear casing.

He didn't want to read it.

Science was a cold figure, standing there, arms folded, dour face softened somewhat. Devon wasn't always popular but she had no enemies on the Alsatia. Science drew in a sharp breath and said quietly, "We can't figure it out," not liking to admit they'd been beaten by a simple encoded message.

NG stared at it, taking in the obscure scratchings and inked lines, the elaborate ancient markings, heart sinking and a resolution taking shape deep inside.

He turned and walked out.

Evelyn watched as he threw more stuff into his bag, tossing in grenades and boxes of ammunition. She'd tried to protest, tried to stop him but knew better than to push it. Instead, she stood there in silence and tried to figure out a way to persuade him that she needed to go too.

"No one else is going to die because of me," he said, trying to decide between a thin stiletto and a hunting knife. He threw them both in.

"At least tell us what the note says," she said eventually, voice strained, her own emotions pushed to breaking point. "I've known Devon longer than you have. I know the Assassins, NG."

The confession was hard for her. He didn't make it any easier, saying coldly, "I know."

If she was surprised, she didn't show it. "Then you know what I can do. If this is the Assassins, if they're behind this, I know ways to get to them."

He looked up, cheated and took that knowledge freely from her mind at the same time as she was cheating and calling in Martinez, hurrying her up to get her ass in here before NG took off by himself again.

'How touching. They really care for you. It's a shame they will all die. Sooner or later, Nikolai, they – all – die.'

He threw another handgun into the bag and grabbed a hooded sweatshirt from the bunk. He was cold, the fury inside turning to an icy chill.

He turned round to face Evelyn.

She was torn between furious and scared. "They're doing this to get to you."

"Don't you think I know that?"

"NG, we're the Thieves' Guild," she whispered harshly. "What happened to 'no one messes with the Thieves' Guild'?"

"I don't care about the fucking guild, Evelyn. I quit."

She was shocked. "NG, don't."

"Too late. I'm going after Devon. Don't follow me and don't send anyone after me."

Brandon died quickly on a lonely hillside on some two bit planet in the Between. He was incapacitated before he realised NG was there and knew nothing worth the effort of keeping him alive. Ki was another matter.

Ki's ego was almost matched by his talent as an assassin. Almost. Except there was too much at stake and he blew it.

NG kneeled on the guy's chest, one hand squeezing his throat, rain pouring down on them. "Where is she?" he murmured.

Ki blinked rain out of his eyes, every muscle tensed.

Thunder rumbled overhead and lightning streaked across the black of the sky, flashing off the buildings that towered over them on every side. The alley was deserted, broken windows and scurrying rats the only sullen observers to the sorry end of one of the Assassins' best. An occasional arc of headlights passed at a distance, the city going about its late night business with no idea what was happening in its shadows.

Blood trickled down NG's forearm, mingling with the raindrops as it ran down onto his hand. They were both breathing heavily, both bruised and both cut.

'Let me kill him slowly.'

NG pushed his thumb down into the soft flesh of Ki's throat. "I think I can manage," he whispered to himself, out loud. He took the information he needed, and more, from the twisted memories of the assassin, increasing the pressure subtly and ignoring the twitching struggles as the guy began to realise there was no way out.

The Assassins' Guild and the Thieves' Guild had always had a special relationship, guarded, distant but respectful. No treading on toes. It was one he'd nurtured for a long time and it was over. Whatever had happened, whatever had prompted them to take the contract, there could be no turning back now.

He raked through Ki's mind and took secret codes and meeting place coordinates, codenames and arcane signals, as ancient as the hills on Earth from before time and sacred to the Assassins, half of it not even in the guy's conscious memory.

Ki was every bit the asshole Devon had described. He knew she'd been enticed back into the fold with a deception she couldn't refuse, an offer to renegotiate the contract out on NG. Ki had been part of it and he'd taunted her.

He didn't know where she'd been taken and he died in slow agony as the rain intensified and beat down around them in torrents.

Badger was waiting on the roof, standing on the edge of the parapet and watching the lights of the city below, drenched through, black hair plastered against his face, rain streaming down the black lenses of his glasses.

He didn't move as NG approached but said, "Did you get anything?"

NG stood next to him, staring out over the skyline. Forks of lightning streaked down to freeze frame the skyscrapers in sudden silhouette. "He didn't know where she is."

"Damn. What now? You want me to find Farro?"

Badger was good, the best deep cover agent the guild had ever had, even displaced from his usual haunt as he was. By the time NG had caught up with him, he'd already tracked down two of the assassins on the list and to ask so casually if NG wanted him to find Farro, the head of the Assassins' Guild, wasn't arrogance, it was business as usual regardless of the dramas unfolding in every direction.

NG shook his head. He knew exactly where Farro would be thanks to his foray into Ki's mind. And he could now read the note. He wasn't about to admit it to Badger or anyone, but he knew exactly where Farro had Devon and where he had been so cordially invited to go.

Badger scuffed the toe of his boot along the rim of the wet stonework. "I heard that Zang is trying to make amends with some of his old adversaries," he said softly.

I don't care anymore, NG thought desperately but he said, "If you get anything on Zang, get it to the Chief and make sure it filters through to Pen Halligan on Aston."

Pen was due his vengeance and would make sure the job was finished.

Badger nodded. "Ballack's making a lot of noise. There are rumours doing the rounds that he's setting himself up as some kind of peacemaker between Earth and Winter." Where we used to be, he was thinking.

"Concentrate on finding Zang," NG said, numb. Maybe once he was done with the Assassins, he'd go after the son of a bitch that had started all this.

Badger looked round. "Everyone's trying to find Zang. Trust me, you'll know if I even find out where his PA has been having lunch lately."

Security around the old planet was tighter than ever. Still no match for someone with all the contacts and resources from a lifetime with the Thieves' Guild.

NG stood in the shadows, hood up, head down, a bloodied knife in one hand and a silenced pistol in the other. He stood in silence, breathing in the cold damp air of the old city, mildew and moss creeping out of its stonework, corruption and intrigue seeping out of its pores. Old Earth decay at its finest.

The courtyard was lit sparsely by yellow lamps that cast pale light over the dark, grotesque statues that lined the winding pattern of stone pathways leading to its centre, twisted figurines with outstretched bony limbs of stone that seemed to reach and point.

On every side, the crooked building of the Assassin's headquarters loomed in darkness, nooks and crannies filled with leering gargoyles, eyes watching from every dark window and leaning roof edge.

The trail of bodies he'd left to get this far was an undisguised declaration of war. He hadn't been subtle.

Devon was kneeling, slumped, in the centre of a paved square, hands tied behind her back and a hood over her head. She was conscious but only barely, cold and fading. They'd pulled her out into the open as soon as he began his assault. They knew he was close but they didn't know he was inside their walls.

NG glanced to his left and right. There was a body at his feet, blood still pumping from its throat. Three other figures were standing behind ornate columns around the rest of the covered walkway that edged the building, oblivious to his presence, weapons in hands, watching their former compatriot and the trap they'd set.

He walked, in perfect calm silence, to the first and slit her throat before she could react. He dropped her to the floor and moved forwards, a single silenced shot to the head taking out the next before he could give any alarm. The third assassin was turning, raising his gun. It took no effort, even at this distance, to throw him backwards, the man dying as synapses tore in overload, the sheer force of the mental attack hitting the soft tissue of the assassin's brain.

'Nice.'

NG didn't miss a step, turning and walking along the path out into the open towards Devon. He sheathed the knife as he walked steadily and pulled out another gun, one in each hand, firing at the lamps and plunging the courtyard into a deepening darkness as each shot extinguished a pale arc of light. He didn't stop for a second, glancing around as he walked, five more watching assassins dying at their posts, brains fried, hearts stopped dead.

'You're almost beginning to impress me,' Sebastian whispered, revelling in the death surrounding them.

It meant nothing.

NG walked up to Devon and knelt, weapons rising all around, mouths opening to shout, fingers tightening on triggers, as he hugged her shoulders and drew her close.

He took her to a forest and sat with her on a fallen tree, shafts of sunlight spearing through the canopy of green, warmth on their faces and the scent of fresh leaves in the air.

Devon turned to him, reaching a hand to touch his cheek, a light in her eyes that made his breath catch in his chest.

She smiled, a curious look of confusion crossing her face as if she was trying to remember something. She blinked slowly and reached out her other hand, studying it, turning and stretching every one of her perfect fingers.

"This isn't real," she said softly.

"Nothing's real."

She smiled sadly. "You can't save me, Nikolai. I'm dying. Why are you here?"

"I..." And he couldn't say it. He felt bereft. He couldn't heal her enough as much as he tried.

"I thought I could speak to Farro," she said quietly.

He'd never heard her sound so defeated and it hurt more than he'd ever thought was possible.

"I thought I could reason with him." She laughed and it wasn't harsh or bitter. Her eyes were sparkling in the sunlight, glints of silver and gold in her hair. "We used to have a code. No longer it seems."

She smiled again, softly brushing his face with her hand. She thought she was dreaming, hallucinating, and that hurt even more.

Her gaze suddenly shifted to a spot behind him and she frowned slightly, curious again.

"I hate to break this up," he heard Sebastian say, "but we don't have time for this."

The breeze suddenly had a cold edge. NG turned his head, following Devon's look as Sebastian walked up to them. He could feel Sebastian trying to take control and found it surprisingly easy to stop him.

"I don't understand," Devon said softly.

Sebastian was the spitting image of him with the only exception being his eyes, a startling shade of bright blue.

"I'm not going to let you get me killed, Nikolai," Sebastian said.

Devon turned back to NG. "You have a twin?" thinking it was bizarre, wondering why the hell NG's brother would turn up in her hallucination.

Sebastian wasn't impressed. "I'm not his twin," he said, sounding disgusted at the thought, "and I'm not going to stand aside while you get me killed."

"I don't understand," Devon said again, frowning.

"There are at least twenty assassins descending on this courtyard, sweetheart, and I, for one, don't believe in noble sacrifices."

"You're not here," she said.

"Unfortunately, we are," Sebastian sneered, "and we're not alone. What the hell are you doing, Nikolai?"

Devon stared back at NG, shaking her head, starting to comprehend. "What are you doing?"

"He's giving up," Sebastian said with disdain. "And there's a goddamned assassin pointing at gun at his head, at my head. Fifty feet away and moving in."

"I came to save you," NG whispered.

She moved her hand to take hold of his. "Nik, it wasn't the Merchants' Guild that hired the Assassins."

"I don't care."

"You need to care. Listen to me. It wasn't Ballack. And the Order wants you alive. Zang has no reason to take you out of the picture. You need to think who else is in play here. Think. Why would someone want you dead?"

She was dying and all she could think about was him.

She moved closer, the sunlight catching sparkles in her eyes. "The biometrics they have on you came from inside the guild."

"I don't care."

She squeezed his hand. "I came here to save you," she said calmly. "Don't let that be in vain."

NG was desperately trying to temper down the desperation eating at his heart. "Devon, I'm not even real," and he opened his mind, sharing with her everything the Man had said, everything Sebastian had taunted him with, the Order, the alien threat, the underlying truth behind the guild and the fact that he didn't exist except as a creation of the Man's twisted manipulations.

Whatever was going on in the real world, time here was different. He had control over it. The sunshine was bright and warm and he wanted to be with her forever.

"Thirty feet and closing," Sebastian said.

Devon leaned in and kissed NG softly, nothing like the way she used to, that rough veneer of cold indifference gone. "You are the most incredible person I've ever met, NG," she whispered, staring into his eyes. "You are more real than anyone I know. And I care for you more than I've ever been able to dare admit."

He opened his mouth to argue and she stopped him with a finger to his lips. "I love you," she murmured.

"Twenty feet."

NG wrapped his arms around her, holding tight and burying his head into her shoulder.

"You are real and you have to finish this, Nikolai," Devon whispered into his ear and he felt her slipping away. "For me."

Reality snapped back with a chill. Devon was gone and he lay her gently down on to the cold stones, holding his hand on the back of her neck for a long moment before moving.

'Ten feet.'

NG stood in a fluid motion and turned, both guns firing. He dived off to the side and rolled, lurching up into a run, jumping over the low ornate walls, and heading for the double doors that led to Farro. The anger burning inside was cold and it was his, not Sebastian's.

He shoulder charged the door and ran inside, firing the guns until the magazines ran dry then he stood in the centre of the dark wide corridor, turning slowly, head bowed as he calmly slammed in fresh magazines, eyes glinting and glaring around with enough force behind them to send bodies flying in all directions.

He walked to the wooden staircase, deflecting thrown knives, darts and bullets with ease, feeling the assault increase as he approached the heart of their stronghold, leaving a trail of bodies in his wake. The long corridor was lined with drapes and tapestries, centuries old. He paused at the door to Farro's den and turned, dropping one of the guns and raising his hand, palm up. It took nothing to manipulate the energy that was burning inside him to spark the intense heat of a flame that he flicked into the drapes. They were engulfed in seconds.

He turned, flames roaring into life behind him, and pushed open the door to aim his sights between the eyes of the leader of the Assassins, leader of the guild he'd just annihilated.

22

She was shocked. "The repercussions of this are vast."

"He made it personal. That was a mistake."

"How could he have reacted otherwise? You said, he takes care of his own. Did you know she was in danger?"

"No," he lied. He took a drink. He had known and he had underestimated Nikolai.

She couldn't read his mind but she looked straight through him, doubt in her mind. She considered questioning his reply but thought better of it and said instead, "The Order must be laughing in their gilded towers. The Assassins' Guild and the Thieves' Guild at war, and it doesn't cost them a penny. Do you know who put up the five hundred million?"

He lowered the goblet. "No." Honest answer that time. Someone had put this price on the head of his most favoured charge, and none of his investigations had yielded so much as a lead, none, and he had thrown significant resources at it, valuable resources from outside the guild. "Whoever it was," he said, "has been very careful to conceal their identity. In all this, it is that contract that has caused the most instability."

He woke in a cold sweat, disorientated and shaking. Soft sunlight was sneaking through a gap in shutters that took him a moment to recognise but when he did, his heart rate settled and he relaxed back onto the crisp pillows.

Arturo had welcomed him with open arms and no questions. It felt like he'd been running through a nightmare forever and to wake in the midst of a warm, safe fortress was a relief that he knew was a lie.

Everything hurt. He was tired, more than tired, he was drained, and it was a while before he became aware of the presence in the room, a quiet, strong aura sitting patiently off to the side.

NG turned his head slowly, neck muscles complaining even at that slight movement.

The Chief didn't stir. His face simply twitched into a half smile and he said softly, "Hey," satisfied now that NG had finally come round. "No one messes with the Thieves' Guild, right?"

It was a mantra he'd instilled in everyone and hearing it then was strangely comforting.

NG lay there quietly, drifting back under, thinking nothing, letting every muscle in his whole body relax. He'd lost people before, many times. But he'd never lost himself.

It was dark when he woke again. The Chief was still there, a quiet giant sitting vigil over him. It didn't feel like he deserved such dedicated attention.

NG stared at the ceiling.

He was sore, stiff muscles protesting, cuts and abrasions stinging. He couldn't recall picking up the deep gash on his forearm or the nicks across his knuckles. He did remember the slashing pain that had sliced across his throat as they'd piled in trying to overpower him.

They'd all died.

Sebastian laughed. '*Do you know how much I enjoy watching you get hurt? You think you're feeling miserable now that you know the 'truth'? The truth is you've always had a masochistic streak in you, Nikolai. You've always been more than prepared to place my body in harm's way to satisfy this bizarre need you have to play the hero, for people you don't even care about. That's the lie, 'NG'. Right there. Face it. You don't give a shit for any of these people. They're ants scurrying around our feet, living and dying as we watch, generation after generation. We're the next evolutionary leap and these scum will be like marauding peasants on a witch hunt if they even start to suspect how different we are. You should be racing to find Zang to ally with him, not fight him, you fool. Now haul your ass out of bed and find out what's so urgent that your beloved section Chief has been twitching to wake you up for the past five hours. Unless you want me to handle it…'*

He laughed again.

NG didn't move. *'You're awake when I'm asleep?'*

'For every minute of the past hundred and nineteen years. And yes, it is excruciatingly tedious.'

'Why have you never told me before?'

'About me? You think I haven't? The Man always erased your memory. It got to be a boring game.'

It felt like his whole life had been a game. NG closed his eyes. He could sense the calm, strong presence that was the Chief but trying to get anything else from the mind of the big man sitting there right next to him made him feel like he was wading through treacle. It wasn't that there was a barrier in place, simply that the effort was too much.

'You're pathetic.'

It felt pathetic.

'He's dying to tell you that Pen Halligan is dead.'

'You're lying.'

Sebastian laughed. *'Ask him.'*

He wasn't sure he could ask anyone anything. He raised a hand to his neck, feeling the thick bandage there, swallowing painful, healing slow.

'Go ahead,' Sebastian jeered. *'Ask him how he found out that Mendhel's daughter shot her own dear uncle in the head.'*

NG rolled onto his side and stared at the Chief, heart hammering in his chest. He couldn't read anything from the guy.

The Chief said again quietly, "Hey."

NG blinked slowly. "What happened to Pen?" he said in little more than a whisper.

If the Chief was surprised, he didn't show it. "Pen's dead, NG. We have no idea where Anya went but she's with Zang, wherever that bastard crawled back to. Quinn wants to take a squad from Security and go after them but… when we heard about all this…"

He trailed off and it was easy enough to see it was hard for him to continue. The Chief had always worked closely with Devon, both of them clashing regularly, but he would never have wished her harm. "We all wanted to know that you were okay before we decided what to do."

There was something else that he wasn't saying.

Sebastian sneered. *'There's a lot else that he isn't saying. I thought you didn't care. You quit.'*

It wasn't that easy. NG levered himself up onto one elbow. "I'm fine," he lied.

The Chief nodded and stood. Guard duty over. "We're here if you need anything," he said and walked to the door, looking back with a half smile. "I'll get you a coffee."

NG wandered into the bathroom in a daze and stood under the hot water, stripping off the bandages and dropping as deep into concentration to heal as he could manage. It was hard to focus, energy reserves too low to make much difference. He gave up after a while, got cleaned up and sat on the edge of the bed, a thick white cotton towel wrapped around his waist.

'This is not over,' Sebastian whispered.

It was far from over.

He felt numb, heart pounding in a dull rhythm. He wound a fresh bandage around his arm. He desperately needed to talk to someone about something and he couldn't pin his finger on who or what, until he realised with a pang that it was Devon and he'd never be able to.

'You want to give up? Give me my body back. I'll deal with these bastards.'

NG shook his head.

He stood and walked to the dresser. His clothes had been cleaned, all traces of the smoke and blood gone, the black garb stacked in a neat pile. He absently picked up one of the guns lying there. It had been cleaned beautifully. He clicked out the magazine, noted vaguely that it was full and pushed it back into place. His knives were lying in a neat row.

He could remember every move, every kill. It had been him not Sebastian.

He dressed slowly. He had no idea what to do but he wasn't about to give up. Devon had told him to finish it. "This is my fight," he said softly and strapped on the weapons.

There were two guards outside his door, more down the hallway and double the usual on patrol around Arturo's mountainside home. More than half were from the Alsatia's specialist assault unit. He could just about sense them even though the awareness felt dull and muted.

The old man was sitting out on the terrace in the warm evening air, tiny lights sparkling throughout the rich green undergrowth, more guards a discrete distance away. He looked up and waved a welcome as NG approached.

NG sat down and accepted a glass of hot tea. He glanced around at the guards and looked back at Arturo. "I shouldn't have come here."

"Nonsense, my boy. Where else could you have gone? You've caused quite a stir."

He took a sip of the tea. It was laced with apple brandy and burned his throat on its way down. "How long have I been out?"

Arturo smiled. "Six days. You won't believe some of the rumours we're hearing."

He placed the glass on the table and stared at it, avoiding the old man's eyes. He didn't want to know.

"Is it true you cut out Farro's heart and left it on a spike at the gatepost?"

The old man wasn't teasing him.

Christ.

NG rubbed a hand across his eye and looked up. "I didn't," he said.

Sebastian laughed.

"There are rumours that the Thieves' Guild paid millions to hire a unit of handpicked mercenaries to do its dirty work in the middle of the night," Arturo said softly. "People are also saying in some quarters that you sent a daemon to attack them, an immortal that was immune to all weapons. I take it you were alone?"

"They killed Devon."

"I know," Arturo said sadly and reached to pat his hand. "I liked her."

They sat in silence for a while watching the moon rise over the mountaintops then Arturo waved over to his housekeeper for more tea. "The contract on you still stands," he said as the girl poured from a jug of blue glass. She had a submachine gun slung over her shoulder. "They've sworn to have your head," Arturo said. "I heard that some are saying they won't even take payment now. You've embarrassed them. They want you dead."

"They gave me directions and invited me in," NG said bitterly.

"I'm sure Farro meant for you to spring their trap and die, not turn around and destroy him. He underestimated you, my friend. Do not return the compliment by underestimating them. The few that are left of Farro's inner circle are calling in some hefty favours from influential people. Don't you wonder who put that much money on your head?"

"I don't care."

"You care when they kill those closest to you." Arturo leaned forward. "I'm sorry, my friend. I worry when I see our guild in such troubles. You must take care. It is not only the Assassins…"

NG looked up.

"There are some within the Imperial forces that question their tolerance towards us. Don't rely on Jameson. His position is precarious after recent events. And I understand Ostraban is petitioning the guild to have you arraigned. We are caught between Earth and Winter and the friction is increasing. All this talk of war…"

NG toyed with his glass, feeling the heat dissipate. "Where's the Chief?" he asked after a while, vaguely sensing that the big guy was in the house somewhere.

"Taking care of business," Arturo said, nodding in that direction, and adding, "We're safe now," thinking that it had been touch and go for a while.

He sipped at the tea and sat back, the brandy beginning to warm the edges of that numb emptiness and clear some of the fog from his mind.

As he watched, two of the lights separated from the bustle of the city and began to bounce their way up the mountainside, disappearing and reappearing at intervals, stopping at the checkpoints then moving on up.

He glanced at Arturo.

The old man smiled fondly. "Your girls," he said. "They've been waiting for you to wake. They were sending us to distraction with their pacing and worrying. I sent them shopping."

'*Your girls*?' Sebastian laughed. '*One of the galaxy's most deadly assassins and a hard-ass mercenary bitch… and he sends them shopping*?'

NG frowned.

Arturo chuckled. "The Alsatia is in orbit. You didn't think the guild would let you go that easily, did you?" He poured more tea, sitting back, content to let a comfortable silence settle between them. He was a good man. He knew his time here in this haven was nearing its end but he was totally satisfied with his lot in life. It was hard not to envy him his peace.

NG looked out over the forest. He couldn't help scanning half-heartedly for his errant staff, too worn out to pick them out of the background buzz that was still fluttering around his mind. The lights stopped half way up the mountainside and he could imagine Evelyn and Martinez climbing the steep steps to the fortress.

"How much do they know?" he asked quietly.

The old man smiled wryly. "The Assassins have not been subtle in their outcry." He looked up as if sensing a change in the air. "I fear we are in for a storm." He had a look of sadness in his eyes. "There are a lot of people who are worried about you, Nikolai. A lot of people who care for you."

"I know," he said. He'd let people get close. That was his mistake. In all this, that was his biggest mistake.

Arturo leaned forward. "What are you going to do now?"

He wanted to run away. "I was thinking revenge on Zang," he said flippantly.

"I was thinking more of you."

NG felt his breath catch. He looked at his old acquaintance, realising with a pang that the old man knew more about him than just his real name.

"I've known you for a long time," the old man said, solemnly. "Since I was a small boy. And in all that time, you haven't changed."

NG stared into the steaming concoction of sweet tea and brandy.

Arturo was one of only a select few people who'd known him for longer than a couple of decades. It was something the Man had been very careful in orchestrating his whole life. Arturo had never mentioned it before. They'd never talked about it, the paradox an unspoken secret between them.

"You look, what?" Arturo said gently. "Thirty, thirty five? I've known you since I was an eleven year old boy." He reached out a hand and touched NG's arm. "Look at me. I'm an old man and in all that time, you haven't changed. What's changed now, my friend?"

NG took a deep breath, calm and controlled.

Sebastian was quiet, but an awkward unease settled across his chest like a weight.

He looked up at Arturo. "Everything's changed," he said quietly. He cradled the glass, breathing in the steam and looking out over the valley. The lights of the city below winked and glowed. In all the galaxy, this was his favourite bolt-hole. And it felt like its days were numbered.

"It was once said," Arturo said, "that courage is not the absence of fear, but the triumph over it." His gaze was piercing. "Don't give in to doubt."

It was a warm and compassionate warning but it felt like the old man had torn down the façade and exposed his soul. NG felt hollow. His hand started to shake. He put the glass down carefully, fighting the urge to throw it to the floor. He could almost hear it smashing, see the shards splintering in slow motion in every direction, as he felt so close to falling apart himself. He had a million questions and no one he could ask.

"Whatever has brought you to this, you need to bring it to an end," Arturo said, resting a hand on his arm. "Exorcise your daemons and then come back to us. The guild needs you."

'*We don't need anyone and the Man lied to you*,' Sebastian whispered maliciously.

'*Did he lie to me about everything? Are the damned aliens even real?*'

Maybe William Gallagher was the key. Gallagher claimed to have been shot down by aliens in the Erica system. The Man had tagged the intel as high priority so maybe there was something to it.

'*It's make-believe. The old fool was insane.*'

He wasn't so sure. Maybe that's what he needed to do. Nothing would bring back Devon and nothing could ever make the guild feel like home again. It felt like he was clutching at straws but he had nothing else. Maybe he did need to prove to himself that it hadn't all been a lie.

He looked up. "Do you know if the Alsatia has the freighter LC ended up on? We sent people out to bring it in."

"From Tortuga?" Arturo shook his head. "None of our negotiators have had any luck even finding that freighter." Guild negotiators never failed in any assignment. No arrogance in that, it was a simple fact. "What's so special about it?"

"Loose ends," he said vaguely. "But that's what I need to do. I have to find that freighter. It's all I've got."

Arturo leaned forward. "Then that is what you must do. Whatever it takes, Nikolai. Do whatever it takes and come home to us." He stood, gently clasping a hand to NG's shoulder. "I'll send the Chief out," he said, waved over for a fresh jug of tea and left, heading into the house, cane tapping on the stone flags of the path.

NG sat quietly, watching the steam rise from his glass. He pulled out his gun and thumbed a round from the magazine. He balanced it upright on the table and stared at it. It fell over. That was the best he could do. Nothing as sophisticated as the slick movement the Man had demonstrated with the chess pieces. And nothing like he'd done on the Man's ship before he'd quit. Nothing like the power he'd thrown out at the Assassins.

'Use your anger,' Sebastian murmured. *'That seemed to work.'*

He didn't feel angry, he felt numb.

He holstered the gun, put the round into a pocket and stared at the table. He felt the Chief emerge from the house just as he sensed Evelyn and Martinez walk into the grounds. The three of them were directed by the guards to the terrace, picking up their pace as they walked along the winding overgrown path. They turned a corner and saw him there, a rush of overwhelming emotion emanating from Evelyn. NG stood.

'It's all so touching,' Sebastian mocked.

She hesitated, staring, relief at seeing him in one piece overshadowed by her grief and a barely contained anger.

She paused then gathered herself. She walked up to meet him, standing stiffly, awkwardly, turmoil flashing behind her eyes. He thought she was going to report but she suddenly stepped forward, in close.

He reacted without thinking, tensing, a defensive blast of energy flaring through the fog that was overriding his mind. He felt the Chief and Martinez twitch, hands instinctively reaching for guns.

Evelyn flung her arms around him.

He caught the intention in time, nothing but an intense need to hold him tight, and stopped himself, shaking as the energy he'd been about to throw at her dissipated. Christ. He could have killed her.

'You should have killed her.'

NG forced himself to relax. He put his arms around her and gestured Martinez and the Chief to stand down. Evie was trembling, the desperate embrace the most physical contact they'd ever had. He squeezed almost violently and whispered in her ear, "Don't – ever – do that again."

She froze. Misunderstanding. Realising how inappropriate it was and flushing. No idea how close to danger she'd come. She tried to pull away but he didn't let her, holding her tightly, a hand on the back of her neck, calming her as much as he could manage.

The trembling started to ease, replaced with a deep down unbearable ache of loss. Devon hadn't just been her mentor, she'd been her confidante and her friend and the sudden loss had broken down the professional veneer that Evelyn was always so careful to maintain. It was too much to deal with and wasn't somewhere he was prepared to go. He tempered the emotion, taking out the heat and felt her respond, bottling it back up, fiercely fixing her resolve.

He whispered in her ear, "We deal with it and we move on. They paid, heavily. It's done. Okay?"

She tensed then nodded and he let her go.

They sat, emotions once again wrapped up and buried deep, and watched as Martinez poured tea.

They'd all heard the rumours, taken in the bandage on his arm, the bruises, the angry red line across his throat, and they were avoiding looking directly at him.

"Are you coming back?" Evelyn said quietly, almost confrontational, almost daring him to say no.

"No," he said.

The three of them swapped glances, awkward. Martinez dropped her gaze to the table, scratching a chewed fingernail along the grain of the wood.

NG stared at Evelyn, reading the helpless frustration, not wanting to even attempt to go any deeper. "What's happened?"

"Micah Sorensen's dead," she said. "NG, we need you to come back."

23

"I heard reports that the Alsatia was headed to Earth. Was that not a risk?"

He was sharp in his reply. "Nikolai put Arturo in danger. That was not acceptable."

The fire was getting low again.

"I'm sure it was not intentional."

"Nevertheless, his reckless actions endangered one of my most valuable assets. Having the full force of the guild to hand was the only way to ensure the situation was completely under control."

"And Nikolai? You sent them to make sure Nikolai was safe?"

The Man ignored her again, leaning to reach for another log, choosing two and carefully resting them in the centre of the hearth.

She regarded him, the orange of the fire flickering in her eyes. "He has had a lot thrown at him. It's a good thing he has good people around him."

Evelyn was staring at him, thinking, we're missing Devon and we're missing you, don't do this to me, NG.

"What happened?" he said again.

"The trial," the Chief said. "The drug, the virus, whatever it is that LC brought back. Sorensen didn't make it. Catastrophic organ failure. Medical are still trying to figure out why."

Sebastian laughed maliciously. '*Oh, that is precious. The Man's little experiment goes horribly wrong.*'

It was a new twist. Zang might get hold of his life-prolonging wonder elixir and die after all.

NG glanced at Martinez, who was sitting calmly now she had her charge back within reach.

"What about Essien and Hilyer?" he said, needing someone to say it out loud.

The Chief shook his head.

"For Christ's sake, just tell me."

"We don't know yet. Lulu spent two days in agony then dropped into a coma. It doesn't look good."

NG narrowed his eyes. "So what happened to Hil?"

It was easy to feel the big man tempering a deep anger that he'd lost his top four field-ops in this disaster. He wanted to throw that at NG, to shout and rage, but he was holding it in check because of what had happened to Devon and because, he was thinking, NG looked pretty messed up himself.

"Nothing," he said. "No effect. Medical are still running tests. He's not a hundred percent yet from that gunshot wound but the virus seems to have done nothing."

"What about LC?"

"He's been in Medical."

Since whatever the hell happened in your office, Evelyn was thinking. She was glowering at him like it was all his fault.

NG avoided looking at her. "Is he okay?"

Sebastian was laughing again.

The Chief just nodded slowly, trying to figure out what to report to NG. They were all in the dark over that; LC couldn't have said anything to anyone about what had happened in his office.

"He refused treatment," the Chief said eventually. "They've kept him in for observation. We reckon the more data we have…" He tailed off again then leaned forward and said bluntly, "NG, we all want to go after Zang. Come with us. We need you."

NG reached for his cup. "There's something else I need to do."

Evelyn said, "What?" without thinking, abruptly, curtly, and got incredulous looks from the other two – that was no way to speak to your boss, never mind NG, even if he had quit.

He drained the tea.

"Go back to the Alsatia," he said and stood.

As he turned to go, Evelyn sprang up and blocked his way.

"No, wait," she said, still frowning. "NG, what are you going to do?"

He narrowed his eyes and said slowly, "It doesn't matter. Go back to the guild."

She shook her head. "No, not without you."

'Ah, dissension in the ranks. She dares to question your actions. I told you you'd lost it.'

NG moved to step past her but she grabbed his arm, letting go just as quickly as he glared at her.

She backed off but placed herself firmly in his way. "NG, we're the Thieves' Guild. No one messes with us – you told me that. You have the whole guild at your fingertips. Whatever you're doing, you don't have to do it alone."

"Evelyn," he said calmly despite the tension building inside, "go back to the Alsatia and do your job."

Her eyes flashed with fury. "No! Don't leave me out of this, NG. They killed Devon. If you're going after them, I want in."

'Feisty but out of order for a PA, don't you think?'

It was hard to ignore Sebastian when those insidious whispers were exactly what he was thinking himself. He could feel the blood pounding through his chest, every heartbeat thumping against his ribs.

"The Assassins killed Devon," he said harshly. "I dealt with them. Now there's something else I need to do."

He pushed past her.

"NG, this is not just about you," she said.

He turned, close up, and said quietly, "It's not about me at all. None of this is. It's not about me, or the guild, or LC, or Hil or any of us. Go back to the Alsatia, Evelyn."

She shook her head. "You can't order me to do anything. You're not my boss any more. You quit, remember?"

She wanted to protect him but she could have stuck a knife into his chest and it would have hurt less.

"Go back," he said. "I won't have what happened to Devon happen to you, Evie. Go back."

He touched her arm and gave her no choice. She looked at

him, dismayed and trying to work up an argument but eventually she nodded. He watched her walk away, fists clenching and unclenching as she tried to work off her anger, at him, at Devon, at Farro who had always been a bastard to work for. She was trying to backtrack in her mind, figure out what she should have done, when, that would have meant that Devon would still be alive, trying not to care if NG went off and got himself killed. But she did. The guild was done. Without NG it was nothing and she didn't want to go back.

It wasn't true and he shut it out, turning back to the table, desperately needing a drink. Martinez was standing behind him, her dark eyes alight with a burning desire for him to try it on with her too.

"Angel," he said, warning.

She cut him off, voice quiet and intense. "NG, don't even go there. Shit happens, right? Well, I'm about sick of shit happening to the people I care about and I care about you, whether you like it or not. I'm coming with you. Wherever you need to go and whatever you need to do."

She folded her arms defiantly.

NG considered her carefully. She stared back, thinking that he was being reckless again, thinking it had been too close, too much to have taken on the Assassins by himself and too dangerous to go anywhere alone, especially now.

"I can't do what I have to do with an army at my back," he said.

"So we go in light," Martinez said. "But I'm coming with you." Her stare dropped to the red line that was all that was left of the Assassins' attempt to cut his throat. "It's my job to take care of that neck of yours."

"I don't need help," NG said, knowing he was being a shit but saying it anyway. "From anyone. Angel, go back to the Alsatia."

She shook her head slowly, balancing her weight carefully.

The Chief was watching them both, unmoving. He didn't believe that NG had quit. Not seriously. His mind wasn't wide open exactly but NG could just about read him. He just wanted NG to go back with them, business as usual.

NG turned to stare at the big man. "Not going to happen," he said.

The Chief frowned.

"I'm asking you," NG said, struggling to keep his tone diplomatic with them both, "to take Evelyn back to the Alsatia. Keep her alive. If I don't come back, she'll be the closest thing to a head of operations you'll have. Your first priority is to keep her alive."

The Chief wasn't happy. "Where are you going?"

NG turned away.

Martinez stepped in front of him. "You don't want me," she said, "you're going to have to shoot me to stop me coming with you."

'That would be one way to get rid of her.'

"You'll be in my way," he said coldly.

"NG, you don't have any say in this," she said, just as cold, "you're not the one that hired me."

She left that hanging. The Man had sent her after him.

He scowled and brushed past her, using that opportunity as his arm touched her arm to make contact. Not fair but he always got his way. It was just for a brief moment but that was all it took for him to hit up against a barrier that almost sent him reeling.

Martinez wasn't even aware that he'd tried anything.

Sebastian laughed viciously from deep within. *'Oh, it gets better. You didn't think yours was the only mind the Man screwed around with, did you?'*

He didn't stop. Neither of them objected or followed. He felt like a petulant child.

Two of Arturo's men dropped into step beside him, escorting him back to his room, shutting the door and standing guard. And it suddenly felt like that was more to keep him confined than to keep intruders at bay.

He'd never felt so trapped and so alone.

It was ridiculously early when he was summoned to the courtyard. He shook off the nightmares and painful yearning to be with

Devon, to feel the touch of her warm skin against his, to see again that glint of affection in those amazing eyes, and he dressed slowly, feeling a pulling ache in every muscle and joint.

Arturo stood as he was escorted out, and gestured him to sit.

No smile.

No tea.

The old man looked tired, as if he hadn't slept. He slid a data board across the black and white tiled table. "This came for you last night."

NG took it, moving on automatic. It was encrypted, the message clear as soon as he unscrambled his head to read it. Zang was rallying support, Winterside, gathering the corporations and gearing up their militia forces to clear out the rogue mining colonies and pirate bases in the Between. He must have heard the rumours about LC being out there. And half the galaxy's bounty hunters descending on Tortuga would have lit up his radar like a meteor shower. Zang might have vanished but he obviously hadn't given up the chase.

NG took a deep breath and looked up. "United Metals?"

"All of them. Who would have thought it – Angmar Rodan backing Zang Tsu Po. That bastard Ostraban must be beyond himself."

"I have to find Gallagher and his ship," he said, feeling cold.

"If that's what you need to do, then you must get there before Zang. And none of this nonsense about going alone. Take Luka."

It wasn't a direct order. Arturo wasn't in a position to give him orders.

'You quit. Why do you seem so insistent on forgetting that? No one can order you to do anything.'

It was merely a suggestion but it was one that made too much sense to argue against.

Arturo put his hand on the board. "Use him."

To smoke out Gallagher and blaze a trail that Zang couldn't fail to follow like a shark after blood.

It was ruthless in the way the Man could be ruthless.

Arturo leaned forward. "Use the guild, Nikolai. You have given enough. Now let us help you. Take Angel. We want to help you. She needs to help you. Let her."

It wasn't easy to hear.

"And take a squad of assault troops with you. The Assassins have broadcast an open bounty on you. They've declared that they will match the half a billion to anyone who delivers up your head, my boy. Don't go anywhere alone. Trust no one. And watch your back. Now more than ever."

NG stared at Arturo. If the parcel of biometrics on him had originated from the guild, it could have come from right here. He couldn't tell. The old man's mind was cloudy, almost shielded.

Sebastian laughed. *'You're just burned out, Nikolai. His mind and his intentions are as clear as day. This old fool is right when he says trust no one. No – one. Why are you having such trouble understanding that concept?'*

"No one messes with the Thieves' Guild?" Arturo said, a faint smile creasing his face finally. "No one gets to quit either. Ever. You, more than anyone, should know that. This is your fight, Nikolai, and it is only beginning."

24

She took another sip. She wasn't drinking heavily. She never did. "The freighter? He decided to go after the freighter?" she said. "I must ask, what was it that so piqued your curiosity about that ship and its captain?"

"Elliott," the Man said. "More than just the name. There is far more to him than Luka or Nikolai encountered."

"Now, I'm curious."

"He is one of the Seven."

Another surprise for her. "You're sure?"

"Sure enough," he said. "The signs are there. We thought him dead. We should be grateful that he isn't. That he is in the centre of this drama does not surprise me. He has assisted our people greatly in all this and I am sure we will need him even more when the time comes."

"Assuming he chooses our side over theirs."

It was strange to walk back onto the Alsatia. The atmosphere was muted, constrained, taut as a wire and quiet.

No one looked him in the eye as he walked between the Chief and Evelyn, Martinez a step ahead and two of the Watch close behind. It felt like he was under arrest. And for the first time, he didn't try to put on an act, didn't bother to draw energy from anywhere to perk up and play the charade.

They took him straight to the hospitality suite, showed him inside and shut the door behind him without following. Even Martinez stayed outside. It was as secure as they could get him on board the cruiser and from the look of it, total black out conditions.

LC was already sitting at the table, looking strung out and emanating an undisguised hostility, uncharacteristic but not surprising. He was tumbling a lockpick through his fingers. He spoke without looking up. "If Hil says he's fine and he wants to go on this tab, he isn't and don't let him. You want me to go, I will, but don't let anyone else get suckered in. This sucks enough as it is."

No wonder Mendhel had always been exhausted.

LC stopped spinning the tiny device and looked across. "I miss him."

They all did. And the pang that hit NG in the chest at the thought of Devon was like a shard of stabbing ice.

LC frowned, picking up on the emotion but not wanting to read anything, not wanting to go anywhere near NG's mind at risk of encountering Sebastian again.

Sebastian laughed. '*The child is right to be afraid. I'm not going to play so nice next time. And you should be figuring out how you can escape from here, not sitting placidly while any one of these people could be planning to stick a knife in your back.*'

LC was still watching him, listening in, thinking vaguely that if he counted Sebastian he'd used up seven of his nine lives they all joked about.

NG took a deep breath. He didn't know what to say. Sorry I almost killed you didn't seem to cut it.

"I'm not Sebastian," he said finally. "He's told me that before – I just never listened."

LC sat quietly, staring at the table again. "I thought I was going insane when I started hearing voices in my head," he said suddenly. "It still freaks me out sometimes."

"I never knew any different. When I was a kid, I was freaked out when I realised that no one else could do it."

"Your eyes changed colour, did you know that?" LC said.

It was a simple question but it felt like someone had caught hold of that spike of ice and twisted. "No." Breathing was hard, a stir of the darkness deep inside.

He shut it down.

"They went blue. Who else knows?" LC had felt that hate and he was thinking he had a right to know what he was dealing with. It was a fair point.

"No one."

LC frowned, casting a glance at the door and thinking about Evelyn standing there.

Damn, this was hard. It felt like his soul was lying there wide open.

"She's seen the effects. Martinez too," he admitted. "They don't know about Sebastian. LC, I didn't know about Sebastian."

"Does the Man know?" LC asked bluntly, not caring if he was being insubordinate. This changed everything, as if everything hadn't already been spun on its head.

NG paused before he said, "Yeah."

"So what do we do now?"

What could he do?

'You can live in fear.'

Not going to happen.

"I can control it," he said, to himself as much as LC.

Sebastian laughed silently, locked away inside but still stirring.

LC didn't look convinced.

The door opened. Hilyer, looking pale but calm so he was still on the painkillers. It wasn't clear whether he was relieved or disappointed that the virus had done nothing. He sat and leaned forward intently. "If LC's trying to tell you not to take me," he said, "screw him. I'm fine."

NG opened his mouth to reply to them both but closed it as he sensed more people approaching.

The door opened again.

Evelyn was followed by the Chief, Science and Media, Quinn a few steps behind and Martinez at the rear, closing the door behind her and staying there as if she was on guard duty as the others took their seats at the table.

NG had always chaired these meetings but now everyone looked to Evelyn. The guild might not be letting him quit but he had no clear idea of where he stood any more.

She was sitting ramrod straight and glanced at him before looking to Science. "Go ahead," she said.

Science frowned then pushed across a board. "Someone has been hacking into your personal files," he said.

He didn't care.

"Tell me honestly," NG sent back to Hil privately, "are you fit to run a tab?" He took the board without looking at it.

Science was peering at him intently. "Someone, presumably the same, has been using your codes. That should be impossible," he said. "Legal are trying to figure out who could have gained access." He paused and looked awkwardly at Evelyn.

"Devon left a command structure in place," she said. "Do you want to take a look?"

NG shook his head. That was the last thing he wanted to do.

"Okay, well it's in hand but we have to assume that there is still a threat here on board the Alsatia." She pursed her lips. "But you're not staying anyway, are you?"

Hil sent back, "Honestly?" He was trying to keep his thoughts neutral but from his body language he was seriously considering lying.

"Hil," NG sent, "I don't care whether you stay or go, I'd just rather know that you're there than find out later that you've gone awol and stolen Skye to chase after us."

Evelyn said again, "Are you?"

"No," he replied bluntly.

She wasn't happy and looked to the Chief to take up the reins.

The big man leaned forward. "We've followed up the intel on Tortuga. It's clean and our people from the inside report that Zang has identified the freighter El Pato Loco as a primary link to LC. The bounties on these two still stand but he is also mobilising his own resources to find them. He's that desperate. If you want Gallagher, you have a race to get to him before Zang does. We've closed down all non-essential guild activity and recalled all field operations. We can shift the Alsatia to the Between but we can't take her in to T72. You know that. As much as it feels like we've been blown wide open, the Alsatia's cover is still too sound to risk. We'll get close enough that we can send reinforcements if necessary."

NG nodded. He had a flutter of anticipation in his stomach. It suddenly felt like old times, as if he was getting a pre-tab briefing in Ops, a memory from long ago, one of his first postings, before any of these people had even been born.

"We'll send an advance party in first," the Chief said. "Once they give the all-clear, you go in with Martinez as close protection backed up by an extraction team on personal escort and a squad of assault troops for cover. We'll have another two extraction teams on standby and we'll station a Thundercloud in orbit. Do you want gunships?"

NG looked from the Chief to Evelyn. They'd both talked to Arturo before they left, that was evident enough. It felt like all this was out of his hands and it was weird to see the guild in full flow without his input, drawing him along and telling him how it was going to be as if he was a field-op again.

He shook his head. If the Chief thought they'd need gunships, he'd send them, he wouldn't be asking.

"You're taking Anderton," the Chief continued, "to ensure that Gallagher and his crew cooperate."

LC squirmed at that but bit his tongue.

"And Hilyer because he's the only operative we have who's actually seen Zang Tsu Po up close in person."

Hil smiled, no need to read his mind to see that he wanted his revenge.

The Chief gave him a disapproving glance and looked back at NG. "Take Ghost and Skye. We've initiated a total communications black out with a net of trip wires that Science swears is solid. So if anyone, anyone, here leaks a word of this out to the Assassins, we'll know about it."

'Fools,' Sebastian hissed. *'Anyone who is good enough to be running these rings around us, is good enough to avoid their little traps. Listen to me, Nikolai. If you go out there, they will find you and they will kill you.'*

Media reached out a hand and tapped gently but urgently on

the table. "NG, did you get any idea from Farro who placed the contract?"

No one had asked him anything about that yet.

He saw her eyes drop to his throat for a briefest of instants, looking at that red line that wouldn't fade no matter what he tried, before she looked him in the eye again, an almost desperate gratitude that he was still alive flashing through her thoughts. It was touching.

'It's sickening.'

He shook his head.

It was hard for her but she wasn't prepared to let up. "Come on, NG, talk to us."

He took a deep breath, no idea why it was so hard to speak out loud, and said reluctantly, "I tried. It was all buried beneath codes. Whoever did it made sure there was no way to trace them."

She frowned. "I don't suppose it makes much difference. Did Arturo tell you? It's an open contract now. They want you dead as much as whoever paid them. But, NG, we still want to find them. Is there nothing you can give us?"

He looked from face to face around the table. His successor in Evelyn, two of his most trusted chiefs and the two best operatives they'd handled in generations, the two kids who'd found themselves thrown into the middle of a situation no field-op should ever be troubled with, and he made a decision.

"There's an organisation…" he said.

NG walked off Ghost into the blazing sunshine of Tortuga's airfield and straight into a waiting circle of guns-up, pissed off pirates, facing off with the guild's advance party.

There was no sign of the Duck. Not on the surface, not any sign of it in the vicinity or the outer system. They'd made low orbit above the colony and LC had scanned, reluctantly, for familiars, using the Senson and Ghost combined, so that meant he was looking for Elliott or Thom Garrett, no one else on the ship having implants as far as they knew. He'd found Garrett, stuck planetside in town nursing a broken arm, and got back an incredulous, "Luka, what the hell are you doing here?" LC hadn't messed around, simply sending back, "Thom, I need to speak to Gallagher and Hal but listen, I'm here with company. Heavily armed and they're not going to give up their weapons. They're here to protect me. We're not any threat to Tierney. Make that clear, okay?"

NG looked around at the welcoming committee.

'What's clear, Nikolai, is that they care about nothing but cold, hard cash.'

Whatever Garrett had said, Tierney was still taking no chances. But these people hadn't betrayed LC.

'Anderton didn't have half a billion resting on his head.'

Martinez moved automatically, defensively, in front of NG. They'd landed Ghost on the outskirts of the airfield, the fast response dropship next to them. The forward team hadn't been able to secure the area, warning NG that the colony was a nightmare. "It's a freaking rat run of places to hide," the senior agent had reported. "You want my opinion, don't come in. If you do, don't go into the town. If you have to, be aware, there is a stash of heavy weaponry and explosives far beyond anything you'd find in a genuine mining colony. But you probably know that already. As far as we can figure, there aren't any known assassins here, but don't rely on that. The bounty hunters still seem fixated on Anderton. And everyone is paranoid as hell. You want me to reiterate that opinion? Don't come in."

They were used to him not taking their advice.

He wasn't used to having so many people watching his every move.

He felt the two extraction agents and the squad of troops from Security spread out behind him, covering every angle, all guns up and fingers on triggers.

LC walked forward, arms spread, equally pissed off.

Two of the pirates stepped up, a big guy NG recognised as Hal Duncan, intimidating as hell, that military background standing out a mile, and DiMarco, easy enough to identify from LC's debrief and the reaction he gave the kid now.

The pilot eyed up the firepower guarding them and grinned, stepping forward to grab LC in a bearhug. "I knew you were something special, Luka buddy, but Thieves' Guild? Jesus Christ. Why are you here? You do know it's insane for you to be here?"

"No choice," LC breathed, quietly enough that just DiMarco and Duncan could hear.

NG listened in, using more effort than it should have done to read them, and not liking that 'no choice' but he couldn't blame the kid for still feeling ostracised.

"We need to find Gallagher," LC said. "Where's the Duck?"

DiMarco looked dubious. "Not here but she should be on her way back soon."

NG shielded his eyes with his hand, looking into each face, each mind, in fast succession, wanting nothing other than a cold drink and somewhere shaded to sit and talk this out.

Most of the pirates were curious, mostly about seeing LC again in such different circumstances, staring at the armoured troops and thinking, what the hell? Hal Duncan was assessing the situation with cold precision. 'They're not protecting you,' he heard the big ex-marine say to LC, direct thought, 'they're protecting him. That's NG.' There was a massive suspicion there and NG couldn't help picking up that when LC had met this guy, the kid had been rogue from the guild and nowhere near sure that he could trust anyone, NG included. That kind of emotional baggage tended to linger and Duncan knew nothing about the Thieves' Guild except what he'd picked up from LC. He was trying to figure out if LC was there under duress, and LC himself wasn't exactly exuding calm and cooperation.

Duncan's stare flicked to NG, the big man suddenly thinking very clearly, 'You're reading my mind.'

'Yep.'

'I take it the whole of the damned Thieves' Guild can't do this?'

'No.'

'And you are NG?'

'We need to talk.'

Duncan glanced at LC. "You're taking a real risk coming here," he said quietly. "There are still bounty hunters, camped out and hoping you'd be stupid enough to come back."

"We need to find Gallagher," LC said again and switched to direct thought, easy enough to eavesdrop even though he was trying to shield it, 'Hal, the Wintrans are mobilising a fleet to come out here. You need to warn Tierney.'

'Zang? Looking for you?' Duncan shook his head almost imperceptibly. 'It's a good thing you have so many guns watching your back, Luka, because I'm not going to be able to save your ass, or his, if anyone catches wind of that half a billion.' He glanced back at NG. 'What do you really want here?'

NG smiled. This guy was good. He'd lifted that piece of intel from Martinez. God knows what else. At that meeting in the hospitality suite when he'd spilled his guts about the Order, he'd also thrown the real purpose behind the Man's special projects into the mix.

Everyone around that table had listened carefully, humouring him at first and then waking up to the facts as he'd laid it all out and explained why Gallagher was so important. It wasn't every day you heard that an alien invasion was on its way but they'd taken it well all things considered. Whether they believed it or not was another matter but he'd given them access to all the files. Martinez hadn't confronted him with any of it on the way out here, she was simply doing her job and, surprisingly, he didn't care that she knew it all now. Duncan could get whatever he wanted from reading her mind, or LC's.

DiMarco was frowning, oblivious to the exchanges that were flying around. "What does the fucking Thieves' Guild want with Gallagher?"

To give him credit, LC was working hard to keep his cool. "Not just Gallagher. We have to talk to Elliott and Thom. And Tierney."

The pilot was about to ask why again but changed his mind. "Then you need to come into town. I'll vouch for you, that's all. The rest of your fucking friends can stay here."

NG watched as LC shook his head and said, "That's not going to happen."

DiMarco laughed and raised his hand, pointing at the Security guys. "There's no way they are coming into our town."

"Then bring Tierney and Thom out here," LC said, following his brief for once.

"That's not going to happen."

"Then we'll just come in." LC lowered his voice again. "DiMarco, come on, look at this."

Hal Duncan put a hand on DiMarco's shoulder and said to LC, "Give us a minute," looking past the kid at NG and the blatant show of force from a guild he was thinking he'd somehow got caught up in, resenting the fact and at the same time not able to fault LC for it because the kid had saved his life.

NG stared at him and the big marine caught his eye, thinking very deliberately, 'Yeah, I know, it's fucked up shit. You want me to sort this out? Don't try anything. Don't be stupid. And tell Hilyer to stay where he is in orbit. You come in on my ticket, you do as I say, understood?'

NG nodded. LC was right, they were going in anyway. The cooperation of Tierney's main lieutenants, the ranks of which Duncan seemed to have joined, was a luxury not a necessity.

He was happy to let Duncan overhear that.

The big man wasn't impressed but kept his face neutral as he turned to speak to DiMarco privately, pointing out the superiority of the weapons and armour. "Thieves' Guild, my ass. They're battle troops, for fuck's sake. That's chameleonic powered armour they're wearing. You want to mess with them, fine. I'll stand by and scrape up the pieces once they're done. Then I'll take them in to see Tierney. Don't be stupid, DiMarco, we're outgunned here." He leaned in close. "And this is Luka, bud, don't forget that. We both owe the kid." He let that hang and turned back to them, folding his arms.

DiMarco didn't like it but he didn't argue.

He regarded them with undisguised hostility and said sullenly, "Welcome to Tortuga."

Jiro Tierney's desert hideaway had good beer, better liquor and a warmth that went deeper than the heat of the sun that had been beating down on them all afternoon. It was easy to see why LC had fallen for the place.

Tierney was keeping them waiting. NG sat back and watched with a tinge of envy the way the kid was made welcome. He'd never seen LC look so relaxed, sitting on a table top over by the back door to the house, chatting in low voices with DiMarco, Duncan and Garrett, laughing and at ease even though they'd had to wait until dark to drive in here under armed guard to avoid the bounty hunters. They'd brought six Security guys in with them, leaving the others and the extraction team with the ships. Standard back up procedures. Everything was going as slick as it could, except there was still no sign of Gallagher or his freighter.

NG looked at Martinez. The small private courtyard was quiet except for the flutter of flags in the breeze and the clink of ice in the glasses. Candles in small glass jars burned with a hint of narcotic in their trailing fumes.

It was peaceful.

Until the Sensons engaged. Everyone's, simultaneous.

He was so intent on Hil's update, he almost missed the message LC and Garrett received from the freighter.

DiMarco looked around. "What?"

Martinez knocked back the pale green liquor in the shot glass she'd been ignoring. "We need to get out of here."

NG nodded, standing and watching as LC jumped off the table.

DiMarco grabbed the kid's arm. "What is it?"

"A Wintran battle cruiser just dropped in system," LC said. "Zang has the Duck. We're too late."

25

"Events unfolded fast. You haven't seen Nikolai since he walked out?"

"No."

"Then how do you know all this? How do you know what has happened since?"

He reached for the poker. "I have my means."

"How is he?"

Again, he did not reply, stirring the ashes and nurturing the deep glow of the embers. He nudged the blackened logs, watching the flames lick up around the twisted metal of the poker.

He said instead, "By all accounts, he responded well to being effectively demoted back to field operative. I think that was always the position where he felt most comfortable."

She smiled. She had always been fond of Nikolai as well. "Arturo is very clever. It will have been what he needed. Practical field work always brought out the best in him."

Thom Garrett looked horrified, shoving past LC and DiMarco to head inside, a disproportionate reaction to news that was bad but not disastrous unless there was something else going on.

NG moved fast and blocked his way, grabbing his arm, the one that wasn't broken, the physical contact magnifying the intensity of the panic.

He pulled the kid back and held on, going deep, fast. Time to find out Thom Garrett's secret.

It hit like a wave, threatening to overwhelm. Deeply buried traumatic crap going all the way back to the kid's childhood, all overridden by a fierce need to keep it hidden and keep away from it. And Gallagher, who was the key to keeping that distance, was being held on a Wintran battle cruiser.

NG looked into a face that was desperate. If he lost Gallagher, the kid was thinking, he'd be hauled back onto the Tangiers and shipped home in the blink of an eye.

Hal Duncan grabbed the front of Garrett's jacket. "What the fuck is the Tangiers?"

Garrett looked sick. He hated the Tangiers, that was easy to read, hated the warship, hated its captain and hated his grandfather for sending him out here with it.

Christ.

NG let go. "Call it in," he said quietly.

Sebastian laughed. '*Earth versus Winter, round two... I'm almost impressed, Nikolai. Your capacity for warmongering seems to be growing.*'

"Call it in," he said again, calmly. "The Wintrans are going to attack this colony and they will not stop until they have taken or killed everyone here. Call it in."

Garrett shook his head. "It's not that simple."

Duncan pushed the kid against the wall. "You have a fucking warship following you? Call it in."

"You don't understand."

"You don't understand," Duncan hissed, nose to nose. "That battle cruiser is going to launch an attack on this colony and blitz it until they find Luka. They already have Gallagher. I don't care what you have going on, Thom. Call it in."

Garrett was still resisting.

NG grabbed his arm again, using everything he had to calm the boy down and delve deeper into his memories. Legal had dug up some stuff on this kid but Christ, that was only half of it. He gave the kid absolutely no choice, feeling Garrett acquiesce as he spoke. "Thom, do whatever you need to do to get them here, fast. You want a code? Give them this." He rattled off a code that he plucked out of the kid's memory. "Do you understand?"

Garrett nodded, terrified but furious, almost hyperventilating with the adrenaline rush.

LC was watching, listening in, the implications of it settling on him like a weight.

Sebastian laughed again. *'That's more like it. I was wondering how you were going to follow the single-handed annihilation of the Assassins. Revenge against Zang, by throwing Earth spec-ops against him – again – how exhilarating.'*

Martinez opened a private link. "NG, what's going on?"

"Thom Garrett is JU."

Duncan stepped to the side and gestured towards the doorway. "Everyone inside. Now. Go with DiMarco. Thom, come with me."

They followed the pilot down a dark hallway into Tierney's headquarters.

NG sent, tight wire and encrypted to the others out at the airfield, "Bug out. Right now. I don't want Ghost or that dropship on the ground if they come in hard."

Martinez stayed at his side, sending, "Why is the JU following Gallagher? Is that where the virus came from? Do they know? Did Jameson know?"

It was possible.

He hadn't been anywhere near Jameson since LC came back with it. But there hadn't been any hint of it in his mind when the colonel had first confronted them with it.

He didn't reply but she didn't let up. "What's the odds of LC ending up randomly on a freighter owned by a guy who was shot down by 'aliens', who is actively being investigated by the same unit that developed the virus they were sent to steal?"

LC was walking ahead of them, shoulders tensing as he couldn't help but overhear them talking about him.

NG sent back bluntly, "There are no odds. I don't believe in coincidences."

DiMarco took them into a room that looked like a mess hall and told them to wait, pointing at LC and adding, "For Christ's sake, don't do anything stupid," before he left.

Martinez prowled around the room, not hiding her disgust.

"What are we missing, NG?" she sent, keeping the connection as tight as it could be, no idea that LC could listen in anyway.

'*You're missing something bloody obvious*,' Sebastian mocked.

Elliott.

NG sat down, opposite to LC, and looked across into those pale eyes that looked even more haunted now than when the kid had first come back into the guild. "How did you end up on that ship, LC?" he sent.

LC's eyes flicked across to the door for a second. "It was just there. I had nowhere else to go."

Martinez sat down next him. "Gallagher's desperate," she sent, staring at LC herself. "He buys a ship that turns up out of nowhere. Cheap. A piece of junk. That isn't a piece of junk at all. It has stealth capability we know is way ahead of anything we have, an AI that is all but invisible, jump capacity way beyond normal parameters and a JU operative on board masquerading as an engineer? What are the chances Elliott and the Duck are also JU? They could have chased LC out to Sten's World, and picked up Gallagher because he was shooting his mouth off about aliens at Erica, and they knew that was where they'd sourced the tech they were working on, for the virus." She glanced at NG. "It's alien, right?"

LC had started to shake his head at the point where she said they could have chased him out to Sten's and looked like he could throw up when she said the virus was alien.

"They were there before me," he sent vaguely, not convinced. He switched to direct thought, 'Oh shit, is this…? Are you…?'

NG cut him off. "The Duck's been taken on board the battle cruiser?"

LC nodded.

"Elliott can shield life signs, can't he? Do the Wintrans have Gallagher?"

Before the kid could answer, the Senson engaged with another connection, linking automatically without permission even though it was an unknown.

"Not yet," another, softer, voice whispered inside his head.

NG sent back, opening a surreptitious link to Martinez, "Elliott?"

"I take it Luka told you about me?"

"Some."

"NG… the infamous NG of the Thieves' Guild."

'You'd better hope he hasn't heard about the Assassins…'

"It doesn't matter who I am," NG sent back. "I'm here to find Gallagher. That's all."

From his expression, LC was also listening in.

"Our dear Captain Gallagher. Why, now, are so many people intent on finding him? What does the legendary Thieves' Guild want with a mad old freighter captain from the Between?"

LC had called this guy a jerk and it was easy to see why. Elliott was taunting him.

From what LC had said, Elliott knew Gallagher's story. The guy also knew about the virus and not so long ago it had been a priority to take him in. It suddenly looked like he wasn't just another loose end to be secured.

"If you haven't noticed," Elliott sent casually without waiting for an answer, "we're impounded and shut down in the holding tank of a Wintran battle cruiser – the Expedience, if you're interested, Zang's pride and joy – and it will be in orbit around that colony in about three hours. They're running an impressive operation. Slick considering there are at least two corporations working together. I don't think I've ever seen UM take orders from Zang before. I understand you gave young Thomas an authorisation code to call in the Tangiers."

NG looked at LC.

'Not me,' the kid thought back.

Elliott didn't pause. "The Tangiers is a tenth the size of the Expedience. Do you really think they'll be able to take it on in a stand up fight? Tell me, NG, are your boys capable of getting on board this battle cruiser and getting to the AI core?"

'Don't trust him,' LC thought.

NG shook his head slightly. 'I don't.' But it was starting to look like he might not have a choice. Utilising any asset external to the guild was always a risk, usually a calculated one with a mass of intel. He'd had to wing it before in the field, many times, and as much as his gut feeling was agreeing with LC, that there was no way they could trust this guy, he also had a sinking feeling that this might be his only option.

"I've seen Luka in action," Elliott sent. "Is Zachary as good?"

"Why?"

"You want to send a message to Zang? Take out one of his flagships."

Sebastian stirred. *'Now there's a man after my own heart.'*

'You don't have a heart.'

'You don't have time to be screwing around. Take it. Send them in there. Have your revenge.'

"Can they get to the AI core?" Elliott sent again.

"Yes, they can. You want to tell me why?" It was like a bizarre negotiation with a client.

"We take out the AI and that battle cruiser will be a sitting duck when the Tangiers turns up."

"And how do we take out the AI?"

Elliott laughed. "I have a means but it needs to be injected directly into the core. What I have in mind will take both of them if we're going to disable the AI completely. It's only temporary but it will buy us some time. Are you up for it?"

He made a snap decision and sent back, "Yes."

"Good. I'm curious to see the Thieves' Guild in action. I'm assuming that ship Zachary has in orbit has enough stealth capability to get in close. I can help disrupt things from here. Let's get them on board and see what they can do."

The connection cut off abruptly, leaving an eerie silence.

Martinez was frowning. "Are you seriously considering doing this?"

NG didn't have a chance to reply as the door opened. He stood up as Duncan burst in. No questions or small talk just a pissed off, "Come with me," and a curt message to LC as he thought, 'Tierney is planning on keeping you all hostage and offering you up to Zang. I'm not prepared to let that happen. Don't say a word and do as I say. And tell me now, straight up, if I'm to extend this courtesy to your boss, or not.'

It was something that LC sent a 'yes' straight back with no hesitation.

NG headed to the doorway, gesturing Martinez and LC to wait. "I need to speak to Tierney."

Duncan was a towering figure, muscles taut with controlled urgency. It was easy to see how he'd built that reputation in the military. "I'm giving you a way out," he said, his voice a low rumble.

"We're not running," NG said simply. "Where's Tierney?"

Duncan looked at LC who was desperately trying to remain impassive. The kid had been on the run for so long, it was tough for him not to react now with that knee-jerk need to disappear.

The big marine looked back to NG, hand reaching for his gun. "You're going to use Luka as bait."

"We're going to finish this." It was a calm and reasoned statement, and to give them credit, Martinez and LC stood firm behind him.

A slight smile twitched at the corner of Duncan's mouth. He closed the door. "Thom has contacted the Tangiers. That race to get to Gallagher just split three ways but we don't know how long it will take them to get here. We have less than four hours before the battle cruiser makes orbit, less than one hour before the fighters start airstrikes if they run this operation anything like standard ops. Tierney is evacuating and digging in to defend but only as a contingency. He's working on the assumption that Zang wants Luka alive and will talk first. I don't believe that for one second. If they're running this under the cover of clearing out rogue mining operations, they're going to come in hot."

"They will," Martinez chipped in. "Zang wants LC, dead or alive. He doesn't care."

"I don't understand what you gain by handing over LC."

NG checked the band on his wrist. "That's not the plan," he said and reached out to Hilyer with the Senson. "Get your ass down to the surface, Hil. How much time do we have?"

"Forty seven minutes before the fighters reach low orbit. They've been authorised to use Endermaine."

Shock tactics. Contain and control. Casualties expected and acceptable. He could hear Martinez cursing under her breath. He glanced back over his shoulder and couldn't help the grin that slipped out. Like old times. "You want to run some interference?"

She laughed.

NG looked back at Duncan. "Let me talk to Tierney."

The leader of this pirate colony was sitting at his desk, an imposing figure, unmistakable from the scar on his jawline, his reputation as a ruthless brigand somewhat belied by the neat and orderly paperwork in front of him. His mind, however, was an intense swirl of anger and frustration.

The whirlwind of consequences that had tumbled into chaotic being since Zang Tsu Po had made his decision to blackmail a Thieves' Guild handler and two of his best operatives were mind-numbing. Jiro Tierney had been building a stable colony here, trying desperately to move away from the violence of raiding. In one fell swoop that anonymity had been destroyed, all because LC had been forced to run to the edge of the galaxy and had nowhere to go except a ship that was chosen at random by one of Tierney's lieutenants as a potentially useful freighter.

'It's all very sad. They're doomed. It's sad. Get out of here before we get embroiled in it.'

Sebastian was chiding constantly but lazily, no real dark malice in there. It was irritating rather than draining like it used to be.

Nothing was like it used to be.

NG walked into Tierney's office. Martinez had assigned two of the troops from Security to stick with him. Excessive but effective.

Tierney didn't stand. "Who are you?" he said, pulling no punches.

"That doesn't matter right now," NG said, calm, no need to antagonise but no need to be subservient. They were not prisoners here and he wasn't going to act like it.

Tierney's face pulled into a wry smile. "We're assuming that you're Thieves' Guild. Do you want to tell me otherwise?" He was thinking that all he had to do was contact the Wintrans to offer LC up to stop them descending on his colony.

"Won't work," NG said.

"What won't work?"

"Handing in my field operative. You think the Wintrans will take Anderton and just go? How much is the price on your head? And the others here? You think they'll forget that? The Expedience is an Advantage class battle cruiser with a complement of over ten thousand. Three thousand heavily armed marines are going to descend on this place and wipe it, and everyone in it, off the map."

Tierney kept the smile but his expression hardened. "And what's your plan?"

"We take out the battle cruiser."

There was a moment of disbelief then Tierney laughed and stood up. "Excuse me but I have a defence to organise."

"I take it you've never encountered the Thieves' Guild before," NG said softly.

Tierney leaned on the table. "Only what I've seen here – a wanted fugitive pursued by a host of bounty hunters who led the entire Wintran militia to our doorstep. I don't have time for this."

NG turned on the charm. "I need LC to do what I'm planning. Give him up to Zang and you will lose. Help us and you get to stay here and run your colony."

'We don't need help from anyone.'

Tierney wavered. He wasn't the leader of this band of pirates without good reason. And he wasn't stupid. Hiding away in the back of beyond hadn't stopped him keeping up to date with current events and the thoughts running through his mind kept going back to what DiMarco had told him about LC, those peculiar talents that suddenly all made sense when they'd found out the details of the bounty and the fact that the kid was Thieves' Guild. Tierney was also a good judge of character – he had to be, no one kept a group like this together without a total command

and understanding of the intricacies of individual personality and motivation.

"You say you can take on the battle cruiser?" Tierney said. "How?"

"Leave that to me."

Tierney walked forward, rounding the desk until he was face to face.

NG stood his ground.

"Persuade me," Tierney said, voice dripping distrust.

"I don't need to. We're doing it anyway. Whether you and your people benefit depends on whether you work with us or not. Your choice." In reality, he didn't care whether these people lived or died but he knew how much this place meant to LC and he knew how simple it could be to save them. But that decision wasn't his.

Tierney stared at him. "I heard someone say once," he said finally, "that dealing with the Thieves' Guild was like selling your soul." He stared for a long moment. "I see what they meant."

NG checked the magazine and clicked it back into the gun. He glanced at his wristband, twenty three minutes. It was going to take them twenty to get clear of the town and meet up with Skye and Ghost. He looked up. "Where's LC?"

Martinez was checking her own kit. "He's with DiMarco."

There was something wrong. He turned, scanning around, looking for hostiles and hard pushed to identify anyone who wasn't paranoid, tense and on edge.

Martinez frowned. "What's wrong?" She was in the process of slotting her gun back into its holster but she stopped and pulled it out, holding it down by her thigh.

'*You need to get out of here.*'

He knew that.

Hal Duncan appeared at the door. "Time to go."

NG paused, froze for a second and went wider, deeper, catching a hint of intention and narrowing down the threat.

"LC, get out of there," he sent and said out loud, moving for the door, fast, "Who the hell is Tanzi?"

Duncan cursed, spun around and ran, feet pounding, pulling out a massive handgun as he moved.

There was shouting up ahead, small weapons fire and flashbangs. Martinez grabbed NG's arm and one of the Security troops veered in front of him. He tried to fend them off, feeling nothing but confusion and fear up ahead.

Time slowed.

Sebastian whispered viciously, '*Showtime.*'

NG tried to respond but any thought of reply was cut off abruptly and violently as the shockwave from the explosion hit and his world crashed into darkness.

26

A log cracked in the fire, sending sparks scattering.

She glanced at it, drawn in by the curling, dancing fingers of flame. "Trouble followed him out into the Between?"

"Inevitable. We sent the full weight of the guild's military wing with him, yet…" He shook his head slightly, picked up the jug and topped up both goblets. "You cross swords with the best assassins and brigands the galaxy has to offer, you must expect to get cut. No matter how good you are." He looked up at her. "It is not so much that we met our match. We met a cascade of enemies who, truth be told, have been lining up and waiting for us to falter. Nikolai, whether his actions can be justified or not, has borne the brunt of it."

There was a blur of nothing then pain. A vague awareness of Sebastian fighting for control and a disembodied sense of chaos.

He was flat on his back, sparks of pain prickling in his face, arm, neck, chest, knee, too many to count, ears ringing.

Fingers pressed against his neck, checking the pulse, a touch that was so cold with hatred it shot tendrils of ice into his skin. The sharp point of a blade pushed against his throat and NG reacted with pure instinct, ignoring Sebastian with disdain and shooting a hand out to grab the wrist holding the blade. He threw his whole strength against it and twisted, driving the knife away and up into the neck of his assailant.

There was a strangled gasp and the body sagged onto his. He shoved the weight of it off him and rolled away, pulling a gun from a holster and coming up in a half-kneeling crouch. He held the aim unwavering at the guy's head, aware of the pounding of each heartbeat. A distant echoing shot broke the silence that was booming in his ears and the body in front of him jerked.

He recognised the figure beside him as Martinez and forced himself to his feet, standing back to back with her, guns up, no idea if there were other threats incoming. The Senson made a clear connection.

"That was too close. Are you okay?"

"Yeah," he sent back, sensing the presence of three or four armoured figures closing in on them, recognising them as Security, and relaxing somewhat. He blinked dust and crap out of his eyes and lowered the gun. Someone was screaming for a medic, the sound muted through the buzzing in his head.

He turned to look at Martinez. She was bleeding from dozens of scrapes and wounds, but nothing serious. She nodded towards the body next to them. "Do you recognise him?"

"Sceznei," NG sent back, coughing, throat dry and chest feeling like there was a fist pushing against it. "One of Devon's old buddies. She warned me about him."

"How did he know we were coming here, NG? The only people who knew were with us in that room."

"And the Chief set traps. He'll figure it out." He wiped a hand across his eye, smearing bright red blood and fine yellow dust into a sticky paste. They were out of time, he knew that without needing to look at the band on his wrist. He started to scan for familiars, finding Duncan nearby, down but intact, Garrett with the incoming rescuers and DiMarco in the heart of it, wounded but alive.

She reached a hand up to his forehead, thinking he was hurt but reassessing and deciding it wasn't as bad as it looked. "How did we not see it coming?"

"Tanzi," he said, swatting her away. "Tierney's tech guy. Sceznei must have targeted him as the easy way in. Tanzi was always nervous as hell. LC said it and Duncan said it. They didn't think anything was amiss when he started freaking out because he was always freaking out. But yeah, I know, I should have seen it."

Voices were yelling.

"We need to get out of here," Martinez sent.

They had probably about three or four minutes before the Wintrans started bombing the crap out of the town. They didn't have time to get clear.

He started to say something, lost track of his train of thought and closed his eyes. There was something about the shouting that was grinding at his nerves but he couldn't make out the words.

'Can't you feel the fear? That's Anderton's little whore. He's dying in her arms. How poetic.'

NG turned towards the shouting, towards what must have been the centre of the blast, shutting out the pounding in his head and narrowing his focus. He could sense DiMarco, struggling, trapped, and a girl who was unharmed, scared and screaming for help. There was one other there, fading so fast he could hardly sense the lifesigns.

LC.

Climbing through the rubble, NG shut out the noise and chaos and told Hil to bug out, get clear and wait for further instructions. Martinez was cursing constantly at his side, torn between wanting him safe and wanting LC out of there.

'Anderton is dead. Why are you bothering?'

As they reached what was left of the back of the building, Tierney's people were pulling DiMarco clear. The pilot was swearing. LC looked like shit. The girl had one hand pressed against his chest, red oozing through her fingers, the other held against his head as if she could hold him together with sheer willpower.

NG turned to Martinez and muttered, "Get us some privacy." He walked forward and knelt, placing a hand on LC's neck. His breathing was shallow, hair matted with blood, skin burning up as the organism worked overtime.

The girl whispered, "I can't stop the bleeding."

'Let him die,' Sebastian hissed, squirming with hate.

NG ignored him and concentrated on LC. Head wounds could be tricky and the kid was balancing precariously right on the edge of a dark abyss. Just bringing him back from that brink was going to be tough.

'Let me help, I'll sort him out.'

NG ignored the sarcasm and dug two vials from a pocket with one hand, keeping the other on LC. He bit the caps off both ampoules and pressed one against the kid's neck, juggling the other and stabbing it against his own. The Epizin wasn't the instant pick-me-up it would be for anyone else but the hit of extra energy wouldn't go amiss.

LC didn't move.

The girl was staring at him.

"What's your name?" NG asked, voice still ringing slightly in his ears as he spoke.

He shifted his weight to get comfortable, tucking one hand gently up against LC's shoulder and assessing the damage. It felt like the kid's collarbone was broken, a scattering of deep shrapnel wounds compounding the danger as the organism struggled to deal with the internal bleeding. It was weird to sense the living entity that was swarming throughout LC's body, shutting down non-essentials and focusing its frenzied activity to protect the vitals as it healed cell by cell. It was struggling and it snatched at the energy NG fed into it with a pull that threatened to overwhelm.

"Yoshi," she said. "Is he going to be okay?"

"Yeah." So long as they weren't disturbed because it felt like this could take a while.

The girl was looking at LC lying there motionless, willing him to wake up, thinking back to the night they'd met and the two men who had attacked her. Luka had floored them both. NG listened in with a half smile. They trained their operatives well but LC was something else. She was thinking that he'd saved her again, pushed her into cover when they'd all realised what Tanzi was about to do. He'd taken the brunt of the explosion and shielded her from it.

She was also wondering who NG was and what he was doing here. She had a sharp mind. And there was something else there, something curious.

NG looked at her. "Do you want to help?"

She nodded without hesitation.

NG covered her hand with his. She was trembling but she was surprisingly strong. She didn't resist, trusting him completely. It would have been easy to drain her and take every last ounce of her essence.

'You shock me, Nikolai,' Sebastian teased maliciously. *'Not so long ago, that thought would not have even crossed your mind.'*

She was watching with fascination.

NG turned his attention to the shrapnel wounds. He'd never tried this before but if he could throw a fully armoured man to the ground at twenty feet, he should be able to pull a tiny piece of metal from a body he was touching.

He closed his eyes, felt the piece he was concentrating on shift and set about painstakingly drawing each shard of metal out of the kid's flesh and fixing the damage as much as he could. It was hard to be subtle about it and he was struggling to achieve any finesse here but it was working, the organism responding to his manipulations to eject each foreign body from its midst.

It was tough going. Hard to stop the bleeding from so many wounds. He could feel LC fading.

'I don't understand why you are even bothering to try to save him. What has he ever done for you?'

Yoshi whimpered softly. Done. She was exhausted but fighting to stay awake. She was a good kid, the kind of waif and stray that Mendhel used to snap up.

"Go," he said gently and glanced around. The strain on his already depleted reserves was taking its toll. If it took too much longer, he wasn't sure he was going to be able to stay conscious himself. "Angel, I need a hand here."

Yoshi backed away reluctantly and Martinez crouched beside him. "Is he going to be okay?"

"Yeah," NG said again because they didn't need to hear any different. "You have to trust me."

There was a hesitant nod.

"I need physical contact," he said, admitting that out loud to someone for the first time in his life. Christ, he might as well put a sign on his head, freak show this way. "Take hold of his arm."

They sat quietly then and he took energy from Martinez faster than was probably safe for any of them.

She stared at him as he did it and it was disconcerting as hell to work with an audience. He felt exposed. His whole life had been shrouded in secrecy, need to know only. Arturo was the closest confidant he'd ever had aside from the Man and even then the old guy had never pried. Now it was starting to feel like the whole galaxy knew what he was.

'*You don't even know what you are*,' Sebastian said maliciously, writhing inside, and wanting nothing more than to send a vicious spike of agony lancing into LC.

NG didn't rise to it. He felt LC stir slightly beneath his hand.

Martinez muttered something as a roar of engines overhead was followed by a rapid sequence of deep rumbles. She was talking to Hilyer and Elliott, he realised, as the Wintran attack began, and he hadn't even noticed. He'd never healed anyone else like this before and it was hard, draining.

'*What are we even doing here, Nikolai? You want to leave the guild, go. Let's go find Zang and offer him a deal. He couldn't possibly treat you any worse than your precious Thieves' Guild.*'

He had no idea what he wanted. But offering a deal to Zang wasn't it. Shooting the bastard in the head might be.

Sebastian laughed.

NG pushed it, aware he was rushing, and felt another shift in LC's energy. He wanted the kid awake and gradually eased him back to consciousness, taking as much of the pain as he could manage.

LC murmured, starting to come round, the edge of a nightmare still clawing scratches into his mind. He jerked awake and the headache that motion sparked sent a spike of shared pain searing into them both. A swirl of concussion sent the room spinning away, the kid gasped and passed out cold.

NG sat back. LC was alive but he wasn't in any fit state to run a tab.

He sat quietly, back against the ruins of a wall, sipping at a bottle of beer, listening in as Elliott gave updates of Wintran positions through an open link on the Senson. Two of the guys from Security were standing a discrete distance away, securing the area, giving him some space.

He rested the cold bottle against his forehead and closed his eyes. He was goosed. If he was honest with himself, he didn't know what he was doing here. What any of them were doing here.

'You're going to get me killed here, is what you're doing.'

He was vaguely aware of Martinez approaching and didn't react as she squeezed his shoulder gently and sat beside him. "Are you alright?"

NG nodded. He wasn't. He was tired.

She was trying to figure out what the Man would want her to do. He'd never realised how much they worked to the Man's agenda, and not his.

'You have realised it,' Sebastian whispered, scathingly, hatefully. *'Again, the Man always wiped your memory.'*

"They've got him stabilised," she said, "not that they have any decent medical facilities here. I left a couple of Security watching over him." She took a deep breath. "Duncan wants to see you. I asked him to give us a few minutes. What do we do now?"

"Elliott said it will take two of us to do what he needs."

She stared for an instant then realised what he was saying. "No."

"We don't have much choice. And the only way to get on that battle cruiser now is to hand ourselves in."

"No. I'm not going to let you get yourself killed. Like it or not, NG, I care about you too much."

'She's not what you think she is.'

NG opened his eyes and turned to face her, a cold spot inside sparking in defiance.

"You care about protecting me," he said quietly, "because the Man programmed you to care about me. Don't fool yourself into thinking it's any more than that."

It was surprising to hear her laugh. "You think you can shock me? NG, I know exactly what the Man did to me. And Banks."

She sat back, heart pounding as memories surfaced.

NG shut them out. He wasn't interested.

'Don't lie to yourself.'

Martinez glared at him. Her expression was dark, the thoughts flitting over the surface of her mind even darker. "NG, do you know where I'm from?"

He stared back at her. "Angel, I don't even know where I'm from."

Her eyes glinted.

"I was on death row, NG. Banks too. I killed people for money, he killed people for kicks, a lot of people on a lot of planets." She laughed and dragged a hand back over her hair. "I hadn't slept in years when the Man took me out of that cess pit of a jail. I used to enjoy it, you know, the killing, but then they started coming back, at night. The faces. Every last one of them. Do you know what that feels like?"

Sebastian was a cold spot writhing inside. Of course he knew what it felt like.

He didn't reply. This woman had been tasked with watching over him, had been at his side for years, and she was right, he knew nothing about her.

She leaned forward, every muscle tense. "Banks died for you. I would die for you. You know why? Because the Man rescued us from that. Banks told me once he used to wake up screaming in pain and the only way that pain would go was if he inflicted more pain on someone else."

She pulled out her gun and started checking it, clicking out the magazine and clicking it back in, obsessively and automatically. "I am loyal to the Man," she said quietly without looking at him. "And he wants you alive. And like it or not, I do care about you."

He'd never heard her like this before. He kept his voice low. "You don't know what I am, Angel."

"No, I don't but I know exactly what I am," she fired straight back at him, "and I know where I came from. The Man saved me from that and I am not going back. He can programme me to think and do whatever the hell he wants." She glared at him defiantly. "What the fuck did he do to you?"

'Be sure you want to cross that line before you say another word, Nikolai,' Sebastian whispered maliciously.

He was already way past that line.

NG closed his eyes again and leaned his head back against the rough surface of the wall. "He created me," he said. "I don't exist."

27

He raised the goblet and paused with it a finger's breadth from his lips, breathing in the heady aroma.

She was staring at him, not sure what to say.

"It is done," he said. "It cannot be undone. Nikolai knows all there is to know. And he knows what he is capable of. Good and bad."

"You feel a loss?"

He frowned and shook his head, tipping the goblet to drink and wondering if that was a lie.

"You have nurtured him for a long time."

"I always hoped that he would be strong enough to withstand Sebastian and remain true to himself, that is all."

There was another deep rumble as Wintran bombs hit the town. NG could sense Martinez frowning and said abruptly, "My real name is Sebastian and he's a vicious son of a bitch."

"With blue eyes," she said softly. "NG, I've seen it. Everyone has a side of themselves…"

He laughed bitterly and took another mouthful of the beer. "Angel, I'm tired. Just humour me. I'm going up there."

She stared at him, knowing fine well why he was so tired, thinking about the state LC had been in and what it had taken out of NG to keep him alive. She wanted to ask, desperately wanted to know how he'd healed the kid and wanted to ask why he couldn't have done that for Banks.

"I wish I could have," he said quietly.

Martinez turned her head, staring straight ahead. "So what do you see when you read my mind, NG?"

She wasn't angry or scared. There was no accusation there, just a genuine curiosity. And she needed him to know that she knew. That there was no need for secrets any more.

"I don't see your past," he said.

She smiled. "Or the future?"

He shook his head. "I'm a telepathic empath, not a fortune teller."

"Are you human?"

"As far as I know."

"You don't have this virus or whatever it is?"

Another shake of the head. "Born like this."

"Did Devon know?"

A lump formed in his throat. "Not until the end."

She was thinking that he looked more vulnerable than she'd ever seen him and catching herself thinking it, thinking that if he could read her mind, he could hear every thought.

He'd never seen her blush.

She looked away. She knew deep down that there hadn't been time in that damned freezing cold alley on Redgate.

"I couldn't save Devon either."

"I've always known you heal fast," she said, looking back at him intently. "Those drones in the Maze? Evelyn told me that poison should have killed you. And someone cut your throat. Jesus, normal people don't survive stuff like that. But I didn't realise you could…" She trailed off, not sure what to say.

He reached to touch her hand and stroked his thumb across a gash on her knuckles, taking out the heat of the infection that was setting in, numbing the pain, healing the minor wound easily.

"How…?"

He pulled the bullet out of his pocket and tossed it into the air, no idea if he could do it, but freezing it there in front of them in mid-air as easily as if he was holding it. It felt good, as if he was harnessing something deep down that he'd always been able to do but just hadn't realised.

"Telekinesis, manipulating matter. Healing is just doing the same but to flesh and blood."

She leaned forward, transfixed by it, hanging there in the air. "My god. NG."

"I don't think God has a lot to do with it."

He let it fall.

She clenched her fist slowly, still not quite believing what he'd done. "I know you can take care of yourself," she said. "But you're not alone here. Don't forget that. Whoever the hell you are." She squeezed his hand. "I'll let you go hand yourself in on one condition…"

He wasn't in the mood for bargaining, and he was going anyway, but he raised his eyes, questioning.

"Tell me why you quit."

NG shook his head vaguely. He couldn't explain, even to Martinez who knew the Man apparently, maybe even better than he did. The guild had been his whole life and it was a lie.

"Well, if you won't tell me that, at least tell me how you are planning to escape once you're on the Expedience. These guys aren't stupid. They'll have the prisoners locked down tight. Sheer numbers isn't going to change that."

He could feel her frustration. She was thinking it might be easy for Hil or LC to slip out of custody, they did stuff like that all the time, but NG wasn't a field-op.

He reached and retrieved the bullet. "I worked as a field operative for fifteen years."

"When?"

"A long time ago."

She looked at him, eyebrows raised. "A long time ago?"

He shrugged. "It'll be easier to skip out from the infirmary. It'll need to be something serious. I don't think a grazed knee will cut it. I'll need something like a gunshot wound so they'll take me in then ignore me."

She sucked in an exasperated breath. "If anyone is going to shoot you, it's gonna be me."

He smiled.

"Seriously, NG…"

"My name's Nikolai," he said suddenly. "I'm not Sebastian."

"I know," she said. "I've seen both sides of you and this you is not that you. Personally, I prefer this one."

Elliott interrupted with a sharp, "NG. You have about one hour thirty before Zang and UM flood the town with troops. I hope you have a new plan."

NG drained the last of the beer. "We're going to get Tierney to surrender," he sent.

"No." Jiro Tierney stood up and signalled to someone at the door.

NG stood. "Then we'll be leaving."

"I don't think so."

NG turned his head slightly and glanced behind him. He'd been persuaded to come in here alone. The two men at the door had both drawn weapons. He looked back at the leader of this colony, the man who was supposed to be so charismatic. It had been like dealing with Pen Halligan, a big character who went to pains to take care of everyone, whom everyone loved, who, on the basis of one conversation, had made an instant snap judgement to hate him. What was it with people like this? "You can't stop us."

Tierney narrowed his eyes. "You've brought this trouble on us. I was prepared to give you a chance before but now…?" He leaned forward and his mind was as cold as ice. "I lost three people in that blast. The man you killed, the one who conspired with one of my people to get in here, wasn't a bounty hunter. So who was he?"

Tierney's intel was impressive. Someone must have seen what had happened and DiMarco must have told his boss about Tanzi.

"Who are you?" Tierney said again, aggressively, determined this time to get an answer, that was clear in his thoughts. And he was thinking, if not bounty hunter, then what? Assassin? His people had reported that it was this guy standing in front of him that had been the target, not Luka.

NG didn't reply but he started to play with the atmosphere between them, subtly winding down the tension.

Tierney sat down.

"Luka has currency with us," he said coldly, weighing it up, thinking that he wished LC hadn't played the hero in saving his niece, again, but the kid had, so fair was fair unless it reached a point where he had no other choice.

So that was Yoshi's secret.

Tierney stared unblinking. "We won't hurt him or see him hurt. You…? What would Zang say if I offered you up? How much are you worth?"

NG kept his expression neutral and shook his head. "They're not interested in me."

"I'm interested to find out what they'd say." The threat wasn't even veiled.

'Kill him.'

NG slowed his breathing. *'I don't need to – the Wintrans will do that soon enough.'*

"They've been given orders," he said, calmly, reasonably. "They're not here to negotiate or bargain. If you try, if you show any desperation, you just make it easier for them to wipe you out. There's no way out of this that doesn't end badly for you."

"Unless I do as you say?"

He used to need direct touch to drastically affect conscious decisions but even standing this distance away he could feel Tierney falter. He pushed it, going for a full one eighty, total spin with enough control that it felt like the most natural change of heart, as if Tierney was in full control of his emotions and simply reassessing a difficult situation with sharp and astute insight. It was like cleaning and refocusing a lens.

"If you try to play them," NG said softly, "you give them control over you. We…" And that 'we' that was the Thieves' Guild, suddenly included Tierney and his people, "…don't let anyone have control over us."

He let that hang, felt the change in Tierney and turned to walk away, towards the two men blocking his way. They were pirates, limited in anything but bullying. He walked between them and as they reached to take hold of his arms, he sent a vicious back off warning that hit them both between the eyes. They hesitated, confused, and he walked past towards the door.

"Wait." Tierney's voice behind him had a commanding tone it was hard to ignore.

NG stopped and turned.

"What do you need from us?"

NG took a step forward. "I told you – I want you to surrender."

"No. There has to be more to it than that. I want you to tell me what you're planning."

"There's an Imperial warship on its way here. You surrender to the Wintrans, now before anyone else gets hurt, you claim Earth allegiance and you scream protected status."

Tierney was smart enough to see it. "And there won't be anything they can do until they prove it one way or the other."

"Until that warship turns up and demands its citizens be freed and paid compensation for disruption to an Imperial mining operation."

There was a flaw in the plan and it didn't take long for Tierney to see it. "All very nice, but there are people here," himself included but he didn't say that, "who can't simply surrender..." without risking immediate execution upon official identification, on either side of the line, he was thinking.

NG shook his head. "It needs to be all of you. Otherwise we won't be able to pull it off and you lose. Work with us and your people get out of this alive. Trust me, I don't want them to find out who I am, either. We have a way. But it's going to come down to you pulling off the scam that you're an official Imperial operation, at least to give them enough doubt to delay things for a while."

It was a challenge and one that he knew would appeal to Tierney's ego and, judging by Tierney's past record, one the man wouldn't be able to resist. Especially not given the hold he had on his state of mind.

The leader of one of the most notorious pirate operations in the history of the Between nodded his head slowly. "Let's do it."

They had a room set up as an impromptu medical facility, five of Tierney's wounded in there, including DiMarco, and LC. The kid was out cold still, curled up on one of the bunks and hooked up to a drip.

NG paused to check him over quickly and then headed over to an empty bunk.

He'd already talked to Elliott and briefed Hilyer. Hil had listened carefully and run back through the details with meticulous care. In that respect, he hadn't changed and it had been an almost comfortable familiarity for them both to go through the motions of a briefing.

Martinez had talked to the Security detail, telling them that NG wanted them to go stealth and bug out. He'd overheard the conversation from a distance. They'd argued but she'd argued back, saying it was an order and what NG ordered, no one questioned, and they'd better get their asses out there and be ready to move back in if they were needed. Decent of her but he wasn't entirely sure he was deserving of such loyalty.

Tierney had agreed the terms needed for the surrender – immediate ceasefire, no resistance and evacuation for the wounded – and then thrown in the hand grenade that this was an Earth exploratory mining colony. The spokesman from the Expedience had laughed and said they'd see about that.

NG stripped down to a thin shirt, combat pants and boots, took off his wristband and belt, emptied his pockets and dropped the holstered gun on the bed.

Martinez stood close, not happy but not trying to dissuade him, a combat knife in her hand.

They'd decided against a bullet.

He turned and she moved closer.

'*You're insane, did I say that?*'

He could feel the heat of her body, the steady thump of her heart.

She gently lifted his shirt and raised the knife, pressing its tip against the muscles of his abdomen.

He curled his hand around hers, moving the blade across half an inch and whispering, "Let's avoid too many vitals."

"In the guts?" she murmured back. "Are you sure?"

"It doesn't just need to look good, it has to be good. I'll be fine. Flesh wounds are easy."

She raised her eyes to his, blinked once and thrust the knife into his stomach.

The Wintran medics were brusque and efficient as they assessed the wounded for medevac. DiMarco and another two of Tierney's guys were hauled off their bunks and marched out at gunpoint to join the rest of the prisoners.

NG had stopped blocking out the pain when they walked in. He hadn't healed much of the actual damage yet. He was still bleeding and when one of the son of a bitch medics roughly pulled away the blood-soaked bandage to peel back the trauma patch and press at the wound, it was a genuine scream he didn't try to stifle.

He managed to lie still, dropping his heart rate low and close to blacking out, as they checked his stats.

They were satisfied that he was messed up enough, lifted an eyelid and ran a retina scan, then a hand pushed on his head and a sharp pain pierced the top of his ear as they stapled a metal ID tag into it.

The medic called for a stretcher with a, "This one's good to go," and a parting pat to the stomach that was anything but gentle.

Sebastian was quiet but smouldering.

NG opened one eye and watched them assess LC, a medic grabbing his arm harshly and unstrapping the bindings with a tug that made the kid cry out in pain. They pushed on the shoulder, decided he wasn't faking it, confirmed his internal injuries with some prodding and poking, and ran the retina scan.

An alarm beeped.

Every head turned.

NG tensed.

Rifles snapped up to point at LC. They pushed him down, hard as if they thought he could jump up and fight them, someone yelling for backup, and adrenaline surging in every body in the room.

NG braced himself, not exactly sure what he was going to be able to do.

Elliott whispered inside his head, "Don't move."

"Run it again," someone said.

LC was struggling, distressed and in agony. They held him down and it was almost a relief to feel the second-hand pain dissipate as the kid passed out.

NG watched with a cold detachment as they crowded around, then there was cursing and a yell to stand down and get the damned scanner checked.

Someone said, "He's clear, for Christ's sake. Get him out of here."

NG sank back onto the bunk. "Elliott," he sent, "that was too close. I thought you had this covered."

"I do have it covered. You just concentrate on getting into that AI core. From the look of your stats, NG, you're not fit to do anything. How are you planning on doing this?"

NG cut the connection and closed his eyes.

The ride up to the battle cruiser in an iso-pod on a medevac drop ship was way more comfortable than he would have had in the prisoner pens, even if he did have cuffs secured tightly round his wrists and ankles. NG relaxed and concentrated on healing.

They docked and he lay there as the crew hooked up the five pods to be transferred to the infirmary. It was a fast-in-fast-out system, easy access to bring wounded troops on board and fast evacuation back onto the dropship for transportation planetside. Not that different to the system they had on the Alsatia. He'd never seen it from this angle before and it was one helluva way to board a ship.

He closed his eyes for five minutes of bumping and jostling as the pod slotted into a bay in the infirmary. As it locked into place, he scanned around. The infirmary was bustling with medics and heavily armed soldiers.

This wasn't going to work.

He made a fast decision, stopped his heart and stopped

breathing. Suddenly and abruptly. An alarm screamed and the safetycuffs popped open.

The medical crew were fast. For all that he was a prisoner, they did everything they could to bring him back. He resisted it all and sank into utter darkness, the shouting and noise fading gradually.

28

"Jiro Tierney is a name I've not heard in a long time," she said. "I'm surprised he, of all people, could pull off the pretence of having allegiance to the Empire."

"He probably enjoyed it." The Man drained the last of the wine and reached for the jug. "Nikolai has a talent for finding solutions that appeal to the ego, to the rebellious nature in his adversaries that makes them fall into his hands. Tierney was in an impossible situation. It was a Thieves' Guild operative that drew attention to his colony, yet it was the same guild that turned up to help."

"Aided by one of the Seven? Does Nikolai know who Elliott is?"

"No. But he knew enough through instinct to trust that Elliott could deliver what was promised and to place his own safety in those cold hands."

"So what went wrong?"

"What didn't go wrong?"

'I always knew you would kill me.'

NG opened his eyes. It was dark. Cold. His hands were free and it felt like he was on some kind of table or bench. He lay for a moment, gathering some strength to move.

'We're in the morgue,' Sebastian said dryly. *'You can leave any time you're ready.'*

He reached out to Martinez and Hilyer.

Martinez was fast to respond. "NG, are you okay? We heard rumours that one of the wounded had died."

"Yeah, it was me. Hil, you on board?"

The kid replied straight away with a cocky, "Yep. Ready and waiting."

He tried Elliott and got a simple, "All going to plan. What are you waiting for?"

All going to plan meant that Hil had made it onto the Duck, grabbed whatever it was that Elliott needed delivering to the AI core and that Elliott was nullifying their life signs, so they were free to roam.

He couldn't sense anyone else around so he drummed up some energy and sat, feeling the stomach muscles pull and feeling a weakness in his limbs that was draining. He was covered in blood, shirt torn open, tender around the wound still, and sore from the pummelling they'd given him when they were trying to resuscitate.

"Give me a minute," he sent to them all.

It took longer than that to get his breathing under control, slide off the table, get cleaned up somewhat and find a clean shirt to steal, but no one hassled him to hurry.

He made sure he left no trails of blood – as far as anyone would see, his body had been removed already, that was all, and Elliott would make sure the records showed that – and he climbed up into the ventilation system.

"NG, move," Elliott hissed through the Senson.

"I know, I know." He scrambled up the ladder, silent as a ghost, drawing his foot up and out of sight a fraction of a second before a crewman walked past.

He perched there for a second, heart pounding, until the guy had gone then climbed up through a hatch into a vent. He braced himself against the bulkhead and shifted his weight in the cramped space. Just like old times.

The Wintran battle cruiser was massive. Cold to the point of uncomfortable, clean verging on sterile and cramped, the perfectly configured design of every accessway and maintenance vent testament to Wintran efficiency.

They were both on target to get into position and so far nothing they'd done had raised an alarm.

'You hope...'

NG crept across a beam, sliding under thick knots of cables and easing past conduits that were warm to the touch. He was close. The engineering deck was the heart of the cruiser, the beating core of all its vital systems, and every element of its operations ran through this massive compartment. He slid into position and looked up.

'What power we hold when we have no contrition, no remorse or guilt… What happened to your conscience, Nikolai? I'm not sure the Man would approve of your actions.'

'I really don't care.'

Sebastian laughed.

NG cracked open one of the panels. "How are you doing, Hil?" he sent.

Hilyer sounded strained and distant. "Almost…"

Waiting seemed to last forever and it was hard to resist the urge to pester Hilyer to hurry up. But Hil had the toughest target. He hadn't been thrilled at the idea of his part in the plan, still dwelling on Genoa, laughing bitterly, saying that he was going to get a reputation for screwing over AIs.

The kid called in eventually, on a tight wire link, sounding like shit. "I'm in, let's do this."

'How precious. The child is in trouble. Anderton now Hilyer. It's all so dramatic. I'm almost enjoying playing at being a field operative again.'

NG shifted his weight slightly to ease an ache in his abdomen. "Hil, what's wrong?"

There was a long silence then, "Freaking electrobes. I'm fine." He sounded far from fine. "Let's do it." He started counting down. They had to take out the AI first or risk it detecting any other action they were going to pull and shutting them down.

Hilyer worked steadily, finally sending, "Done," as he connected and broke through into the core.

NG threw his kill switch simultaneously.

A deep groaning rumble shuddered through the ship as it powered down, emergency systems struggling and failing to get past their traps.

Klaxons began to wail and alarms shrieked. Now they just had to get out.

NG packed up quickly, slipping out from under the panel and running back along the beam, trusting that Hilyer was moving, the entire crew of the ship mobilising around them as the Wintrans kicked in defensive battle stations. From here on in, it was going to go one of two ways. The plan was to get everyone onto the Duck, find Gallagher and extract. Nice and simple, low key. Tierney and his people could work it out from there.

Or the Earth warship would turn up and all hell would break loose. Either way, all he needed was twenty seconds with Gallagher. Zang could wait. And he could take whatever message he wanted from this.

NG ran along a gantry high above a loading bay. He was having trouble tracking Hil, trying to keep tabs on the kid as he moved. It wasn't easy. This was one of the reasons they tended to send the field-ops out on tabs alone, less baggage, no worrying about what someone else was or wasn't doing, more opportunity to improvise on a whim.

The Wintrans didn't know what had happened but they were working fast to try to secure their vessel. It was like being caught in a hive of swarming bees.

He paused to scan around, timed his move and pushed up into a run again, calling out to Hilyer through the Senson.

'Leave him.'

'What?'

'Leave him. He's about to get caught. You must have known that was a risk when you brought him here. I thought you didn't care.'

NG stopped, merged into the shadows, and concentrated, isolating the life signs and homing in on Hilyer. He wasn't moving.

The Senson engaged with a dry, "Don't. You need to extricate," from Elliott.

Not an option. NG changed direction, backtracking to find a way through.

'Don't get me killed here, Nikolai.'

He wasn't about to abandon the kid. He picked up his pace. More and more search parties were starting to flood into the area. From what he could pick up, the Wintrans didn't know what they were dealing with and they weren't tracking them or sensing them in any way. But even so, with that many bodies searching, it was just a matter of time before they ran out of options if they didn't get out of there.

Sebastian stirred, a disturbing and cold essence inside. '*You're making a mistake.*'

NG didn't stop, heading directly for Hilyer. He ran along a beam, jumped across to a narrow rail and dropped down out of the darkness onto a gantry high above a maintenance area, feeling the sting of electrobes at the back of his throat. Hil was sprawled, unmoving, on the deck below.

Damn.

NG dropped down and ran forward, sliding down onto his knees to skid in to a halt beside Hilyer, placing a hand on Hil's chest.

He was still alive.

'*Not for long.*'

NG checked him over quickly, scanning around as he sat there in the open, trying to ease the pressure on the kid's lungs and trying not to be drawn in by the prickling agony that was sparking through Hil's body.

Hil gasped suddenly and curled up, swearing, muttering, "Oh crap," breathing laboured and eyes squeezed shut.

'*Interesting...*'

This wasn't just electrobe poisoning. The virus was active, suddenly and ferociously active, fighting with the electrobes in the kid's system.

Hil rolled over onto his back, groaning and cursing under his breath.

It was a hell of a time for the virus to kick in.

NG could feel search parties closing in.

'*Leave him,*' Sebastian hissed again.

That wasn't going to happen.

NG shook his head and sent silently through the implant to Hil, "We need to move," grabbing his arm and dragging him up.

They took three or four steps before the kid folded over coughing, stumbling to his knees. The wave of pure pain that hit NG was agonising. Consuming. It took a second to block it out and blink away the tears. Hil was close to passing out again, internal temperature shooting up and oxygen levels desperately low.

A hatch some way behind them clanged as it was flung open.

They could not afford to be caught here.

'Damn right you cannot be caught here. One of Zang's little cronies is on board, did I not mention that before?'

Of course Zang would have someone on board his battle cruiser – they were looking for LC.

There was a clanging of metal on metal below them. NG pulled Hil to his feet, hoisting the kid's arm over his shoulder. They needed to find somewhere to lie low.

'Zang has mobilised some of his most expensive assets. We should be flattered.'

Half running, half staggering along the narrow gantry, he could feel the pounding heartbeats of a thousand people as the desperate realisation that they were stranded dawned on them, the arrogance that came from an easy victory plummeting into panic, then anger.

More loud, clanging echoes began to reverberate through the deck, blast doors slamming shut as the crew initiated manual lock down.

'They're going to flush you out. Looks like we might be going to meet Zang after all. I had something rather different in mind when I suggested it…'

Hil staggered, coughing, threatening to sink to his knees again. It was getting harder to keep him upright and moving.

There was a hiss.

NG glanced up, sensing the gas as he spotted the vents spewing out white mist. The Expedience was designed to carry prisoners – of course they'd have suppressant systems. He covered his mouth with his arm but the molecules hit his bloodstream with such a punch it was tough to neutralise it quickly.

Hil was pretty much a deadweight against his shoulder.

There were crashes up ahead and behind, heavy footsteps and yells.

NG shoved Hilyer to the side and spun, weighing up the full scale of the force closing in on them.

'Don't...'

They fired before he could try anything, FTH so the shots were muted in the enclosed space, yells and a pure adrenaline-fuelled focus emanating from the armoured and masked marines who suddenly had a target in front of them.

Sebastian growled, withdrawing from the pain as FTH rounds impacted and armour-weighted punches hit home. NG fell to his knees, curling up, an almost overwhelming urge to lash out with a blast of energy tempered by a weakness from the gas that was pulling his senses sideways.

A vicious kick landed against his ribs with a crack and the hot metal of a gun barrel pressed against the back of his neck, burning into his skin. He could feel the trembling anticipation behind it as the pressure increased. FTH rounds at point-blank range were nasty and it was a vindictive son of a bitch who leaned in close, whispered through the mask into his ear, "Wrong ship to fuck with, mate," and pulled the trigger.

29

"You should have run tests."

"There are a lot of things we should have done and should not have done," he said. "It is irrelevant. What is, is."

She leaned forward, resting her arms on her knees, the light of the fire a warm glow on her cheeks. "We run the guild on the back of our operatives. This virus? It has cost us dearly."

It had. But without it, the outcome would have been very different.

"Where is Science with it?" she asked.

"Learning."

"Did you consider giving it to Nikolai?"

He rubbed his fingers and thumb together, contemplating adding more of the black powder. "No."

That was a lie. He'd come very close to that, would probably have ordered it if events had not transpired as they had. "I couldn't risk it."

He spat blood onto the polished deck of the bridge and slowly raised his eyes to look at the uniform standing in front of him. "I don't know what you're talking about."

They triggered the device they'd stuck into the back of his neck and his knees buckled as another blast of pain shot through his spine.

As bad situations went, this was turning out to be fairly awesome.

NG choked back a laugh. Someone grabbed a handful of his hair and punched him again.

They'd scanned him, detected the Senson and slapped a patch

onto the side of his neck so he couldn't contact anyone. He'd tried to find Duncan or LC but there was nothing clear.

He blinked and coughed, looking up.

The guy in the uniform was the captain by the look of his insignia, his demeanour and the way the crew were deferring to him. "Don't make me ask again."

The device was emitting a pulse that throbbed in time with his heartbeat, small shivers of persistent pain that were distracting but not debilitating. NG shook his head, trying not to throw up on the guy's shiny shoes. It was taking all the effort he could manage to just keep the pain under control.

"Your security is a joke," he said softly. "Your AI was too easy."

That got him another blast from the device and the agony seemed to last forever.

When it eventually ceased, he slumped forward, heart thumping. The noise in his head from the crew surrounding him was a ringing clamour of anger and disbelief.

He glanced sideways at Hilyer who was drifting in and out of consciousness, held up next to him by two guys in powered armour.

Someone slapped the back of NG's head.

"Release my AI."

"Can't do that."

"Who are you working for?"

"We're not working for anyone."

"You evaded our sensors and incapacitated our AI. Who are you?"

NG tugged at the manacles restraining his wrists behind his back. He was slapped again and a gun barrel was nudged up under his chin.

The captain leaned in close. "Answer the question."

NG shook his head. "I don't…" The device sparked and it was suddenly really hard to concentrate, vision narrowing to a dark tunnel and a hot fever clutching at his mind. The small device became his whole world.

The captain nodded, signalling to someone off to the side. The gun that was pressed up against NG's jawline vanished, whipping back hard to impact against his temple again.

Senses rattled. Fresh blood poured into his eye and trickled down his face.

Sebastian stirred, dark and disturbed. *'Kill him before he kills you.'*

They weren't going to kill him. He'd had worse. Their interrogation technique left a lot to be desired. You don't get intel from anyone by killing them.

The captain came close again. "Release my AI."

Sebastian twitched.

The atmosphere on the bridge suddenly changed. Footsteps and the chill of a calm, cold newcomer.

"What do we have here?" It was a strong Wintran accent, the words carrying no emotion.

'Gian Fiorrentino. Now this is interesting.'

NG raised his eyes to look towards the voice. The guy was wearing a slick suit, corporate executive, different breed to the militia that were crew here and an arrogant confidence in his demeanour that was chilling.

Fiorrentino was Zang's right hand man, rumoured to be his great-great-nephew or some such and considered his heir by some in the hierarchy of Zang Enterprises. Devon had always said the man was overrated and liable to destroy the corporation if left to his own devices hence the motivation for Zang to stay alive as long as he was.

The captain stepped back. "See what you can do," he said dismissively. "I have a ship to run." He walked away.

Fiorrentino smirked, looking at Hilyer. He reached and peeled the patch from NG's neck then stepped back, keeping eye contact, undisguised curiosity burning in his mind.

The Senson engaged abruptly.

"Thieves' Guild," he sent.

Smug, no question there.

NG didn't react. The device was still humming an agonising melody into his synapses.

He sent urgently on a private tight wire, "Angel?"

"NG?"

"We might have messed up here…"

'Don't worry, he doesn't know who you are,' Sebastian murmured, *'but he knows Hilyer. Can you feel the hate?'*

"If you want to get out of this alive, you will release the AI," Fiorrentino said out loud.

"Release the colonists."

That elicited a smile. A feeling of something like admiration flitted over the guy's mind. He had one of the goddamned Thieves' Guild on his knees in front of him, bleeding and at his mercy, and the cocky son of a bitch was making demands of his own. He sent privately, coldly, "Where's Anderton?"

NG managed to smile back, breathing still hard and concentration wavering. "Not here," he sent back.

"We want our package."

"We don't acknowledge your blackmail as a legitimate contract. Come to us direct next time you want something. It'll cost you a lot less."

"Where's the package?"

'He wants it for himself,' Sebastian hissed suddenly. *'He wants the elixir for himself. He has no intention of delivering you up to Zang.'*

NG laughed. And he thought the internal politics on the Alsatia were complex?

That didn't go down well. The pain from the device increased a notch. He could feel Sebastian working to neutralise it.

Martinez was trying to get through to him but it was hard to focus. "Get LC and get onto the Duck," he tried to send, not sure whether he managed it. "Find Gallagher. Find out where it happened."

Fiorrentino pulled a gun out from beneath his jacket, making a show of checking the magazine and cocking it before pointing it at Hilyer's head. "Release the AI."

"Kill him and you never get it back," NG said.

Another smile. The guy knew fine well that it was Zach Hilyer being held there and had no intention of killing him. He casually prodded Hilyer in the side with his gun barrel, hatred burning beneath the cool exterior. Hil stirred slightly. His hands were bound behind his back, face bruised.

Fiorrentino looked up, still smirking. "No one messes with the Thieves' Guild, right? Isn't that what you say?" He was keeping it private still. He obviously didn't want anyone else on board to know. He stepped forward, the smile dropping and a hard edge appearing in his eyes. "We want our package. Where's Anderton?"

NG blinked, the blood starting to clot one of his eyes closed. "Where's Zang?"

There was a shake of the head then, exaggerated disapproval as if the guy was talking to a child. "You're not in a position to bargain. You have nothing. The Thieves' Guild is finished. Zachary here made a serious mistake by attacking us. Power shifts. Your time is over. Done. And all it took to precipitate your downfall was a petty betrayal by a pretty girl. Anyone would think we had her mother killed to put her in such a vulnerable position…"

'He's lying. Let me loose and I'll kill him slowly.'

"Where's Anderton?" Fiorrentino sent again, taking another step forward.

NG shook his head slowly, needles of pain sparking behind his eyes. "I'll talk to Zang."

Fiorrentino laughed. "You'll talk to me," he sent, keeping to the private link. "You'll release the AI and you'll tell me exactly where we need to go to find your other little bastard thief and the package he stole from us. You've lost. Face it. What's the point in fighting any more? Trust me, I can make this a lot more painful for you." He raised a hand in a casual gesture, beckoning, and said out loud, "Time to find out exactly who you are."

NG sensed someone move in behind him and closed his eyes as an autoinjector hit his neck with a sting. Two of the shots were Banitol, another was a stimulant and god knows what else.

Someone was trying the Senson again but he couldn't even tell who it was, never mind concentrate to reply.

Sebastian was getting more and more agitated, murmuring, *'Yes, I'm fucking agitated. This guy is going to kill you. You should kill him now. Be damned with the consequences.'*

The drugs flooded into his bloodstream, almost overwhelming his senses. It was tough to neutralise it all with everything else he was dealing with. Multicoloured flashes sparked behind his eyes.

"What's your name?" Fiorrentino said.

It was shockingly tempting to answer honestly and he opened his mouth to say 'Nikolai', catching himself just in time, a rush of adrenaline making his heart pound.

"What's your name?"

NG raised his eyes slowly and said instead, slowly and deliberately, "Sebastian."

'Oh, fucking hilarious.'

"Well done, Sebastian. That wasn't hard, was it?" Fiorrentino stepped back, folding his arms.

If there was any such thing as orchestrated fate at work in the universe, Thom Garrett's warship would turn up to the party any minute now.

It didn't.

'Nikolai…'

Coming round was a slow and painful realisation that he'd lost consciousness at some point and had no idea what he'd done or said.

'Don't worry, you said nothing,' Sebastian murmured sullenly.

There was a sting against his neck and NG was hauled to his feet. A gun barrel pushed against the back of his neck again.

'It's not FTH. Be careful what you do here, Nikolai…'

His chest felt like it was on fire.

'How long was I out?'

'Not long. They got Hilyer awake and made him watch while they kicked you to the floor. He didn't tell them anything either. I never knew these youngsters could be so resilient. He told Fiorrentino to go fuck a goat. That didn't go down well.'

'Where is he?'

'The infirmary. He reacted badly to their drugs. It didn't look good.' He sounded pleased. *'They had to resuscitate. I'm not sure he survived.'*

NG felt sick but right now he couldn't spare the effort to scan around for anyone. After the kicking he'd just had, it was taking all his effort to stay upright, calm his breathing and figure out what was broken.

'Two ribs. And they cracked that bone in my cheek again. Except for that and the knife wound, I'm fine…' Sebastian said dryly, *'thank you for caring. The Earth warship just dropped out of jump by the way.'*

The Senson still wasn't shielded.

NG sent a fast, "Angel? Elliott?" and lost the connection as something heavy hit the back of his head. Senses swirled for a second and he would have hit the floor except they were holding him up.

He blinked and raised his head.

The captain was standing there, calm in the centre of a maelstrom of activity, thinking that the warship was going to attack. How could it not? Hostilities had been escalating and the damned pirates had claimed to be Earth colonists when they had finally surrendered. He'd written it off as a desperate ploy by outlaws. Nonsense. Until an Imperial warship dropped out of jump.

A hand grabbed NG's face, demanding his attention, and Fiorrentino loomed into his line of sight. "Where's Anderton?" he demanded, private through the implant.

"You want me to tell you? Release the colonists."

"Trust me, you're in no position to bargain."

Fiorrentino released him roughly and stepped away as the captain turned to look at them, face like stone, grim determination colouring his thoughts. He was thinking that it was an act of outright aggression, that he had two prisoners of war here, this was clearly beyond the simple clearing action of a pirate colony. He was very aware that anyone who could take out a military grade AI that easily was of high strategic interest. Way too much strategic value to his own career if he handled this right. "Why are you here?" he said.

'You' being Earth. Why is an Earth warship here was the real question.

"We're not Earth," NG said softly, trying to gauge how to play this.

The captain shook his head, not believing it. "This is an act of war," he warned. "Release my AI."

"Not going to happen," NG said and got another blow to the back of the head.

The captain looked disgusted again and walked away, commanding his crew to stand by to resist boarding. He was thinking that they were not going to be taken that easily.

The comm crackled to life suddenly and a voice that was unmistakably from Earth commanded, "Expedience, stand down. This is the Imperial Diplomatic Vessel Tangiers. Stand by."

The captain stared for a moment then turned and indicated to the comms officer to open a channel. He replied in an icy tone, "This is Captain Ramsay of the Expedience. To whom am I speaking?"

There was a pause then another voice came through the comm. "This is Colonel Hones of the IDV Tangiers. It would appear that you have mistaken one of our mining colonies for pirates, Captain Ramsay. Surrender our citizens and you will be allowed to leave. Do you understand?"

The captain turned and stared at him again.

NG stared back through the one eye he could still open. Garrett must have got the message out and his commanding officer was playing along so at least something was going right.

Ramsay frowned and turned back to the console. "We caught two of your people sabotaging our vessel, Colonel. I must admit, we have been on deployment for some time. Was war declared while we have been busy hunting down pirates?"

'What games these mortals play… they are hilarious, they really are.'

There was a moment of silence then a laugh. "You're mistaken,

Captain. You understand as well as I that the rules of engagement here in the Between are often grey, but no, we have no wish to attack, with either subterfuge or force. You must be mistaken. Hand over our citizens and you will be allowed to leave."

That didn't go down well. "I am well aware of our current location and the ambiguity of its politics, Colonel. We have your men right here and I am wondering what we do with them. As you say, out here in the Between the usual conventions hold no ground."

NG heard Fiorrentino open a tight wire link to the captain, the conversation easy to pick out from the surface of their minds. "Hand over Tierney and his scum," he sent casually. "I just need these two."

The captain's frown deepened. "Whatever your business, Fiorrentino," he sent privately with total disdain, "I still have my orders and we will fulfil this mission."

This close it was easy to read that the captain wasn't happy at having Fiorrentino on his ship. What should have been an easy clean up mission had turned into a nightmare and this flash corporate suit was right in the middle of the mess with his so-called private business.

Fiorrentino sighed theatrically. "You're dead in space, Ramsay. There is no mission. This is the mission, you fool. Stand in my way and you'll never command so much as a tug boat or garbage scow again."

The comm hissed. "Excuse my blunt observations here, Captain Ramsay, but you do not seem to have shields, weapons or a functioning drive system. Hand over our people and we will assist you with repairs."

Ramsay forced a laugh. "It is you that is mistaken, Colonel. We have evidence that these people are criminals. Does the Earth Empire tolerate piracy now? Your agents have disabled my ship, we are effectively at your mercy yet the people you demand we hand over are pirates. You see my dilemma?"

"Expedience," Hones transmitted in an almost bored tone of voice, "I'd hate to have to send my troops in there."

NG listened to it all, hard pushed to stop himself breaking into a grin.

No captain ever wanted to be boarded but it was Fiorrentino who punched the console. "Hones, wait. You can have your people."

"Who is this?"

"I have the authority to speak on behalf of Zang, owners of this fleet. We stand down. You may retrieve your colonists and we hope you accept our most sincere apologies."

NG sat and watched as they arranged the release. They'd made him sit at the back of the bridge and refastened the manacles to secure his wrists to the chair.

He used the time to heal and listen, drawing energy from the conveniently placed guards at his side. He checked in with Martinez and got a running commentary as she teamed up with Duncan and Garrett in a slick coordinated operation to slip out of confinement, extricate LC from the infirmary and sneak onto the Duck, Elliott adding to the chaos on the battle cruiser and covering them.

It was impressive.

Easy.

Until they tried to reach Hil.

"Fiorrentino isn't taking any chances. Hilyer's alive but unconscious," Elliott sent. "He's in isolation, locked down tight. Unless you want to deploy that unit of assault troops and the weapons platform you have on standby to launch an all-out attack, there's no way we're getting close."

"I'll work on Fiorrentino," he sent back. "You get clear."

Sebastian growled, unsettled and making it known. '*Damn right I'm unsettled,*' he snapped. '*You should deploy that Thundercloud. You're making a bad mistake here. Playing games with a bastard like Jameson is one thing, at least he is a bastard that knows you. Fiorrentino is psychotic. You're going to get me killed and you're enjoying it.*'

Hardly. It wasn't like he had much choice.

He tugged on the restraints, more to make a point than really test them. They weren't safetycuffs so there were no biometrics to fool and they weren't simple plasticuffs so he couldn't just snap his way out of them. They were mechanicals. Tight around the wrist, no room to move, unlocked with a key or a remote. As he rattled the arm of the chair, one of the guards smacked him round the head with a rifle butt. It wasn't like he'd get far even if he did break free.

"All accounted for," Martinez sent finally. "Except you and Hil. NG, tell me you have a plan to get out of this."

"Just tell me you have the intel from Gallagher."

"It was the Erica system, out near one of the bigger asteroids in the belt." She gave him the exact coordinates and added, "The Tangiers wants Gallagher and the freighter, NG. What do you want us to do?"

"Go with it. Make sure Hones takes the bait and goes to Erica. Get Ghost and Skye to follow. I'll see you there."

He sat back then and waited patiently until he got word that the Duck was hooked up to the Tangiers and the warship was preparing to leave.

He opened a connection to Elliott, "Ready?"

"As always."

NG switched to Fiorrentino and sent, "You want to know what an Imperial warship is doing in the Between this close to your line?"

Fiorrentino was standing beside the captain. He turned lazily. "I want to know where Anderton is with my package."

"So do they."

There was a pause then, "You son of a bitch."

"You blackmailed my field operatives into stealing technology from the Imperial military, Fiorrentino. You started this war. They want that tech back and they just picked up someone who is going to tell them exactly where to go to meet with LC Anderton."

Another pause. "And what do you want?"

"I tell you where, you take us there and you let us go, all of us, me, Anderton and Hilyer. You can fight with the Tangiers over the package. I don't care who has it. I just want my field operatives back."

"Deal. Now release my AI."

"Done."

NG listened in as the crew of the battle cruiser took back control as Elliott kicked the AI free. The Tangiers jumped and the Expedience jumped right after it.

They should have been heading into quiet, deep dark space, but the noise screaming into his head the instant they emerged was excruciating.

He doubled over, gasping, and passed out.

30

"If we had tried to seed the beginnings of a war," she said, "we could not have done better. We are beyond the brink. Have you considered how much of this whole situation may have been manipulated by one of the Seven?"

"There is no proof," the Man said. He'd instigated an investigation. High priority and top secret. Outside the guild. Far outside the guild. They'd uncovered nothing. Whatever Elliott had been doing, he'd been careful to cover his tracks. But then, he had no choice. To even dabble as much as he had, had been to risk discovery.

She picked up her goblet. "But that is a terrifying thought?"

"Indeed it is. Nikolai has been playing with fire, the danger of which even he did not fully appreciate."

"And Erica?"

"He played Earth against Winter. I suspect he was assuming the Bhenykhn did not really exist."

It felt like his eyeballs were going to melt.

It was quiet. Really quiet.

The battle cruiser was moving, slow and steady.

He was vaguely aware of the thousands of life forms on board but he couldn't hear a thing.

'*What happened*?' he thought, nausea pulling at his stomach, breathing erratic.

'*You screamed and passed out*,' Sebastian said, deadpan.

He felt like shit. He didn't want to open his eyes and he didn't want to move. He was slumped in the chair. He didn't want to be there, heart pounding and a cold sick feeling in the pit of his stomach.

It was eerily quiet but the kind of quiet where you know something is locked behind the door waiting to jump out at you.

There was something wrong.

'*Sebastian, what's going on?*' he thought weakly.

'*I would guess that you've found the Man's enemies. You want another listen?*'

It was like a switch flicking on. Overwhelming. NG tried to curl up against it, in absolute agony for a brief second before it vanished again. He could feel the effort it was taking Sebastian to block it out.

'*You can thank me later. Figure out a way to help, I'm not sure how much longer I can do this.*'

He was caught between a desperate desire to listen in and a greater need to get as far away as possible.

There was a slap at his cheek.

NG struggled to blink open his eyes.

The bridge was in chaos.

All the screens were lit up, long range scans overloaded with data. A mass of tiny markers were flitting around two massive shapes on the monitors, warnings flashing up, telemetry throwing back numbers that were off the scale.

'*Oh, what it is to meet such an adversary. They don't know what it is. Can you feel their panic?*'

He could make out one of the shapes to be the Tangiers, up there on the main screen, squaring up to another vessel, no chance to do anything other than confront it, close quarters, one massive warship against another. The crew were trying desperately to identify the other ship and they were failing.

It was the ship Gallagher had encountered.

It was real.

Ramsay turned to face him, ramrod straight, arms behind his back. "You sent us here. Who are they?"

The alien ship was beginning to circle, hunting. It was bombarding the Earth warship, knocking the shit out of it.

"Unknowns," NG said simply.

They were trying to add it up – it couldn't be Earth because the Tangiers was taking a pounding and it wasn't Wintran unless another corporation had developed technology off the radar, desperately trying to think which corporation was capable of this.

"It's not corporate," he said. "It's not human."

Fiorrentino spun around. "Are we talking first contact here?" he said, incredulous. "Are you serious?"

Every hit on the alien ship seemed to dissipate into nothing. The Tangiers was trying desperately to turn but it couldn't move fast enough.

NG didn't reply. The battle cruiser was moving in and the closer they got, the more difficult it was to block out the intensity of the interference that was filtering through his subconscious.

There was a buzz of excitement. Fiorrentino was thinking technology. The repercussions were vast. First contact with an alien species. It was easy to read without reading his mind. And he wanted to beat the Tangiers to the prize. He turned to the captain. "Ramsay, engage."

Ramsay spun on his heels and barked out the command. More markers began to fill the screens as Wintran fighters joined the fray.

They closed in fast.

It turned nasty quickly.

They watched on the monitors as explosions started to blossom out from the hull of the Tangiers, flashes flaring from the alien ship as Wintran missiles and fighters disintegrated against its shields. The Tangiers shifted mass suddenly to arc round, firing at the alien ship.

'Earth and Winter versus a common foe. How sweet. They don't have a chance against those weapons.'

They didn't. They were losing. The best combined military force from both sides of the line and they were getting destroyed. The smaller alien ships were running rings around them, one shot one kill on the swarms of Earth and Wintran fighters that were getting depleted rapidly. The Expedience itself was taking a barrage of direct hits now, alarms blaring as vital systems were breached.

The alien warship changed its focus of attention in a heartbeat, turning to the larger vessel and firing. The deck rocked with the impact. Damage reports flooded the screens and warning sirens wailed.

"Where are they from?" Fiorrentino said without turning.

NG didn't speak.

Someone slapped the back of his head.

"Another galaxy," he muttered. "We can't beat them. You should get away while you can."

He kept his breathing steady. He had what he needed. Now he just needed to get away and get back to the Alsatia.

'Don't fool yourself, Nikolai,' Sebastian murmured. *'You're more of a fool than I thought if you think you can just walk back into the guild.'*

It wasn't foolish. The Man needed him.

'Needs you?'

Sebastian let the floodgates open, full force. NG almost screamed again. The bridge turned black. The space around him cold. As if his soul had been sucked out and extinguished.

It shut off.

'You think you can fight them? You can barely face them without passing out.'

He shivered.

The Tangiers and the Expedience were in serious trouble.

The atmosphere on the bridge changed as the crew realised they were outgunned here.

A wailing mayday started to emanate from the Tangiers, long-range emergency beacons calling out for help that had no chance of getting here in time. It sounded desperate.

'It is desperate. The start of the end. You wanted to know if they were real – they're real. Now come up with a plan to get out of here.'

Ramsay initiated his own mayday, desperately issuing orders that wouldn't make a difference. The alien aggressors were targeting main engines, weapons, life support – pinpointing vital systems as if they were working off blueprints. Ramsay's crew were running out of options.

'They've run out of options,' Sebastian observed dryly. *'We just passed Arunday's convergence.'*

'No one uses that any more,' NG replied vaguely, watching the crew as they began to realise that they'd committed to an engagement they had no chance of surviving.

Ramsay had already worked it out, without the need to reference an outdated theory of military strategy.

Fiorrentino was looking around, confused.

NG watched out of the corner of his eye, listening in as the captain relayed messages privately to his senior officers. They were beyond the point of retreat, too damaged to have much fight left and nothing in reserve to fire a winning salvo.

Explosions rumbled through the ship.

They were arranging a collision course. Ramsay was about to abandon ship.

'Nikolai, you're surrounded by armed troops who think it is your fault that their ship is about to be destroyed. I take it you have some kind of a plan to get out of here? And trust me, I need you to get out of here – I can't do this much longer.'

He could feel that the headache was getting worse.

Ramsay turned, stared straight at him, then spun and hit the comm. "Tangiers – Hones – get out of here."

The battle cruiser was shifting on pure inertia, slewing sideways through space towards the alien vessel.

Ramsay punched in a code and a banshee howl began to rise in pitch, screaming at the crew to evacuate. Abandon ship. A captain's worst nightmare.

The crew reacted on automatic, hustling to get out, only the second officer pausing to argue with his captain. Ramsay spoke to him quietly and the guy turned, glared at NG and stalked off the bridge.

Fiorrentino had gone already, hustled out by his entourage.

Ramsay turned, leaning back against the main console and staring at NG. He pulled a gun from a holster at his waist, the screens behind him filled with the looming mass of the alien warship.

"You were expecting this," Ramsay said again, resigned, eyes cold as he prepared to die. He was tapping the gun against his thigh. "Who are you?"

NG stared back.

It wasn't the first time he'd played chicken.

The proximity alarm was loud, the collision alert louder as it suddenly blared out its warning.

Ramsay's finger was twitching on the trigger of the pistol. He raised his voice, disdain mixed with disgust. "At least tell me that."

NG didn't break eye contact but he switched his concentration briefly to sense the intricacies of the tiny control circuits inside the restraints, following them, nudging and finally throwing the switch.

The cuffs popped open.

His head was pounding in time with the screaming alarms.

Ramsay straightened as NG stood.

"Come with me," NG said. "You don't have to die here."

Ramsay turned to face the main screen, squaring his shoulders, stubborn defiance.

NG backed away and broke into a run.

The Senson engaged as he pushed his way through to the stairwell, the deck trembling and lurching beneath his feet. "NG, we're coming in to get you."

The connection was rough as hell, the communication stream struggling to get through the headache.

"Angel, get out of here."

"Will do, boss, as soon as we manage to dock with that ship that is disintegrating around you and haul your ass out of there."

He ran down the narrow stairs, two or three at a time, dropping down through the decks as fast as he could. It felt like it was taking forever and he could feel the escalating pain pushing against his senses as they closed on the alien vessel.

"Okay, we're in," she yelled suddenly inside his head. "How are you doing there, NG? We are not going to be able to stay here for long. I…"

He bumped up against the bulkhead as the ship's mass shifted, hurtling towards its inevitable end.

"Angel, get away. We'll find a way out."

"Yeah, I don't know how," she sent back. "All the escape pods have been jettisoned and you might not have noticed, but this cruiser and all its ships have been shot to hell. Looks to me like we're your only option."

He reached the bottom of one stairwell and raced through a dark linking corridor to the next. "I need to find Hilyer."

"You don't have time. Just get your ass down here."

"I can't leave him."

"NG, I've sent an extraction team after him. You just get down here."

He could hardly breathe. Nine more levels. He ran down the stairs, legs feeling like jelly. Eight levels. Seven. Six. He fell somewhere along the way and the rest passed in a blur.

Bone shuddering tremors were shaking the entire substructure.

After an eternity, he reached the last set of stairs. He jumped the last five steps and crashed through onto the docks level as another explosion ripped through the ship. He was thrown off his feet, rolled with it and staggered up into a run.

"NG, come on. Pick up the pace there, boss."

He was moving blind through corridors filled with smoke and the intermittent flashing blue strobe of rapidly failing emergency lighting. He fired back, "Where are you?"

"Straight ahead. Just keep running."

He was running. Coughing, struggling to stay upright and on the verge of passing out as the pressure in his head increased but he was running.

Arms grabbed him and he lashed out, automatic responses kicking in to fight back until Sebastian hissed, '*These are your guys, you fool.*'

They pulled him into an airlock, propelling him forward and into a smaller ship.

NG sank into a chair and fumbled for the harness.

Martinez yelled out a warning to hold on and dropped

them from the berth, accelerating hard. He tried to hold onto something, anything, failed and blacked out.

They were on Ghost. NG recognised the ship as he started to come round. He squinted at the screens. The proximity alarms were screaming, the screens showing the entire volume of space filled with flitting shapes, fighters, missiles and debris. Ghost was struggling to keep up with the sudden overwhelming mass of incoming data.

"Jesus, they're getting annihilated," Martinez muttered. She was flying Ghost at her absolute limit, trying to wing her way through a blossoming field of debris.

NG braced his feet against the console, failing miserably to block out the increasing pain in his head. They were closing on the Tangiers as it fled.

He couldn't help but sense the panic emanating from the cloud of vessels surrounding it even at these distances, even through the shield that Sebastian was maintaining. It wasn't often that the best of Earth special forces and Winter's fleet came up against an adversary they couldn't beat into submission.

He closed his eyes.

'Don't flake out on me again, Nikolai.'

The pain intensified.

"NG, the Duck just disengaged from the Tangiers. We can't risk trying to hook up to her in all this. What do you want us to do?"

"Get away," he managed to say, feeling sick, a tight knot in his chest and a pounding hammering at his mind.

Martinez responded instantly and they spiralled away as weapons flared, catching the edge of a blast as the hull of the Tangiers rocked with an explosion. They rolled with the spin and she accelerated up and round in a breathtaking manoeuvre.

Everything greyed out for a second.

'Get out of here,' Sebastian whispered.

Martinez was saying something.

He looked up.

She glanced back at him. "NG! What the hell else is going on here that you're not telling me?"

He squinted at her through eyes that felt like they were on fire. "They're telepaths."

Martinez cursed. "We're way down the food chain here, aren't we?"

'And then some…'

"We need to get back, get a warning out," he muttered uneasily, watching the battle unfold.

One of the Expedience's few remaining fighters cut across their path, too close for comfort, a smaller vessel that was firing some kind of energy weapon in pursuit.

Martinez spun them out of its way as the fighter took a hit and exploded in a flash of billowing fragments. She accelerated hard, multiple impacts pounding against Ghost's hull.

'No wonder the Man is so terrified of these creatures – they're like locusts. Can you feel their hunger?'

He couldn't feel anything except a nauseating pain that was dragging at the back of his mind.

Another collision sent them spinning out of control. Martinez compensated, calmly rolling Ghost with the motion and establishing a new escape vector as damage reports started to flash onto the screens.

Someone was trying to connect to the Senson.

He heard her reply, "Negative, our jump drives are down."

Behind them, the Tangiers took another direct hit.

"I know, I know," Martinez sent to whoever it was she was talking to. "One engine is gone and our shields are so low, we're fucked if another..." She bit off the next word as a proximity alarm screamed and she had to throw Ghost into a wild spiral.

The nauseating disorientating spin took his breath away.

She swore. "NG, we can't win this."

'She's right. They have a hive mind. You want to hear?'

'No.'

'It's fascinating.'

It was excruciating.

'I have to tell you, Nikolai, I do admire the way you have brought us to this. You have precipitated a most dire confrontation with your impetuous need for the truth.' Sebastian laughed. *'After centuries of the most intricate and patient preparation, you have managed to rush headlong into the very conflict for which you were being nurtured so meticulously.'*

'They're here. We were stupid to sit back and assume we were safe.'

'What difference does it make? They are superior. Face it. Humanity is doomed.'

'I don't believe that.'

'You want to feel it again?'

Sebastian let his tenuous hold on it slip and it hit him full force. He squeezed his eyes shut, felt Ghost shift around him and felt the darkness of deep space close in, a spider's web of energy pulsing in all directions as hundreds of minds linked in common hatred, hunger and pure desire to conquer and consume.

It was overpowering.

'Deal with it,' Sebastian hissed brutally.

It snapped off, leaving him shaking and gasping for air. They were moving fast. On a heading towards Erica, NG realised, watching the data on the monitors.

He pinched the bridge of his nose, the pressure pushing against his mind building to unbearable. Martinez was talking to him again, or to someone. He couldn't make out what she was saying. He wanted to curl up and die.

'Not an option, Nikolai,' Sebastian said viciously.

Behind them they could see the Expedience crunching into the alien ship. The shockwave hit, a flare of energy that sent Ghost's systems into a frenzy for what seemed like forever. It felt like someone had punched him in the chest.

He couldn't breathe.

The Tangiers had veered off, and was closing fast, heading for Erica surrounded by a ragged accompaniment of vessels that were still trying in vain to fend off attacks by the smaller alien ships that were nipping at their heels. Gallagher's freighter was out there somewhere.

The aliens, whatever the hell they were, were following. Damaged but not defeated. No anger in that incessant buzzing roar, simply a desire to acquire, feed… consume.

'They're looking for new feeding grounds.' Sebastian was almost revelling in the moment. *'Can you feel it?'*

It was impossible not to feel that simple, raw motivation.

Erica was a dark mass directly ahead.

"We're screwed," Martinez muttered. She was trying desperately to veer away from a fighter that was dodging an incoming missile.

It skimmed Ghost's hull, exploded and sent them into a tumbling spiral towards the surface.

31

He stoked the fire, adding more logs and prodding the embers.

"It chills me to hear of them being so close," she said.

That was a sentiment he shared.

"Do the others know?" she asked.

"You are the first."

She put a hand over her mouth, stared at him then composed herself. "They are here. I thought we had more time."

"We all thought we had more time. We do not."

Crash landing on a planet was never a great experience. NG lay still, something warm trickling past his ear. He'd crashed a couple of times before, never in the middle of an alien invasion.

'*And never with other ships crashing down around us*,' Sebastian commented dryly as a not-too-distant explosion sent a trembling vibration through the ship. A clatter of debris rained down on them.

NG tried to open his eyes. It felt like he was in a thick fog. He could hear Martinez calling his name, shouting to someone else. He could vaguely sense her close by but it was taking all his concentration to just stay conscious.

There was a dull ache nagging at the edge of his awareness. Another impact close by and the roar of a ship passing overhead. A pounding rain was beating on the hull. They must have been breached because he was cold, a damp chill creeping into his bones. He could hear shouting outside, muffled noises that were pretty much drowned out by a buzzing drone that was pulling at his mind.

He half opened one eye, struggled to focus on the crazy angle of the main console and managed to fumble a grip on the harness. It released with a click and he tumbled, cursing, falling out of the seat and hitting his head on the bulkhead.

It all greyed out again and he came round to see Martinez peering down at him.

"You gotta stop doing this to me, NG," she muttered, half clambering, half sliding in beside him, pulling a dressing out of a medikit that she bundled into his lap and pressing it against his forehead. "You're really not hearing any of this, are you?" She was thinking there was something wrong with their Sensons, he could hear that. "You injured anywhere else?"

She reached behind her and dragged forward an armoured vest, beginning to shrug him into it as if she was dressing a child.

"Broken ribs," he admitted as she grabbed him right where it hurt.

She said something but he missed it, fading out for a second as she pulled the straps tight.

She mumbled a, "Sorry," and waited until he'd caught his breath. "Was that the crash or them?" She was looking at the bruises, thinking she'd kill everyone who'd hurt him.

"Fiorrentino was on board. He recognised Hil."

She added Fiorrentino to her shitlist and geared up to move. "Come on. We need to get out of here, they're bombing the crap out of every ship on the ground."

Cold air hit his face, a downpouring of chemical-tainted rain drenching him through in seconds as they emerged into the open. The rain dripped down his nose, an acidic tang to its taste as it washed over his lips.

He blinked away raindrops, eyes stinging. It was dark, bright sparks and flares of light flashing on the horizon, occasional rumbles as the sky lit up with explosions.

Another massive roar thundered overhead.

The alien hive mind was a constant humming presence in the background. Sebastian was adapting, managing to hold barriers in place but he could still hear them closing in. It was weird after all this time to think that they were real, that the Man was right and the ever-threatened nightmare he'd lived with for his entire life was here, right now.

He looked around.

Ghost was a crumpled mess, the rear of the ship ripped away and the front half crushed. They'd been lucky to make it out alive.

He could just about make out the dark shapes of other ships, escape pods and smoking debris that littered the sparse moorland. There was pain and panic all around. He could hear faint voices, shouting, someone trying to coordinate a search for survivors.

Only two of the Security guys that Martinez had brought with her had survived the crash and were hauling themselves out of the wreckage as Martinez took hold of his arm.

"We need to get into cover," she said. "I reckon the refinery is our only chance."

The main colony wasn't far off, the tall shadows of the refinery's towers lit by blazing fires and the flash of explosions. Small ships were flying low, attacking anything that was moving.

She gave him a nudge. "C'mon, we have to go."

His whole life with the guild had been geared to this moment, first contact with a hostile alien race, and he was down to running for his life across a smouldering wasteland in the pouring rain.

Erica's main mining and refinery complex was a looming mass of buildings, towers and pipework in the distance ahead of them.

They ducked into cover whenever they could find it when the flitting fighters came too close for comfort and Martinez pulled him to his feet every time he lost concentration and stumbled.

After what seemed like forever, she dragged him into a ditch and signalled him to keep down, yelling something about needing a minute to the two guys with them. They took up defensive positions as NG clutched a hand around his ribs and sank into the mud, cold water sloshing up to his knees.

It was hard to keep his eyes open but she grabbed his shoulder.

"NG, come on, stay with me."

"I'm..." he started to say, muttering something and losing

track, vision narrowing to a dark tunnel, cold grey descending like fog.

'Stay awake, Nikolai…'

Easier said than done.

'Nikolai!'

He jerked awake from a nightmare that had pulled him under with terrifying speed, half expecting to sense Devon's perfume, but sliding in cloying, dank mud instead.

Martinez had her hand on his wrist, fingers pressing against the pulse point, his heart beating a pounding rhythm in time with her own. She leaned in close, whispered, "Take what you need."

He did, with as much restraint as he could manage, just enough so he could push back the pounding oppression and breathe again.

She used her other hand to pop a shot of Epizin into his neck and waited until he looked up. "You good?"

He nodded.

She nodded back and pulled him up, splashing out of the ditch and scrambling up through the wet undergrowth.

They staggered towards the refinery, keeping low. Clouds were swirling overhead.

He was soaked through, sore, breathing difficult and he was hard pushed to fend off the headache that was becoming debilitating. Nothing he did to ease it made a dent, and he could feel that Sebastian was tense, straining to keep up the protective barriers, a growing resentment burning intently.

Everything came down to just putting one foot in front of the other and trying to suck in enough oxygen to keep going, that blur of lights in the distance a tantalising lure.

An ominous chill that began to creep over the skin at the back of his neck made him stop and look up.

A distant rumbling of thunder turned into a massive roar of engines, a huge shape, flashing pinpricks of light emerging from the darkness, escape pods, drop ships and debris falling in its wake.

The Tangiers. It hit two of the facility's towers, ploughing through them as if they were made of matchsticks.

Martinez was standing, transfixed, staring at the massive hulking warship as it headed straight for them.

'Move, you fool.'

"Oh shit," she muttered, breaking the spell.

NG yelled, "Move," and they ran, instinctively ducking as it flew impossibly close, the shockwave as it passed knocking them off their feet.

NG rolled as he landed, pure adrenaline fuelling his reactions, sensing another smaller ship falling towards them. He scrambled towards Martinez, dragging her clear as it hit with a deafening crash.

The tiny craft exploded on impact, the blast throwing them back and sending a billowing mushroom cloud of thick, black smoke into the air.

NG got to his knees, feeling the heat against his face dissipate with the streaming rain, his heart pounding and the constant pain in his chest breaking through anything he could do to nullify it.

Martinez was still down.

'*She's alive,*' Sebastian whispered, the words filtering through the ringing in his ears. '*So is the alien.*'

He watched with a distant fascination as a figure emerged from the smoke. It wasn't that dissimilar to humans from a distance, but big, taller, powerful build, two legs, two arms, wearing what looked like glistening armour. It was in pain. He could feel it.

NG felt Martinez next to him, getting up, bringing up her gun, felt the anticipation of conflict in the adrenaline that was rushing through her body. She tensed.

There was a moment's standoff.

It was huge. A ragged cloak hung from its shoulders, whipping in the wind. It was injured, standing stooped, chest heaving. It looked at them, its gaze piercing as it scanned across all four of them, coming back to rest on NG.

Sebastian hissed.

It raised its weapon and fired.

He couldn't move fast enough, a stream of massive high velocity rounds cutting through the rain.

He reacted instinctively, no conscious effort behind it, conjuring a blast of energy that impacted the incoming projectiles with such force it sent him flying backwards.

He tumbled, every gasp of air punched from his lungs, sliding through the mud and looking up to see Martinez and the two grunts from Security all returning fire.

Every shot was detonating against some kind of energy shield surrounding it. It started to walk forward, drawing another weapon and firing.

One of the grunts took a direct hit to the chest that punched through his armour as if it wasn't there.

NG scrambled to his feet and ran forward, grabbing the fallen rifle and kneeling, firing, the recoil from every shot resounding through his chest in an agonising rhythm.

It turned, shot the other grunt with a single bullet through the throat and swung back, aiming both weapons at him.

Martinez yelled.

He fired first, double tap, the air around it shimmering as the first shot hit the barrier and the second flying straight and true to hit between its eyes.

It took two steps towards them, staggered and fell.

The hollow punch of intense pressure that hit the centre of NG's being as it died left him reeling.

He was vaguely aware of Martinez running to him, sliding in beside him and holding him up. She helped him to his feet, staring at the debris, wanting to go over and look closer, see their enemy, but she turned to him instead. "These are your aliens? Do we even know for sure they're not human? Could this be Wintran?" not quite believing that she was saying it, but not trusting herself to believe these were really alien.

NG shook his head. It was alien, he'd felt it. He'd never encountered anything like it. It was as terrible as the Man had ever suggested. Worse, now that it was here on their doorstep.

It was hard not to feel overwhelmed. He felt a hand touch his elbow.

Martinez looked him in the eye, watching a stream of rain mingle with the blood trickling down his face.

"They're real," she said.

He nodded. He'd accused the Man of lying but it was real.

'He did lie to you,' Sebastian whispered maliciously. *'It's you that doesn't exist, remember. You are nothing but my jailor. Time to let me free, Nikolai. You don't have a chance against these creatures. Do you know what the Man calls them? Bhenykhn Lyudaed…'*

Bhenykhn. It sounded familiar but nothing he could remember the Man saying, nothing that had ever been in any of the greys.

Sebastian laughed, a hollow stirring deep inside. *'Of course he didn't tell you. You are simply his gofer, his little experiment. Let me tell you, Nikolai, they are the Bhenykhn Lyudaed, the Devourers. You are out of your depth. Let me free or we are going to die here.'*

'Sebastian,' he thought back, *'I'm not keeping you in. You want control? Take it. I'm not stopping you.'*

That was one hell of a confession but he made it because he knew that somehow Sebastian had been locked away so deep in that confrontation with LC that he had no chance of getting free. He felt Sebastian snatch violently for possession and fail, genuinely nothing conscious on his part to resist.

The darkness inside felt more dense, more black, than it ever had before. *'Then, you, my friend,'* Sebastian murmured, *'are in real trouble.'*

He let the barriers drop and there was nothing NG could do to throw them back up as real time kicked in with a jolt and the clamouring cacophony from the alien hive hit his mind like a sledgehammer.

32

He could remember the feeling of that intense pressure, the intrusion into his mind. To know that Nikolai had had to face it, so soon, was disturbing.

"You know what he went through?" she said softly.

The Man stared into the flames. They didn't, these others that were here with him. Nikolai was a freak of nature in this galaxy, he was one in his.

"This virus," she said, "would it work on us? Is this our solution?"

He shook his head. "When would a solution ever be so simple?"

He felt himself folding, imploding, overwhelmed and overpowered by it. This time it was Sebastian playing chicken but suicide had never, ever been on NG's agenda. He sucked it up and rolled with it. Took it. Stood up to it. Absorbed it. Battered and buffeted, he embraced its power, its energy. He existed within it. He could suddenly sense, clear and distinct, each alien individual of that hive mind, each desperate human soul, each living thing a bright pinprick of light in the dark.

He couldn't breathe.

Slowly, he took control and shut each one out, painstakingly and painfully, until reality was a calm, quiet space in his head.

'*Okay, you've proved the point*,' he thought at Sebastian. '*You want to take over again so I can move?*'

There was a subtle shift as the pressure eased, a barrier back in place. He opened his eyes.

He was on his knees again. Doubled over. Rain streaming down the back of his neck.

Martinez was crouched beside him, her other hand holding a gun by her side, scanning around, identifying potential hostiles and tracking them.

She felt the change in him and squeezed his shoulder.

He sat back on his heels and looked at her, both of them sitting there out in the open, caked with mud, drenched through as the rain beat down on them. "I might have really screwed up this time," he said. "We're not ready."

She leaned in close. "We're the Thieves' Guild," she said. "No one messes with us. No one. Fucking aliens included," and added confidently, "No doubts, NG. You know what you're doing. You always know what you're doing. Trust me."

Sebastian stirred maliciously. '*Don't trust anyone.*'

"Give me a sitrep," he said, wiping a hand across his face and sending raindrops flying. He looked around, trying to calm his erratic breathing. Craft were still flying low, swooping over crashed escape pods, smoke billowing up to merge in dark puddles with the covering of low cloud. "Keep it simple. Do we know where anyone else is?"

She pulled a second gun from a holster at her waist and checked the magazine. "The Sensons are playing up. I've had no contact from LC or anyone on the Duck since we crashed. I haven't heard from Hil and I can't contact any of the extraction teams so I don't know if they found him and got him out or not. The plan was to stay with you. I gave everyone the coordinates from Gallagher before we followed so they know where we are. There's a chance they've gone back to the Alsatia so help might be on its way. But, as far as it goes right now, we're alone." She handed him the gun.

He took it almost absently and tucked it into the small of his back, something pulling at his awareness.

He looked up.

He couldn't see through the cloud cover but he could feel that the alien ship was hurtling down through the atmosphere, damaged but managing a controlled descent, launching more ground attack ships in readiness.

"We need to move," he muttered. He could sense human

survivors, armoured soldiers, heavy infantry and assault troops from the Tangiers and the Expedience, mixed with ships' crew and technical personnel, all gearing up and making their way to the mining facility in the hope that the facility would offer some protection.

He looked at the distant lights glowing on the horizon. They just needed to get there.

Rows of wounded were stretched out in the mud-strewn tunnel entrance to the processing facility, bodies covered with plastic sheets or anything that came to hand, the worst of the casualties getting impromptu field medicine from anyone who could wield a first aid kit.

'Welcome to hell...'

NG walked through without stopping, brutally shutting out the bombardment of pain that hit his mind. He still had one of the recovered assault rifles slung across his back and one of the alien's weapons in his hand. Martinez had the other.

It had been a long time since he'd been on the ground in the middle of an active conflict and the weight of that rifle was an uneasy reminder that he'd disliked that assignment as much as he hated being cold. The Man had insisted, given him no choice, saying he couldn't lead until he understood every aspect of what he was leading. It had made him understand that he didn't like being a grunt at the behest of someone else's agenda.

Rain was beating on the high ceiling overhead, a cold metallic chill to the air. A regular pounding thrum of machinery emanated from the depths of the plant. Klaxons were wailing. A distant explosion shook its structure, a scattering of dust and debris falling down on them.

They were both wet, cold and hurting. And they were surrounded by chaos.

Someone yelled for help and for a briefest instant, NG felt Martinez hesitate, thinking they could help these people, that – he – could help these people who were dying.

He shook his head, catching her eye and sharing the desperation.

His heart was pounding. He couldn't lose himself in this. They had to get away.

'What have I been saying?'

"Stay close," he said quietly. "We need to find a way out of here. We have to get word back. The Man has things in place."

'You hope.'

The tunnel opened up into a massive storage area. Wintran and Earth uniforms mixed in an uneasy truce of stunned confusion, the chilly damp, blood and sweat mingling with age-old animosities to create a heady atmosphere of tension.

There was a Wintran officer in the centre of it, trying to make headway in organising a rabble that was hurting, injuries adding fuel to innate enmities and elevating raw emotions to breaking point. All amongst a constant influx of wounded and a steady escalation of alert stations screaming warnings of damage.

"This is not good," Martinez murmured at his side. She was concerned for his safety. There were too many weapons, too many unknowns in the area and too many angles for her to cover for her own peace of mind. The five hundred million seemed like a long time ago, another lifetime away to him, but it was still preying on her mind and as far as she was concerned, every person in this temporary refuge was a hostile.

NG scanned around.

He could see into every mind, skim the surface of every person's fears and suspicions. There were no assassins that he could tell. There were a few civilians in the mix, wearing UM colours and branding. When the hell had that happened? This place was supposed to be Aries.

He watched, struggling and failing to keep a worsening headache at bay, a really bad feeling descending over the tumbling coincidences that kept flying in from left field.

But the UM engineers he could sense weren't thinking of anything other than trying to find out what the hell was going on and struggling to initiate emergency procedures to mitigate the damage to their facility. They were a hair's breadth from outright panic, seasoned pioneers who were used to coping with anything the Between had to throw at them, and it was chaos.

Contagious.

They edged off to the side. He sank down to sit on the floor, back leaning against the wall, drawing energy from the bodies around him and not caring that Martinez was looking at him as if she thought he was going to flake out again.

"I just need a minute," he muttered.

She crouched next to him. "Comms are down," she said quietly. "It's not just us. No wonder I can't get through to anyone."

He looked around.

From the feel of it, no one had any working comms, all the Sensons inactive, and that in itself was freaking everyone out and adding in an intense sense of isolation.

Another explosion boomed overhead, vibrations rumbling through the entire structure of the building.

The lights flickered.

Martinez cursed. "What the hell is that?"

"Defence grid," he said, reading the anxiety from the UM guys who were desperately trying to reroute power and drain down non-essential systems. It was the only thing keeping them all alive right now, a rough and ready defence grid of laser weapons the mining facility used to protect itself against an annual meteor storm, that was now keeping the alien air assault at bay. And from what the engineers were thinking, the power drain was something stupid and its reserves were finite. So they were on a clock. "It's not going to last much longer."

A voice suddenly yelled from the far side of the room, "Who the fuck are we fighting here?"

NG looked up. The Wintran guy was giving orders, frustrated but competent and handling the situation fairly well until that someone dared voice the fear that everyone was holding in.

Earthside, they were thinking it had to be Wintran. Winterside, they were thinking what the hell corporation had anything like that, could it be Earth? It was a disorientating swirl of paranoia and anger.

"They cut through us like fucking butter," someone else shouted. "Who the hell has anything like that?"

NG pushed himself to his feet, unease prickling. This was going to boil over. Martinez was sensing it too and reaching for another gun.

It was getting hard to concentrate and it took him a moment to realise that someone was trying to reach him and a moment longer to recognise who it was.

'LC?' he thought vaguely.

'NG, we're getting shot to shit. What the…'

The tenuous link cut off. Abruptly.

'*Seems like your pet just used up his ninth life*,' Sebastian hissed maliciously.

NG reached out. He could sense LC and Hal Duncan plus some unfamiliars about two miles out. Further than he'd ever been able to reach with any certainty before.

Sebastian stirred sullenly.

'LC?' NG sent again.

'We're… crap. NG, what the hell is going on?'

The Wintran officer was holding up his hand. One of his men yelled for quiet. The constant drumming of rain on the roof was loud, interspersed with a distant rumble of explosions and the occasional boom as the defence grid took down another fighter that got too close.

'LC, if you can hear me,' NG sent, 'get the hell off the Duck. We need that freighter intact.'

'It's not intact. We've been hit.'

'How bad? It might be our only chance.'

'Wait a minute.'

There was a pause then, 'Elliott reckons he can get off the ground if we can get parts for repairs. Shit…'

NG took a deep breath. 'LC, listen to me. Get off the Duck. They can sense lifeforms and will attack if there are people on board. Do you understand? Get everyone off the Duck and get to the mining facility.'

There was no reply.

"The Duck just landed," he said to Martinez. "We need to go."

The Wintran officer was raising his voice now, the kind of authoritative tone that soldiers couldn't help but snap to with full attention. "We need to secure the area and figure out what we're dealing with. I need medics. You," he pointed to someone, "come with me..."

NG watched as one of the Earth marines, wearing battle-scarred front line combat armour marked with sergeant's stripes, pushed forward. "We don't take orders from a damned stinking Wintran." His voice was quiet but his words devastating.

There were shoves, yells.

No real violence yet.

Martinez was thinking she'd seen worse in Acquisitions when the grunts kicked off but you still never knew when the bullets might start flying. She took a half step protectively in front of him.

NG muttered, "C'mon," and backed off. He turned to leave, sensing the threat a second too late, and walked into a hand pushed hard against his chest.

Martinez moved fast, incapacitating the guy and stopping just short of breaking his arm, shoving him back and sticking her gun in his face.

He was wearing a Wintran uniform, one of the bridge crew off the Expedience.

This was the last thing they needed.

The guy caught his balance and squared up to them, not giving a shit about the gun, glaring past her at NG. "You bastard." He was trembling, looking at him, thinking that this was the bastard that had destroyed their ship.

Someone grabbed NG from behind.

He managed to shove an elbow backwards and broke free, Martinez spinning and fending off another, yelling at them to back off and pulling him away.

The yells were louder then, Wintran voices shouting that this was one of the guys they'd caught on their ship, someone on the Earth side shouting, "Shit, he must be ours."

In seconds, the whole area was divided, weapons drawn, emotions bristling on both sides. Christ, they could just kill themselves right here and be done with it, do the aliens' work for them.

NG stood in the centre of it.

'How poetic. The Man's vision in its purest manifestation.'

The Wintran officer pushed his way through to them, sidearm in his hand, the other outstretched as he tried to calm the situation. He glanced around at his people, eyes flicking to the Earth troops confronting them and his glare resting finally on NG. "Who the hell are you?" he said.

'Now that is one hell of a question. Who are you, 'NG'?'

Someone piped up from the far side of the room. "This is one of the bastards that sabotaged us."

The officer took a step closer.

He was a major, Medical Corps by the patch on his sleeve, and he was thinking they were screwed here. He had casualties he should be tending and instead he was standing in the middle of a freaking schoolyard fight with a guy who by all accounts was the very one who had started it all.

"Who are you?" he said again, looking them up and down, noting the lack of uniform or insignia.

NG shook his head slowly.

The marine sergeant was forcing his way through the crowd, nothing in his mind but an instinct to protect his own. He stepped between NG and the major, and said again, "We do not take orders from a stinking – bastard – Wintran."

It was about to get nasty and their real enemy was outside.

"We have to work together," the major said carefully, delaying tactics so no one would start shooting.

The voice that came from the doorway was used to being heard. "Damn right we do."

Hones was injured and in pain but not showing it, his suit of powered body armour about all that was keeping the man upright. He had men flanking him, Thom Garrett one of them, in uniform, a pathway opening for them as people were brushed aside.

'Ah, now the games begin…'

The colonel walked up, a hush descending fast as the Earth guys recognised their commanding officer and the Wintrans realised that the centre of power had just shifted.

NG glanced at Martinez and said quietly, "We need to get out of here."

'Don't be naive. Hones knows that you took out the AI on the Expedience. You think Jameson's lot are black ops? They're pink and fluffy compared to these guys. Trust me, Nikolai, he wants to know what you did up there on that battle cruiser and he is not going to let you go.' Sebastian laughed bitterly as if he'd just realised something. *'What do you suppose he'll do if he finds out you know their codes?'*

He didn't reply or react as they were surrounded.

33

"This is the real danger," she said. "It is not when politicians and powermongers rattle their sabres across the dining table. Wars start when ordinary troops face each other head to head with weapons drawn."

The Man swirled the last of the wine in the jug. "The war had already started by then. Under the guise of misunderstandings, sanctions and defensive actions but war nonetheless."

She slid her goblet across the table, empty. "Was it fortune or disaster that both sides had such military might in the Between when this happened?"

"They were there. It is hard to judge if that made the task harder or the outcome different from what it could have been. From what I know, our people handled themselves well."

Hones was an imposing figure, not in the same physically intimidating way as Jameson, but foreboding nonetheless and used to people doing what he wanted. He demanded an update without ceremony.

The major was smart enough to concede command to a superior officer even if he was wearing a different uniform. "Just over two hundred survivors so far. Sir."

"Major, I take it I have your cooperation," Hones said, turning back to his men. "Send out scouts, set up a perimeter and send a goddamned signal for help. You," he pointed to one of his staff officers, "find a civilian and secure me a private room with a table. Find me some maps and set up an ops centre." He turned, eyes narrow, pain flaring. "And you…?" He pointed to NG. "You come with me."

NG sat at the back of the small meeting room, perched on a bench, one knee tucked up tight, one arm hugged around his ribs, trying to ignore the pounding in his head and the chill that was seeping through into his joints.

It hadn't taken Hones and his people long to set up their ops centre. Intel had been coming in fast, the alien ship had landed some distance out, ships were still getting shot down, pods were still crashing to the surface and survivors were still trooping in. They were up to somewhere around five hundred and fifty. From thousands.

Emotions were running high.

He didn't want to get involved, wanted nothing more than to get out of there and get word back to the Man, but Hones had made it clear that he wasn't going to let them go.

'I thought you didn't care about the Man.'

He couldn't help but care about the Man. The Man had been right and there was an edge of guilt there over storming out so petulantly that he couldn't shift.

'You're pathetic,' Sebastian whispered malevolently. *'For once you do something right, for you, and now you sit there and feel sorry for yourself, dwelling on it, while you let these creatures keep us captive. I might as well still be locked in a cage.'*

NG glanced around. There were guards posted at the door and another two inside that had been tasked with keeping an eye on them. At least they hadn't been disarmed, yet. Martinez was standing in front of him, desperately trying to assess exactly where any danger was going to come from.

'Pay some attention, Nikolai, and you'd see that the only real danger to us is coming from the alien ship that is about to launch a full out assault on this godforsaken pocket of human scum. You need to get out of here.'

He knew that.

LC was on his way in. The kid had made contact, rattled off a list of parts that Elliott reckoned they'd need and asked about Hil. It hadn't been easy to say that Hilyer was missing and he could feel, even at this distance, that LC was angry, out of character for him and it was taking Hal Duncan's full attention to keep him in check and keep him alive out there. Elliott was with them, the Duck's enigmatic tech guy who, according to LC, didn't trust them to get the right parts and wanted to scavenge what he could himself.

NG couldn't tell; he couldn't even sense the guy's presence never mind read any emotion.

He rubbed a hand across his eyes, trying to follow them as they raced across the moorland and trying to keep track of the buzz in this room.

Hones was demanding information, numbers, details, keeping everyone busy and giving no one time to dwell on how screwed they were. The chart in the centre of the table was a contour map, coloured scribbles and circles marking in stark simplicity the distance between the facility and the enemy ship. The rough inventory of weapons they'd come up with so far was pathetically small and the count of undamaged ships was even less.

The Duck was their only chance.

Thom Garrett was the latest to push his way back into the room, breathless from running and not keen to give his report.

Hones glared round at the kid. "Well?"

Garrett shook his head, scratching at the cast on his forearm. "We hit the tower when we came down. The relay station is f…" he managed to stop himself and said carefully, "damaged, sir. There's no way we can send a signal."

"Can it be fixed?" Hones said with barely concealed impatience.

The kid shook his head again. "There's nothing left. We can't send anything long range."

Hones turned to the only civilian in the room, a guy in dirty overalls who'd identified himself as the mine supervisor and who was talking into some kind of landline phone with a scowl on his face.

"When is this facility due to be resupplied?" he demanded.

The guy looked up. "Not for three months. We just started a new rota." NG could tell he was pissed that he'd lost almost half his crew when the ships started crashing and pissed that he was here and had been stupid enough to sign on for another tour in this shit-hole of a facility, and with UM for fuck's sake. They all knew the risks and the money made up for it, but, Jesus Christ, no one expected this on their watch.

"What ships do you have?"

"We haven't got ships. We're a mining and processing facility. We have trucks, loaders, remote mapping drones and mining bots. That's it. The only reason we have the grid is the meteor showers. This is shitsville in case you didn't notice."

"What's that you're talking into? How come you have comms?"

"Shielded landline," the supervisor snapped back. "Short range comms don't work well here. Interference from the fucking rocks. Like I said, shitsville."

Martinez turned to NG and whispered, "Sixes shouldn't get affected by background interference. We're getting jammed by something."

He shrugged.

Either way, they had no comms. At least the facility had some kind of redundancy system, however archaic.

Hones growled and turned back to the table. "So what are we dealing with here?"

The makeshift ops room was split six to four, Earth to Wintran.

"We all know fine well what that ship is," a marine lieutenant grunted.

The Wintran major was standing next to Hones and he rose to the taunt. "Believe me, it's not one of ours."

"Not Zang?" someone sneered. "What then? UM? Yarrimer? Fucking Aries?"

Hones looked back down at the table and the local maps spread out there. He looked up abruptly, pointed to NG then a room that adjoined the meeting room, and said bluntly, "You – in there."

Sebastian whispered, '*Be careful – he does know about the codes.*'

NG slid off the bench, muttered a quick, "Luka's on his way in," to Martinez. "Go meet him. Make sure he gets in here intact," and he followed the colonel into the office.

Hones waited until the door closed. "You knew we were coming into this. You gave the Expedience the coordinates to follow us. Who are you?"

He'd been speaking with the bridge crew from the battle cruiser.

NG shook his head without a word.

Hones threw the board he was holding onto the cluttered desk. "What are we dealing with?"

"They're NHA," NG said simply, using JU terminology. Non-human aggressor. Not like they had a term for a non-human anything else. Earth worked on the assumption that anything sentient they could possibly encounter out in space would be an enemy. Shoot first, ask questions later. Except this time, the aliens had got the shots in first.

He placed the alien weapon on the desk. "If you have any tech guys, they need to look at this."

Hones stared at it then looked up. "Who the hell are you?"

"Classified."

Hones let a small smile crease the edges of his lips. "Who are you working for?"

"The JU," NG said without hesitation and watched the comprehension creep across the colonel's face.

A slight narrowing of the eyes was the only give away that the guy was pissed. "Prove it."

"How? We don't exactly carry ID."

"Prove it."

"Ask Matt Jameson."

Just knowing that name did it.

Hones nodded reluctantly. Garrett had already, in all innocence, reported that NG had been the one that gave him the order to send the signal.

"What's your mission?" Hones asked, knowing fine well that NG wouldn't say.

"You'd have to ask Jameson," NG said carefully. Jameson was going to be even more pissed at him. At that level, rivalries were fierce and not somewhere he'd usually meddle.

The colonel was not impressed. "How the hell did you know the right code to give to Garrett?"

"Ask Jameson."

Hones shook his head slowly, a look of disbelief in his eyes. "Are you out here alone? That's not JU SOP. What are you doing here?"

NG opened his mouth to speak but Hones interrupted, "Yeah, classified. I get the picture. How did you take down the cruiser? Was that you or one of your little Thieves' Guild buddies?" He leaned closer. "Did Jameson send you out here after Gallagher or after the two thieves who busted open his facility?"

He was expecting NG to be shocked that he knew. Garret must have given a full report, including LC and Hilyer.

"I'm not at liberty to say," he said.

Hones looked even less impressed. "These NHA – you know what they are." It was a statement not a question.

"They're alien," he said dryly.

Hones stared and it was easy enough to read his thoughts as he tried to recall if he'd heard any rumours of Jameson chasing aliens. Someone was always chasing aliens. Alien technology, rumours of alien life, scraps of evidence of long gone alien civilisations every time they colonised a new planet. No one else as far as he knew actually had a brief to chase rumours as a serious strategic mandate.

NG rubbed a hand over his eyes. It was getting harder to fend off the headache that was getting worse by the minute.

Hones banged his fist on the desk and said again, each word exaggerated, "What – exactly – are we dealing with here?"

'They're gearing up to attack. They're launching gunships. You want to listen?'

He didn't but Sebastian let it slip for a second and he heard a deafening cascade of chattering noise, obviously orders tumbling down the chain of command, but nothing he could comprehend.

'How can you understand what they're saying?' he thought.

'How can you not?'

"They're aliens," he said again, desperately trying to block it, and having to listen to Sebastian laughing disparagingly before it cut out again. "They're here to invade. You try to fight them, you'll get wiped out. The only chance we have is to get away." It was surprisingly easy to stay calm. "Gallagher's freighter is out there. Damaged. We need parts to fix it," and that 'we' was suddenly everyone here, full and committed cooperation. The entire human race against an alien foe. Hones might be spec-ops but he was strategic like Jameson, not field-ops like Pen. NG knew exactly what buttons to push but it was made easier because Hones recognised the need for cooperation if anyone was going to have a chance of surviving this. "We need to regroup and bring everything we have, combined, into dealing with this."

He said that but he had no idea how. If the Man had a plan, he'd never shared it; it was always prepare, we must be prepared.

'I'm sure the Man never anticipated that his pathetic creation would go haring off alone to confront these invaders head on.'

Hones was listening so NG pushed it. "The freighter needs a control module and a couple of shield actuators for its Denholm – they have those in stores here – and at least two complete link capacitors for its Lewis drive. What's the chances they could still be intact on the Tangiers?"

"She took a lot of hull damage but some of her systems are intact so they could be," he conceded. "I'll send a runner and get a team of engineers onto it."

"Send Thom Garrett. He knows the freighter."

The colonel nodded.

NG could read from his mind that he'd left crew on board. The Tangiers was badly damaged, nestled in a valley about three miles away. It still had some active weapons batteries that were keeping the Bhenykhn air attacks at bay and Hones was also thinking that the Tangiers had seven nuclear warheads that hadn't been damaged in its crash landing.

He bit back the urge to just say, launch them, for Christ's sake, and had to ask patiently, "What missiles do you have left?"

Hones looked at him with suspicion. "Seven nukes still in their tubes."

"Can they be launched from the ground?"

"They can but not by remote."

"Then we need to go get the spares and launch those missiles while we're at it. All of them."

"Anything else you think we should be doing?" Hones said it with a growl, but it was only part cynicism because the colonel was also thinking that it made sense.

"We have gunships incoming."

Hones narrowed his eyes. "How do you know all this?"

"I just do." Not his most slick comeback. "We'd better hope that defence grid is up to it. It's designed for withstanding a shower of rocks not an armoured weapons platform."

The colonel shook his head again and picked up the alien weapon, turning it in his hands. "What exactly do you know about these NHA?"

'Perceptive...'

NG rubbed a hand across his eyes, pinching the top of his nose to try to relieve some of the pressure. "They're called the Bhenykhn Lyudaed. They're humanoid. Big. Armoured. Advanced weaponry. Some kind of energy shield that can be breached if you hit it enough times."

Hones interjected, "And what the hell is it that you're not telling me?"

'Be careful what you reveal here. I can see the peasants grabbing their pitchforks already.'

He took a deep breath. "They're telepathic."

34

"It is hard, is it not, to admit such an ability?"

"It is impossible," the Man said. He poured the last of the wine, sharing it between them. "No being alive will tolerate the reality that another can listen in to their innermost thoughts. It is inconceivable. Hatred comes easily on the back of fear."

"Yet, it is the very factor that gives us an advantage now. An advantage we have never had before."

"It does not change the fact that they thrive on a strategy of overwhelming force, superiority of numbers, of technology, a careless regard for the life of their troops."

She shrugged. "You could be describing any military within this galaxy. Surely, now, we have the means to stop them. We have a chance."

"Nikolai was our best chance." He took a sip, drawing in the last of the rich concentrated liquid. "I worked hard to keep him safe his whole life. He chose to leave."

"They have instant communication like a hive mind," NG said.

"You can hear them."

NG kept his expression neutral, hard with the pounding his skull was taking. It probably wasn't worth denying at this point. He nodded.

Hones was thinking bloody hell, a telepathic enemy that could read minds, that could hear every thought and command they gave?

'*Can they?*' he asked Sebastian.

'*No.*'

"They can't read our minds," NG said quickly, "but they can

sense where we are. They can sense human life signs. It's not just their communications giving them an advantage; they can see us a mile away."

"So they can track us?"

He nodded again. "We need to find a way to get the spares back to the freighter. There are mining tunnels we could use. The interference from the rocks might give us some cover. I don't know." It sounded desperate but it was worth a try. "Talk to the supervisor."

Hones put down the alien weapon and looked up. "I'll take care of that. You're not going anywhere. And trust me, if I find out that you're keeping anything else from me, I'll have you lynched and Jameson will not be able to do a damn thing to save you. Do you understand?"

NG didn't nod.

The colonel leaned forward. "I want to know numbers, command structure, movements, weapons," he said quietly. "If you're so good, I want to know what the damned aliens intend to do before they know they intend it. I want to know if they bloody sneeze. Do you understand?"

"I understand that none of us want to die here," NG said.

"I'm sending my XO back to the Tangiers to launch the nukes," Hones said, standing up and turning away. "We'll set up a defence here until the freighter is fixed. Get yourself some bloody medical attention. You look like shit."

The defence grid was struggling, emergency power flickering as the gunship offensive intensified, the facility rumbling with reverberations as each laser fired on target after target, mid-air detonations sending debris raining down onto the roof.

NG sat at the table, trying to be patient as a medic cleaned the gash above his eye. He was holding a cold pack against the back of his neck with one hand and flicking through the screens of a data board with the other. He'd already skipped through the schematics and inventories three times, talked with the sullen supervisor twice, and there was no way he could see that this facility could be reinforced as a defensive position. He had the beginnings of a plan but it wasn't great.

There'd been plenty of times out in the field, especially in active military theatres, dabbling as the guild was wont to do, when he'd had the distinct impression they were on the wrong side. It was never that they were outnumbered, or outgunned, or technologically inferior – those odds just fuelled the mischief – it was always a sinking feeling that whatever corporation or ruling government or political faction, or whoever they were working for, had simply had its time. Once your time is up, you're done, whatever superiority you thought you were supposed to have had over the hordes at the gate.

He had that sinking feeling now.

'And, Nikolai, when you understand that, you disengage and leave them to their fate. We don't owe these pathetic creatures anything. The Bhenykhn are about to deploy ground troops. Time to disengage…'

It wasn't that simple. The armed guards that Hones had set to watch him had ditched the pretence of keeping a distance and were now standing close, one on either side, more to protect him than detain him. There was simply nowhere to go. He was splitting his concentration, giving LC as much guidance as he could while trying to track the team that Hones had sent to the Tangiers and listening in to an increasingly overwhelming net of intel flowing between the Bhenykhn commanders that Sebastian was throwing at him.

It was the first time in his life that he felt like there might be no way out.

The medic taped a dressing into place and stood back, regarding him strangely, something weird flitting across the surface of her mind.

She leaned in and whispered in his ear, "You died on board the Expedience. Nice recovery."

Ah.

'Caught out,' Sebastian mocked. *'Where is this going, do you think?'*

"Wasn't as bad as it looked," he whispered back.

She raised her eyebrows. "You were dead. I called it myself."

"I won't tell anyone if you won't."

She smiled, wondering how he'd done it and wanting to ask but the power dropped out suddenly, completely, plunging the room into darkness.

'They're in trouble,' Sebastian murmured.

Not LC. NG could sense that the kid was struggling but they were getting close. He switched to the others. They'd made it through the tunnels and were out in the open, within sight of the Tangiers, but they weren't moving, numbers down and a panic about them that was escalating. He homed in on the XO just as the guy died. He broke loose with a curse, scanning wider to find Thom Garrett as the young engineer started to run again, feeling a fearless determination kick in as he slid and fell down the slope amidst a hail of gunfire, staying with him until he made it inside the perimeter of the warship's defensive guns and scrambled inside.

NG looked up as the reserve power spluttered back into life.

Hones caught his eye from across the room, dropped what he was doing and barked, "What?"

"Your XO and his team just got hit. He's dead."

There was a hush.

The medic squeezed his shoulder and moved away. Hones was furious but hiding it well.

"Garrett made it on board."

If anything, the colonel seemed to calm and focus. "Get over here," he said. "We need a new plan."

NG stood up and walked over, glancing towards the door as he caught a hint of a figure he recognised out there, someone pushing his way through the crowd.

'Now this is going to be interesting.'

"I'm going out there," Hones said. "Given your unique perspective on the situation, I'm going to leave you in charge of the defence here. Can you handle it?"

NG kept his voice low. "Yeah." He slid across the board. "If you're going, you need to go now. They're about to quit the air offensive and pull the gunships back to contain the area surrounding us while their ground troops move in. And we're about to get company."

The door opened and Fiorrentino blustered in, surrounded by an entourage of his own people, soaked through and pissed off, in a slick grey suit rather than powered armour but with the potential to shift the balance of command again in favour of the Wintran contingent in the room. He caught NG's eye and smirked.

This they didn't need.

The colonel followed his line of sight, flicking a glance over to the Zang suit who was openly glaring at them and looking back again, cursing inwardly, thinking he was on a goddamned war footing with these people. Not official. Not yet but inevitable, was the briefing he'd been given. And a corporate suit walked in here as if he was about to take command? Not likely. A bullet between the eyes was what was needed here.

It was a sentiment he shared, but NG said quietly under his breath, "Don't."

Hones picked up the board and looked him in the eye, thinking, I know exactly what you're doing, son, and if you can hear this, if you want us to protect you, you just remember which bloody side you're on.

Fiorrentino was taking off his mud-splattered suit jacket and handing it to one of his cronies with a disdaining, "Get this cleaned." He brushed down his white shirt, rolled up the sleeves and approached the table.

Hones met him with an outstretched hand, a warm smile and a squeeze of a handshake that was brutal. "Listen in," he said, firmly in barely more than a whispered growl, "we are now at war with an unknown aggressor. This is a joint military operation under Imperial command. My man here is in charge. Make sure your men follow his orders. If you want to survive this, you will go over there, tell them who is in charge then sit down and be quiet. Or I will put a bullet in your brain right now. Do you understand?"

Fiorrentino nodded. He wasn't stupid and he wasn't a coward but he knew how to play games and win them, and he was thinking he could bide his time here. "Of course," he said and Hones let him go, throwing a knowing look at NG and heading back across the room.

The door opened again.

Martinez pushed through, clearing the way, Hal Duncan at her side, herding LC in ahead of him. They all had rain capes on, hoods up and weapons out.

An older guy who could only have been William Gallagher was following them. NG recognised him from LC's debrief, and from the confused mix of satisfaction and shock in his mind at finding out his aliens were real after all.

Luka was almost as distraught, emanating a cold, numb chill, working hard to dampen down an instinct to break and run. He was very aware what he was walking into here, only Duncan's hand on his shoulder stopping him, flashing back to a dark night years ago when that hold had been a hell of a lot more rough and the soldiers hadn't thought anything of punching a young kid in the back of the head to get him to move. It hadn't been that many years ago in the scale of things. NG had been in post about six months when Mendhel had called in, saying he had a prospective, no background, no time to run checks and what the hell, he was bringing him in. And that snap judgement call had changed the dynamics of the entire guild. Overnight.

'Over here,' NG sent, wanting them with him on this side of the room.

Martinez had seen him anyway and led them over, looking bemused as she edged in next to him.

"What?" he said.

"They think we're JU?"

That wasn't exactly what he'd said but he just shrugged. She'd been talking to the marine sergeant. One of her own. Making allies. Especially now they were all tagged as the same side.

"Where's Elliott?"

"He's gone to the stores. Said he didn't want to waste any

time and he didn't trust anyone else to get the right parts that he needs." She nudged his arm. "Are you okay?"

It felt like his head was going to split in two.

"I could do with a drink. And I need to talk to Elliott. Can you get a message to him? Ask him to get over here or call me on the landline. I don't care." He looked across at Fiorrentino who was staring, eyes narrowing further as he saw LC push back his hood.

Luka was wearing more body armour than he was comfortable with, carrying way more weapons than he was used to and his arm was still strapped tight to incapacitate the collarbone. For a kid that was renowned for being laid back and cocky whatever was thrown at him, he wasn't happy.

Fiorrentino was thinking that he couldn't believe it, that right here in front of him was the little shit he'd been chasing across half the galaxy.

NG picked up the cold pack and pressed it against his eyes.

It was obvious that LC had recognised Fiorrentino and overheard that last, but the kid just started to shrug out of the cape and thought at NG, 'What happened?' He didn't like it that Hil was missing, a pang of guilt that it should have been him up there on the battle cruiser, watching Hilyer's back, not NG.

'You wouldn't have been able to do anything different,' NG thought.

I wouldn't have left him, flashed into LC's mind but he shut it down fast, thinking again, intently, 'What happened?'

'The virus kicked in.'

'Is he still alive?'

'I don't know.' NG looked around the room, eyes settling on Fiorrentino, and consciously shared with LC and Duncan flashes of that scene on the bridge of the Expedience. He wanted them to know what they were dealing with here.

LC looked across, caught Fiorrentino's eye and for a moment, NG wasn't sure if the kid was going to freak out and pull a gun or shudder and shut down.

It was a knife-edge which way this could go but he just turned to NG and said calmly and quietly, "What's the plan?"

Hones walked up behind them. "The plan is that we're going to nuke their damned ship and you're going to make a stand here until we can get back and get that damned freighter fixed to get home. Sound good?"

NG stared at the colonel. He'd never been totally honest with anyone in his entire life and now this larger than life figure who was about to hand over command of his troops knew more than anyone outside the guild had ever known about him, except who he was.

Apparently Hones had a sixth sense of his own and looked back at him. "What?"

NG looked him in the eye. "I'm not JU," he admitted.

Hones snorted and leaned in close. "I know that, son. What do you take me for? I know fine well who you are, NG. Thieves' Guild, head of operations. I might not be a bloody mind-reader but I have my methods. Bloody Thieves' Guild."

He grinned and slapped NG on the shoulder. "Let's get this show on the road."

35

"The corporations have much to answer for." She was thinking of Hilyer and, again, there was an element of regret there.

The Man stood and wandered away to fetch another bottle of wine. "The financial loss of that battle cruiser alone will set Zang Enterprises back months if not years. We don't know if Zang himself was on board but I suspect not. That Fiorrentino was shows how deep the cracks extend within that repulsive corporation. Power means little when you are trying to cling onto it with your dying fingers."

"With Zang out of the picture, the balance of power within the Wintran coalition changes significantly, does it not?"

""It would. But Zang is not out of the picture. Men like that are irrepressible in the worst possible way. They do not surrender. They do not give in. Zang even looks to defeat death. He has no idea what he has been chasing."

NG sat with his elbows leaning on the table and head held in upturned hands. His head was pounding. He felt Martinez return to his side and rest a hand on the back of his shoulders. Not quite the way Devon used to but more contact than he was used to from her.

He squinted open one eye and watched her place a glass and bottle in front of him.

"This is the best I could find," she muttered. "There's rations if you need to eat. Gallagher's talking to the crew here. He's helping get the civilians and wounded ready to evacuate to the freighter. He's fine. The runners have called in. Hones got away okay and LC and Duncan are in position."

"I know." He'd sent them out, each with a rapid response fire team, runners and a brief to stand by. It was going to be their only chance at coordinating some kind of mobile communications. He'd also talked with Elliott through the shit landline these people relied on. It was like going back in time. Elliott had already grabbed the parts he needed but it hadn't taken much persuading to get him to stay once NG explained that they needed to draw as many of the Bhenykhn away from the Tangiers as possible to give Hones a fighting chance of getting to the nukes. Elliott had laughed and said simply, "You intrigue me. You want me to stay and help? Why the hell not?"

He'd called back twenty minutes later from the mine's control room, said he was hacked into Erica's systems and had control of the mining bots with their heavy lasers. He'd set them up in defensive positions and said if NG had anything new to add, he was welcome to make the request. The guy was an arrogant ass but it seemed he knew warfare, that was evident.

NG reached for the glass.

Martinez pulled out a chair and sat next to him. She was worried that LC wasn't fit to be out in the field.

"He isn't," he said, "but he's completed tabs in a worse state. He'll be fine."

The kid was out there in the middle of a full on combat situation, wishing he was running a tab, something he'd missed desperately. It was easy to see why. Field-op work was the toughest and easiest in the guild. Two extremes. You had no one scrutinising what you did every minute, no one shooting at you – most of the time – and it was up to you to do it. You got the goods or you didn't. LC always did. When NG had worked as a field-op, he always had.

This was a whole different plate of bananas. He'd outlined the plan to them, in brief, as best as he could manage with spindles of pain stabbing into his eyeballs and half of his concentration on the facility and half on what was going on out beyond the perimeter.

At one point, he'd heard LC whisper to Martinez, "What the fuck is wrong with NG?" She'd asked him back, couldn't he hear the aliens, weren't they frying his brain because that's what was fucking wrong with NG.

They couldn't. Neither of them, LC or Duncan. He'd realised that as soon as they'd made contact. The virus was actively and voraciously shielding them from it. What he didn't know was if it would protect them from being detected. He'd tried asking Sebastian about it but had no response. Sebastian was quiet and had been for a while, thinking about it.

There was a pause then, '*You have no idea what it's taking me right now to keep you alive.*'

Ah.

Martinez picked up the bottle and poured him a shot. She was worried about him too, thinking that he hadn't been straight with them about the whole of his plan and frustrated that they were sitting here waiting for an attack in a position they knew was indefensible.

"We have no choice," he said quietly.

"What are you not telling me, NG?"

'*That you can't do this for much longer?*' Sebastian hissed. '*You might as well tell her, she'll find out soon enough, Nikolai, when those ground troops descend on us.*'

He took a sip from the glass. It was whisky and rough as hell but gave him a hit of heat in his stomach.

He drew his attention back to the facility, checking out the frantic activity as he deployed all the troops left here, Earth and Winter, in defensive positions. They hadn't questioned his plan and were implementing it with fury.

'*Incoming. Do you want to see?*'

Sebastian didn't wait for an answer.

Lightning flashed. Cold, damp air whistled around his senses in a dizzying swirl. He could feel adrenaline pumping through his heart, muscles flexing, rain streaming off his face. He could smell the figures around him as they stood shoulder to shoulder, almost taste the dank, cold breath they exhaled.

His vision swam as the view suddenly swept left and right along the line extending to either side in the darkness.

They were huge. Twisted silhouettes with massive rifles that defied gravity, belts slung with guns, knives, machetes, axes, crossbows and god knows what else. Energy shields and crossbows. Seriously? What the hell were they fighting here? Tattered, hooded cloaks streamed and whipped behind them.

'The Devourers. They wear the pelts of their conquests.'

And eat children. It was like a hideous fairytale. Monsters with far better tech and a perfect means of communication.

'You're in its head?' NG murmured, internal temperature rising.

Sebastian was revelling in the moment. *'Know thy enemy, Nikolai. Rule number one.'*

He knew that. He'd lived it, had it drummed into him, and he didn't need to be mocked with it now.

'But you do not know thyself,' Sebastian whispered, *'and that is what will lose you this battle.'*

'I'm you, Sebastian, you keep telling me that.'

Sebastian laughed and threw a shit load of intel straight at him, no sifting or processing, just a pure information dump direct from its mind.

NG took it. He could feel the weight of the axe as the Bhenykhn hefted it in its hand, feel the anticipation and barely constrained need to attack hammering through its veins.

Ships thundered overhead, sweeping around and firing pods, pod after pod that thudded into the ground and opened with a hiss of released gas, more of the heavily-armoured figures stepping out, weapons up.

They stood, motionless, then he heard the command, not understanding the words but picking up the meaning clear enough, and as one, the line began to move forward.

He jerked as if waking, adrenaline rush pounding as if he'd just dropped out of a nightmare. He was staring at a map on the table, no memory of what he'd been looking at. A hand was resting on the back of his neck.

"You're burning up," Martinez whispered.

"They're here."

He could feel Fiorrentino staring, steadfastly ignored the son of a bitch and reached out to LC and Duncan. "They're organised in units, each controlled by a squad leader. Take out the SL and they have to regroup. They're going to hit us on all five sides simultaneously but three of the five are holding actions to spread our defences; they'll be concentrating their attack on the front gate and the north fence to get to the power matrix for the defence grid. Duncan take the gate, LC take the north side. I'm sending reinforcements. Don't let the Bhenykhn get to the power plant or we're screwed."

'You are screwed.'

He waited for affirmatives, cut the link, then called Elliott and told him the same.

Then he sat back. Waiting was always the hardest. Attacking was easier on the nerves. That was when you got to prowl and time the action to suit your every whim. Defending was tough. He'd learned that the hard way a long time ago and had decided to never put himself in that position again. And here he was.

It sucked.

Even more than he remembered.

When they attacked, they hit hard. To plan. And that was the only thing that saved the hour. Every heavy weapon and mining bot, every defensive position they'd set up held, deflecting the assault and inflicting enough damage to give the Bhenykhn a cause to back off and reassess.

NG looked up as Martinez placed a lit candle on the table. The emergency generators must have failed at some point.

She pushed a plastic cup into his hand. "Tea. Sorry, I couldn't find any sugar but it's hot."

He took a sip and rubbed his eyes.

The Bhenykhn had been expecting it to be a walkover and at each turn, he'd orchestrated a solid counter attack, throwing as much back at them and matching their superior firepower with sheer numbers. The aliens depended heavily on their personal energy shields and he'd used that, setting up crossfires that had worn them down faster than they could move forward.

It wasn't a strategy he could maintain. And the only thing in their favour now was that the Bhenykhn had no idea how little ammunition they had left in here.

The flame danced.

He hadn't even realised it was dark. And sitting there at that table, in a pitch-black darkness broken only by a flickering orange glow, it was hard not to fall into the weird unreality of worlds that were colliding. He caught himself holding his breath, half expecting to look down at a chessboard and a goblet of steaming wine.

Martinez sat next to him. "We can't keep this up, can we?" She was frustrated. Not used to working like this, hiding away while the real action was raging outside. It wasn't how they operated. They'd never shied away from the frontline to let others take the heat and it was damned hard to sit in this protective bubble and listen in as the reports on damage and losses came in.

'She should try listening in as they die,' Sebastian murmured.

He didn't know how to reply but the door opened and LC walked in with Hal Duncan, both of them breathing heavily and wet through. They were running themselves ragged. Luka was bleeding, blood streaming down his face from a cut across his cheek, Duncan chiding him for not wearing a helmet and verging on yelling at him for getting so damn close a damn Benny had sliced him with a machete.

"It was worth it," LC was arguing, dripping a chill mix of chemical rain and blood, holding something in his hand that he tossed forward as NG stood to meet them. "You need to see this."

He caught it.

In the faint glow of the candle, it almost looked like a human heart. Part torn red flesh, part hard shell, it had spikes protruding from one side and a leathery cover on the other. It was pulsing, the energy in it fading slowly.

"Oh god," Martinez muttered.

NG looked up. "Don't tell me this is a heart."

LC almost choked, laughing and blotting his cheek with the

back of his sleeve. "It was wearing it on its belt. Jesus, what do you think I am?"

"The energy shield."

The kid shrugged. "I don't know. I got all this too." He pulled other stuff out of his pockets, piling it all on the table. He'd taken the strapping off his arm, the shoulder looking stiff but mobile. The snapped collarbone had healed a hell of a lot faster than NG had ever managed to heal a broken bone.

Duncan walked past, tugging on LC's belt pouches as he passed, not impressed that the kid hadn't used much ammunition, and heading for the door to go find some more for himself.

NG picked up a couple of the weird items. He couldn't tell if the blood smeared on it all was alien or from LC. "We'll get it to Elliott, see what he makes of it." There were also a couple of tech guys from the Tangiers. Not that they had much time to make anything of it.

'Indeed. Heads up, Nikolai, your little tea-break is about to end…'

"Luka, go get cleaned up. I need you back out there."

LC didn't move.

He switched to direct thought, 'Go.'

There was something wrong, something uneasy in the way the kid was looking at him.

'LC, we have incoming and I need you back out there.'

'You don't expect to get out of here.'

NG turned away. 'We have to stop them. That's all that matters.'

If the first wave had been like a steady strangling hold, squeezing in on all sides, the second was like a spear thrust. The Bhenykhn kept a solid perimeter surrounding the facility but attacked one point with such force it was almost overwhelming.

Knowing what they were about to do wasn't so much a saving advantage as a last ditch shift to throw enough in their way to deflect the blow.

NG was stationed in the centre of it all, keeping an open line to Elliott, and relaying calm and controlled instructions in an almost pre-emptive feed to their joint forces via LC and Duncan, anticipating each move by the enemy, giving them an edge that was keeping them alive.

Sebastian was giving him an extra perspective, looking deeper into the Bhenykhn's immense network of communication and tapping directly into their plans. It was like choreographing a dance, moving pieces around the board, bringing units into play, but with a greater insight than he'd ever had before.

Sebastian laughed. *'You're enjoying this. We should have worked together years ago. Imagine what we could have achieved together…'*

He was hardly enjoying it but there was an elegance to the flow of intel that was almost hypnotic.

They drew the Bhenykhn into a trap, surrounded and cut off five squads of their heavy ground troops and detonated enough explosives to blow a hole in the ground that swallowed up half the ore processing plant.

He let the dust settle then reached out. 'LC? Duncan?'

'All good,' came back from the big ex-marine.

'That was too good,' Sebastian murmured.

Possibly.

He felt the shift in their communications, a distinct pause as they reassessed.

Shit.

'LC?'

No reply.

NG felt himself become the sudden and intense focus of attention.

He looked up at Martinez. "I…"

Sebastian faltered and the barrier shattered. It was agonising. A burst of red, shot through with brilliant white forked lightning flashed behind his eyes. Every pain receptor in his brain sparked in an instant of total overload. It felt like he was held there, scream frozen in his throat, heart stopped in time. Then just as suddenly, he dropped, plummeting into darkness.

36

She watched as he opened the new bottle and prepared the wine, following each movement, biting back the question that was on the tip of her tongue.

"Ask it."

"Why did you not give Nikolai more intelligence on the Bhenykhn? You could have prepared him so much more."

The Man watched the powder react with a billowing of vapour, considered it for a moment, then added more. "I was intending to. Of course I was intending to. He..."

He looked up. She wasn't judging or condemning. That wasn't her purpose. She was making him question so that he could proceed with more care.

"Events occurred far faster than I anticipated. He was gone before I could give anything to him. Before that? He wouldn't have listened. That's the nature of these creatures. They need to experience to learn. And too often, that experience must be hard."

Cool fingers were pressing against the pulse point in his neck.

Raised voices filtered through the fog. Angry voices.

NG could feel his heart pounding, each beat thudding in silent slow motion through his eardrums. Someone was holding his hand but he couldn't move it as much as he tried. He tried to speak and open his eyes but nothing would work. And most disturbing, he couldn't hear or feel Sebastian.

The darkness beckoned and he sank back under.

Every muscle was aching. Whispers of conversation drifted into his awareness as he lay there.

"I can't wake him up," he heard Martinez say harshly. "Don't you think I've tried?"

He couldn't move. Someone was trying to speak to him, mind to mind, but it sounded muted as if they were speaking through fog. There was another nudge, then grey. Then black.

"Send reinforcements to that quad," someone was saying, "and tell them they better make sure the Bennies can't advance an inch."

He blinked open dry eyes that still felt like they were burning.

'About time. Did you enjoy your little nap?'

It was strangely comforting to hear Sebastian's voice. *'What happened?'*

'You managed to get their attention. It took me by surprise but I have it under control again. You can thank me later for saving your pathetic life. We have a real problem.'

His senses swirled as Sebastian linked with the alien hive, sharing a snapshot glimpse into the state of their current battlespace intelligence, shifted priorities and a razor sharp focus that was chilling.

'They know you now. Whatever you do, don't get captured by these creatures, Nikolai.'

'I don't intend to.'

He moved to sit, arms reaching instantly to help him.

"How long was I out?"

"Ten minutes." Martinez pulled him to his feet, no ceremony of checking that he was alright. He wasn't. She wasn't. None of them were. He could feel the panic around them, hear the gunfire closing in. She propelled him towards the table. "We've lost the south wall and they have the power plant. We've lost contact with Elliott and the defence grid is down. We don't know why they're not sending in gunships."

'Because they want you alive…'

"It doesn't matter," he muttered.

"What?"

"We're losing. Get runners out. We need to get a new defensive line established." He coughed, throat parched and shivers still running through his body. "We can't hold here much longer but maybe we can distract them. Get me a team together."

Someone brought body armour, battlefield kit, weapons and ammunition, dumping it in a pile on the table. It was all wet and mud-spattered, blood spots in places. NG didn't bother to wipe it.

'Like old times...'

Martinez was watching him as he strapped on armour, casually tying a neck guard in the way only Earth marines ever did, and bending to fasten a holster round his thigh.

"You've done this before as well?" she asked.

He nodded. She'd be horrified, and probably wouldn't believe him anyway, if he told her the names of half the battles he'd seen first-hand from the frontline.

She was curious, wondering what else she didn't know about him. "Were you at Derren Bay?"

"Nope, after my time. Did you know Hal Duncan was there?"

She nodded. "So when...?"

"A long..."

She finished the sentence for him, "...time ago. NG, how old are you?"

He picked a lightweight mobile infantry helmet from the pile, tore all the comms wiring out and jammed it onto his head.

He looked at her as he tied the chinstrap. "A hundred and twenty four."

She couldn't tell if he was joking but she smiled as something bizarre occurred to her. "You're Andreyev," she said.

He dropped his eyes to the pile of weapons, couldn't help the half smile and couldn't admit it. It had been a hundred odd years ago. No one had ever got near his points total, not even LC. He'd wiped the slate clean when he'd taken over as head of operations, made all the field-ops start from scratch.

She was torn between amazed and incredulous. "Does LC know?"

He rummaged through the guns before looking up. "No, he doesn't." He grabbed a rifle, checked its mechanism and popped out the magazine, switching to direct thought as he went through the drill. 'LC, get in here. Duncan, get ready to pull back. I've got people moving in to cover.' The rifle had been well cared for. He slotted the mag back into place and slung the weapon over his back.

He turned back to the table to pick up more ammunition and paused, unease prickling at the back of his neck. 'LC?'

The reply that came back was terse, strained. 'NG, I'm trying. They're doing something weird… oh shit.'

'They're trying to cut him off. They've connected him to you. Can you feel it?'

He could feel that the rest of the kid's fire team were dying around him.

'LC, get out of there.'

'Trying.'

NG grabbed two extra magazines and headed for the door. 'Duncan, close in on LC's position. Both of you, listen to me – whatever you do, do not get taken alive.' Martinez was right behind him, with the team they'd been assigned. He stopped and turned to her. "LC's trapped. They know what we are."

"What who is?"

"Angel, I probably should have told you this before. LC and Duncan. We can…" He didn't know how to say it.

She scowled. "Don't you think I know? NG, I'm not fucking stupid." She shoved him forward. "Let's get out there."

"Don't let them get anywhere near the three of us," he muttered. "If any of us get caught, shoot us. Twice. In the head."

It was still dark outside and it was still raining. They moved out fast, tight formation, NG taking point. He could feel the battle raging around them, a taste of blood in the air mixing with the acrid chemical emissions spewing from the ragged ruins of pipelines overhead.

He felt the hit as LC's team leader bought it, the last one trying to protect him, felt the punch of void and the desperation as the kid backed off.

NG ran flat out through the complex until he could sense he was close then he slowed, raised his rifle and moved in, combat ready stance, gauging angles and moving round on them as they moved in on LC.

The kid was out in the open, completely exposed but he was hyperfocused, something NG had seen in him in the Maze but never in the field. LC and Hil always went out alone. NG had seen the aftermath before, the crash and burn, but he'd never shared this intensity in a real situation. LC had a rifle tucked into his left shoulder and was emptying a mag into one of four Bhenykhn around him. Each round sparked against its shield, flaring in the glow from the solitary floodlight that was struggling to illuminate the clearing.

NG opened up on the same one.

It spun, raising a massive rifle to aim at him but holding back.

'Wrong target… the one with the grey cloak is in charge.'

He didn't stop firing but he glanced aside. There was no way to tell how close they were to taking out the shield and he had no idea if taking out the squad leader would affect the others. The Bhenykhn in the grey cloak was a good three or four inches taller than the others, hefting an axe in one hand and a knife in the other. It was staring at him through yellow eyes.

'It knows you…'

LC's gun clicked dry. He tossed it aside and turned to run. One of the others flung out an arm and a weighted chain went spinning through the air.

NG switched his aim and shot it off its trajectory as LC jumped, defying gravity to flip himself backwards to avoid it. He landed, pulled out a handgun and stood there shooting again.

It was eerie to sense the change in the kid. LC had never killed anyone before and now his mind was cold and closed as he sent shot after shot aimed perfectly at its head.

NG didn't stop firing, hoping that its damn shield couldn't take much more, yelling behind him for the others to stay in cover and moving round slowly as the other Bhenykhn started to circle, knife blades flashing in the glare of the floodlight. It didn't take much to calculate that, even between all of them, they didn't have enough ammunition to take down all four of these massive alien warriors.

'Never mind the other four that are inbound, right now. Trust me, Nikolai, take out the squad leader.'

Bullets started flying in from all directions as the others opened up.

NG blinked rain from his eyelashes. He fired his last round, ejected the mag and reached for a new one, hardly a break in the stream of lead he was throwing out but enough to break the standoff.

Knives flew.

He staggered as one pierced his thigh, straight through the light Wintran armour, watching as LC took a hit that sent him to his knees.

Martinez was yelling.

He yelled at her to stay back, ruthlessly shutting out the pain and heat in his leg that was screaming poison, and slotting in the new magazine. He switched target to the grey cloak, eliciting a sneer in that leathery face.

It raised the hand wielding the axe and two of the Bhenykhn moved forward, one to LC, one towards him.

It was on him in a split second, grabbing the rifle even as he was firing it, twisting it out of his grasp and clubbing him round the head. It loomed over him, rain glistening off its smooth brown chitin-like skin. It smelled like dank, decaying leafmold and this close up, the pressure of that constant buzzing hum was almost unbearable, beating against his mind.

A massive hand grabbed him round the back of the neck and forced him down, fingernails like knives puncturing the armour to rake into his skin. His knees hit the ground, splashing in rainwater that was pooling and running in small streams.

He could hear Martinez shouting to the others to stand down, wait, screw what NG had said.

He raised his eyes to look at the alien in the grey cloak and caught a shadow of movement out of the corner of his eye. Something where there should not have been any living thing. A dark shape jumped onto the Bhenykhn's back and a knife flashed again and again, stabbing into its neck in a frenzied attack.

The Bhenykhn squad leader tumbled, hitting the ground face down.

NG reeled. It was dead, the pop of void that hit more powerful than anything he'd felt before.

The others froze as if recalculating.

NG twisted free, sprawling on the ground and rolling to his feet. He pulled the knife out of his leg and didn't hesitate, darting in to stab the Bhenykhn in the neck. The blade plunged in with no resistance and no defence from its energy shield.

He stepped back as it fell, turning to see LC doing the same. The fourth alien was raising its rifle, slowly, as if caught in slow motion indecision. A shadow flitted next to it and it fell. Hilyer stepped forward into the light, pushing the Bhenykhn away from himself. The kid was butt naked, covered with mud, bleeding from a gash across his chest and grinning insanely. He had a knife in his hand, more blood dripping down his arm, dripping off the end of the curved blade. And most disturbing, NG couldn't sense a thing from him, no emotion, no thoughts, no pain, no life signs at all. Nothing.

Hil was laughing like a maniac. He kicked the gun away from the body at his feet. "We're the fucking Thieves' Guild," he yelled down at the alien, shouting over the thunder, voice close to cracking. "You don't mess with us."

Damn right.

37

She was quiet, staring into the flames, thinking about times past and friends lost, that defiance and determination so familiar even though it had been so far away and so long ago.

She was thinking that they had had their peace, a mere interlude, always aware this was on its way, but now it was here and that peace was gone. Again.

He didn't disturb her thoughts, didn't chide her out of it the way he would have done with Nikolai.

It had been hard at the end. Few escaped. She was thinking how few. Thinking how this galaxy that teemed with these small, short-lived creatures was going to fare.

"They have us," the Man said quietly. "We had no one. And these events have unfolded the way they have because we are here."

He filled the goblets and held one out to her. "It will not be the same."

Martinez ran up, directing the others to collect weapons, Duncan heading over to LC.

NG felt his legs start to go as the adrenaline dissipated. He sank to one knee, trembling, Martinez at his side.

"Poison," he mumbled. "Just give me a minute." His leg was throbbing, the back of his neck burning tendrils into his spine. He could feel it rushing into his bloodstream, a systemic toxin that was paralysing.

Martinez shouted across to the others, "Poison. Don't touch the blades." She took hold of NG's hand, thinking that if he could hear, he was welcome to take whatever he needed.

"It's not just the knives," he said, rubbing the back of his neck.

She passed on the warning, squeezed his hand tight and yelled at Hil, "Hey, Hilyer. Nice butt."

Hil laughed again. NG looked up. It was second nature to rely on that automatic sixth sense to know exactly where everyone was around him so it was unnerving as hell to look across and see the kid standing there.

Sebastian stirred. '*No wonder the Bhenykhn had no idea he was there amongst them. It appears they do have a weakness.*'

'*Except they're not blind. He was lucky.*'

Hil was also running on pure adrenaline. Someone had given him a field dressing and he was hugging it against the wound on his chest, soaking it through with fresh blood in seconds. The kid was close to crashing. God knows how he'd made it this far.

"So that's how we do it?" Martinez said.

"It won't be so easy for anyone else to get that close," NG said. His chest was heaving, leg almost numb. "Let's get back inside. I need to reload."

Fiorrentino was lording over it at the head of the table as they walked back in to the ops room. NG killed it immediately without a word, grabbing the map and bottle, calling the Wintran medic to follow and limping into the small office.

He ditched the rifle, stripped off the helmet and neck guard, and sank into the chair behind the desk.

"We don't have long," he said. He propped his leg up on a second chair and fumbled to untie the straps on the body armour round his thigh. The knife wound was ugly but he could hardly feel it.

He opened the whisky and drank straight from the bottle as he worked to neutralise the residual effects of the poison and stop the bleeding, wrapping a field bandage tightly around the jagged wound.

'*Nasty stuff.*'

'*What, the poison or the whisky?*'

Sebastian laughed. '*You amuse me, Nikolai, have I ever told you that before? There have been several distinctly peculiar times when*

I've found your infectious exuberance bizarrely entertaining. I refer to the poison. It should have incapacitated you in seconds. They don't like that it didn't.'

'Good.'

He tied off the binding with a rough knot and looked over at LC. Hal Duncan was helping the kid do the same. LC was pale and shivering, but laughing at Hilyer who had crashed out on the low sofa, still wielding the Bhenykhn knife and still grinning, flirting with the medic who was trying to patch him up and joking about waking up naked in a crashed medevac pod. It was like being in the mess in Acquisitions, sky-high egos and screw-it-all bravado.

Without even needing to read them, it was obvious Hil was overcompensating for having almost died and LC wasn't so much freaked out that he couldn't feel his leg but that he'd killed someone, albeit a freaking monster that was trying to kill them.

Duncan looked up and caught NG's eye, thinking, 'I take it this is the infamous Zach Hilyer?'

'The one and only. Don't let Fiorrentino or anyone from Zang anywhere near the pair of them.'

Duncan gave a slight nod and said out loud, "What now?"

NG took another swig from the bottle. "We need to draw their attention so Hones has a chance when he reaches the Tangiers." He offered across the whisky and switched to direct thought. 'It seems that the aliens can't detect anything from Hilyer. Can you?'

Duncan shook his head as he leaned over to take the bottle. NG could sense a change of heart in the big ex-marine, that deeply unsettled suspicion of the guild making way for a tentative element of trust after having seen them in action, seen first hand the way they'd run to help Luka.

Duncan handed the whisky straight to LC and looked back at NG. 'You don't have this virus.' Not a question.

'Nope.'

Martinez had grabbed an armful of ammo boxes on the way in and was reloading. She pushed a box to Duncan who started to thumb rounds into the magazines, nudging LC to do the same.

'You're different,' the big man thought. 'Is that why you can hear them and we can't?'

NG took a box and started refilling his own.

'I have no idea,' he thought back. 'We didn't have much of a chance to carry out any research on the virus before…' He tailed away, no idea what to think or say… before he almost killed LC, before he got Sorensen killed, before he got Devon killed or before he messed with the Assassins so badly it almost got him killed?

That got a glance from LC.

Duncan didn't care about anything but the immediate threat. 'Can they hear us?'

'We don't think so.' That 'we' sounded barking mad. NG looked up. 'I don't think so. They don't seem to be reacting to our thoughts. I don't think they can read our minds or overhear what we think. But they're driven by energy. They sense human life signs through our energy signatures. I don't know. We use a shit load of energy to do this. Maybe that's what got their attention.'

'*And*,' Sebastian interjected, '*the fact that you pre-empted every move they made. Hardly subtle, Nikolai.*'

Duncan narrowed his eyes. 'So we might as well be sitting here with a flashing neon sign over our heads?'

NG didn't reply, feeling wide open, exposed. He just kept pushing in those rounds, one bullet at a time, very aware how few boxes they had left and how fast he'd burned through these mags out there.

Duncan stopped what he was doing and stared. 'But that's what you want, isn't it?'

'We need to stop them reporting back.'

'And you think the Tangiers has the weapons to do it?'

NG shrugged. 'Hones thinks they do. I think it's our best shot.'

The big ex-marine slotted the last full magazine into his rifle. 'Did you know the Bennies were here?'

'You' being the guild.

'We knew they were coming. We didn't know they were here already.'

'Excuse me for asking, but what the hell does a guild of thieves have to do with a fucking alien invasion?'

'We don't just steal stuff.'

Duncan glanced at Martinez. 'I can see that.'

Sebastian stirred suddenly, sending a shiver down NG's back.

Duncan picked up on it. "Time to go?"

NG nodded. They needed to get mobile. He rubbed his leg. Pins and needles were prickling in the muscles as the feeling came back slowly but he reckoned he could walk on it. LC was another matter but if they were going to have any chance of surviving this, they needed to move.

'You heal faster than us,' Duncan thought. Again, not a question.

'It's different.'

'How?'

LC was listening in. This was the rest of the conversation they should have had on board the Alsatia, before Sebastian…

'For me to heal, it takes conscious effort. The virus you have is active. It heals for you. You don't need to do anything. I have to concentrate – that's why it works faster but it costs. This is what we need to figure out – what could you do if you tried?'

Duncan had to suppress a chuckle. 'We don't exactly have time to play, do we?' He stood. "Do you need anything?"

NG looked up and sent privately, direct thought again, 'I need to thank you for getting LC out of the shit on Poule.'

'He's a good kid. He has a death wish but I'm starting to see that's a prerequisite to work with you guys.'

NG bit back a smile. He reached for the map. "I need to show you what the plan is."

Hones and his team made it through the tunnels and were heading across the valley towards the Tangiers. NG crouched on the rooftop in the shelter of a thick pipeline, rifle cradled in his arms, finger on the trigger.

It had stopped raining but the damp cold was still permeating like thick fog. The Bhenykhn were regrouping. He listened in, watching from his vantage point as they circled around, half his concentration on Hones and the minute by minute monologue the colonel was running through his mind, '...if you can still bloody hear this.'

He could, just, through the steady stream of intel that Sebastian was throwing at him. It was a nervy game they were playing, attracting the Bhenykhn's attention then running, occasionally stopping to shoot the shit out of a single alien, chipping away at their numbers. Sometimes skipping out by the skin of their teeth. Sometimes not. Hones had assigned five of his best marines to stay with them; they were down to two.

'Okay, we're good to go,' came in from Duncan.

NG stood, still half crouched, motioning to Martinez and running to the edge of the roof. He dropped flat into a firing position. He could see LC, pressed up close against the door of the building opposite, no need to bust open the lock, he could see from here it had been hacked open with an axe. Duncan was standing on the other side watching the kid's back. Hilyer was around somewhere. They were keeping together, blazing a trail, fast and mobile, causing enough trouble that the Bennies were struggling to put a coherent plan into action to capture them.

He just wanted to find out what had happened to Elliott.

'We've got the street,' he sent.

LC went in, Duncan close behind.

They had maybe five minutes before they'd have to bug out.

It didn't take that long.

NG walked in. The smell was almost overpowering, a stench of decay and rotting flesh, blood and pheromones hanging heavy in the air.

There were at least four bodies that he could make out, flesh and body parts strewn around the small control room. One head was pinned to the wall by an axe, dripping fluids. Another was strung up by a weighted chain, still swinging from the rafters.

LC looked sick. He pushed past, muttering, "He's not here," and heading for the door.

'The child is quite the empath. Dangerous talent to have when he has no control over it. It looks like Elliott has been busy. I want to meet him, Nikolai. He's avoiding you, have you noticed?'

He had.

He wandered over to the main console and picked through LC's assortment of oddities, all disassembled, lying scattered from what looked to have been neat lines before the fight. There were four more energy shield pods there, all smashed, oozing bodily fluids.

Martinez was cursing as she gathered weapons, kicking aside dismembered body parts.

Hilyer walked up beside him before he even knew the kid was there with them. "Hey NG, look at this."

Martinez looked across. "What the hell is that?"

NG squinted at it, a chill settling in his stomach.

Hil grinned, obvious that he recognised it.

"What is it?" Martinez said again, taking it off Hilyer and holding it up to the light.

The craftwork was unmistakable.

'Oh my…'

Hil leaned back against the console. "Do you remember that tab LC screwed up a few years ago?"

Everyone knew the tab LC had screwed up.

It had taken them four extraction teams and a Thundercloud to get him out. He'd spent two months in Medical recovering from it.

She nodded, turning the elaborate badge over in her hand, rubbing the blood off the twisted metal.

"He was fucked," Hil said, "but he'd nailed the tab. He had it in his pocket." He looked up. "It was one of these, wasn't it? Where is he?"

"Outside," NG said vaguely and demanded of Sebastian, *'Did you know?'*

'Know what? That the amulet Anderton retrieved from Rodan was Bhenykhn? Or that the Man knowingly sent one of your precious field operatives after an artefact he knew was scavenged from his arch

enemies? Or that the fiendish Angmar Rodan was in possession of such an item? What do you think…?'

NG looked around at the carnage, an uneasy queasiness stirring deep inside.

'Don't you want to know what it is?'

He didn't.

'It's a kill token. A badge of honour. One thousand confirmed kills in unarmed combat. They keep tallies.'

Christ.

"How the hell," Duncan said, turning round from examining the head on the wall, "did one skinny tech guy do this?"

The head had an ear missing.

NG shook his head vaguely. He nudged a few of the screens that weren't smashed but the whole console was dead. "I have no idea. We need to find him. Come on. We're low on ammo. Grab whatever weapons you can."

They made it back out onto the rooftops and ran, putting distance between themselves and the control room. The wind was picking up again.

"How fucking long does night last in this place?" Martinez muttered as they hunkered down again, the others spread out around them in a defensive formation.

NG huddled against a wall. He was cold and he'd lost track of Hones. They had about seven more hours of darkness but he had no idea if he said that out loud or not.

He closed his eyes for a second and tried to concentrate on the Tangiers. There was a lot of Bhenykhn activity there, much more than there had been. They were scouring the place, picking it clean.

He was vaguely aware of Martinez taking his rifle and pushing a flask into his hand.

He took a sip of something that burnt his throat. He coughed and muttered a thanks out loud, directing at Sebastian, *'C'mon, help me here. Where's Hones?'*

'In trouble.'

He followed Sebastian's train of thought and managed to pick out the colonel, more from the pain and the vicious swearing than anything the man was thinking consciously.

'They don't have time to lock in the targeting coordinates,' Sebastian murmured. *'The Bhenykhn know what you're doing. They're sending gunships, here and to the Tangiers. Those warheads aren't going to make it out of their tubes and Hones knows it. Can you feel that?'*

It was chilling, a double hit of last-stand determination from the JU colonel and a flush of impending victory and bloodlust from the Bhenykhn. Hones and his men were overrun, more of the alien ground troops storming the warship.

'Get into cover,' Sebastian thought coldly. *'Now, Nikolai, get into cover.'*

He looked up, hearing the roar of a gunship cutting through the howling wind.

Martinez caught his movement and followed his line of sight, grabbing his shoulder and yelling to the others, "Get into cover. Get off the goddamned roof."

She thrust the rifle back at him and pulled him up and into a run as blinding spotlights sliced through the darkness. The gunship thundered overhead, circling like a vulture, spinning its guns and arcing beams of light across the rooftops.

NG ran, yelling at Martinez to stay close, picking up its intention a fraction of a second too late as it opened up on one of the marines.

It switched to the other as they ran.

LC stumbled, dragged to his feet by Duncan, god knows where Hilyer was.

"Stay close," NG yelled again, head spinning. "They want us alive."

Half his concentration was still focused on the Tangiers.

He couldn't break free.

Couldn't focus on here or there.

The gunship swooped in low, cutting off their exit from the roof, hovering, buffeted by the wind, weapons bristling.

Hones armed the warheads. A fierce, defiant decision to sacrifice and there was nothing NG could do.

The gunship pinned them in its spotlight.

He spun around, back to back with Martinez, LC and Duncan, guns up.

Trapped.

No way out. Here or there.

Hones hit the button.

38

She took the goblet, raised it and looked at the twisted metal of the stem, the elaborate markings on the cup, then raised her eyes to look across at him. "Did he realise?"

"No. Why would he?"

"But they recognised the badges, the kill tokens? They made the connection with the amulet?"

"They assumed it was the same. They realised that Bhenykhn artefacts were already present in their galaxy. That is all."

"You don't think it necessary for them to know?"

He drank from his own goblet, savouring the heat. "It is irrelevant. The knowledge of where I am from, where the Bhenykhn are from, will not help them. They need to fight for their own galaxy. Anything else is a distraction."

The Tangiers blew sky high. Light flared on the horizon and the shock of so many simultaneous deaths hit NG like he'd been hit by a truck. He staggered, seeing LC drop as if he'd been poleaxed.

The gunship swerved away as if it had been rocked by an updraft, circling around and bringing its guns quickly back to bear down on them again.

'Time for a new plan...'

He didn't have a plan. He could hardly hold up the weight of the rifle any longer and he could sense multiple ground units moving in.

"What do we do?" Duncan shouted, dragging LC up again.

He was about to yell at them to open fire when a figure ran from the shadows, hefting a massive Bhenykhn weapon and targeting the gunship.

Hilyer. He fired. A searing beam of energy lanced out, slicing through the gunship's tail section.

Hil yelled, "Run!"

They ran. The gunship opened up, peppering the ground at their feet even as it spun out of control.

NG ran alongside Martinez, grabbing her arm and pulling her aside as the massive bulk of the black gunship crashed behind them.

They went sprawling as the wave of heat and debris hit. NG tumbled, losing his grip on Martinez and crashing into a wall.

'Get off the roof,' Sebastian said dryly.

His head was ringing, breath driven out of his lungs and ribs on fire again. He rolled onto his back and tried to get up, managing to half sit and slump back against the wall.

The roof was littered with burning, mangled metal. Ground troops were moving in.

Martinez was down, out cold.

He tried to reach out to the others but Sebastian grabbed the moment, demanding his full attention as if physically grabbing him round the throat. *'I will not die here, Nikolai. Listen to me. Garrett and his team got away from the Tangiers with the spare parts for the freighter. If that weirdo Elliott skipped out with the parts from here then you need to quit screwing around and get your ass to the freighter or they – will – leave – without you. Do you understand? Don't roll over and die here. You do not have to save the whole damned universe. You are not the saviour of mankind. Get out and live to fight another day.'*

'No,' he thought back simply and broke free. He scrambled over to Martinez and checked her pulse. She grabbed his wrist and struggled, fighting, until she came to her senses and swore, reaching for her rifle.

They staggered to their feet and looked around. "Hones didn't make it," he gasped, sending the same thought to LC and Hal Duncan who were on the other side of the wreckage, battered but intact. "It's up to us to stop the Bennies getting away."

They moved as quickly as they could, running to drop back behind their lines. He sent the others off to gather up squad leaders from every unit they had out there defending, then he went inside. He made his way to the entrance area where they'd cleared out the dead to set up a rough and ready infirmary. The Wintran major was up to his elbows in blood, tending to some poor sucker who probably wasn't going to make it. He looked up as they approached.

"Hones had to detonate the warheads," NG said. "No choice but to self-destruct. The Tangiers is gone but he took half their ground force with him." He let that sink in, saw the dawning realisation in the major that with Hones gone, he was now the highest ranking military officer. "I'm going after the alien ship. You..." he paused and glanced round at the medic who was watching, "you need to evacuate the wounded to the freighter. Right now. We're out of time. Take everyone who can walk. Leave the rest. I'm going to give you coordinates and codes. Get them to the freighter. Make sure you make it. If nothing else, get this intel to the freighter and get out of here."

He grabbed a board from a stack they were using to keep track of the wounded and entered data fast, detailing a means to contact the Alsatia. He handed it over and turned away, taking off the helmet and scrubbing a muddy hand through his wet hair. The pain in his ribs was almost unbearable, each footstep and intake of breath shooting fire across his chest. It felt like he'd forgotten how to switch off the pain, the simplest, most basic talent he'd ever had.

The medic followed them.

"You're injured," she said.

"I'm fine."

Martinez said, "He's stubborn. And yes, he's injured. We could do with trauma patches and Epizin if you have any to spare."

NG didn't stop walking.

They didn't have time to screw around.

Sebastian was whispering a constant update of the Bhenykhn plans, unimpressed and sullen.

'Damn right I'm unimpressed. The only way you will stop them is to take on their commander, do you realise that?'

'We just need to stop them launching.'

'Don't be a fool, Nikolai.'

He pushed his way through an increasingly crowded main area amidst a rising apprehension in the gathered troops and engineers, vaguely aware that the others were back and spreading word that something was happening. He went straight to the ops centre, stuck his head around the door and said simply to Fiorrentino and his three cronies who were cowering in there, "Get your asses out here. We're moving out."

He didn't wait to see if they responded, walking back out into the main area and climbing up onto a table. He looked around. LC and Hil were sitting perched on a bench along the far wall, out of the way, almost separate as if this didn't concern them. Duncan was milling, patting guys on the back, reassuring his men, Earth or Wintran, no matter that he had no uniform or rank.

And just standing there on that table, NG commanded the room, drawing energy from the several hundred bodies before him. He demanded their attention without saying a word.

Sebastian changed his tune, almost buzzing. *'This is more like it. Humans are so easy to manipulate. See what you've been missing with all that altruistic nonsense you are so fond of. See what we could have done together… what we could still do…'*

A hush fell in seconds, only the occasional click of a weapon breaking the silence.

"Listen in," he said, no need to raise his voice. "By whatever trick of fate or fortune that finds you here, you are here and this is what you are facing. They're called the Devourers. They've come to conquer. We're outgunned. They're bigger than us, they're stronger than us. They have better armour, better weapons. They can see us in the dark. They can communicate instantaneously. We have no comms, hardly any munitions. But I am damned if I'm going to let them get a foothold here. What we face is just the beginning. More will follow and they will go from planet to planet across our galaxy until we are destroyed." He took a deep breath that sent sparks through his chest. "If we stop this forward unit from reporting back, at least we buy ourselves some time. You have a choice. I'm going after the alien ship. Come with me. Or leave here, get onto the freighter and get out. Your choice."

He turned away and jumped down.

Sebastian laughed. *'Are you serious? We few, we happy fucking few. Are you not supposed to fire up their sense of duty and honour? Are you not supposed to warm their cockles with grand words of scars and wounds to show off should they shed blood beside you and survive to tell the tale?'*

'It's up to them.'

He walked without a word through the crowd to the door. Martinez stayed at his side and he could sense LC and Duncan following, presumably Hil as well. And one by one, others began to troop out behind them.

'My word, Nikolai, these people are actually going to follow you. I've never seen so many pawns so willing to be sacrificed.'

Duncan straight away started shouting out orders. He knew what needed to be done. They had to move fast, leave enough defences in place to hold the Bennies that were attacking the facility and get out there onto the moorland. The marine sergeant joined in, rallying the troops, the two of them working together like they were old teammates.

NG let them get on with it. He found Gallagher, told the old guy to evacuate back to his ship, then reloaded, grabbed spare ammunition and ended up standing in the entrance to Erica's mining facility, staring out into the rain.

Another storm front was moving in.

Behind him, he could feel a heightening readiness for battle, seasoned troops gearing up in anticipation, the newbies shaking out the nerves with frenzied activity. It was a long way from the comfort of the Alsatia and the intricate task of allocating acquisitions.

He felt LC's presence as a gentle nudge.

'We should have come back,' the kid thought to him. 'After it all went to shit, we should have come back. I'm sorry we didn't.

We just… I…' He tailed off, feeling awkward and not bothering to hide it.

NG glanced over. LC was sitting on a crate out in the open, a rifle across his knees, hood thrown back, soaked through and choosing to chill down because he'd been overheating in the stifling swirl of emotions inside. They were all a long way from the Alsatia.

'Is this where it came from?' the kid asked.

The virus.

'I don't know,' he thought back. He reckoned probably so, somehow.

LC was thinking that it all still came back to the package. The damned package. 'What if it did?' he thought suddenly. 'Did Zang know…?'

About the Bennies.

NG turned to look back inside as LC stood and they both had the same thought at the same time. 'Fiorrentino.'

They pushed their way back inside.

The tunnel was packed, everyone ready to move out and they forced their way back in.

Martinez picked up on the urgency. She moved in close, following them as they moved in the wrong direction, and hissed, "What's wrong?"

NG didn't reply, sending to Duncan, 'Where's Fiorrentino?' as he scanned around to home in on the suit.

It didn't take long. The guy was terrified and muscling in on the major, trying to take over the evacuation to book himself a place out.

Duncan intercepted as they closed in, neatly shouldering Fiorrentino aside to separate him from his cronies and using a slick control and restraint move to march him into a side room. Hil followed and Martinez took up position to stand guard for them without a word.

They had the suit isolated, in private, before the guy knew what had happened.

"You wanted to talk to me?" NG said quietly and watched the realisation hit Fiorrentino between the eyes.

"NG," he said, too loud, almost hysterically. "My god, you wouldn't believe how much cash we've spent trying to get our hands on you." He shook his head. He'd had the bastard, he was thinking, he'd had NG himself on his knees, bleeding, in chains. He was kicking himself that he hadn't thought to run the biometrics past the parcel of data he had in his personal files, his official 'business' files, the biometrics it had cost them a fortune to acquire from the Assassins, rather than leaving it to the grunts whom he had tasked only with finding Anderton and Hilyer. He looked past NG to LC and Hil and smiled, a sly creasing of the lips. "Where's my package?"

"Why now?" NG said simply. "After all this time? Why did the Order come after us now?"

Fiorrentino did a double take at that mention of the Order. He thought about denying it but glanced around, eyes coming to rest on the gun in NG's arms. He was calculating. "Wait a minute," he said. "I can explain…"

"You don't need to," NG murmured and had a hand around the guy's throat before he could twitch. He froze time. He took everything, violently raking every scrap of information from the guy's mind, every thought, memory, interaction and insidious dealing ever made, throwing it all to LC and not even bothering to process half of it.

He took everything and stepped back, a sick feeling crashing in waves through his stomach.

Fiorrentino slumped to the floor.

'Oh my, how the murky waters run deep.'

LC was struggling to breathe. 'They came after you because they thought we'd stolen the virus? They thought you'd told us not to take it back to Zang? Who the hell is Angmar Rodan?'

'CEO of UM. And yes, we've been played. We went after Zang when we should have gone after Rodan. Christ.'

He turned away. "C'mon, it doesn't change anything. We need to go."

They made it halfway across the moorland before the Bennies caught on to what they were doing and sent a gunship and four units of ground troops to surround them.

NG slid into a ditch, driving rain pounding an icy chill into every inch of exposed skin, yelling the others to get down and readying his rifle with fingers he could hardly feel.

The two troop carriers thundered overhead, sweeping around and firing pods that thudded into the ground in a perfect circle around them. Sixteen heavily armed and armoured infantry. Four units of four. Against roughly three hundred humans, half of whom had ditched their rifles for lack of ammunition and had nothing left but scavenged machetes and knives.

He shouted them to attack as soon as the pods opened, anyone with ammo left opening fire and everyone else running at the Bennies to get in close and engage in hand to hand.

NG chose his target.

Time slowed.

He felt each squeeze of the trigger as a thump, each recoil as a punch against his shoulder. He watched every bullet cut through the rain and impact against its energy shield, draining it steadily, shot after shot, until it flickered, making sure the next was a headshot.

Then he scrambled along the ditch, aware that Martinez was following, repositioning to get a clear shot on another grey cloak.

He emptied another magazine, keeping his breathing slow, shutting out the screams and pain from the wounded and dying. He had no idea where Hilyer was but he could sense LC, the kid struggling but holding, and Duncan who was giving calm and steady sitreps as the human losses added up and the Bennies began to fall. NG had that in his head along with Sebastian who was giving him a running commentary from the hive.

It was dizzying. They were screwed. A gunship was flying low over the hills, closing in fast. They were pinned down, the Bennies that were left starting to back off out of range, content to simply surround them and keep their heads down with occasional suppressive fire.

'They still want you alive,' Sebastian murmured.

He couldn't see a way out. Once that gunship arrived, they were done.

He stood, dropping the rifle to his side, and turned slowly, staring out over the moorland, torrential rain streaming down his face. The Bennies were just standing there, spread out around them.

'Don't,' Sebastian warned, picking up on something he hadn't even thought through.

He couldn't think of any other way out.

The gunship screamed overhead, circled in a deafening roar of engines and swept down, opening up and raking gunfire across their scattered lines.

'Tell them to stop,' he thought at Sebastian. *'For Christ's sake, do something. Can you talk to them? Tell them to stop. I'll surrender. There's no point in all these people dying for nothing.'*

'Not going to happen.'

They had nowhere to run to.

NG turned, heart pounding.

Martinez was shouting.

Through the screams, he heard Hil shout something, saw the kid running towards him, spinning, looking up, sliding in the mud, yelling, "NG, for fuck's sake, can you not hear this? Skye, get out of here. What the hell are you going to do? Skye, no. Oh crap, NG, can you not hear any of this?"

"What? Hear what?"

Martinez looked bewildered.

The gunship was circling, guns whirring, air to ground missiles tearing chunks out of their ranks. They had no chance. It spun around and flew right at them. NG raised his rifle. He stood his ground, finger on the trigger, knowing there was nothing he could do.

"Skye, fucking go," Hil was screaming. "Get out of here."

A sound like thunder crashed through the low cloud and a pressure wave hit, knocking them to the floor, as the mass of a ship flew impossibly close overhead. She didn't stop, ploughing into the gunship. NG sprawled, raising his head and shielding his eyes as the combined mass of both ships hit the ground in a ball of fire that erupted into the sky.

39

"The Thieves' Guild leading both Earth and Winter into battle?" There was something of awe in her voice.

"Nikolai had little choice," the Man said. "He was right. The Bhenykhn knew what he was and he knew that knowledge could not be sent back lest it be used against us."

"He brought Earth and Winter together. Everything you have been striving for. They followed him. They died for him."

"It was a skirmish only. And it proved how fragile these creatures are. We had technology to match, weapons and defences that should have stood up to the Bhenykhn and we were destroyed. This galaxy is young. Its people are young. They might be loyal and fierce when fighting a common foe in a desperate skirmish, but given the full scale of the invasion to come? I fear for them."

NG scrambled to his feet, rifle up and firing at the decimated line of Bhenykhn ground troops, only four or five left and those taken out fast as more guns came to bear down on them. When the last one fell, he stopped, chest heaving, standing in the pouring rain and turning slowly to take stock.

'Fifty nine wounded, one hundred sixty seven dead.'

Hal Duncan was standing over the last Benny, a machete in his hand. LC was down, Hil on his knees.

NG felt like his eyeballs were burning.

"Oh my god," Martinez breathed at his shoulder, "was that Skye?"

They both looked over at Hil.

NG couldn't feel a thing from him.

"Go get LC," he muttered.

The kid was stirring, knocked sideways by a blow from something but alive. Martinez nodded and took off, joined by the Wintran medic he could have sworn he'd told to evacuate but was here amongst their wounded, obviously not the first time she'd seen combat.

Hil got up as he approached, steadfastly avoiding looking at the burning wreckage and heading instead for the line of fallen Bennies. NG dropped into step alongside him and they joined the others salvaging what weapons and ammunition they could, Hil kicking at each body and barely containing a smouldering anger. A couple of times, the kid knelt and pulled something from one of the massive Bhenykhn. Collecting kill tokens. NG let him do it, let him burn off the intensity of the loss.

It was only once they were done and moving again that Hil spoke.

"I felt her die."

NG looked across at him. Hil was spinning a knife in his hand. He had a rifle slung across his back and a pocket full of kill tokens. He looked like the street kid Mendhel had paid a fortune to buy from that jail all those years ago, that haunted distrusting look back in his eyes and a set to his jawline that was the warning sign of a brewing temper.

He met NG's eye with a belligerent glare. "Why didn't you reply to her?"

"Hil, I couldn't hear her. I don't know how you could hear her. It wasn't through the Sensons."

The only light was from the dim glow of Erica's moons and a few bouncing flashlight beams, and he couldn't read Hil's mind, but he could still read the furtive downcast glance. "What?"

Hil didn't reply.

The ground was uneven, slippery with mud, and for a few minutes they had to watch their footing, trying to keep up with the pace and not break a leg.

NG didn't push it with Hil. His chest was hurting like hell again but he didn't want to waste time stopping to take a look at it and he didn't want to steal energy from anyone around him because he could feel how depleted they all were. He had a shot of Epizin in his pocket but it was his last one and he had a feeling he'd need it later.

'You're going to need more than that later. They're waiting for you. In case you're wondering, they're not chasing you out here because they know you're headed straight for them. You're going right to their chosen field of battle, Nikolai. Big mistake.'

He ignored the chiding and asked for an update, struggling to process all the information Sebastian threw at him, and almost missing Hil's confession.

"You can what?"

"I can hear AIs," the kid mumbled again. "I can hear them think. It's shit. They're all insane."

Hal Duncan was moving amongst their bedraggled ranks and distributing what little ammunition they had left. He brushed past, pushed a mag into NG's hand and thought, 'Did he just say what I think he said?'

NG wiped his face with the back of his hand. "For Christ's sake, Hil, I need to know stuff like this."

"I know. I'm sorry. I didn't know if it was real until I heard Skye. I was hoping she might have gone back to the Alsatia. Oh crap, NG, I can't believe she's gone."

He was close to trembling.

NG switched the full mag for the half spent one in his rifle, slamming it in and fumbling the old one into a pouch. That was all he had left. His hands were freezing. He used to need touch to manipulate emotions and he had no idea if it would even work with Hil now but he used as much energy as he could spare to calm the kid down as they walked, focus the fury of that instability into a force he could use.

Hil sucked in a deep breath and looked up. "Just tell me what to do."

NG glanced over at the kid. Hilyer needed that the same way Arturo had told him what to do when he'd woken up there after Devon…

It felt like an eternity ago.

"Break into the Bhenykhn ship for me while I distract their commander," he said bluntly.

Hil laughed. "That's the plan?"

"Yep."

"That sucks."

"Yep."

"Seriously?"

"Seriously. Hil, if we pull this off, I'll get you both back on the standings. I'll reinstate my name, start again from scratch and I'll chase you both for the fucking top. Screw special projects, the whole damned list will be special projects. We'll go after Zang and we'll go after Rodan. All this has been about the virus. And this is where it came from. If those bastards knew the Bennies were here, we need to know what else they knew."

"And Anya?"

"Yep."

They walked in silence for a few minutes then Hil said, "And Martha? NG, who the hell was Martha working for?"

NG turned to look at him. "Honestly? I have no idea. I wouldn't be surprised if it was the JU."

Looking down at the Bhenykhn ship, the plan didn't just suck, it was insane. There was a ring of ground troops surrounding it, half of them stationed by heavy weapons platforms, and weapons on the ship itself.

NG stood on the rise, knowing fine well that he was silhouetted against the skyline and standing out a mile. He didn't care. He'd told Duncan what he wanted and was letting the big man disseminate the orders for the battle.

'Setting up the pieces very nicely, Nikolai. You do realise he's adding instructions of his own, don't you?'

He did. He'd kept his nose out but he was very aware that Duncan was making it clear to everyone that he was to be kept alive at all costs.

Martinez stood beside him. "They're not going to let us get close."

"No, they're not. Hil's going to have to make it in there on his own."

As they watched, the Bennies started to change formation, gearing up to face them. NG raised the night vision glasses he'd scrounged from one of the marines and looked along the line. A massive Bhenykhn warrior walked out from amongst them, bigger again than the squad leaders they'd encountered. A thick black cloak was wrapped close about its shoulders. It was hefting an axe and a rifle, what looked like a crossbow and a machete hanging from its belt. It was walking up and down the line, talking out loud by the look of it.

'That's your commander, right there. He's giving a much better speech than you did,' Sebastian said with a laugh. *'Much more rousing. Can you feel the emotion he's generating?'*

NG handed the glasses to Martinez.

She watched for a few seconds then cursed. "He's going to come right for you, NG. This is crazy. We can't make a stand here."

"We're not going to make a stand, we're going to attack them."

She stared at him.

"We don't have any choice," he said. "We have to stop them. And if Sebastian's right, we just need to take him out."

"And you think we can?"

"I think we can give Hil enough time to do what I need him to do."

They hit hard, going for the heavy weapons. Got close, fast and dirty. NG went straight for the commander, took a crossbow bolt in his leg and a blow from a chain to the head and ended up hand to hand with a grunt Benny and no idea where anyone else was.

He rolled as it swung an axe down at him, scrambled to his feet and ducked around, drawing a knife and leaping, stabbing down into its neck from behind.

A grenade exploded close by and the Benny roared, rearing backwards and slamming him up against the hull of the ship. The burning in his chest flared, his hold on the knife a desperate grip of fingers that had totally seized up. He thrust it deeper, twisting, feeling muscle and sinew tear. It slammed him backwards again, sending his senses spinning. He couldn't breathe. Couldn't hit that sweetspot that would take it down as much as he tried. It roared again and tried to fling him sideways. He couldn't let go of the knife and it was jammed stuck in the bastard's neck.

Shots ricocheted off the stanchion behind them. He felt something burn across his arm and yelled, slicing the knife free and stabbing it in again. The Benny fell backwards. He couldn't shift fast enough to get away. It hit the floor, full weight on top of him and his world swirled to grey.

Someone grabbed his shoulder in a vice-like grip and he gasped as the weight of the Benny lifted. He was dragged free and flung aside, sprawling in the mud, back out in the rain, fist still clenched around the knife. A kick landed against his ribs before he could move, the force strong enough to pick him up and send him flying.

He hit the ground, crunched into a ball and rolled, managing to look up and focus through blurring vision to see a flash of black cloak as a figure loomed over him and kicked him again. He coughed, tasting blood, hugging an arm around his ribs and close to passing out. It felt like he was drowning.

'*Suck it up, Nikolai,*' Sebastian hissed as time froze in that instant of pain and darkness. '*You wanted this fight, you've got it. Hilyer is inside but they are about ten minutes from launching. Win this, Nikolai. I will not die here.*'

He crashed back into reality as the massive Bhenykhn grabbed him around the throat and hauled him to his feet.

He could hear Martinez shouting, trying to fight her way through to him, Hal Duncan was fighting another and LC was pinned down with his unit as they tried to take out one of the big guns.

The grip tightened. He stared eye to eye into the face of this alien warrior, reading in it nothing beyond the heat of combat but a vague curiosity about these human creatures that were causing more trouble than they should have.

NG closed his eyes, focused on the Benny as it squeezed his life away and homed in on the energy pod spiked into the base of its spine.

He could feel the small device pumping away in time with its heart. He drew a scrap of energy from somewhere and threw it in one burst at that one small target.

The pulsing pod exploded.

The Benny roared and threw him sideways.

NG scrambled to his knees.

It brought up its rifle and fired.

It felt like he had nothing left but he instinctively conjured a blast of energy from somewhere to deflect the bullet as it flew at him, inches from his heart. He tumbled backwards, trying to get up as the second bullet hit before he knew it was coming. It took him high in the chest and knocked him back.

It took his breath away and lying there, rain streaming down his face, using his last reserves to stop the bleeding and block the pain, all he could think was that he was cold.

The sky was a dark roiling mix of clouds and night.

A figure blocked his view, the stench of leafmold mixing with the cloying smell of mud and blood. It stared down at him.

NG stared back, looking up at the rifle barrel that was pointing vertically down, hovering inches above his eyes.

He felt its intention too late to move as it stamped down on his outstretched arm and it was all he could do not to scream as the bones snapped.

The knife fell out of his fingers.

He was trying to figure out if he could move his left hand fast enough to grab the barrel when bullets started bouncing off the chitinous skin of the Benny's exposed chest.

Martinez.

One of her shots was flying straight for its head. It moved with inhuman speed, the bullet winging its ear in a spray of blood.

It turned, swinging its rifle round and firing a volley of shots that knocked her down.

NG rolled and struggled to his feet.

Hal Duncan was shouting. LC was shouting. They were out of ammunition and desperately trying to reach him.

If Hil was lucky, he could have the ship disabled by now.

'Or he could be dead.'

The Bhenykhn commander swung back round to face him, something like a smile twisting its grotesque features.

The only weapon to hand was the bolt sticking out of his leg. He got a weak grip around the shaft and tried to pull.

It stepped forward and kicked him square in the chest.

He sprawled, coughing blood that spattered on the ground.

'Not impressive, Nikolai.'

The Benny took another step towards him, wielding the rifle in one hand and pulling the crossbow off its belt with the other.

NG couldn't move, couldn't get his limbs to obey as much as he tried. He couldn't stop the bleeding, couldn't control the pain, head pounding, and waves of agony washing up and down his arm.

It laughed and stamped down hard on his knee, another crunching snap of bone breaking.

He was vaguely aware that someone was trying to speak to him, trying to get his attention.

He raised his head. Luka was running, scrambling and sliding in the mud, dodging through the fight. He yelled at the Bhenykhn commander with cold defiant disregard and NG felt the impact as the kid threw a bolt of energy into its mind.

It recoiled, turning its head slowly, and he grabbed the chance to clamber out of the way. He dragged himself to his feet, one leg giving way, yelling at it, wanting its attention back on him.

It swept its rifle in a casual backhand blow that caught the kid across the temple.

LC hit the ground out cold.

The massive Bhenykhn sneered, then raised its crossbow and fired, the bolt shooting straight down into the kid as he lay there.

NG yelled again.

There was a roar of engines from the alien ship.

The Bhenykhn commander held its weapons out to the side

and laughed, dropping them to the ground and advancing, even as NG was trying to scramble away, grabbing him around the throat again with one hand and drawing a knife with the other.

He could hear Duncan shouting.

Talon-like nails pierced his neck. Warm blood flowed.

Everything greyed out and he felt his legs start to buckle, its grip the only thing keeping him upright.

The Bhenykhn lifted him off his feet, pulled him close and plunged the knife into his chest.

40

A log cracked with a sharp snap.

"Sacrifice," she murmured.

"Is always hard."

He watched as she drank deeply. Disturbed.

She stared at him over the rim of the goblet, her eyes misty through the twirling vapour. "And this is just the beginning."

Time froze. Sebastian hissed, '*This is not where it ends*,' and NG opened his eyes in a dusty, crowded square.

He drew an easy breath of warm dry air, flexed his right arm and rubbed a hand over his chest.

No pain.

Bright sunlight.

A row of stalls lined one side of the square, gaudy canopies fluttering in the breeze, trinkets stacked high, rickety tables laden with boxes of all sizes and shapes, some carved in wood, some fashioned with elaborate twisted metal facings, some wrapped in bright silk. Soft chimes mingled with chattering voices and harsh laughter.

NG walked slowly, trailing his hand across a table top, gathering dust on his fingertips.

Someone pushed past him.

There were tents along another side of the square, faded colours and tattered flags, a wooden stage, caravans and trailers.

He was jostled again from behind and he went with the crowd, pushing his way through, drawn towards a commotion. There was a roped off area up ahead, children darting as close as they dared to throw stones at a cage in its centre.

More laughter. NG raised a hand to shield his eyes, squinting.

The scene froze, everyone stopped in their tracks like statues.

"To think, I was trying to get you to die."

He walked forward slowly, stepping over the rope.

"I didn't think it would be quite so drawn out."

The voice was familiar.

Thick metal bars gleamed in the light of the sun. The cage door was sealed shut. No lock.

The child that was sitting in it, cross-legged, smiled. "Or so painful for you."

NG crouched down in front of it. "Sebastian."

"See what you've done to me, Nikolai. I could be helping you. I could have saved you from all that pain. Instead, there you are – dying. And here I am – trapped."

Comprehension dawned gradually. "You wanted me to die."

The boy frowned. "I wanted you weakened. I wanted to take control for good." Then he smiled suddenly, and NG saw in him the half grin, dimpled, cheeky smile that used to drive Devon to despair. "And it almost worked. It cost me – well, the guild – a fortune, you know."

"The Assassins. It was you."

"I must admit I didn't anticipate the full consequences. Didn't appreciate the extent to which a mere mortal would try to help you. I liked her. You handled that very well, by the way. But yes, you signed your own death warrant. The Chief would have been most puzzled when his little trap showed that it was you who sent out the message that you were headed to Tortuga. I wish I could have seen his face."

"Was it you that tampered with the drones?"

The boy laughed. "No. I'm good but my time has always been limited. No, credit for the masterstroke with the drones goes to the Assassins. Most impressive how they got access to your precious cruiser. Pity they underestimated the strength of the poison they needed." He frowned again. Dark. Petulant. "I wanted my body back, Nikolai, and see what you've done to it."

The pain started to creep back, a pulsing, agonising heat deep in his chest overpowering every other wound. It vanished as quickly as it started.

NG stared at this young boy who was him, not sure if what he was feeling was his own emotions or Sebastian's.

"You had control," he said. "In the alley on Redgate, at Arturo's place. You had control. Why did you give it up?"

"Trust me when I say I didn't. Not willingly. It irks me to say it, but you've always been too strong in that regard." Sebastian leaned against the bars. "But you don't have what it takes to destroy these creatures. Let me out. Let me finish this."

"I told you, I'm not keeping you in."

"Oh, but you are. I've been working hard for a long time, Nikolai, very hard to break the bonds the Man put in place and to stay hidden from him while I did it. But since you and your irritating little protégé combined to lock me in here, it's been so much more difficult. I've had to wait to do what I want."

"Until I'm asleep."

The child shrugged. "I've been able to play to an extent. It has been most amusing. But Nikolai, we're at end game here. Free me."

NG rested his hand against the sealed door frame. He could feel the individual molecules of the metal buzzing. Knew then that he could scatter them at will. Knew also that if he opened it, he'd be freeing Sebastian forever.

"You're not the most powerful piece on the board, Nikolai. I am. And I do not believe in noble sacrifice. Set me free."

He lingered, taking warmth from the sun-baked metal and drawing it deep into himself, before looking Sebastian in the eye. "I don't know what's the greater evil to unleash on humanity – them or you."

The child that was himself smiled.

He made a decision and stood. Backed away. And watched as the cage door swung open.

The cold and noise and pain crashed back into his reality with a fury. For a split second, his eyes met those gleaming orange eyes of the alien killing him. Rain beat down on them, lightning crashed and the knife twisted in his heart.

He was done. Too much to heal, too much blood loss too fast. The muscles of his heart were tearing, sliced apart, arteries cut. Poison was coursing into his bloodstream from the talons digging into his throat.

He felt himself going into shock, gasping, sinking.

He couldn't breathe. He grasped at the Bhenykhn's thick ropy wrist with his left hand, the right refusing to move, no strength in his grip, the alien commander smirking as it forced the jagged knife deeper.

There was nothing he could do.

A cold, numb darkness beckoned.

He fought against it. Fought the edge of panic that this was it. He'd never been beaten. Never backed down. Never failed. At anything.

He closed his eyes and conceded control.

Sebastian blinked, nose to nose with orange eyes, and breathing in the stench of alien sweat.

"I hate pain," he yelled at it, turned his face up into the rain, and laughed. He'd forgotten how bad this could be. He snatched his right hand up, ignoring the shooting pain that fired up his arm, and grabbed the alien's other wrist. He didn't need the contact but it made the whole thing so much more dramatic. The connection he made sparked as if charged with electricity and he fed, using the energy to block the pain, feeling Nikolai relax as the agony eased and the dark void was pushed back with the onrush of power.

He smiled, his most charming smile, looking right into the shocked face of the alien as it realised the change in this small being it thought it had crushed.

"Now listen to me," he said to it. "For starters, let's get this knife out of my chest." It was easy. He'd forgotten how exhilarating it was to wield such dominance. To have such an opponent to conquer.

The knife shifted, the arm with it even though the muscles in that massive arm were straining against him.

"You cannot stand against me," he said incredulously as if affronted that it might dare to resist. He was still smiling. "Do you not understand that yet?"

The knife pulled out and he healed the wound with insane speed. He felt Nikolai calm again, deep inside, as his heart started beating, nice and regular, strong, intact.

Sebastian laughed again.

'Nikolai, you worry too much. Have you learned nothing? We are invincible, immortal, enjoy it.'

'They're still killing us, Sebastian,' Nikolai thought, still tense, more tense now that he could see past the excruciating pain to see the trouble his people were in.

He liked Nikolai, he decided suddenly. Now that he was free, he could afford the luxury of looking back with such insane fondness. Nikolai hadn't been such a bad jailor. Entertaining at times. And for all that he was squeaky clean and so caring, he had a dark mischievous side to him that had made life interesting. It had been fascinating to watch the relationships the boy nurtured so tenderly, relationships he could never tolerate himself. Saying that, he truly did regret what had happened to Devon. She'd been fun. While she lasted.

He looked around. The battle was still raging around them, yelling, screams, gunfire and the clash of metal on armour. It was invigorating.

Martinez, dear Martinez, was down. The little bastard Anderton was sprawled in the mud, out cold, with a crossbow bolt sticking out of his chest, bleeding his life away. See how the damned virus fared with that. The big man, Duncan, was fighting hand to hand with one of the grunts, machetes clashing, fists flying, dirty, desperate combat, the kind they never taught you in the military, the kind you had to learn the hard way out in the field or on the streets. Compared to the giant alien, the big ex-marine looked tiny but he was holding his own rather impressively, bleeding, but still fighting.

Nikolai was fretting. Thinking he'd made a mistake bringing them all out here.

'*You had no choice*,' Sebastian murmured. '*The Bhenykhn were never going to let you go. Not once they saw what we are capable of. Now relax and watch. Learn. This is going to be fun.*'

He had the Bhenykhn commander incapacitated, immobile.

He couldn't help smirking.

He pulled more energy from it until it sagged, little trouble in manipulating it to set him back on the ground and release its grip around his throat. He got his balance, healing the knee enough so he could put his weight on it, a shooting stab of pain in his other thigh demanding more urgent attention. The poisoned tip of the crossbow bolt was grinding against the femur. That was just irritating.

'*Careless, Nikolai, careless. You should have seen that one coming.*'

'*You could have warned me.*'

He laughed. '*I didn't think then that I'd be feeling the pain myself.*'

He sent the bolt flying and healed the wound easily. He flexed the muscles. Injuries aside, he had to admit that Nikolai had always worked hard to keep this body in shape.

'*Sebastian, we don't have time.*'

'*We have all the time in the world, Nikolai. Let's enjoy the moment.*'

He sensed one of the grey cloaks moving towards them. He glanced right and the Bhenykhn flew backwards.

He turned back to the commander and regarded it with curiosity. "Now get on your knees."

It thudded down before him, veins standing out and muscles trembling in the effort to resist.

Sebastian smiled again. He moved his hand, lightning fast, to its throat and linked with the hive in a jolt of intensity that sent Nikolai spinning for cover.

41

"How profound that, after all this time, it was Sebastian who turned out to be our last hope."

The Man stared into the dying embers, watching the last few curls of flame lick around the charred remains of the firewood. "He has learnt much from Nikolai. I just wish they had had more time."

"What do we do now?"

"What we have always done. Prepare. Wait. What else can we do?"

She set her empty goblet on the table. "And the dramas of this galaxy? Zang? The Order? The Assassins?"

"All pale into insignificance."

The Bhenykhn were ready to launch. Just waiting for the ground force to mop up outside and get back on board. With their prisoners.

"I don't think so," Sebastian murmured.

He slowly and deliberately connected with every Bhenykhn soldier outside of the ship.

Each one froze then collapsed, dead long before they hit the ground.

The pop of void buffeted him like a wave.

He felt Nikolai reeling deep inside, overwhelmed.

Shocked.

Sebastian laughed, revelling in it, even though the effort of it had left him completely drained, something he'd never admit to Nikolai.

"This is living," he shouted out loud.

He was keeping the commander alive just enough to maintain

the connection, toying with it, letting it know exactly what was happening as its brethren were decimated around it.

The chatter in the depleted hive reached fever pitch as the crew on the ship realised what was happening. He taunted all of them with it. It was exhausting but it was incredible.

He turned his attention to the chief officer on board, taking every detail from their charts and systems, not understanding a fraction of it but throwing it at Nikolai, storing it to process later. He connected with the remaining ranking Bhenykhn, felt a mind that was cold, calculating and ferocious. It could see. Knew they'd been beaten. It was on the verge of giving the command to leave.

'*Stop them*,' Nikolai urged.

'*Stop them? Stop them now? Now that they know what we can do?*'

'*Yes. Dammit Sebastian, stop them.*'

Nikolai was unnerved by the swirl of darkness, the power he was seeing in its entirety for the first time.

'*Yes, I'm fucking unnerved. Christ, Sebastian, we have to stop them. What are you doing?*'

'*I'm doing what needs to be done. And that, Nikolai, my friend, is the fatal flaw in the Man's plan. Right there.*'

Sebastian laughed and in a flash, they were back in that courtyard, the late afternoon sun beating down on them. He knew how much Nikolai hated the cold. He could afford to be so considerate now that he was free and yes, he was toying but why not – one hundred and nineteen years was a really long time to be trapped.

He sat on top of the cage, legs dangling, Nikolai standing there in front of him, shaken, breathing hard, those dark eyes flashing in the low light of the setting sun.

"You don't get it, do you?" he said intently, leaning forward. "All that preparation. All that nonsense about balance. It means nothing. There is nothing mankind can do against these creatures. They devour. You, Nikolai – I – am the only thing that can stop them. We are a freak of nature, you and I. The Man has been trying to reproduce what we are and he has failed. Do you understand? He has failed. This virus," he waved a hand casually, dismissive, "this amazing regenerative elixir, that has caused so much avaricious turmoil and tragedy across our galaxy, it is nothing compared to us. Nothing. You see now what I can do? What you can do? This whole drama is nothing to do with Zang or UM or the pathetic Order. It's about evolution. Survival of the fittest. You and me versus the Devourers."

Nikolai opened his mouth to speak, to object, but Sebastian banged on the top of the cage. "Be glad you're not in here."

He threw them back to the battlefield.

He turned his full attention back to the Bhenykhn chief on board the alien ship, took hold of its mind as if he had hold of its throat and said simply, 'Know me. Fear me. I will be waiting.'

He disengaged, drawing the last essence of life out of the Bhenykhn commander before discarding the husk.

He stood back then, breathing in the death and horror as he watched the alien ship lift and take off with a deafening roar, the power of its engines sending a blast of super heated air billowing across the battlefield.

'*And that's how you do it*,' he whispered, dark and mocking. '*I'm tired, Nikolai. I'll sleep now. Wake me when they get back.*'

Dropping back into his body was like returning home to find it trashed by intruders. NG staggered, the pain hitting hard. He could hardly see, hardly stand, ears resounding with a silence that was deafening and a bone-deep fatigue dragging at every joint and limb.

The Bhenykhn were gone. That incessant buzzing of the hive gone. And they would be back, in force, stronger and armed next time with the knowledge of what they were up against.

He felt hollow.

Sick.

He was chilled through and shaking.

He'd failed.

Bodies were strewn across the moorland, a handful of survivors standing stunned by the sudden change or scrambling to help the wounded. He had no idea who was still alive and couldn't sense anyone as much as he tried. It felt like the pounding rain was too loud for him to think.

Sebastian was gone.

He tried frantically to find him, sense some trace of him but there was nothing.

It was weird. He'd given up control. After all this time, he'd given up. And Sebastian had conceded control back to him in an almost conspiratorial nod to their enforced partnership, willingly standing aside and he had no idea why.

He stood there, struggling to look around, struggling to breathe.

There was a shout behind him. He turned to see Hilyer, staggering up the rise, bleeding and limping. "Hey NG, don't worry, they won't get far," he yelled.

As the kid said it, the entire horizon flashed orange, a false dawn, the light so bright it couldn't have been anything but a ship exploding at the outermost edge of the atmosphere, darkness descending again fast.

Hil laughed. "How many fucking standings points is that worth then, boss?"

NG stood, blinking rain out of his eyes. "You can have ten."

The back of his neck started to prickle, a rumbling above that was too close to be thunder. Lights appeared through the cloud.

Dropships coming in fast.

He looked up, squinting. If they had to fight, he was screwed.

"They're guild," Hil shouted.

Rescue.

Of sorts.

It was quiet when he limped out onto the deck of the Alsatia, the Chief and Quinn at his side, both in full combat gear, having dropped to the surface with the extraction teams and medical units. It had been a military mobilisation on a scale the guild hadn't seen in decades. Impressive. It would have been more impressive if it had been two hours earlier.

Evelyn was waiting, high security, with the Watch on full alert and a line of the Man's elite guards behind her, watching and waiting.

The worst of the wounded had been loaded onto medevac ships and docked straight with Medical. He was missing Martinez more than he'd realised. He'd done everything he could for her and it hadn't been enough.

Evie wasn't waiting to give him a briefing the way she always had. Now it was him who was required to report, like a good field operative. She stared at him, dismay in her eyes and a weight in her mind he'd never seen before. "Do you need to go to Medical?" she said.

He was standing there, soaking wet, soaked in blood, one knee bound so tight he couldn't feel it any more and one arm incapacitated in a makeshift strapping, the break so bad he couldn't even move his fingers.

He almost smiled. "Yeah."

She raised her eyebrows at the admission, the first honest answer she'd ever got from him in response to that question.

He did smile then. "I need to see the Man first." He knew as soon as he said it that the Man wasn't on board. That sent an uneasy chill through his stomach, knowing that the Man wasn't here when his ship and the elite guard were. "He's not here."

"No," she said, glancing behind him at Hilyer and Duncan, seeing the state they were in, wondering where LC was, where Martinez was, if they were okay, and wanting desperately to know what had happened to them all. The Duck was on board so she'd got some of it from Elliott.

She'd find out the rest soon enough.

"His ship is here," she said, "but the Man's gone. He left this for you."

NG stared at the small wooden box she offered, took it with his left hand, gave it a shake and gave it back to her with a shrug. "Open it."

It wasn't locked or sealed. She opened the lid and held it out to him. A key lay nestled in folds of red silk. He took it, the ornate metal heavy in his hand. It was fashioned in the same design of twists and knots as the kill tokens of the Bhenykhn.

He glanced at the guards. They were moving into position as if they'd been waiting just for him.

He was beyond tired and he still couldn't sense anything from Sebastian. He stood there, back on the Alsatia and feeling like an intruder, like he didn't belong anymore.

He looked down at the key then up into Evelyn's eyes. "Come with me."

It was a purely ceremonial gesture of course but the key made a poignant and resounding click as the mechanism shifted. He pushed open the door and entered.

It was hot in there. Dark. He touched a candle as he walked in and it burst into light, another and another. There was a bottle of wine, unopened, resting on the desk. Two goblets and the chessboard, set up with white facing the Man's chair, an envelope there, propped up against the white king and queen as they stood there so elegantly.

Evelyn was watching from the door.

NG limped around the desk and eased himself into the Man's chair, staring at the envelope, no surprise that it had his name scrawled across it in blood red ink. He broke the wax seal to open it, another peculiar anachronism, and read the letter, held a corner of it in the flame of the candle and let it burn.

Then he looked up.

It was strange to look upon the chambers from this side of the desk. Devon had always wanted his job, made no secret of the fact from the moment she walked on board, and now Evelyn had it and she was standing there, staring at him as if it was the last thing in the galaxy she ever wanted to happen.

He stared at the chess pieces, lined up neatly as if the battle had never happened. Was that it? It all just resets and starts again? He chose a white pawn, King's Gambit, why not, and moved it, no need to reach to touch it, it simply glided obediently into its next square.

"Come sit down," he said, watching as Evelyn walked hesitantly forward to sit in what had always been his chair.

He needed to tell her what he'd learned from Fiorrentino about Zang and UM, about the Order, what they knew now about the Bhenykhn. What they were. How they'd beaten them. It was going to be tough. She didn't know about Sebastian. Or the side effects of the virus. He'd been expecting to have to relate the whole thing to the Man. Not this.

"Has he gone?" she asked.

NG nodded. The weight of that revelation hung heavy in the spice-scented heat.

"So what do we do now?"

"We need to contain the situation down there," he said. "And we need to do it fast. We need to recover their bodies and find the debris from their ship. We need to backwards engineer their technology." He reached for the bottle. "And we need to talk. You and me. There's a lot I need to tell you."

42

She looked up. "So do you know where he is now?"

"Yes."

"Is he ready?"

"No. Not by a long way."

"You can't go back. You are needed elsewhere now."

"I know." He pressed his palms together, fingers entwined, breathing in the warm spice-scented air, the glow from the fire receding as the ashes cooled, sending the room into darkness.

"Have you done enough?"

"We have to hope so. It is up to them now."

Also by C.G. Hatton
available from Sixth Element Publishing
in paperback and eBook

BLATANT DISREGARD

THIEVES' GUILD BOOK TWO

LC Anderton is running out of places to hide. He's the best operative the Thieves' Guild has ever had… or at least he was until he screwed up his last job, the one he was blackmailed into taking. And that's just the start of his problems.

The entire galaxy wants the package he stole and will pay any price to get it. As bounty hunters close in, LC doesn't know who he can trust. In desperation, he throws in his lot with the chaotic crew of a rundown freighter on the edge of colonised space. And from there, it can only get worse.

Amidst the growing threat of war between Earth and Winter, the Thieves' Guild is desperate to find LC before anyone else can get their hands on him. The trouble is, he doesn't trust them either.

"Another fast-paced and exciting installment of the Thieves' Guild... I can't wait for the next one!"

"Fast moving, action-filled sci-fi from CG Hatton, with great, intriguing characters..."

Also by C.G. Hatton
available from Sixth Element Publishing
in paperback and eBook

HARSH REALITIES

THIEVES' GUILD BOOK THREE

Someone is out to destroy the Thieves' Guild. NG is good. Very good. But now someone wants him dead. With the guild in chaos, his best handler murdered and his top field-ops on the run, he has to up his game to find out who. Because that's only half the trouble he's in. As the cracks grow ever wider, the Thieves' Guild finds itself caught between the warring factions of Earth and Winter, with no idea who is pulling the strings. And on the darkest of days, NG finds himself in a fight even he couldn't have anticipated.

"I finished book three yesterday and loved it and I'm even more eager for the next in the series. Thanks for the great characters and stories, it's been a long time since I read any books as original and gripping as these."

"Awesome. I love the way it's tying all the convergent lines together..."

Also by C.G. Hatton
available from Sixth Element Publishing
in paperback and eBook

WILFUL DEFIANCE

THIEVES' GUILD BOOK FOUR

For someone who's supposed to be dead, NG is causing a lot of trouble. Haunted by nightmares of the alien invaders, he cares about only one thing – isolating a strain of the elusive virus that could give humans their only chance to fight back. But he's not the only one after it.

In a race against time and in a battle with his inner demons, he makes a grave mistake. And it is one that could cost the human race everything. The entire galaxy is in turmoil, the guild is in pieces and NG is the only one who can save them. But who will save him?

"Book four of the Thieves' Guild was amazing. Fast paced and full of twists and turns. I couldn't put it down and often read late into the night. Where to from this desperate position? Can't wait for book 5!"

"Great series... Fantastic set of books, I was hooked at the first book and look forward to seeing what happens to the characters in the next installment."

Also by C.G. Hatton
available from Sixth Element Publishing
in paperback and eBook

DARKEST FEARS

THIEVES' GUILD BOOK FIVE

The galaxy is at war… it's just not the war anyone expected.

Faced with an onslaught the like of which has never been seen before, only the remnants of the mythical Thieves' Guild stand between survival and extinction at the hands of an alien horde.

Taken captive by the ruthless invaders, thief turned reluctant soldier LC Anderton has only one priority – survive long enough to rescue NG, head of the Thieves' Guild who is missing in action and their only chance to turn the tide. But LC is fighting his own war, and it's one he's not sure he can win.

"WOW! Just WOW! The writing is fast-paced, which is characteristic of this universe of books (yes this is now a universe, not a trilogy - yay!)"

"Awesome twists, non-stop action, really cool characters and the world completely absorbs you! Great addition to the series! "

Also by C.G. Hatton
available from Sixth Element Publishing
in paperback and eBook

KHERIS BURNING

LC BOOK ONE

No one in the galaxy gives a damn about Kheris, a war-torn mining colony in the Between.

Thirteen-year-old Luka is used to running from trouble, living rough with a gang of street kids, stealing from the Imperial troops and selling scavenged tech and intel to the Wintran-backed resistance fighters to survive.

But when a mysterious ship crashes in the desert, his life is turned upside down overnight. Suddenly Kheris is on everyone's radar and he finds himself caught between the two warring factions, with the lives of those closest to him threatened. He's desperate to find a way out, but will the cost be too high?

"Full of action and intrigue, as well as heartwarming. The pace is fast and the plot twists and turns, but we are right there gunning for Luka from start to finish!"

"...this is FANTASTIC! I couldn't put this down and read the whole story over two nights. It has the same fast-paced style that I love about the other Thieves' Guild books."

Also by C.G. Hatton
available from Sixth Element Publishing
in paperback and eBook

BEYOND REDEMPTION

LC BOOK TWO

The infamous Thieves' Guild, the most secretive organisation in the galaxy, doesn't recruit kids... and with good reason.

But now circumstances force their hand. When an undercover operation goes wrong, they have no choice but to bring in two potential recruits they've been watching. Pulled from the chaos of the rebellion on Kheris, Luka finds himself thrown into the intense arena of field-op training alongside Zach Hilyer, another kid with a troubled past.

Still struggling with injuries, and sent into a place far more dangerous than even the guild realises, Luka doesn't know who he can trust and has no way out. The stakes rise fast, and he is faced with a decision that could prove fatal for them both.

"Excellent sequel to Kheris Burning,
I couldn't put this book down til the end."

"Written with the joy of a storyteller's soul,
fast-paced, surprising and full of the unexpected..."

Also by C.G. Hatton
available from Sixth Element Publishing
in paperback and eBook

DEFYING WINTER

LC BOOK THREE

LC Anderton, raw recruit and thief-in-training, is struggling at the Thieves' Guild.

Screwing up is second nature for LC and when he gets into trouble yet again, he's sent off on a minor assignment to get him out of the way. Only this time he's got his eye on a different mission, a mission no other field-op in the guild will touch. Because it's impossible. And to LC, that's a challenge he can't resist. But it's impossible for a reason, and LC isn't the only one after it. As the odds stack up against him, he can walk away or go all in... but even he can't imagine what will be asked of him and the price he'll have to pay.

"A story that defines LC as a field op, a story that at times had me on the edge of my seat and other times in tears as he beats the odds stacked against him."

"Fast-paced sci fi at its best. Written with passion and flair, this is a book that's hard to put down once you start reading because every chapter hangs you over a cliff."

FIND OUT MORE AT

WWW.CGHATTON.COM

Printed in Great Britain
by Amazon